作家及作品

余华

卡夫卡和K

《城堡》中的土地测量员K在厚厚的积雪中走来，皑皑白雪又覆盖了他的脚印，是否暗示了这是一次没有回去的走来？因为K仿佛是走进了没有谜底的命运之谜。贺拉斯说："无论风暴将我带到什么岸边，我都将以主人的身份上岸。"卡夫卡接着说："无论我转向何方，总有黑浪迎面打来。"弥漫在西方文学传统里的失落和失败的情绪感染着漫长的岁月，多少年过去了，风暴又将K带到了这里，K获得了上岸的权利，可是他无法获得主人的身份。

在有关卡夫卡作品的论说和诠释里，有一个声音格外响亮，那就是谁是卡夫卡的先驱？对卡夫卡的榜样的寻找凝聚了几代人的不懈努力，瓦尔特·本雅明寻找了一个俄国侯爵波将金的故事，博尔赫斯寻找了芝诺的否定运动的悖论。人们乐此不疲的理由是什么？似乎没有一个作家会像卡夫卡那样令人疑惑，我的意思是说：在卡夫卡这里人们无法获得其他作家所共有的品质，就是无法找到文学里清晰可见的继承关系。当《城堡》中的弗丽达意识到K其实像一个孩子一样坦率时，她仍然很难相信他的话，因为——弗丽达的理由是"你的个性跟我们截然不同"。瓦尔特·本雅明和博尔赫斯也对卡夫卡说出了类似的话。

同时，这也是文学要对卡夫卡说的话。显然，卡夫卡没有诞生在文学生生不息的长河之中，他的出现不是因为后面的波浪在推动，他像一个岸边的行走者逆水而来。很多迹象都在表明，卡夫卡是从外面走进了我们的文学。于是他的身份就像是《城堡》里K的身份那样尴尬，他们都是唐突的外来者。K

是不是一个土地测量员？《城堡》的读者会发出这样的疑问。同样的疑问也在卡夫卡生前出现，这个形象瘦削到使人感到尖锐的犹太人究竟是谁？他的作品是那样的陌生，他在表达希望和绝望、欢乐和痛苦、爱和恨的时候都是同样的令人感到陌生。这样的疑惑在卡夫卡死后仍然经久不息，波将金和芝诺的例子表明：人们已经开始到文学之外去寻找卡夫卡作品的来源。

这是明智的选择。只要读一读卡夫卡的日记，就不难发现生活中的卡夫卡，其实就是《城堡》中的K。他在1913年8月15日的日记中，用坚定的语气写道："我将不顾一切地与所有人隔绝，与所有人敌对，不同任何人讲话。"在六天以后的日记里，他这样写："现在我在我的家庭里，在那些最好的、最亲爱的人们中间，比一个陌生人还要陌生。近年来我和我的母亲平均每天说不上二十句话，和我的父亲除了有时彼此寒暄几句几乎就没有更多的话可说。和我已婚的妹妹和妹夫们除了跟他们生气我压根儿就不说话。"

人们也许以为写下这样日记的人正在经历着可怕的孤独，不过读完下面的两则日记后，可能会改变想法。他在1910年11月2日的日记中写道："今天早晨许久以来第一次尝到了想象一把刀在我心中转动的快乐。"另一则是两年以后，他再一次在日记中提到了刀子。"不停地想象着一把宽阔的熏肉切刀，它极迅速地以机械的均匀从一边切入我体内，切出很薄的片，它们在迅速的切削动作中几乎呈卷状一片片飞出去。"

第一则日记里对刀的描绘被后面"快乐"的动词抽象了，第二则日记不同，里面的词语将一串清晰的事实连接了起来，"宽阔的熏肉切刀"、"切入我体内"、而且"切出很薄的片"，卡夫卡的描叙是如此的细致和精确，最后"呈卷状一片片飞出去"时又充满了美感。这两则日记都是在想象中展示了暴力，而且这样的暴力都是针对自我。卡夫卡让句子完成了一个自我凌迟的过程，然后他又给予自我难以言传的快乐。这是否显示了卡夫卡在面对自我时没有动用自己的身份？或者说他就是在自我这里，仍然是一个外来者。我的答案是卡夫卡一生所经历的不是可怕的孤独，而是一个外来者的尴尬。这是更为深远的孤独，他不仅和这个世界和所有的人格格不入，同时他也和自己格格不入。他在1914年1月8日的日记中吐露了这样的尴尬，他写道：“我与犹太人有什么共同之处？我几乎与自己都没有共同之处。”他的日记暗示了与众不同的人生，或者说他始终以外来者的身份行走在自己的人生之路上，41年的岁月似乎是别人的岁月。

可以这么说，生活中的卡夫卡就像《城堡》里的K一样，他们都没有获得主人的身份，他们一生都在充当着外乡人的角色。共同的命运使这两个人获得了一致的绝望，当K感到世界上已经没有一处安静的地方能够让他和弗丽达生活下去时，他就对自己昙花一现的未婚妻说：“我希望有那么一座又深又窄的坟墓，在那里我们俩紧紧搂抱着，像用铁条缚在一起那样。”对K来说，世界上唯一可靠的安身之处是坟墓；而世界上真正的道路对卡夫卡来说是在一根绳索上，他在笔记里写道：“它不是绷紧在高处，而是贴近地面。它与其说是供人行走不如说是用来绊人的。”

人们的习惯是将日记的写作视为情感和思想的真实流露，在卡夫卡这里却很难区分出日记写作和小说写作的不同，他说：“读日记使我激动。”然后他加上着重号继续说：“一切在我看来皆属虚构。”在这一点上，卡夫卡和他的读者能够意见一致。卡夫卡的日记很像是一些互相失去了联络的小说片断，而他的小说《城堡》则像是K的漫长到无法结束的日记。

应该说，卡夫卡洁身自好的外来者身份恰恰帮助了他，使他能够真正切入到现存制度的每一个环节之中。在《城堡》和其它一些作品中，人们看到了一个巨大的官僚机器被居民的体验完整地建立了起来。我要说的并不是这个官僚机器展示了居民的体验，而是后者展示了前者。这是卡夫卡叙述的实质，他对水珠的关注是为了让全部的海水自动呈现出来。在这一点上，无论是卡夫卡同时代的作家，还是后来的作家，对他们自身所处的社会制度的了解，都很难达到卡夫卡的透彻和深入。就像是《城堡》所显示的那样，对其官僚机构和制度有着强烈感受的人不是那里的居民，而是一个外来者——K。《城堡》做出了这样的解释：那些在已有制度里出生并且成长起来的村民，制度的一切不合理性恰恰构成了它的合理。面对这至高无上的权威，村民以麻木的方式保持着他们世代相传的恐惧和世代相传的小心翼翼。而K的来到，使其制度的不合理性得到了呈现。外来者K就像是一把熏肉切刀，切入到城堡看起来严密其实漏洞百出的制度之中，而且切出了很薄的片，最后让它们一片片呈卷状飞了出去。

在卡夫卡的眼中，这一把熏肉切刀的锋刃似乎就是性，或者说在《城堡》里凡是涉及到性的段落都会同时指出叙述中的两个方向，一个是权威的深不可测，另一个是村民的麻木不仁。

关于权威的深不可测，我想在此引用瓦尔特·本雅明的话，本雅明说："这个权威即使对于那些官僚来说也在云里雾里，对于那些它们要对付的人们来说就更加模糊不清了。"当卡夫卡让他的代言人K在积雪和夜色中来到村子之后，在肮脏破旧的客栈里，K拿起了电话——电话是村民也是K和城堡联系的象征，确切的说是接近那个权威的象征，而且所能接近的也只是权威的边缘。当K拿起电话以后，他听到了无数的声音，K的疑惑一直到与村长的交谈之后才得以澄清，也就是说当一部电话被接通后，城堡以及周围村子所有的电话也同时被接通，因此谁也无法保证K在电话中得到的声音是否来自于城堡。由此可见，城堡的权威是在一连串错误中建立起来的，而且不断发生的新的错误又在不断地巩固这样的权威。当K和村长冗长的谈话结束后，这一点得到了进一步的证实。尽管村长的家是整个官僚制度里最低等的办公室，然而它却是唯一允许K可以进入的。当村长的妻子和K的两个助手翻箱倒柜地寻找有关K的文件时，官僚制度里司空见惯的场景应运而生，阴暗的房间、杂乱的文件柜和散发着霉味的文件。因此，K在这里得到的命运只不过是电话的重复。而对于来自城堡的权威，村长其实和K一样的模糊不清。在《城堡》的叙述里，不仅是那位端坐在权威顶峰的伯爵先生显得虚无缥缈，就是那个官位可能并不很高的克拉姆先生也仿佛是生活在传说中。K锲而不舍的努力，最终所得到的只是与克拉姆的乡村秘书进行一次短暂的谈话。因此，村长唯一能够明确告诉K的，就是他们并不需要一个土地测量员。村长认为K的来到是一次误会，他说："像在伯爵大人这样庞大的政府机关里，可能偶然发生这一个部门制定这件事，另一部门制定那件事，而互相不了解对方的情况……因此就常常会出现一些细小的差错。"作为官僚机构中的一员，村长有责任维护官僚制度里出现的所有错误，他不能把K送走，因为"这是另外一个问题"，他所能做的无非是将错就错，给K安排了一个完全是多余的职位——学校的看门人。

关于村民的麻木不仁，我想说的就是卡夫卡作品中将那个巨大的官僚机器建立起来的居民的体验，这样的体验里充满了居民的敬畏、恐惧和他们悲惨的命运，叙述中性的段落又将这样的体验推向了高潮。弗丽达、客栈老板娘和阿玛丽亚的经历，在卡夫卡看来似乎是磨刀石的经历，她们的存在使权威之剑变得更加锋利和神秘。克拉姆和索尔蒂尼这些来自城堡的老爷，这些《城堡》中权力的象征，便是叙述里不断闪烁的刀光剑影。

人老珠黄的客栈老板娘对年轻时代的回忆，似乎集中了村民对城堡权威的共同体验。这个曾经被克拉姆征召过三次的女人，与克拉姆三次同床的经历构成了她一生的自我荣耀，也成为了她的丈夫热爱她和惧怕她的唯一理由。这一对夫妇直到晚年，仍然会彻夜未眠地讨论着克拉姆为什么没有第四次征召她，这几乎就是他们家庭生活的唯一乐趣。弗丽达是另外一个形象，这是一个随心所欲的形象。她的随心所欲是因为她曾经是克拉姆的情妇，这样的地位是村里的女人们梦寐以求的，可是她轻易地放弃了，这是她性格里随心所欲的结果，她极其短暂并且莫名其妙地爱上了K，然后她以同样的莫名其妙又爱上了K的助手杰里米亚。在卡夫卡眼中，弗丽达代表了另一类的体验，有关性和权力的神秘体验，也就是命运的体验，她性格的不确定似乎就是命运的不确定。这个曾经有着无穷的生气和毅力的弗丽达，和K短短地生活了几天后，她的美丽就消失了。卡夫卡的锋利之笔再次指向了权力："她形容憔悴是不是真的因为离开了克拉姆？她的不可思议的诱惑力是因为她亲近了克拉姆才有的，而吸引K的又正是这种诱惑力。"尽管弗丽达和K与客栈老板夫妇绝然不同，可是他们最终殊途同归。卡夫卡让《城堡》给予了我们一个刻薄的事实：女人的美丽是因为亲近了权力，她们对男人真正的吸引是因为她们身上有着权力的幻影。弗丽达离开了克拉姆之后，她的命运也就无从选择，"现在她在他的怀抱里枯萎了。"

阿玛丽亚的形象就是命运中悲剧的形象。在客栈老板娘和弗丽达顺从了权力之后，卡夫卡指出了道路的另一端，也就是阿玛丽亚的方向。顺着卡夫卡的手指，人们会看到一个拒绝了权力的身影如何变得破碎不堪。

事实上在卡夫卡笔下，阿玛丽亚和村里其他姑娘没有不同，也就是说她在内心深处对来自城堡的权力其实有着难以言传的向往，当象征着城堡权威的索尔蒂尼一眼看中她以后，她的脸上同样出现了恋爱的神色。她的悲剧是因为内心里还残留着羞耻感和自尊，当索尔蒂尼派人送来那张征召她的纸条时，上面粗野和下流的词汇突然激怒了她。这是卡夫卡洞察人心的描述，一张小小的纸条改变了阿玛丽亚和她一家人的命运，阿玛丽亚撕碎纸条的唯一理由就是上面没有爱的词句，全是赤裸裸的关于交媾的污言秽语。然后，叙述中有关权力的体验在阿玛丽亚一家人无休止的悲惨中展开，比起客栈老板娘和弗丽达顺从的体验，阿玛丽亚反抗之后的体验使城堡的权威显得更加可怕，同时也显得更加虚幻。

也许索尔蒂尼并没有把这事放在心上，对于那些来自城堡的老爷，他们床上的女人层出不穷。问题是出在村民的体验里，一旦得知阿玛丽亚拒绝了城堡里的老爷，所有的村民都开始拒绝阿玛丽亚一家。于是命运变得狰狞可怕了，她的父亲曾经是村里显赫的人物，可是这位出色的制鞋匠再也找不到生意了，曾经是他手下伙计的勃伦斯威克，在他们一家的衰落里脱颖而出，反而成为了他们的主子。两位年轻的姑娘奥尔珈和阿玛丽亚必须去承受所有人的歧视，她们的兄弟巴纳巴斯也在劫难逃。

在卡夫卡的叙述里，悲惨的遭遇一旦开始，就会一往无前。这一家人日日夜夜讨论着自己的命运，寻找着残存的希望。他们的讨论就像客栈老板夫妇的讨论那样无休无止，不同的是前者深陷在悲剧里，后者却是为了品尝回忆的荣耀。为了得到向索尔蒂尼道歉的机会，他们的父亲在冰雪里坐了一天又一天，守候着城堡里出来的老爷，直到他身体瘫痪为止；出于同样的理由，奥尔珈将自己的肉体供给那些城堡老爷的侍卫们肆意蹂躏。巴纳巴斯曾经带来过一线希望，他无意中利用了官僚制度里的漏洞，混进城堡成为了一名模棱两可的信使。然而他们所做的一切丝毫没有阻止命运在悲剧里前进的步伐，他们的努力只是为了在绝望里虚构出一线希望。卡夫卡告诉我们：权威是无法接近的，即便是向它道歉也无济于事。索尔蒂尼对于阿玛丽亚一家来说，就像城堡对于K一样，他们的存在并不是他们曾经出现过，而是因为自身有着挥之不去的恐惧和不安。

卡夫卡的叙述如同深渊的召唤，使阿玛丽亚一家的悲剧显得深不见底，哪怕叙述结束后，她们的悲剧仍然无法结束。这正是卡夫卡为什么会令人不安和战栗的原因。阿玛丽亚和她家庭悲惨的形象，是通过奥尔珈向K的讲述呈现出来的，这个震撼人心的章节在《城堡》的叙述里仿佛是节外生枝，它使《城堡》一直平衡均匀的叙述破碎了，如同阿玛丽亚破碎的命运。人的命运和叙述同时破碎，卡夫卡由此建立了叙述的高潮。其他作家都是叙述逐渐圆润后出现高潮的段落，卡夫卡恰恰相反。在这破碎的章节里，卡夫卡将权威的深不可测和村民的麻木不仁凝聚到了一起，或者说将性的体验和权力的体验凝聚到了一起。

有一个事实值得关注，那就是卡夫卡和性的关系影响了《城堡》中K的性生活。在卡夫卡留下的日记、书信和笔记里，人们很难找到一个在性生活上矫健的身影；与此相对应的叙述作品也同样如此，偶尔涉及到的性的段落也都是草草收场。这位三次订婚又在婚礼前取消了婚约的作家给人留下了软弱可欺的印象，而且他的三次订婚里有两次是和同一位姑娘。他和一位有夫之妇密伦娜的通信，使他有过短暂的狂热，这样的狂热使他几次提出了约会的非份之想，每一次都得到了密伦娜泼来的一盆凉水，这位夫人总是果断地回答：不行！因此，当有人怀疑卡夫卡一生中是否有过健康有力的性经历时，我感到这样的怀疑不会是空穴来风。退后一步说，即便卡夫卡的个人隐私无从证实，他在性方面的弱者的形象也很难改变。确切的说，卡夫卡性的经历很像他的人生经历，或者说很像K的经历；真正的性，或者说是卡夫卡向往中的性，对于他就像是城堡对于K一样，似乎永远是可望而不可及。

他在给密伦娜夫人的信中似乎暗示了他有这方面的要求，而在他其他的书信和日记里连这样的迹象都没有。他只是在笔记里写下了一句令人不知所措的话："它犹如与女人们进行的、在床上结束的斗争。"没有人知道这样的比喻针对什么，人们可以体验到的是这句话所涉及到的性的范围里没有爱的成分，将性支撑起来的欲望是由斗争组建的。另一个例子是K的经历，这位城堡的不速之客在第一夜就尝到了性的果子。在那个阴暗的章节里，卡夫卡不作任何铺垫的叙述，使弗丽达成为了K的不速之客。这一切发生得是如此的突然，当人们还在猜测着K是否能够获得与象征着权力的克拉姆见面的机会时，克拉姆的情人弗丽达娇小的身子已经在K的手里燃烧了。"他们在地上滚了没有多远，砰地一声滚到了克拉姆的房门前，他们就躺在这儿，在积着残酒的坑坑洼洼和扔在地板上的垃圾中间。"然后，卡夫卡写道："他们两个人像一个人似的呼吸着，两颗心像一颗心一样的跳动着。"这似乎是性交正在进行时的体验，接下去的段落似乎预示着高潮来临时的体验："K只觉得自己迷失了路，或者进入了一个奇异的国度，比人类曾经到过的任何国度都远，这个国度是那么奇异，甚至连空气都跟他故乡的大不相同，在这儿，一个人可能因为受不了这种奇异而死去，可是这种奇异又是那么富于魅力，使你只能继续向前走，让自己越迷越深。"

与卡夫卡那一段笔记十分近似，上述段落里K对性的体验没有肉体的欲望；不同的是K和弗丽达的经历不是床上的斗争，卡夫卡给予了他们两人以同一个人的和谐，当然这是缺乏了性欲的和谐，奇怪的是这样的和谐里有着虚幻的美妙，或者说上述段落的描写展示了想象中的性过程，而不是事实上的性过程。卡夫卡纯洁的叙述充满了孩子般的对性的憧憬，仿佛是一个没有这样经历的人的种种猜测。当卡夫卡将其最后的体验比喻成一个奇异的国度，一个比人类曾经到过的任何国度都要远的国度时，卡夫卡内心深处由来已久的尴尬也就如日出般升起，他和K的外乡人的身份显露了出来。"连空气都跟他故乡的大不相同"，于是K和弗丽达的性高潮成为了忧郁的漂泊之旅。

是否可以这么说，就是在自身的性的经历里，卡夫卡仍然没有获得主人的身份。如果这一点能够确认，就不难理解在《城堡》的叙述里，为什么性的出现总是和权力纠缠到一起。我的意思是说卡夫卡比任何人都更为深刻地了解到性在社会生活中可以无限延伸。就像是一个失去了双腿的人会获得更多的凝视的权利，卡夫卡和性之间的陌生造成了紧张的对峙，从而培养了他对其长时间注视的习惯，这样的注视已经超越了人们可以忍受的限度，并且超越了一个时代可以忍受的限度。在这样的注视里，他冷静和深入地看到了性和官僚机器中的权力如何合二为一，"两颗心像一颗心一样跳动着"。因此在《城堡》的叙述里，同时指出权力深不可测和村民麻木不仁的，就是性的路标。

最后我要说的是，究竟是一个什么样的内心造就了卡夫卡的写作？我的感受是他的日记比他的叙述作品更能说明这一点。他在1922年1月16日的日记中写道：“两个时钟走得不一致。内心的那个时钟发疯似的，或者说着魔似的或者说无论如何以一种非人的方式猛跑着，外部的那个则慢吞吞地以平常的速度走着。除了两个不同世界的互相分裂之外，还能有什么呢？而这两个世界是以一种可怕的方式分裂着，或者至少在互相撕裂着。”卡夫卡的一生经历了什么？日记的回答是他在互相撕裂中经历了自己的一生。这有助于我们理解阿玛丽亚一家的命运为什么在破碎后还将不断地破碎下去，也使我们意识到这位与人们格格不入的作家为什么会如此陌生。

内心的不安和阅读的不知所措困扰着人们，在卡夫卡的作品中，没有人们已经习惯的文学出路，或者说其它的出路也没有，人们只能留下来，尽管这地方根本不是天堂，而且更像是地狱，人们仍然要留下来。就像那个永远无法进入城堡的K一样，悲哀和不断受到伤害的K仍然要说：“我不能离开这里。我来到这儿，是想在这儿呆下来的。我得在这儿呆着。”K只能呆在城堡的边缘，同样的命运也属于卡夫卡和《城堡》的读者，这些留下来的读者其实也只是呆在可以看见城堡的村庄里，卡夫卡叙述的核心就像城堡拒绝K一样拒绝着他们。城堡象征性的存在成为了卡夫卡叙述的不解之谜，正是这样的神秘之谜召唤着人们，这似乎是地狱的召唤，而且是永远无法走近的召唤。然后令人不安的事出现了，卡夫卡和K这两个没有主人身份的外来者，也使走进他们世界的读者成为了外来者。K对自己说：“究竟是什么东西引诱我到这个荒凉的地方来的呢，难道就只是为了想在这儿呆下来吗？”被卡夫卡和K剥夺了主人身份的读者，也会这样自言自语。

1999年8月30日

Contents

Contents

PUBLISHER'S NOTE

"Dearest Max, my last request: Everything I leave behind me . . . in the way of diaries, manuscripts, letters (my own and others'), sketches, and so on, [is] to be burned unread. . . . Yours, Franz Kafka"

These famous words written to Kafka's friend Max Brod have puzzled Kafka's readers ever since they appeared in the postscript to the first edition of *The Trial,* published in 1925, a year after Kafka's death. We will never know if Kafka really meant for Brod to do what he asked; Brod believed that it was Kafka's high artistic standards and merciless self-criticism that lay behind the request, but he also believed that Kafka had deliberately asked the one person he knew would not honor his wishes (because Brod had explicitly told him so). We do know, however, that Brod disregarded his friend's request and devoted great energy to making sure that all of Kafka's works—his three unfinished novels, his unpublished stories, diaries, and letters—would appear in print. Brod explained his reasoning thus:

> My decision [rests] simply and solely on the fact that Kafka's unpublished work contains the most wonderful treasures, and, measured against his own work, the best things he has written. In all honesty I must confess that this one fact of the literary and ethical value of what I am publishing would have been enough to make me decide to do so,

> definitely, finally, and irresistibly, even if I had had no single objection to raise against the validity of Kafka's last wishes. (From the Postscript to the first edition of *The Trial*)

In 1925, Max Brod convinced the small avant-garde Berlin publisher Verlag Die Schmiede to publish *The Trial,* which Brod prepared for publication from Kafka's unfinished manuscript. Next he persuaded the Munich publisher Kurt Wolff to publish his edited manuscript of *The Castle,* also left unfinished by Kafka, in 1926, and in 1927 to bring out Kafka's first novel, which Kafka had meant to entitle *Der Verschollene* (The Man Who Disappeared), but which Brod named *Amerika.* Wolff later noted that very few of the 1,500 copies of *The Castle* he printed were sold. The first English translation of *The Castle,* by Edwin and Willa Muir, was published in Britain in 1930 by Secker & Warburg and in the United States by Alfred A. Knopf. Though recognized by a small circle as an important book, it did not sell well.

Undeterred, Max Brod enlisted the support of Martin Buber, Hermann Hesse, Heinrich Mann, Thomas Mann, and Franz Werfel for a public statement urging the publication of Kafka's collected works as "a spiritual act of unusual dimensions, especially now, during times of chaos." Since Kafka's previous publishers had closed during Germany's economic depression, he appealed to Gustav Kiepenheuer to undertake the project. Kiepenheuer agreed, but on condition that the first volume be financially successful. But the Nazi rise to power in 1933 forced Kiepenheuer to abandon his plans. Between 1933 and 1938 German Jews were barred from teaching or studying in "German" schools, from publishing or being published in "German" newspapers or publishing houses, or from speaking and performing in front of "German" audiences. Publishers that had been owned or managed by Jews, such as S. Fischer Verlag, were quickly "Aryanized" and ceased to publish books by Jews. Kafka's works were not well enough known to be banned by the government or burned by nationalist students, but they were "Jewish" enough to be off limits to "Aryan" publishers.

When the Nazis introduced their racial laws they exempted Schocken Verlag, a Jewish publisher, from the ban against publishing Jewish authors on condition that its books would be sold only to Jews. Founded in 1931 by the department store magnate Salman Schocken, this small publishing company had already published the works of Martin Buber and Franz Rosenzweig as well as those of the Hebrew writer S. Y. Agnon as part of its owner's interest in fostering a secular Jewish literary culture.

Max Brod offered Schocken the world publishing rights to all of Kafka's works. This offer was initially rejected by Lambert Schneider, Schocken Verlag's editor in chief, who regarded Kafka's work as outside his mandate to publish books that could reacquaint German Jewry with its distinguished heritage. He also doubted its public appeal. His employer also had his doubts about the marketability of six volumes of Kafka's novels, stories, diaries, and letters, although he recognized their universal literary quality as well as their potential to undermine the official campaign to denigrate German Jewish culture. But he was urged by one of his editors, Moritz Spitzer, to see in Kafka a quintessentially "Jewish" voice that could give meaning to the new reality that had befallen German Jewry and would demonstrate the central role of Jews in German culture. Accordingly, *Before the Law*, an anthology drawn from Kafka's diaries and short stories, appeared in 1934 in Schocken Verlag's Bücherei series, a collection of books aimed to appeal to a popular audience, and was followed a year later—the year of the infamous Nuremburg Laws—by Kafka's three novels. The Schocken editions were the first to give Kafka widespread distribution in Germany. Martin Buber, in a letter to Brod, praised these volumes as "a great possession" that could "show how one can live marginally with complete integrity and without loss of background." (From *The Letters of Martin Buber* [New York: Schocken Books, 1991], p. 431)

Inevitably, many of the books Schocken sold ended up in non-Jewish hands, giving German readers—at home and in exile—their only access to one of the century's greatest writers. Klaus Mann wrote in the exile journal *Sammlung* that "the collected works of Kafka, offered by the Schocken Verlag in Berlin, are the noblest and most significant publications that have come out of Germany." Praising Kafka's books as "the epoch's purest and most singular works of literature," he noted with astonishment that "this spiritual event has occurred within a splendid isolation, in a ghetto far from the German cultural ministry." Soon after this article appeared, the Nazi government put Kafka's novels on its blacklist of "harmful and undesirable writings." Schocken moved his production to Prague, where he published Kafka's diaries and letters. Interestingly, despite the ban on the novels, he was able to continue printing and distributing his earlier volume of Kafka's short stories in Germany itself until the government closed down Schocken Verlag in 1939. The German occupation of Prague that same year put an end to Schocken's operations in Europe.

In 1939, he re-established Schocken Books in Palestine, where he had lived intermittently since 1934, and editions of Kafka's works in the renewed Hebrew language were among its first publications. In 1940, he moved to New York, where five years later he opened Schocken Books with Hannah Arendt and Nahum Glatzer as his chief editors. While continuing to publish Kafka in German, Schocken reissued the existing Muir translations of the novels in 1946 and commissioned translations of the letters and diaries in the 1950s, thus placing Kafka again at the center of his publishing program. Despite a dissenting opinion from Edmund Wilson in *The New Yorker* (where he nonetheless compared Kafka to Nikolai Gogol and Edgar Allan Poe), a postwar Kafka craze began in the United States; translations of all of Kafka's works began to appear in many other languages; and in 1951 the German Jewish publisher S. Fischer of Frankfurt (also in exile during the Nazi period) obtained the rights to publish Kafka in Germany. As Hannah Arendt wrote to Salman Schocken, Kafka had come to share Marx's fate: "Though during his lifetime he could not make a decent living, he will now keep generations of intellectuals both gainfully employed and well-fed." (Letter, August 9, 1946, Schocken Books Archive, New York)

Along with the growing international recognition of Franz Kafka as one of the great writers of our century, scholars began to raise doubts about the editorial decisions made by Max Brod. The notebooks in which Kafka had written *The Castle,* for instance, contained large crossed-out sections with the last part in a fragmentary state, forcing Brod to make editorial decisions. Intent on securing an audience for his friend, Brod sought to improve the readability of the unfinished novel by normalizing spelling, introducing standard High German punctuation, changing the way Kafka's chapters were broken, and deleting the final chapters (although by 1951 this material had been reinserted into the German edition, and in 1954 was translated by Eithne Wilkins and Ernst Kaiser and placed in the English edition with the final paragraphs in an appendix). Brod's main concern was to make the novel appear as a unified whole, although Kafka had not supplied an ending; indeed, he appears to have broken off the novel in mid-sentence.

Salman Schocken was among the most eager for new, critical editions of Kafka's works. "The Schocken editions are bad," he wrote in an internal memo. "Without any question, new editions that include the incomplete novels would require a completely different approach." (September 29, 1940, Schocken Archives, Jerusalem) However, Max Brod's refusal to give up the Kafka archive in his Tel Aviv apartment or to allow scholars access to it made such new editions impossible until 1956, when the threat of war in the Middle East prompted him to deposit the bulk of the archives, including the manuscript of *The Castle,* in a Swiss vault. When the young Oxford Germanist Malcolm Pasley learned of the archives' whereabouts, he received permission from Kafka's heirs in 1961 to deposit them in Oxford's Bodleian

Library, where they were subsequently made available for scholarly inspection.

Since the 1970s an international team of Kafka experts has been working on German critical editions of all of Kafka's writings, which are being published by S. Fischer Verlag with financial support from the German government. The first of these editions, *The Castle,* appeared in 1982, edited by Malcolm Pasley in two volumes, one for the restored text of the novel drawn from Kafka's handwritten manuscript, the second for textual variants and editorial notes. (See the afterword to the German critical edition in the appendix to this volume for Pasley's discussion of his work.)

Our new English translation of *The Castle,* by Mark Harman, is based on the restored text in the first volume of the Pasley German critical edition, which corrected numerous transcription errors in the earlier editions and removed all of Brod's editorial and stylistic interventions. Although many of the novelties of the German critical text (such as Kafka's unorthodox spelling and his use of an Austrian German or Prague German vocabulary) cannot be conveyed in translation, the fluidity and breathlessness of the sparsely punctuated original manuscript have been retained, as Mark Harman explains in his preface. We decided to omit the variants and passages deleted by Kafka that are included in Pasley's second volume, even though variants can indeed shed light on the genesis of literary texts. The chief objective of this new edition, which is intended for the general public, is to present the text in a form that is as close as possible to the state in which the author left the manuscript. Thus, for the first time, English-speaking readers will be able to read Kafka's haunting novel as he left it.

ARTHUR H. SAMUELSON
Editorial Director,
Schocken Books, New York

TRANSLATOR'S PREFACE

W. H. Auden once said that anybody who presents a new translation of a literary classic ought to justify the endeavor—a task, he adds, "which can only be congenial to the malicious."[1] I have no desire to malign the translations of the Muirs, a gifted Scottish couple who were in Prague learning Czech while Kafka was in Silesia writing *Das Schloß*. Their elegant translations, beginning with *The Castle* (1930), quickly established Kafka's reputation in the English-speaking world.

Yet translations eventually do show their age and the Muirs' Kafka is no exception. The literary sensibility of Edwin Muir, the primary stylist, was molded by nineteenth-century figures such as Thackeray and Dickens, and he had little sympathy with contemporary writers such as Virginia Woolf and James Joyce. He had this to say about *Ulysses:* "its design is arbitrary, its development feeble, its unity questionable."[2] Small wonder, then, that he and Willa Muir should have toned down the modernity of *The Castle*.

The datedness of the Muirs' translations has not gone unnoticed. In 1983, the centenary of Kafka's birth, the critic Siegbert Prawer summarized the case in favor of new translations: "Scholar after scholar has told us of the Muirs' tendency to tone down Kafka's ominousness and make his central figures more kindly than they are in the original. . . . They misunderstood some of Kafka's phrases and sentences . . . [and] tended to obscure Kafka's cross-references by elegant variation. . . . At other times, the Muirs import connections where there are none in the original. . . . "[3]

Moreover, the Muirs' translation furthers the rather simplistic theological interpretation proposed by Brod, who saw the Castle as the seat of divine grace. Edwin Muir even outdid Brod by stating bluntly that "the theme of the novel is salvation"; he also suggested that it was a kind of updated version of Bunyan's seventeenth-century prose allegory, *The Pilgrim's Progress*. That allegorical reading, which dominated the critical debate about the novel for several decades, is now widely discredited. Muir himself was firmly convinced that literature could not survive the demise of religious belief: "If . . . that belief were to fail completely and for good, there would be no imaginative art with a significance beyond its own time. But it is inconceivable that it should fail, for it is native to man." Those strong convictions leave their mark on the Muirs' translation, which fits a religious mold more neatly than does the original.

Literary translators must forge a prose style that mimicks the original. How best to describe Kafka's style in *The Castle*? Thomas Mann speaks of its "precise, almost official conservatism." Yet that is only part of the story. The writers in Kafka's eclectic pantheon mirror his oscillation between conservative-classical and modern styles. Among his favorites were Goethe, Kleist, the nineteenth-century Austrian novelist Adalbert Stifter, the rustic Alemannic moralist Johann Peter Hebel, Dickens (though Kafka disliked his verbosity), Flaubert, Dostoevsky, and the quirky Swiss modernist Robert Walser.[4]

The prose style of *The Castle* reflects its origins as a first-person novel. Kafka changed his mind while working on the third chapter and went back, crossing out each "I" and replacing it with "K." Nevertheless, that original conception left an imprint on his style. As in much first-person fiction, the tempo of the prose charts the state of the central character. When K. is agitated, it is choppy. When K. loses himself in the labyrinth of his paranoid logic, it is tortuous and wordy. When the emphasis is on K.'s actions rather than on his thoughts, the prose becomes terse. At such moments—chapters 2 and 3 are striking instances—the stark prose becomes a miracle of precision. Kafka can be both taut and fluid. His prose seems meticulously chiseled, but he did not labor over it. The flowing handwriting in the manuscripts with relatively few corrections suggests the intuitive certainty of a somnambulist. Perhaps that is why there is so much life in his extraordinarily compact sentences.

At times, however, the prose slows downs and is almost asphyxiated by clotted passages of opaque verbosity. That wordiness may well parody the prolixity of Austro-Hungarian officials, which, incidentally, occasionally amused Kafka, who once embarrassed himself by erupting in uncontrollable laughter during a speech by the president of the Workers Accident Insurance Company in Prague. In the course of one key chapter in *The Castle* an official called Bürgel drones on in almost impenetrable pseudo-officialese, which I have tried to keep as murky in English as it is in German.

In the second half of the book Kafka chooses to narrate the story largely through conversations and reported speech. As a result, his prose becomes increasingly fluid, culminating in a breathless monologue by a barmaid called Pepi. One can sense the pleasure that he takes in mimicking the envious, spiteful voice of Pepi. And indeed, though a notoriously severe critic of his own work, he himself notes in a letter to Max Brod (September 11, 1922) that he is quite pleased with the last chapters he has written. Yet this uncharacteristic sense of satisfaction does not prevent him from announcing in the very same letter that he is giving up on the book for good. It therefore seems only fitting that the new edition of this unfinished but seminal modern novel should halt, tantalizingly, in mid-sentence. Kafka lifts his pen from the paper, and his words fade into the page.

It is difficult to discuss translation without giving specific examples, which I shall now do. First I shall compare three versions—my translation, the Muirs', and the German original, in that order—of a central, if rather dense, passage in the novel, in which K. compares the church tower in his hometown with the tower of the Castle:

> And in thought he compared the church tower in his homeland with the tower up there. The church tower, tapering decisively, without hesitation, straightaway toward the top, capped by a wide roof with red tiles, was an earthly building—what else can we build?—but with a higher goal than the low jumble of houses and with a clearer expression than that of the dull workday. The tower up here—it was the only one in sight—the tower of a residence, as now became evident, possibly of the main Castle, was a monotonous round building, in part mercifully hidden by ivy, with little windows that glinted in the sun—there was something crazy about this—and ending in a kind of terrace, whose battlements, uncertain, irregular, brittle, as if drawn by the anxious or careless hand of a child, zigzagged into the blue sky. It was as if some melancholy resident, who by rights ought to have kept himself locked up in the most out-of-the-way room in the house, had broken through the roof and stood up in order to show himself to the world.

> And in his mind he compared the church tower at home with the tower above him. The church tower, firm in line, soaring unfalteringly to its tapering point, topped with red tiles and broad in the roof, an earthly building—what else can men build?—but with a loftier goal than the humble dwelling-houses, and a clearer meaning than the muddle of everyday life. The tower above him here—the only one visible—the tower of a house, as was now evident, perhaps of the main building, was uniformly round, part of it graciously mantled with ivy, pierced by small windows that glittered in the sun—with a somewhat maniacal glitter—and topped by what looked like an attic, with battlements that were irregular, broken, fumbling, as if designed by the trembling or careless hand of a child, clearly outlined against the blue. It was as if a melancholy-mad tenant who ought to have been kept locked in the topmost chamber of his house had burst through the roof and lifted himself up to the gaze of the world. (Muirs, 12)

> Und er verglich in Gedanken den Kirchturm der Heimat mit dem Turm dort oben. Jener Turm, bestimmt, ohne Zögern, geradenwegs nach oben sich verjüngend, breitdachig abschließend mit roten Ziegeln, ein irdisches Gebäude—was können wir anderes bauen?—aber mit höherem Ziel als das niedrige Häusergemenge und mit klarerem Ausdruck als ihn der trübe Werktag hat. Der Turm hier oben—es war der einzige sichtbare—, der Turm eines Wohnhauses, wie sich jetzt zeigte, vielleicht des Hauptschlosses, war ein einförmiger Rundbau, zum Teil gnädig von Epheu verdeckt, mit kleinen Fenstern, die jetzt in der Sonne aufstrahlten—etwas Irrsinniges hatte das—und einem söllerartigen Abschluß, dessen Mauerzinnen unsicher, unregelmäßig, brüchig wie von ängstlicher oder nachlässiger Kinderhand gezeichnet sich in den blauen Himmel zackten. Es war wie wenn irgendein trübseliger Hausbewohner, der gerechter Weise im entlegensten Zimmer des Hauses sich hätte eingesperrt halten sollen, das Dach durchbrochen und sich erhoben hätte, um sich der Welt zu zeigen. (*Schloß*, 18)

Catching the tone is particularly important in pregnant passages such as this, passages that "foreground" language itself—a term coined by the Linguistic Circle in Prague—with the help of techniques more commonly encountered in poetry than in prose.[5] The Muirs' version of this passage still reads well. Indeed, critics who regard smooth readability as the prime criterion in translation might prefer their version of this passage to mine. My English is stranger and denser than the Muirs'; it is also less vivid than theirs. But then so, too, is Kafka's German.

In the above passage the Muirs transform the cryptic original into a sermon about the gulf between the human and the divine. The words with which they characterize the church tower—"soaring unfalteringly," "loftier," etc.—have spiritual undertones that are more pronounced than those in the original. They also lessen the negative implications of Kafka's description. In their translation the church tower is "graciously mantled" by ivy—a phrase I render as "mercifully hidden by ivy" ("gnädig mit Efeu verdeckt"). The voice we hear at such moments in the Muirs' translation is not so much Kafka's as Brod's.

Since the Muirs see K. as a pilgrim in search of salvation, they tend to overlook the criticism that Kafka directs at his namesake. I have sought to make K. as calculating and self-serving in English as he is in the original. For instance, in the first chapter Kafka uses the potentially ambiguous phrase "nach seinen Berechnungen" to describe K.'s thinking (*Schloß*, 30). The Muirs translate that phrase as "by his reckoning" (Muirs, 23); I render it as "according to his calculations" because I hear in it a covert allusion to K.'s calculating nature. Besides, the phrase may be doing double duty here; it could also refer to the ostensible occupation of K., the surveyor, the would-be professional calculator, who is also calculating ("berechnend")—a charge, incidentally, that Kafka often leveled against himself.

Like other modernists, Kafka leaves it up to the reader to discern his transitions, which are often hidden under the surface. Sudden changes of tone, even within a single sentence, can catch the reader off guard. Take, for instance, the following sentence, with its puzzling final clause:

> He moved about more freely now, rested his stick here and there, approached the woman in the armchair, and was, incidentally, the biggest in the room.

> He felt less constrained, poked with his stick here and there, approached the woman in the arm-chair, and noted that he himself was physically the biggest man in the room. (Muirs, 17)

> Er bewegte sich freier, stützte seinen Stock einmal hier einmal dort auf, näherte sich der Frau im Lehnstuhl, war übrigens auch der körperlich größte im Zimmer. (*Schloß*, 24)

The first three elements describe a sequence of actions and clearly belong together; the fourth clause is in a different category since it describes an attribute of K.'s. The Muirs, in an effort to close this seeming gap in narrative logic, insert an explicit link such as one would find in a nineteenth-century novel—"and noted that he himself"—a linking phrase for which there is no counterpart in the original. As a result, their English sounds more conventional than the German.[6]

In *The Castle* the process of interpretation becomes an integral part of the novel. This obsession with meaning is most evident in the second chapter, where K. subjects a six-sentence letter from an official called Klamm—whose name could suggest secretiveness ("klammheimlich")—to a probing analysis that would satisfy even the most exacting of New Critics. Fittingly, that chapter ends with an explicit reference to interpretation:[7]

> "But you're spending the night with us," said Olga in astonishment. "To be sure," said K., leaving it to her to interpret the words he had spoken.

Unlike the Muirs, who translate the last clause as "leaving her to make what she liked of it," I have retained Kafka's explicit reference to interpretation—"und überließ ihr die Deutung der Worte"—because it seems significant in a novel largely made up of K.'s endlessly proliferating interpretations.

Kafka's prose can also be laconically expressive. For instance, when K. attempts to locate Barnabas, his messenger, by shouting his name, we can almost hear the shout:

> Nevertheless, with full force K. shouted out the name, the name thundered through the night.

> None the less K. yelled the name with the full force of his lungs. It thundered through the night. (Muirs, 36)

> Trotzdem schrie K. noch aus aller Kraft den Namen, der Name donnerte durch die Nacht. (*Schloß*, 47)

In German the instant repetition of "name" mimicks K.'s yell, an effect I echo in English. Of course it is always possible to quibble with a translator's solutions. To some ears, my placement of the phrase "with full force" may sound jarring. Yet it is the best compromise I could find. The ideal solution would be to re-create Kafka's wonderfully elastic syntax without making him sound less natural or more jarring—and he can be both—than he is in German. However, modern English shies away from inversions of word order, and this restricts the options available to the translator. One must simply strike the best balance one can.

Among the many such compromises I would like to single out a couple here. For instance, in the first pages we meet the "Wirt" and "Wirtin." Initially I experimented with "innkeeper"—the perfect match for "Wirt." But the "Wirtin" then became "the innkeeper's wife," which turned out to be misleading as well as cumbersome. She is no mere appendage to her husband. I therefore decided to use "landlord" and "landlady"—in their older and now infrequent meaning as proprietor of an inn or similar establishment.[8]

The English-language translator must also grapple with the often conflicting demands of Kafka's tone and style. Colloquial German, especially in the hands of a master like Kafka, can sound both colloquial and terse. Colloquial English tends to be less succinct. For instance, at the end of the first chapter K. asks his two would-be assistants where they have put their surveying equipment, and they respond: "Wir haben keine." The translator must choose between a phrase such as "We have none," which captures the terse style of the original but introduces an inappropriately wooden tone, and the tonally accurate but somewhat less pithy English "We don't have any." In that particular case I selected the latter; at other times I chose less colloquial language in order to echo Kafka's terseness.

While Kafka generally plays off lofty and down-to-earth diction in his usual contrapuntal fashion, sometimes he simply piles one on top of the other. At such moments the translator must choose between preserving the tone and capturing the interpretative nuances under the surface. A simple instance: at one point K. tells the villagers that they have "Ehrfurcht" for the authorities. While that word could mean something as lofty as "reverence" or even "awe," it can also be used in a more everyday sense, simply as "respect." The translator is obliged to choose between the colloquial and elevated tones. I hesitated a long time, since that particular choice could affect how readers interpret the mysterious Castle. Yet in the end I opted for the less lofty term "respect." The word "Ehrfurcht" occurs several times in the same conversation, and to have the characters speak repeatedly of "reverence" or "awe" seemed tonally inappropriate.

Punctuation is another thorny issue. In Germany some critics objected to Kafka's frugal use of punctuation in *Das Schloß*, which Malcolm Pasley respected in the critical edition. One could reasonably argue that Kafka might have gone through the manuscript and inserted conventional punctuation had he prepared the text for publication. Yet, as a diary passage of 1911 suggests, he was highly conscious of the impact punctuation—or its absence—can have on listeners:

> Omission of the period. In general the spoken sentence starts off in a large capital letter with the speaker, bends out in its course as far as it can towards the listeners and with the period returns to the speaker. But if the period is omitted, then the sentence is no longer constrained and blows its entire breath at the listener.[9]

The paragraphs in *The Castle* are extraordinarily long even by the standards of literary German. At the risk of trying the patience of English-speaking readers, I decided to retain them. For one thing it would be difficult to break up the paragraphs without making arbitrary decisions about which portions of dialogue to print in separate paragraphs and which to leave in the narrative. Besides, Kafka's decision to embed the dialogue in the narrative and to omit most punctuation except for commas and an occasional period lends his prose a breathlessly modern tone.

The relentless momentum of Kafka's prose in *The Castle* was not lost on Samuel Beckett. In a rare 1956 interview with a journalist from the *New York Times* Beckett had the following to say about Kafka's style: "I've only read Kafka in German—serious reading—except for a few things in French and English—only *The Castle* in German. . . . You notice how Kafka's form is classic, it goes on like a steamroller—almost serene."[10]

Kafka himself could not always tell where his words would lead him: "Where, then, shall I be brought?"[11] he asks himself in the diaries not long before sitting down to write *The Castle*. That is a question that we, too, constantly ask ourselves. Although we are often unsure what is happening in the strange world of the village and the Castle, Kafka holds us in thrall through a startling combination of breathless intensity and ironic—and at times even drily humorous—detachment.

MARK HARMAN

Notes

I should like to thank Lina Bernstein and David Kramer for graciously hosting readings from the translation-in-progress, and other participants—too numerous to name individually—whose responsiveness spurred its gestation. I am especially indebted to David Kramer's keen ear and linguistic acumen. A grant from the Austrian Ministry of Education and Art provided needed support for the translation. I am also grateful to Fred Jordan, who gave the original commission, to Melanie Richter-Bernburg for her fruitful suggestions and patience with my many revisions, and to Arthur Samuelson, who supported the project and shepherded it into print.

A related essay "Digging the Pit of Babel: Retranslating Franz Kafka's *Castle,*" which appeared in *New Literary History* 27, no. 2 (1996): 291–311, and also, in somewhat different form, in Lenore A. Grenoble and John M. Kopper, eds., *Essays in the Art and Theory of Translation* (Lewiston, N.Y., 1997), 139–64, contains a more complete bibliography than can be included here.

1. W. H. Auden, "Lame Shadows," in *Forewords and Afterwords*, selected by Edward Mendelson (New York, 1973), 404.

2. Edwin Muir, *The Structure of the Novel* (London, 1928), 127.

3. S. S. Prawer, "Difficulties of the Kafkaesque," *Times Literary Supplement,* October 14, 1983, 1127–28.

4. See Kafka's letter about Walser in Mark Harman, ed., *Robert Walser Rediscovered: Stories, Fairy-Tale Plays, and Critical Responses* (Hanover, N.H., 1985), 139–40.

5. The term "foregrounding" was developed by the Prague Linguistic Circle only a few years after Kafka's death. See Jan Mukařovsky, "Standard Language and Poetic Language," in *A Prague School Reader on Esthetics, Literary Structure, and Style,* ed. Paul L. Garvin (Washington, D.C., 1964).

6. In German this sentence sounds more convincing if one reverts to Kafka's initial wording and reads it in the first person. However, that is an isolated instance. Usually, the lingering presence of that erased yet still audible "I" makes K.'s voice all the more compelling. For a comparable phenomenon in Robert Walser, see Mark Harman, "A Secretive Modernist: Robert Walser and his Microscripts," in *Review of Contemporary Fiction* 12, no. 1 (1992): 114–17.

7. Around the time Kafka was writing the "letter chapter" in *The Castle,* he confided the following to Milena Jesenská: "All my misfortune in life . . . derives from letters or from the possibility of writing letters" (late March 1922). Kafka, *Letters to Milena,* trans. Philip Boehm (New York, 1990), 223.

8. Another possibility I considered for "Wirt" and "Wirtin" was "proprietor" and "proprietress"; however, they are too Latinate and emphasize possession in a way that Kafka—who could have chosen the German equivalents, "Inhaber" and "Inhaberin"—does not.

9. Franz Kafka, *Diaries 1910–1923* (New York, 1988), 45.

10. *New York Times,* May 6, 1956, 25.

11. Kafka, *Diaries,* 399.

CONTENTS

I.

ARRIVAL

It was late evening when K. arrived. The village lay under deep snow. There was no sign of the Castle hill, fog and darkness surrounded it, not even the faintest gleam of light suggested the large Castle. K. stood a long time on the wooden bridge that leads from the main road to the village, gazing upward into the seeming emptiness.

Then he went looking for a night's lodging; at the inn they were still awake; the landlord had no room available, but, extremely surprised and confused by the latecomer, he was willing to let K. sleep on a straw mattress in the taproom, K. agreed to this. A few peasants were still sitting over beer, but he did not want to talk to anyone, got himself a straw mattress from the attic and lay down by the stove. It was warm, the peasants were quiet, he examined them for a moment with tired eyes, then fell asleep.

Yet before long he was awakened. A young man in city clothes, with an actor's face, narrow eyes, thick eyebrows, stood beside him with the landlord. The peasants, too, were still there, a few had turned their chairs around to see and hear better. The young man apologized very politely for having awakened K., introduced himself as the son of the Castle steward and said: "This village is Castle property, anybody residing or spending the night here is effectively residing or spending the night at the Castle. Nobody may do so without permission from the Count. But you have no such permission or at least you haven't shown it yet."

K., who had half-risen and smoothed his hair, looked at the people from below and said: "What village have I wandered into? So there is a castle here?"

"Why, of course," the young man said slowly, while several peasants here and there shook their heads at K., "the Castle of Count Westwest."

"And one needs permission to spend the night here?" asked K., as though he wanted to persuade himself that he hadn't perhaps heard the previous statements in a dream.

"Permission is needed" was the reply, and this turned into crude mockery at K.'s expense when the young man, stretching out his arm, asked the landlord and the guests: "Or perhaps permission is not needed?"

"Then I must go and get myself permission," said K., yawning and pushing off the blanket, as though he intended to get up.

"Yes, but from whom?" asked the young man.

"From the Count," said K., "there doesn't seem to be any alternative."

"Get permission from the Count, now, at midnight?" cried the young man, stepping back a pace.

"Is that not possible?" K. asked calmly. "Then why did you wake me up?"

The young man now lost his composure, "The manners of a tramp!" he cried. "I demand respect for the Count's authorities.

I awakened you to inform you that you must leave the Count's domain at once."

"Enough of this comedy," said K. in a remarkably soft voice as he lay down and pulled up the blanket: "You are going a little too far, young man, and I shall deal with your conduct tomorrow. The landlord and those gentlemen there will be my witnesses, should I even need witnesses. Besides, be advised that I am the land surveyor sent for by the Count. My assistants and the equipment are coming tomorrow by carriage. I didn't want to deprive myself of a long walk through the snow, but unfortunately lost my way a few times, which is why I arrived so late. That it was too late then to report to the Castle is something that was already apparent to me without the benefit of your instructions. That's also the reason why I decided to content myself with these lodgings, where you have been so impolite—to put it mildly—as to disturb me. I have nothing further to add to that statement. Good night, gentlemen." And K. turned toward the stove.

"Land surveyor?" he heard someone asking hesitantly behind his back, and then everyone was silent. But the young man soon regained his composure and said to the landlord, softly enough to suggest concern for K.'s sleep, yet loudly enough to be audible to him: "I shall inquire by telephone." So there was even a telephone in this village inn? They were certainly well equipped. True, certain details took K. by surprise, but on the whole everything was as expected. As it turned out, the telephone hung from the wall almost directly above his head, in his sleepiness he had overlooked it. If the young man had to use the telephone, then even with the best intentions he could not avoid disturbing K.'s sleep, it was simply a matter of deciding whether or not to let him use the telephone, K. decided to allow it. But then of course it no longer made sense to pretend he was asleep, so he turned over on his back again. He watched the peasants gathering timidly and conferring, the arrival of a land surveyor was no trifling matter. The door to the kitchen had opened; filling the doorway was the mighty figure of the landlady, the landlord approached her on tiptoes in order to report to her. Then the telephone conversation began. The steward was asleep, but a substeward, one of the substewards, a Mr. Fritz, was there. The young man, who introduced himself as Schwarzer, said that he had found K., a man in his thirties, rather shabby-looking, sleeping quietly on a straw mattress, with a tiny rucksack for a pillow and a knobby walking stick within reach. Well, he had of course suspected him, and since the landlord had obviously neglected his duty, it was his, Schwarzer's, duty to investigate the matter. K.'s response on being awakened, questioned, and duly threatened with expulsion from the Count's domain had been most ungracious but perhaps not unjustifiably so, as had finally become evident, for he claimed to be a land surveyor summoned by the Count. He was duty-bound to check this claim, if only as a formality, and so Schwarzer was asking Mr. Fritz to inquire at the central office whether a land surveyor of that sort was really expected and to telephone immediately with the answer.

Then there was silence, Fritz made his inquiries over there while everyone here waited for the answer, K. stayed where he was, did not even turn around, seemed completely indifferent, stared into space. With its mixture of malice and caution Schwarzer's story gave him a sense of the quasi-diplomatic training that even lowly people at the Castle such as Schwarzer could draw on so freely. Nor did they show any lack of diligence there, the central office had a night service. And obviously answered very quickly, for Fritz was already on the line again. Yet it seemed to be a brief message, since Schwarzer immediately threw down the receiver in a rage. "Just as I said," he shouted, "no trace of a land surveyor, only a liar and a common tramp, and probably worse still." For a moment K. thought that everybody, Schwarzer, the peasants, the landlord and landlady, was about to jump on him, and he crawled all the way under the blanket to escape at least the first assault, when—he was slowly stretching his head back out—the telephone rang again, especially loud, it seemed to K. Although it was unlikely that this call also concerned K., everyone froze, and Schwarzer came back to the telephone. After listening to a fairly long explanation, he said softly: "So it's a mistake? This is most unpleasant. The department head himself telephoned? Odd, very odd! And how am I supposed to explain this to the land surveyor?"

K. listened intently. So the Castle had appointed him land surveyor. On one hand, this was unfavorable, for it showed that the Castle had all necessary information about him, had assessed the opposing forces, and was taking up the struggle with a smile. On the other hand, it was favorable, for it proved to his mind that they underestimated him and that he would enjoy greater freedom than he could have hoped for at the beginning. And if they thought they could keep him terrified all the time simply by acknowledging his surveyorship—though this was certainly a superior move on their part—then they were mistaken, for he felt only a slight shudder, that was all.

After waving aside Schwarzer, who was timidly approaching, K. rejected their insistent pleas that he move into the landlord's room, accepted only a nightcap from the landlord and a wash basin with soap and towel from the landlady, and did not even have to request that the room be cleared, for all rushed to the door, averting their faces so that he wouldn't recognize them tomorrow, then the lamp was extinguished and he finally had some peace. He slept soundly until morning, only briefly disturbed once or twice by scurrying rats.

After breakfast, which the landlord said would be covered by the Castle along with K.'s full board, he wanted to go immediately to the village. Recalling the landlord's conduct yesterday, K. spoke to him only when strictly necessary, but since the landlord kept circling him in a silent plea, K. took pity on him and let him sit down for a moment beside him.

"I still haven't met the Count," said K., "they say he pays good money for good work, is that so? Anybody traveling as far from his wife and child as I am wants to have something to take home with him."

"The gentleman need have no worries in that regard, one doesn't hear any complaints about bad pay here."

"Well," said K., "I'm not at all shy and am quite capable of saying what I think, even to a Count, though it is naturally far better if one can remain on friendly terms with those gentlemen."

The landlord sat opposite K. on the edge of the window seat, not daring to sit more comfortably and keeping his large, anxious brown eyes fixed on K. At first he had thrust himself on K., but now it seemed as if he wanted to run away. Was he afraid of being questioned about the Count? Was he afraid that the "gentleman" whom he saw in K. was unreliable? K. had to distract him. He looked at the clock and said: "Well, my assistants will be here soon, can you put them up?"

"Certainly, sir," he said, "but won't they be staying with you at the Castle?"

Was he parting that easily and that gladly with his guests, especially K., whom he was quite determined to transfer to the Castle?

"That hasn't been settled," said K., "first I must find out what kind of work they have for me. For instance, if I'm to work down here, then it would make more sense for me to live here, too. And I fear that the life up there at the Castle wouldn't appeal to me. I want to be free at all times."

"You don't know the Castle," the landlord said softly.

"Of course," said K, "one shouldn't judge matters too hastily. All I can say about the Castle for now is that they know how to choose the right land surveyor. There might be other advantages there, too." And he stood up in order to release the landlord—who kept anxiously biting his lips—from his presence. It certainly wasn't easy to win the confidence of this man.

On the way out, K. observed on the wall a dark portrait in a dark frame. He had already noticed it from his bed, but unable to discern any details from that distance, he had thought that the actual picture had been taken from the frame, and only the dark backing was to be seen. But it was indeed a picture, as now became evident, the half-length portrait of a man around fifty. He held his head so low over his chest that one barely saw his eyes, the drooping seemed to be caused by the high, ponderous forehead and the powerful, crooked nose. His beard, pressed in at the chin owing to the position of his head, jutted out farther below. His left hand was spread out in his thick hair but could no longer support his head. "Who is that," asked K., "the Count?" K. stood before the picture and did not even turn to glance at the landlord. "No," said the landlord, "the steward." "They do have a handsome steward at the Castle, that's for sure," said K., "what a pity his son turned out so badly." "No," said the landlord, drawing K. down and whispering in his ear, "Schwarzer exaggerated yesterday, his father is only a substeward, and one of the lowest at that." Just then the landlord seemed like a child to K. "The rascal," said K., laughing, but the landlord said without laughing: "Even *his* father is powerful." "Come on!" said K., "you consider everyone powerful. Me too, perhaps?" "No," he said, timidly but gravely, "I do not consider you powerful." "Well, you're very observant, then," said K., "for, speaking in confidence now, I'm really not powerful at all. And so I probably have no less respect for those with power than you do, only I'm not as honest as you are and don't always care to admit it." K. tapped the landlord on the cheek in order to comfort him and to gain his affection. And now he even gave a little smile. He was really a boy with his soft, almost beardless face. How had he come by his stout, older wife, whom one could see through a small window, bustling about with her elbows sticking out? Yet K. did not want to question him any further and risk chasing away the smile he had finally elicited, so he merely signaled to him to open the door and stepped out into the beautiful winter morning.

Now he saw the Castle above, sharply outlined in the clear air and made even sharper by the snow, which traced each shape and lay everywhere in a thin layer. Besides, there seemed to be a great deal less snow up on the hill than here in the village, where it was no less difficult for K. to make headway than it had been yesterday on the main road. Here the snow rose to the cottage windows only to weigh down on the low roofs, whereas on the hill everything soared up, free and light, or at least seemed to from here.

On the whole the Castle, as it appeared from this distance, corresponded to K.'s expectations. It was neither an old knight's fortress nor a magnificent new edifice, but a large complex, made up of a few two-story buildings and many lower, tightly packed ones; had one not known that this was a castle, one could have taken it for a small town. K. saw only one tower, whether it belonged to a dwelling or a church was impossible to tell. Swarms of crows circled round it.

Keeping his eyes fixed upon the Castle, K. went ahead, nothing else mattered to him. But as he came closer he was disappointed in the Castle, it was only a rather miserable little town, pieced together from village houses, distinctive only because everything was perhaps built of stone, but the paint had long since flaked off, and the stone seemed to be crumbling. Fleetingly K. recalled his old hometown, it was scarcely inferior to this so-called Castle; if K. had merely wanted to visit it, all that wandering would have been in vain, and it would have made more sense for him to visit his old homeland again, where he had not been in such a long time. And in thought he compared the church tower in his homeland with the tower up there. The church tower, tapering decisively, without hesitation, straightaway toward the top, capped by a wide roof with red tiles, was an earthly building—what else can we build?—but with a higher goal than the low jumble of houses and with a clearer expression than that of the dull workday. The tower up here—it was the only one in sight—the tower of a residence, as now became evident, possibly of the main Castle, was a monotonous round building, in part mercifully hidden by ivy, with little windows that glinted in the sun—there was something crazy about this—and ending in a kind of terrace, whose battlements, uncertain, irregular, brittle, as if drawn by the anxious or careless hand of a child, zigzagged into the blue sky. It was as if some melancholy resident, who by rights ought to have kept himself locked up in the most out-of-the-way room in the house, had broken through the roof and stood up in order to show himself to the world.

Again K. stood still, as if he had greater powers of judgment at a standstill. But he was distracted. Behind the village church, beside which he had stopped—it was actually only a chapel with a barnlike annex to accommodate the congregation—was the school. A long, low building, an odd combination of makeshift and ancient features, it lay behind a fenced-in garden, which was now a field of snow. Just then the children came out with their teacher. Bunched about the teacher, the children all had their eyes on him, there was constant chatter from all sides, K. could not follow their rapid speech. The teacher, a small narrow-shouldered young man but also, without thereby seeming ridiculous, quite erect, had fixed his eyes from afar on K., who was the only person anywhere around, aside from the teacher's group. As a stranger, K. was the first to say hello, especially faced with such a domineering little man. "Good day, Teacher," he said. All of a sudden the children fell silent, having this sudden silence before he spoke must have pleased the teacher. "You're taking a look at the Castle?" he asked, more gently than K. had expected, but as though he did not approve of what K. was doing. "Yes," said K., "I'm a stranger here, I only arrived in the village yesterday evening." "You don't like the Castle?" the teacher said quickly. "What?" countered K., somewhat baffled, but then, rephrasing the question more delicately, he said: "Do I like the Castle? What makes you think I don't like it?" "Strangers never do," said the teacher. To avoid giving offense then, K. changed the subject and asked: "You must know the Count?" "No," said the schoolteacher, and he was about to turn aside, but K. did not give up and asked again: "So you don't know the Count?" "How could I know him?" the schoolteacher said softly, adding loudly in French: "Keep in mind that there are innocent children present." To K. this was sufficient justification for asking: "Teacher, could I call on you? I'll be staying for some time and already feel a little isolated, I don't belong among the peasants nor in all likelihood at the Castle." "There is no difference between the peasants and the Castle," said the teacher. "Maybe so," said K., "but that has no effect on my situation. May I call on you?" "I live in Swan Street at the butcher's." Though this sounded more like an address than an invitation, K. said: "Very well, I shall come." The schoolteacher nodded and moved on with his little bunch of children, who instantly resumed their shouting. They soon disappeared down a steep side street.

But K. was distracted, the conversation had irritated him. For the first time since coming here, he felt truly tired. At first, the long journey hadn't seemed like much of a strain to him—how he had kept wandering through the days, steadily, one step at a time!—but the consequences of those exertions had to go and make themselves felt now, at the worst possible time, of course. He felt an irresistible urge to seek out new acquaintances, but each new acquaintance had only increased his weariness. In his present state, if he could force himself to prolong this walk to the Castle entrance, that would be more than enough.

So he set off again, but it was a long way. The street he had taken, the main street in the village, did not lead to the Castle hill, it only went close by, then veered off as if on purpose, and though it didn't lead any farther from the Castle, it didn't get any closer either. K. kept expecting the street to turn at last toward the Castle and it was only in this expectation that he kept going; no doubt out of weariness he was reluctant to leave this street, what amazed him, too, was the length of this village, which wouldn't end, again and again those tiny little houses and the frost-covered windowpanes and the snow and not a living soul—finally he tore himself away from this clinging street, a narrow side street took him in, the snow here was even deeper, lifting his sinking feet was hard work, he broke out in perspiration, suddenly came to a stop and could go no farther.

Well, he certainly wasn't abandoned, there were peasant cottages right and left, he made a snowball and threw it at a window. The door opened right away—the first door to open on his way through the village—and standing there was an old peasant in a heavy brown fur jacket, head tilted sideways, friendly and weak. "May I join you for a little while?" said K., "I'm very tired." He didn't hear anything the old man said, but gratefully accepted the plank being pushed toward him, which immediately rescued him from the snow, and after taking a few steps he stood in the room.

A large dimly lit room. At first, the new arrival from outdoors could not see a thing. K. stumbled against a washtub, a woman's hand held him back. From one corner came the sound of children crying. From another, smoke billowed, turning the dim light to darkness, K. remained standing there as if in the clouds. "He must be drunk," someone said. "Who are you?" cried an imperious voice, and then, probably to the old man: "Why did you let him in?" "Can we let in everything that is slinking through the streets?" "I am the land surveyor of the Count," said K., trying to justify himself in front of these as yet invisible people. "Ah, it is the land surveyor," a woman's voice said, and then there was complete silence. "You know me?" asked K. "Of course," the same voice said, curtly. Their knowing K. did not seem to recommend him.

Finally the smoke dispersed a little, and K. was gradually able to get his bearings. It seemed to be washday. By the door, clothes were being washed. Yet the smoke had actually come from the left-hand corner, where in a wooden tub, larger than any K. had ever seen, it was about the size of two beds, two men were bathing in steaming water. But even more surprising, though one still couldn't make out the exact nature of the surprise, was the right-hand corner. Through a large garret window, the only one in the back wall, came pale snow-light, surely from the courtyard, which lent a luster as of silk to the dress of a woman who almost lay wearily in a tall armchair set deep in the corner. She held an infant at her breast. A few children were playing around her, peasant children by the looks of them, but she seemed out of place among them, though illness and weariness can make even peasants seem refined.

"Sit down!" said one of the men, who had a full beard in addition to the mustache over his mouth, which he kept open, snorting, and pointed—a comical sight—with one hand over the rim of the bath at a trunk, splashing warm water all over K.'s face. Seated on the trunk, already dozing off, was the old man who had let K. in. K. was glad he could finally sit down. No one was paying the slightest attention to him now. The woman at the washtub, blond, youthfully ample, sang softly as she worked, the men in the bath stomped their feet and thrashed about, the children tried to approach them but were repeatedly driven back by great splashes of water, from which not even K. emerged unscathed, the woman in the armchair lay there as if lifeless, without even glancing down at the infant on her breast, merely gazing vaguely upward.

K. must have spent a long time looking at them, at this unchanging, beautiful, sad picture, but then he must have fallen asleep, for when a loud voice called out to him he awoke with a start, his head was resting on the shoulder of the old man beside him. The men were finished with the bath—in which the children now romped under the blond woman's supervision—and stood before him fully clothed. The loudmouthed man with the full beard turned out to be the slighter of the two. The other one, no taller, but with a smaller beard than that of his full-bearded colleague, was a silent, slow-witted man, of stout build, with an equally stout face, he kept his head lowered. "Surveyor," he said, "you cannot stay here. Forgive the impoliteness." "I didn't want to stay," said K., "I simply wanted a rest. Now that I have had it, I am leaving." "This lack of hospitality may surprise you," said the man, "but there is no custom of hospitality here, we do not need guests." Somewhat refreshed after his sleep, somewhat keener of hearing than before, K. was glad to hear such frank words. He moved about more freely now, rested his stick here and there, approached the woman in the armchair, and was, incidentally, the biggest in the room.

"Certainly," said K., "what would you need guests for? But every now and then someone is needed, such as me, the land surveyor." "I don't know about that," the man said slowly, "if they summoned you, then they probably need you, this may be an exception, but we little people go by the rule, you shouldn't blame us for that." "No, no," said K., "I simply want to thank you, you and all the others here." And, to everyone's surprise, K. turned around almost in one bound and stood before the woman. With tired blue eyes she looked at K., a transparent silk kerchief had slipped down to the middle of her forehead, the infant was sleeping at her breast. "Who are you?" asked K. Dismissively, it was unclear whether the contempt was meant for K. or her own answer, she said: "A girl from the Castle."

All this had taken no more than an instant; now two men, right and left, seized K. and pulled him to the door, silently but with full force, as if there were no other means of communication. Something about this pleased the old man, who clapped his hands. The washerwoman laughed over near the children, who suddenly began making noise like mad.

Yet K. soon stood outside on the street, the men watched him from the threshold, it was snowing again, although it now seemed a little brighter outside. The man with the full beard cried impatiently: "Where do you want to go? Here's the way to the Castle, this way to the village." K. did not answer, but turned rather to the other man, who, despite his superiority, struck him as the more congenial of the two: "Who are you? Whom should I thank for the visit?" "I am Master Tanner Lasemann," came the reply, "but you needn't thank anybody." "Fine," said K., "perhaps we shall meet again." "I do not think so," said the man. Just then the man with the full beard, raising his arm, cried: "Good day, Artur, good day, Jeremias!" K. turned around, so other people were showing up on the streets of this village! Coming from the Castle were two young men of medium height, both quite slender, in tight-fitting clothes, with very similar, dark-brown faces and strikingly black goatees. They were going astonishingly fast for the state of these roads, flinging out their slender legs in step. "What's the matter?" cried the man with the full beard. One had to shout to make oneself heard, they were going so fast and did not stop. "Business," they shouted back, laughing. "Where?" "At the inn." "That's where I'm going," K. cried all of a sudden, louder than everyone else, he so wanted these two to take him along; though he did not consider this acquaintanceship all that rewarding, they were good traveling companions and could cheer one up. Yet, though they heard K.'s remark, they simply nodded and were gone.

K. was still standing in the snow, he had no great desire to lift his foot out of the snow only to sink it back in a little farther on; the master tanner and his colleague, satisfied at having finally rid themselves of K., slowly pushed their way, eyes still fixed on him, through the barely open door into the house, leaving K. alone in the blanketing snow. "Cause for a slight attack of despair," was the thought that came to him, "if I were only here by accident, not on purpose."

Just then in the cottage to the left a tiny window opened; closed, it had seemed deep blue, perhaps in the reflection from the snow, and so tiny now that it was open that one couldn't see the full face of the onlooker, only the eyes, old brown eyes. "There he is," K. heard the tremulous voice of a woman saying. "It's the surveyor," a man's voice was speaking. Then the man came to the window and asked, not in an unfriendly way but as if he wanted everything to be in order on the street in front of his house: "Who are you waiting for?" "For a sleigh to take me," said K. "No sleighs come along here," said the man, "no traffic comes through here." "But this is the road that leads to the Castle," objected K. "Even so, even so," the man said rather implacably, "no traffic comes through here." Then the two of them fell silent. But the man was obviously contemplating something since he still hadn't closed the window, from which smoke was pouring. "A bad road," K. said to help him out. But all he said was: "Yes, indeed." After a little while, however, he said: "If you like, I will take you on my sleigh." "Please do," said K., delighted, "how much do you want?" "Nothing," the man said by way of explanation. K. was astonished. "You are after all the surveyor," said the man, "and you belong to the Castle. So where do you want to go?" "To the Castle," K. said quickly. "Then I will not go," the man said at once. "But I belong to the Castle," K. said, repeating the man's own words. "Maybe so," the man said dismissively. "Then take me to the inn," said K. "Very well," said the man, "then I'll be out right away with the sleigh." This did not leave the impression of any great friendliness but rather of an extremely egotistical, anxious, almost pedantic effort to get K. away from the street in front of his house.

The courtyard gate opened and let out a small sleigh, made for light loads, quite flat, without any seats, pulled by a small weak horse, and then the man himself, not old, but weak, bent, limping, with a lean red congested face, which seemed especially tiny because of the woolen shawl wrapped tightly round his neck. The man was clearly ill and had obviously only come out to carry K. away. K. said something to that effect, but the man shrugged it off. K. learned only that he was Coachman Gerstäcker and that he had simply chosen this uncomfortable sleigh because it happened to be ready and it would have taken too long to pull out another one. "Sit down," he said, pointing with his whip to the back of the sleigh. "I shall sit beside you," said K. "I will walk," said Gerstäcker. "But why?" asked K. "I will walk," repeated Gerstäcker, so shaken by a fit of coughing that he had to brace his feet in the snow and grasp the side of the sleigh with both hands. Without saying another word, K. sat down in the back of the sleigh, his coughing gradually eased, and they set off.

The Castle up there, oddly dark already, which K. had still been hoping to reach today, receded again. Yet as though he still had to be given a cue for this temporary parting, a bell up there rang out cheerfully, a bell that for a moment at least made one's heart tremble as if it were threatened—for the sound was painful too—with the fulfillment of its uncertain longings. Yet this large bell soon fell silent and was followed by a faint, monotonous little bell, perhaps still from up there, though perhaps already from the village. This tinkling was better suited to this slow journey and this wretched but implacable coachman.

"You there," K. cried suddenly—they were already near the church, the inn wasn't far off, K. could now afford to take a risk—"I'm very surprised you risk driving me around like this, on your own responsibility. Are you allowed to?" Gerstäcker ignored him and continued walking along quietly beside his little horse. "Hey," K. cried, then, rolling some snow from the sleigh, he threw it at Gerstäcker, hitting him right on the ear. Now Gerstäcker stopped and turned around; but when K. saw him standing so close by—the sleigh had slid forward a little—his bent and almost maltreated figure, with the red lean face and cheeks that were somehow different, one flat, the other sunken, and his rapt open mouth with only a few scattered teeth, he was obliged to repeat what he had just said out of malice, only this time out of compassion, and to ask Gerstäcker whether he might not be punished for conveying K. "What do you want?" asked Gerstäcker, baffled, but without waiting for further explanation, he called his little horse, and they moved on.

When they were almost at the inn—K. could see this from a curve in the road—it was, much to his astonishment, quite dark. Had he been away that long? But it was only about an hour or two, by his calculations. He had set out in the morning. And he hadn't needed to eat. And till a moment ago there had been steady daylight, then just now darkness. "Short days, short days," he said to himself as he slid off the sleigh and walked toward the inn.

Standing above on the small front steps of the inn, a welcome sight for K., was the landlord, raising a lantern and shining it at him. Suddenly remembering the coachman, K. stopped, someone coughed in the dark, it was he. Well, he would be seeing him again soon enough. Not until he was on the steps with the landlord, who greeted him deferentially, did he notice the two men, one on either side of the door. He took the lantern from the landlord's hand and shone it at them; these were the men he had already met whose names had been called out, Artur and Jeremias. They saluted. Thinking of his time in the army, those happy days, he laughed. "Who are you?" he asked, glancing from one to the other. "Your assistants," they answered. "Those are the assistants," said the landlord softly in confirmation. "What?" asked K., "you are the old assistants whom I told to join me and am expecting?" They said yes. "It's a good thing," said K., after a little while, "it's a good thing that you've come." "By the way," said K., after another little while, "you're very late, you've been most negligent!" "It was such a long way," said one of the assistants. "A long way," repeated K., "but when I met you, you were coming from the Castle." "Yes," they said, without further explanation. "Where did you put the instruments?" asked K. "We don't have any," they said. "The instruments I entrusted you with," said K. "We don't have any," they repeated. "Oh, you're a fine sort!" said K., "do you know anything about surveying?" "No," they said. "But if you are my old assistants, then you must know something about it," said K. They remained silent. "Well, come along, then," said K., pushing them ahead into the inn.

II.

BARNABAS

*T*hey then sat together rather quietly over beer in the taproom, at a small table with K. in the middle and the assistants on either side. Only one other table was occupied, by peasants, as on the previous evening. "This is difficult," said K., comparing their faces as he had often done before, "how am I supposed to distinguish between you? Only your names are different, otherwise you're as alike as—" he hesitated, then went on involuntarily—"otherwise you're as alike as snakes." They smiled. "People usually can distinguish quite easily between us," they said in self-defense. "I can believe that," said K., "for I witnessed it myself, but I can only see with my eyes and cannot distinguish between you with them. So I shall treat you as one person and call you both Artur, that's what one of you is called—you perhaps?" K. asked one. "No," he said, "my name is Jeremias." "Fine, it doesn't matter," said K., "I shall call you both Artur. When I send Artur somewhere, both of you must go, when I give Artur a task, both of you must do it, the great disadvantage this has for me is that I cannot use you for separate tasks, but the advantage is that the two of you bear undivided responsibility for carrying out all my instructions. How you divide up the work is immaterial to me so long as you do not try to excuse yourselves by blaming each other, I consider you one person." They thought this over and said: "That would be quite unpleasant for us." "Why, of course!" said K., "it must indeed be unpleasant for you, but that's how it's going to be." For some time now K. had been watching one of the peasants slinking about the table; at last the peasant came to a decision, approached an assistant, and was about to whisper something in his ear. "Excuse me," said K., banging his hand on the table and standing up, "these are my assistants, and we are having a meeting. Nobody has the right to disturb us." "Oh sorry, oh sorry," the peasant said anxiously, walking backward toward his companions. "One thing above all else you must keep in mind," said K., sitting down again, "you're not to speak to anyone without my permission. I'm a stranger here, and if you are my old assistants, then you are strangers, too. We three strangers must stick together, give me your hands on that." All too eagerly they stretched out their hands. "Drop your paws," he said, "but my order stands. I shall go to bed now and suggest you do likewise. We have lost a full workday and have to start work very early tomorrow. You must get hold of a sleigh for the journey to the Castle and have it ready at the door at six o'clock." "Fine," said one, but the other broke in: "You say 'fine,' though you know it's impossible." "Be quiet," said K., "you're simply trying to show you're different." But now the first one, too, said: "He's right, that's impossible, no strangers are allowed into the Castle without permission." "Where must one apply for permission?" "I don't know, at the steward's, perhaps." "Then we shall apply there by telephone, telephone the steward at once, both of you." They ran to the telephone, obtained a connection—how they jostled each other there, outwardly they were ridiculously obedient—and inquired whether K. could go with them tomorrow to the Castle. The "No" of the answer reached K. at his table, but the answer was more explicit, it went, "neither tomorrow nor any other time." "I myself shall telephone," said K., getting up. While K. and his assistants had attracted little attention up to now, aside from the incident with the peasant, his last remark attracted general attention. They all stood up with K., and though the landlord tried to push them back, they gathered round him in a tight half-circle at the telephone. The majority thought that K. would get no answer. K. was obliged to ask them to be quiet, he had no desire to hear their opinion.

From the mouthpiece came a humming, the likes of which K. had never heard on the telephone before. It was as though the humming of countless childlike voices—but it wasn't humming either, it was singing, the singing of the most distant, of the most utterly distant, voices—as though a single, high-pitched yet strong voice had emerged out of this humming in some quite impossible way and now drummed against one's ears as if demanding to penetrate more deeply into something other than one's wretched hearing. K. listened without telephoning, with his left arm propped on the telephone stand he listened thus.

He had no idea how long, not until the landlord tugged at his coat, saying that a messenger had come for him. "Go," shouted K., beside himself, perhaps into the telephone, for now someone answered. The following conversation came about: "Oswald here, who's there?" said a severe, arrogant voice with a slight speech defect, for which, it seemed to K., the speaker tried to compensate by sounding even more severe. K. was hesitant to give his name, against the telephone he was defenseless, the person could shout him down, lay down the mouthpiece, and K. would have blocked a path that was perhaps not insignificant. K.'s hesitation made the man impatient. "Who's there?" he repeated, adding, "I should be greatly pleased if less use were made of the telephone there, someone telephoned only a moment ago." K. did not reply to this remark and announced with sudden resolve: "This is the assistant of the gentleman who came as surveyor." "What assistant? What gentleman? What surveyor?" K. recalled yesterday's telephone conversation. "Ask Fritz," he said curtly. It worked, to his own astonishment. Yet what amazed him even more than its working was the consistency of the official service there. The response was: "I know. The eternal land surveyor. Yes, yes. Go on? What assistant?" "Josef," said K. Having the peasants mumbling behind his back was somewhat annoying, they evidently disapproved of his not giving his right name. But K. had no time to deal with them, for the conversation required all his attention. "Josef?" came the reply. "The assistants are called—" a short pause, he was apparently asking somebody else for their names—"Artur and Jeremias." "Those are the new assistants," said K. "No, those are the old ones." "Those are the new ones, I'm the old one who came today to join the surveyor." "No," the voice was now shouting. "Who am I, then?" K. asked as calmly as before. And after a pause, the same voice, which had the same speech defect but sounded like a different, deeper, more imposing voice, said: "You're the old assistant."

K. was still listening to the sound of the voice and almost missed the next question: "What do you want?" Most of all he would have liked to put down the receiver. He was no longer expecting anything from this conversation. Only under pressure did he quickly add: "When can my master come to the Castle?" "Never," came the answer. "Fine," said K., replacing the receiver.

Behind him the peasants had already edged up extremely close to him. The assistants, who kept casting side glances at him, were busy keeping the peasants away. But this seemed no more than a comedy, and the peasants, satisfied with the outcome of the conversation, gradually yielded. Just then their group was divided in two by a man who came from behind in rapid stride, bowed before K., and handed him a letter. K. held the letter in his hand and looked at the man, who seemed more important to him just then. He greatly resembled the assistants, was as slender as they, just as lightly dressed, had the same quickness and agility, and yet he was quite different. If only K. could have had him as an assistant! He reminded K. somewhat of the woman with the infant whom he had seen at the master tanner's. He was dressed almost entirely in white, the material could scarcely be silk, it was winter clothing like all the rest, but it had the delicacy and formality of silk. His face was bright and open, with enormous eyes. His smile was uncommonly encouraging; he brushed his hand across his face as though trying to chase away the smile, but he didn't succeed. "Who are you?" asked K. "My name is Barnabas," he said, "I am a messenger." As he spoke, his lips opened and closed in a masculine but gentle way. "How do you like it here?" asked K., pointing to the peasants, who still hadn't lost interest in him and who, with their bulging lips, open mouths, and almost tortured faces—their heads looked as if they had been beaten flat on top and their features shaped in the pain of the beating—were staring at him but then again not staring at him since their eyes sometimes wandered off and rested a while on some indifferent object before returning to him, and then K. pointed to the assistants, who were embracing each other, cheek to cheek, and smiling, whether in humility or mockery one could not tell, he pointed all this out as if introducing an entourage forced on him by special circumstances in the hope—this suggested familiarity, which was what mattered to K.—that Barnabas had the sense to tell the difference between these people and K. Yet Barnabas completely ignored this, though in all innocence as one could see, letting the question pass, just like a well-trained servant faced with a comment only seemingly addressed to him by his master, and in response to the question merely looked about, greeting his acquaintances among the peasants with a wave and exchanging a few words with the assistants, all this freely and independently, without mingling with them. Rejected but not abashed, K. turned to the letter in his hand and opened it. It read as follows: "Dear Sir! As you know, you have been accepted into the Count's service. Your immediate superior is the village council chairman, he will furnish you with all further details concerning your work and terms of employment, and you, in turn, will be accountable to him. Nevertheless, I too shall keep you in mind. Barnabas, who brings you this letter, will occasionally call on you to ascertain your wishes and relay them to me. You will find that I am always ready, insofar as possible, to oblige you. Having satisfied workers is important to me." The signature wasn't legible, but printed beside it were the words: The Director of Bureau No. 10. "Wait!" K. told Barnabas, who was bowing, then he asked the landlord to show him his room, since he wanted to spend some time alone with the letter. At the same time it occurred to him that regardless of his affection for Barnabas he was merely a messenger, so he had them bring him a beer. He observed him to see how he would accept it; he accepted it with seeming eagerness and drank it right away. Then K. left with the landlord. In that little house they had only been able to prepare a small attic room for K., and even that had caused problems, for the two maids who had slept there until then had had to be lodged elsewhere. Actually, they had only moved out the maids, aside from that the room was probably unchanged, there were no sheets on the one bed, just a few pillows and a horse blanket left in the same state as everything else after last night, on the wall there were a few saints' pictures and photographs of soldiers, the room hadn't even been aired, they were evidently hoping the new guest wouldn't stay long and did nothing to keep him. Yet K. agreed to everything, wrapped himself in the blanket, sat down at the table and in the light of a candle began to read the letter again.

It wasn't consistent, some passages treated him as a free man and conceded that he had a will of his own, such as the initial greeting and the passage concerning his wishes. There were other passages, though, that treated him openly or indirectly as a lowly worker who was barely noticeable from the director's post, the director had to make an effort to "keep him in mind," his superior was only the village chairman, to whom he was even accountable, his only colleague was perhaps the village policeman. Undoubtedly these were contradictions, so obvious they must be intentional. The thought—a crazy one in the case of such authorities—that indecision might have played a role here, scarcely occurred to K. He saw it more as a choice that had been freely offered him, it had been left up to him to decide what he wanted to make of the provisions in the letter, whether he wanted to be a village worker with a distinctive but merely apparent connection to the Castle, or an apparent village worker who in reality allowed the messages brought by Barnabas to define the terms of his position. K. did not hesitate to choose, nor would he have hesitated to do so even if he had never had certain experiences here. It was only as a village worker, as far from the Castle gentlemen as possible, that he could achieve anything at the Castle, these people in the village who were so distrustful of him would start talking as soon as he had become if not their friend then their fellow citizen, and once he had become indistinguishable from, say, Gerstäcker or Lasemann—this must happen very quickly, everything depended on it—all those paths would suddenly open up, which if he were to rely solely on the gentlemen above, on their good graces, would always remain blocked off and invisible too. Yet there was certainly a risk, and the letter stressed this and even dwelled on it with a certain delight, as though it were inevitable: it was his status as a worker. "Service," "superior," "work," "terms of employment," "accountable," "workers," the letter was crammed with such terms and even if it referred to other, more personal matters, it did so from the same point of view. If K. wanted to become a worker, he could become one, but then only in dreadful earnest, without any prospects anywhere else. K. knew that there was no threat of actual compulsion, he had no fear of that, especially not here, but the force of these discouraging surroundings and of the increasing familiarity with ever more predictable disappointments, the force of scarcely perceptible influences at every moment, these he certainly did fear, but even in the face of this danger he had to risk taking up the struggle. Indeed, the letter made no secret of the fact that if it came to a struggle, K. was the one who had been reckless enough to start, this was delicately put and could only have been noticed by a troubled conscience—troubled, not bad—namely, the three words "as you know," concerning his being accepted into the Castle's service. K. had announced his presence and ever since then he had known, as the letter put it, that he was accepted.

K. took a picture from the wall and hung the letter on the nail, this is where he would be living, so the letter should hang here.

Then he went down to the taproom, Barnabas was sitting at a small table with the assistants. "Ah, there you are," said K., for no reason, simply because he was glad to see Barnabas. He jumped up at once. K. had no sooner entered than the peasants rose to get close to him, they had already formed the habit of following him about constantly. "What is it you always want from me?" cried K. They did not take offense and slowly withdrew to their places. As one of them walked off, he said casually with an indecipherable smile, which several others adopted: "One always gets to hear some news" and he licked his lips as if the news were edible. K. didn't say anything conciliatory to him, it was good if they learned to respect him, but no sooner was he seated beside Barnabas than he felt a peasant's breath down the back of his neck, the peasant said he had come for the salt shaker, but K. stomped his foot in anger, and the peasant ran off without the salt shaker. It was really easy to get the better of K.; one simply needed, say, to set the peasants on him, their stubborn concern seemed more malicious to him than the aloofness of the others and it, too, was a form of aloofness, for if K. had sat down at their table, they would certainly not have remained seated. Only Barnabas's presence prevented him from making a commotion. Nonetheless, he swung around menacingly toward them, they were also facing him. Yet seeing them sitting there like that, each one on his own chair, neither conversing with one another nor visibly connected, connected only because all of them were staring at him, it seemed to him that they weren't pursuing him out of malice, perhaps they really wanted something from him but just couldn't say what it was, and if that wasn't it, perhaps it was merely childlike behavior on their part, the childlike quality that seemed very much at home here; wasn't it also childlike of the landlord to be standing there, holding in both hands a glass of beer, which he should have taken to some guest, gazing at K. and missing a cry from the landlady, who had leaned out of the kitchen hatch.

Calmer now, K. turned to Barnabas, he would have liked to remove the assistants but couldn't find a pretext, besides they were staring silently at their beer. "I have read the letter," K. began. "Do you know the contents?" "No," said Barnabas. His expression seemed to convey more than his words. Perhaps K. was being mistakenly positive now, just as he had been mistakenly negative with the peasants, but the presence of Barnabas remained a source of comfort. "There is also talk of you in the letter, you must carry messages back and forth between me and the director, that's why I assumed you knew the contents." "I was simply instructed," Barnabas said, "to hand you the letter, wait until you had read it, and bring back a verbal or written reply, should you find this necessary." "Fine," said K., "no letter is required, convey to the director—but what's his name? I couldn't read his signature." "Klamm," said Barnabas. "Well then convey my thanks to Mr. Klamm for the acceptance and also for his exceptional kindness, which I, as one who still hasn't proved himself here, certainly appreciate. I shall act entirely in accordance with his intentions. I have no special wishes for today." Barnabas, who had followed this closely, asked whether he could repeat the message in K.'s presence, K. gave permission, and Barnabas repeated everything word for word. Then he stood up in order to take his leave.

Throughout all this K. had been examining his face and now did so one last time. Though Barnabas was about as tall as K., his eyes seemed to look down on K., but almost deferentially; it was inconceivable that this man could ever put anybody to shame. Of course, he was only a messenger and wasn't familiar with the contents of the letters he had to deliver, but his expression, his smile, his gait, seemed to bear a message, even if he himself was unaware of it. And K. stretched out his hand, which clearly surprised Barnabas, for he had merely intended to bow.

As soon as he had left—before opening the door he had leaned against the door with his shoulder for a moment and looked around the taproom, with a glance no longer directed at anyone in particular—K. said to the assistants: "I shall get my notes from my room, then we'll discuss the next project." They wanted to go with him. "Stay here!" said K. They still wanted to go with him. K. had to repeat the command in a more severe tone of voice. Barnabas was no longer in the corridor. But he had just left. And yet outside the inn—it was snowing again—K. could not see him. He cried: "Barnabas!" No answer. Could he still be in the building? This seemed the only possibility. Nevertheless, with full force K. shouted out the name, the name thundered through the night. And from a distance a faint answer came, so Barnabas had already gone that far. K. called him back as he went toward him; where they met, they were no longer visible from the inn.

"Barnabas," said K., unable to suppress a tremor in his voice, "there is something else I must tell you. I see now that this is actually quite a bad arrangement, my having to depend entirely on your chance appearances whenever I need anything from the Castle. If I hadn't managed to catch you just now by chance—the speed at which you fly, I thought you were still at the inn—who knows how long I should have had to wait before you came again." "Well," said Barnabas, "you can ask the director to ensure that I always come at times set by you." "But that wouldn't do either," said K., "perhaps for a whole year I won't want to send any messages, and then only fifteen minutes after you're gone, something that cannot be delayed." "Should I report to the director, then," said Barnabas, "that there needs to be another means of communication between him and you, other than through me." "No, no," said K., "absolutely not, I'm only mentioning this in passing, for I had the good fortune to catch you just now." "Should we go back to the inn," said Barnabas, "so that you can give me the new instructions?" He already had taken a step toward the inn. "Barnabas," said K., "that isn't necessary, I shall go part of the way with you." "Why don't you want to go to the inn?" asked Barnabas. "Those people there keep disturbing me," said K., "you yourself have seen how intrusive those peasants are." "We can go to your room," said Barnabas. "It's the maids' room," said K., "it's dirty and dank, I wanted to go a bit of the way with you so I wouldn't have to stay there, only," K. added in an attempt to overcome Barnabas's hesitation, "you must let me take your arm, your footing is surer than mine." K. took his arm. It was quite dark, K. couldn't see his face, his form was indistinct, a little while ago he had tried to grope about for his arm.

Barnabas gave in, they moved away from the inn. Still, K. felt that however hard he tried he couldn't keep up with Barnabas and was restricting his freedom of movement and that a little thing like that could ruin everything even under ordinary conditions, let alone in side streets like the one where K. had sunk into the snow that morning and from which he could extricate himself only if Barnabas lifted him out. Yet he put aside those worries for now, besides he found Barnabas's silence comforting; if they went on like this in silence, it meant that for Barnabas, too, the only reason for being together was to keep going.

They went on, where to K. had no idea, he couldn't recognize anything, didn't even know whether they had passed the church. Due to the sheer effort of walking he could no longer control his thoughts. Rather than remaining fixed on the goal, they became confused. His homeland kept surfacing, filling him with memories. On its main square, too, was a church, partly surrounded by an old cemetery, and it, in turn, by a high wall. Only very few boys had ever climbed this wall, K. still hadn't succeeded either. It wasn't curiosity that drove them, the cemetery no longer held any secrets for them, they had often enough gone in through the small wrought-iron gate and had merely wanted to conquer the smooth high wall. And then one morning—the calm, empty square was flooded with light, when before or since had K. ever seen it like this?—he succeeded with surprising ease; at a spot where he had been often rebuffed, with a small flag clenched between his teeth, he climbed the wall on the first attempt. Pebbles were still trickling down, but he was on top. He rammed in the flag, the wind filled out the cloth, he looked down, all around, even over his shoulder at the crosses sinking into the earth; there was nobody here, now, bigger than he. By chance the teacher came by and with an angry look drove K. down, in jumping off K. hurt his knee and only with difficulty reached home, but still he had been up on the wall, it had seemed to him then that this feeling of victory would sustain him throughout a long life, and this hadn't been entirely foolish, for now, after many years, on the arm of Barnabas in this snowy night it came to his aid.

He tightened his grip, Barnabas almost dragged him, the silence was not broken; of this particular route K. could say only that judging by the state of the road they had not yet turned off into a side street. He vowed not to let any difficulties along the way or worries about the way back keep him from going on, for after all he surely had sufficient strength for being dragged along. And could this path be endless? All day the Castle had lain before him like an easy goal, and this messenger certainly knew the shortest way.

Just then Barnabas stopped. Where were they? Couldn't they go on? Would Barnabas send K. on his way? He wouldn't succeed. K. gripped Barnabas's arm so tightly that he almost hurt himself. Or might the incredible have happened and they were already in the Castle or at its gates? Yet, so far as K. knew, they still hadn't gone uphill. Or had Barnabas led him along such an imperceptibly rising path? "Where are we?" K. asked quietly, more to himself than to Barnabas. "Home," said Barnabas in the same tone. "Home?" "Now take care, sir, that you don't slip. The path goes downhill." "Downhill?" "Only another step or two," he added, and he was already knocking on a door.

A girl opened it, they were now standing on the threshold of a large room that lay almost in darkness, for there was only a tiny oil lamp hanging over a table on the left toward the back. "Who is with you, Barnabas?" the girl asked. "The surveyor," he said. "The surveyor," said the girl, repeating his answer more loudly in the direction of the table. At that, two old people, a man and his wife, stood up, and a girl as well. They greeted K. Barnabas introduced him to everyone, it was his parents and his sisters, Olga and Amalia. K. scarcely looked at them, they removed his wet coat to dry it by the stove, K. let this happen.

So it was not they who were at home, only Barnabas was at home. But why were they here? K. took Barnabas aside and said: "Why did you go home? Or do you live in the Castle precincts?" "In the Castle precincts?" Barnabas repeated, as if he did not understand K. "Barnabas," said K., "you wanted to go from the inn to the Castle." "No, sir," said Barnabas, "I wanted to go home, I only go to the Castle in the morning, I never sleep there." "So," said K., "you didn't want to go to the Castle, only as far as here"—to K. his smile seemed fainter, and he himself more insignificant—"why didn't you say so?" "You never asked, sir," said Barnabas, "you merely wanted to give me another message, but neither in the taproom nor in your own room, so I thought you could give it to me here at my parents' house without anybody disturbing you—they will go away at once, if that's the order you give—besides, if you prefer to be with us, you can spend the night here. Haven't I done the right thing?" K. was unable to answer. So it was a misunderstanding, a low vulgar misunderstanding, and K. had completely abandoned himself to it. He had let himself be spellbound by the shimmering, silky, tight-fitting jacket, which Barnabas now unbuttoned, revealing underneath a coarse, dirt-gray, often-mended shirt over the powerful square chest of a farmhand. And everything else was not only in keeping with this but even outdid it, the old gout-ridden father, who moved more with the help of his groping hands than of his stiff trailing legs, and the mother who, hands clasped on her breast, could because of her girth only take the tiniest of steps; ever since he had entered, Barnabas's father and mother had been trying to approach him from their corner, but they were still nowhere near him. The sisters, blondes, who resembled each other and Barnabas, too—though with harsher features than Barnabas—were big strong country girls; they surrounded the new arrivals, expecting some greeting from K.; yet he couldn't say a word, he had been convinced that everyone in the village mattered to him, and this was probably true, but these people in particular meant absolutely nothing to him. If he could have managed the way back to the inn alone, he would have left at once. The possibility of going to the Castle with Barnabas tomorrow morning did not tempt him at all. He had wanted to press on to the Castle, at night, unnoticed, led by Barnabas, but by Barnabas as he had struck him till now, a man who was closer to him than everyone else he had met here thus far and who, so he had also believed then, possessed close connections with the Castle far exceeding his apparent rank. But as for the son of this family, who fully belonged to it and already was sitting at the table with them, a man who significantly enough wasn't even allowed to sleep at the Castle, to go arm in arm with him to the Castle in broad daylight was impossible, a ridiculous, hopeless endeavor.

K. sat down on a window seat, determined to spend the night there and not to accept any other services from this family. The people in the village, who sent him away or at least feared him, were less dangerous, it seemed to him, since they essentially threw him back on his own resources and thus helped him to preserve his strength, whereas those seeming helpers who, instead of taking him to the Castle, led him by means of a little masquerade to their family, distracted him, whether intentionally or not, and were draining all his strength. Completely ignoring an invitation from the family table, he remained on his window seat, with his head bent.

Then Olga, the gentler of the two sisters, rose, came over, and with a touch of girlish embarrassment asked him to join them at the table, they had already put out bread and bacon, she would go to get beer. "But from where?" K. asked. "From the inn," she said. K. was pleased to hear this, he asked that instead of getting beer she accompany him to the inn, important tasks still awaited him there. It now turned out, though, that she did not want to go to his inn, only to one much closer by, to the Gentlemen's Inn. Nonetheless, K. asked whether he could accompany her, they might have a place for the night, he thought; no matter what it was like, he would rather have it than the best bed in this house. Olga did not answer at once, she glanced back at the table. Her brother stood up, nodded eagerly, and said: "If that's what the gentleman wants—" This approval almost prompted K. to withdraw his request, anything that man could approve must be worthless. Yet when they brought up the question whether K. would be admitted to the inn and everyone doubted it, he insisted all the more urgently on going, though without troubling to invent a plausible reason for his request; this family had to accept him as he was, somehow he had no shame where they were concerned. Only Amalia shook his confidence slightly in that respect with her grave, fixed, imperturbable, and perhaps rather dull gaze.

On the short walk to the inn—K. took Olga's arm and let himself be pulled, what else could he do, much as he had done earlier with her brother—he discovered that this inn was reserved exclusively for the Castle gentlemen, who, whenever they had anything to do in the village, would eat and sometimes even spend the night there. Olga spoke with K., softly and as if on familiar terms, it was pleasant walking with her, almost as pleasant as with her brother, K. struggled against this sense of well-being, but it persisted.

Outwardly the inn was very similar to the inn where K. was staying, there were hardly any great outward differences in the village, but one could detect certain minor differences right away, there was a balustrade on the front steps and a handsome lantern attached over the door; as they entered, a cloth fluttered over their heads, it was a flag with the Count's colors. In the hallway they immediately encountered the landlord, evidently on a tour of inspection; with small eyes he looked quizzically or sleepily at K. in passing and said: "The surveyor may go no farther than the taproom." "Of course," said Olga, immediately taking K.'s side, "he only came with me!" But K., ungrateful, let go of Olga and took the landlord aside, meanwhile Olga waited patiently at the end of the corridor. "I would like to spend the night here," said K. "Unfortunately, that's impossible," said the landlord, "you don't seem to realize yet that this house is reserved exclusively for the gentlemen from the Castle." "That may be the regulation," said K., "but you can surely let me sleep in a corner somewhere." "I should very much like to oblige you," said the landlord, "but, leaving aside the severity of the actual regulation, which you speak of in the manner of a stranger, that is simply impracticable since the gentlemen are extremely sensitive, I am convinced that they cannot bear the sight of a stranger, or not without forewarning at least; so if I let you spend the night here and by chance—and chance is always on the gentlemen's side—somebody were to come across you, not only would I be lost, but so too would you. This sounds ridiculous, but it's true." This tall, rather reserved gentleman, who had one hand braced against the wall, the other on his hip, his legs crossed and body tilted slightly toward K., and was speaking to him in confidence, no longer seemed to belong in this village, though his suit was festive only by peasant standards. "I believe you completely," said K., "and don't by any means underestimate the importance of the actual regulation, however clumsily I may have expressed myself. There's only one other thing to which I wish to draw your attention, I have valuable connections at the Castle and will obtain others that are even more valuable, these will shield you from any danger possibly arising from my overnight stay and guarantee that I can express fitting gratitude for this small favor." "I know," said the landlord, and then he repeated: "I know that." K. could have stated his wish more emphatically, but distracted by this particular response, he merely asked: "Are many gentlemen from the Castle spending the night here?" "In that respect the situation tonight is quite favorable," the landlord said, almost enticingly, "only one gentleman has stayed." K. still found it impossible to insist, he was hoping that by now he almost had permission to stay, so he simply asked for the gentleman's name. "Klamm," the landlord said casually, turning to his wife, who came rustling along dressed in clothes that were oddly threadbare, outmoded, and laden with pleats and frills, but city finery nonetheless. She came to get the landlord, the director desired something. Before he left, the landlord turned to K., as though the decision about the overnight stay no longer rested with him but with K. K., however, was unable to say a word; especially surprising to him was the presence of his superior; unable to explain this to himself, he felt that he couldn't deal as freely with Klamm as he generally did with the Castle, and though it wouldn't have been as terrifying as the landlord assumed if Klamm had caught him there, it would nonetheless have led to an awkward unpleasantness, as if he had, say, frivolously inflicted suffering on someone he was indebted to, yet it still oppressed him greatly to see that the consequences he feared, such as his being a subordinate, a worker, were becoming evident and that he couldn't overcome them even here, where they were so blatant. He stood thus, silently biting his lips. Before disappearing into a doorway, the landlord looked back at him again, K. stared after him and did not move from the spot until Olga came and pulled him away. "What did you want from the landlord?" asked Olga. "I wanted to spend the night here," said K. "But you're spending the night with us," said Olga in astonishment. "To be sure," said K., leaving it to her to interpret the words he had spoken.

III.

FRIEDA

In the taproom, large but empty in the middle, there were a few peasants along the walls, leaning against barrels or sitting on them, but they looked different from the people at K.'s inn. The ones here were more neatly and uniformly dressed in a coarse gray-yellow material with bulky jackets and tight-fitting trousers. Small men, at first glance they seemed quite alike, with their flat bony yet round-cheeked faces. All were quiet and barely moved except to train their eyes on the new arrivals, slowly and indifferently. Still, because they were so numerous and because it was so silent they had a certain effect on K. He took Olga's arm again to let these people know why he was here. In a corner a man, an acquaintance of Olga's, rose and was about to approach them, but with her linked arm K. turned her in another direction, she alone could notice this, and she accepted it with a smiling side-glance at him.

The beer was served by a young girl called Frieda. A nondescript little blonde with sad features, thin cheeks, and a surprising gaze, a gaze of exceptional superiority. When this gaze descended on K., it seemed to him to be a gaze that had already decided matters concerning him, whose existence he himself still knew nothing about, but of whose existence that gaze now convinced him. K. kept watching Frieda from the side even while she spoke with Olga. Olga and Frieda didn't seem to be friends, they merely exchanged a few cold words. K. wanted to help them out, so he asked abruptly: "Do you know Mr. Klamm?" Olga burst out laughing. "Why are you laughing?" K. asked irritably. "But I'm not laughing," she said, though she kept on laughing. "Olga is still a rather childish girl," said K., bending down over the counter so as to draw Frieda's gaze firmly back toward him. But she kept her eyes lowered and said softly: "Do you want to see Mr. Klamm?" K. said yes. She pointed to a door right beside her on the left. "Here's a little peephole, you can look through here." "And what about these people?" asked K. She pouted out her lower lip, and with an uncommonly soft hand pulled K. to the door. Through the small hole, which evidently had been drilled for the purpose of observation, he could almost see the entire room next door. At a desk in the center on a comfortable armchair sat Mr. Klamm, harshly illuminated by a lightbulb hanging in front of him. A medium-sized, fat, ponderous gentleman. His face was still smooth, but his cheeks had begun to sag a little under the weight of the years. His black mustache stuck out on the sides. A precariously balanced pince-nez, which reflected the light, concealed his eyes. Had Mr. Klamm been sitting directly facing the desk, K. would have seen only his profile, but since Klamm was turned straight toward him, he had a full view of his face. Klamm had put his left elbow on the desk and his right hand, which held a Virginia cigar, was resting on his knee. On the desk was a beer glass; since the desk had a high rim, K. could not see clearly whether there were any documents lying there, but to him the desk seemed empty. In order to make sure, he asked Frieda to look through the hole and tell him what she saw. But since she had just been in the room, she could confirm right away that there were no documents lying there. K. asked Frieda whether he had to leave now, but she said he could look as long as he wanted. Now K. was alone with Frieda; Olga, he fleetingly noted, had indeed found her way to her acquaintance and sat high up on a barrel, kicking her feet. "Frieda," said K. in a whisper, "do you know Mr. Klamm very well?" "Oh, yes," she said, "very well." She leaned over next to K., playfully arranging her blouse, which, as K. only now noticed, was a thin low-cut cream-colored garment, hanging like a foreign object from her poor body. Then she said: "Don't you remember how Olga laughed?" "Yes, the rude thing," said K. "Well," she said in a conciliatory tone, "there was cause for laughter, you asked whether I know Klamm, actually I'm"—at this point she involuntarily straightened up a little and her victorious gaze, which had absolutely nothing to do with the conversation, passed over K. again—"actually I'm his mistress." "Klamm's mistress," said K. She nodded. "Well," said K., smiling, so that things wouldn't get too serious between them, "then I consider you a very respectable person." "You're not alone in that," Frieda said affably, though without returning his smile. K. had a means of combatting this arrogance and employed it by asking: "Have you ever been at the Castle?" But this didn't work, for she responded: "No, but isn't it sufficient that I'm here in the taproom?" Her ambition was obviously boundless and it was on K., apparently, that she sought to appease it. "Of course," said K., "here in the taproom it is you who does the landlord's work." "That's true," she said, "and I began as a stable maid at the Bridge Inn." "With those delicate hands," said K. half-quizzically, not knowing whether he was merely flattering her or had himself really been conquered by her. Her hands were indeed small and delicate, but they could also be called weak and expressionless. "Nobody paid any attention to that then," she said, "and even now—" K. looked at her quizzically, she shook her head and broke off. "Of course," said K., "you have your secrets and aren't about to tell them to someone you've only known for half an hour, someone who still hasn't even had a chance to tell you about his situation." This remark proved inopportune, it was as if he had awakened Frieda from a slumber favorable to him, she took from the leather bag hanging from her belt a small wooden stick, stopped the peephole with it, and said to K., clearly checking herself so that he wouldn't notice the change in her attitude, "As for you, I know all about you, you're the surveyor," and then she added, "but I must get back to work now," and she went to her place behind the counter while here and there several of the people rose to get their empty glasses refilled. K. wanted to speak with her again, unobtrusively, so he took an empty glass from a stand and went up to her: "Just one more thing, Miss Frieda," he said, "the achievement of working one's way up from stable girl to barmaid is quite extraordinary and one that requires exceptional strength, but does this mean that such a person has reached the ultimate goal? Absurd question! Your eyes, don't laugh at me now, Miss Frieda, your eyes speak not so much of the past struggle as of that to come. But the world puts up great resistance, the higher the goals, the greater the resistance, and it's no disgrace to secure help, even that of a little man without influence who is struggling just as much. Perhaps we could get together sometime for a quiet talk, without all these eyes staring at us." "I don't know what you want," she said, and her voice now seemed to echo not the victories of her life but its infinite disappointments, "perhaps you want to take me from Klamm. Good heavens!" she said, clapping her hands. "You've seen through me," K. said as if wearied by such great mistrust, "that precisely was my most secret goal. You were supposed to leave Klamm and become my mistress. And now of course I can go. Olga!" cried K., "we're going home." Obediently Olga slid from the barrel, but she couldn't immediately free herself from the friends encircling her. At that, Frieda said softly, with a menacing glance at K.: "When can I speak with you?" "Can I spend the night here?" asked K. "Yes," said Frieda. "Can I stay here now?" "Go with Olga, so I can get rid of these people here. And then after a while you can come back." "Fine," said K., and he waited impatiently for Olga. But the peasants wouldn't let her go, they had made up a dance with Olga in the middle, and during this round dance one of them, always at a cry from the whole group, went up to Olga, grasped her firmly by the hips, and whirled her about several times, the round went ever faster, their hungrily rattling shouts gradually merged into a single sound, Olga, who had tried earlier to break out of the circle with a smile, was now simply reeling about from one to the other, with her hair undone. "That's the sort of people they send me," said Frieda, biting her thin lips in anger. "Who are they?" asked K. "Klamm's servants," said Frieda, "he always brings these people with him, their presence shatters me. I barely know what I have been telling you, Surveyor, if I said anything bad, forgive me, it's the presence of these people that's to blame, they're the most despicable and repulsive creatures I know, and yet it's their beer glasses I have to fill. How often have I asked Klamm to leave them at home; even if I have to put up with the other gentlemen's servants, he, at least, could show some consideration, but it's useless asking, an hour before he comes they always burst in, like cows into a shed. But now they're really going to be put in the shed, where they belong. If you weren't here, I would tear open this door and Klamm would have to drive them out himself." "Well, can't he hear them?" asked K. "No," said Frieda, "he's asleep." "What!" cried K., "he's asleep? But when I looked into the room, he was still awake, sitting at his desk." "And he's still sitting there like that," said Frieda, "even when you saw him, he was asleep—if not, do you think I would have let you look in there?—that was his sleeping position, the gentlemen sleep a great deal, it's hardly possible to understand this. Besides, if he didn't sleep so much, how could he stand these people. But now I'll have to drive them out myself." Taking a whip from the corner, she leaped toward the dancers in one high but not entirely secure leap, the way, say, a little lamb leaps. At first, they turned to face her as if a new dancer had come, and indeed for a moment it seemed as if Frieda were about to drop the whip, but then she raised it again. "In the name of Klamm," she cried, "into the shed, all of you into the shed," they saw now that this was serious, and in a fear that K. found incomprehensible began rushing toward the back, where under the pressure of the first arrivals a door opened, night air streamed in, all of them disappeared with Frieda, who was evidently driving them across the courtyard into the shed. But in the silence that had suddenly fallen K. heard steps in the corridor. In order to shield himself somehow, he leaped behind the counter, which was the only place to hide; being in the taproom wasn't forbidden K., but since he wanted to spend the night here, he had to avoid being seen. So when the door actually was opened, he slid under the counter. Of course, being found here wasn't without danger either, but then the excuse of having hidden from the peasants, who had suddenly gone on a rampage, wouldn't sound implausible. It was the landlord, "Frieda!" he cried, pacing up and down the room several times, fortunately Frieda soon came back and didn't mention K., she merely complained about the peasants, and then in an effort to find K. went behind the counter, K. could touch her foot there and from then on he felt safe. Since Frieda didn't mention K., the landlord finally had to do so. "And where is the surveyor?" he asked. He was in any case a courteous man, who had acquired his cultivation through constant and relatively open dealings with people far outranking him, yet he spoke to Frieda in an especially deferential manner, this was all the more striking since he didn't stop talking like an employer dealing with an employee, and a rather cheeky one at that. "I forgot all about the surveyor," said Frieda, putting her small foot on K.'s chest. "He must have left long ago." "I didn't see him, though," said the landlord, "and I was in the corridor almost the entire time." "But he's not here," said Frieda coolly. "Perhaps he hid somewhere," said the landlord, "if my own impression is any indication, one oughtn't to put anything past him." "He could hardly be that impudent," said Frieda, pressing her foot down more firmly on K. In her being there was something gay and free, which K. hadn't noticed before, and it got out of hand, quite unexpectedly, when she laughingly said: "Perhaps he's hiding down here," bent down to K., kissed him lightly, jumped back up, and said sadly: "No, he isn't here." But the landlord, too, gave cause for astonishment when he said: "I find it most unpleasant not knowing for certain whether he has left. This is not simply a matter of Mr. Klamm, it is also a matter of the regulation. But the regulation applies to you, Miss Frieda, as well as to me. You're responsible for the taproom, I shall search through the rest of the house. Good night! Sleep well!" He could scarcely have left the room when Frieda switched off the electric light and joined K. under the counter. "My darling! My sweet darling!" she said in a whisper, but without touching K.; as if unconscious in her love she lay on her back and stretched out her arms, time must have seemed endless in her happy love, she sighed rather than sang some little song. Then she started, for K. was still silent, lost in thought, and like a child she began to tug at him: "Come, it's stifling down here," they embraced each other, her small body was burning in K.'s hands; they rolled a few paces in an unconscious state from which K. repeatedly but vainly tried to rescue himself, bumped dully against Klamm's door, and then lay in the small puddles of beer and other rubbish with which the floor was covered. Hours passed there, hours breathing together with a single heartbeat, hours in which K. constantly felt he was lost or had wandered farther into foreign lands than any human being before him, so foreign that even the air hadn't a single component of the air in his homeland and where one would inevitably suffocate from the foreignness but where the meaningless enticements were such that one had no alternative but to go on and get even more lost. And so, initially at least, it came not as a shock but as a consoling glimmer when from Klamm's room a deep, commanding, yet also indifferent voice called out for Frieda. "Frieda," said K. in Frieda's ear, relaying the cry. With almost innate obedience Frieda was about to jump to her feet, but then, realizing where she was, she stretched, laughed softly, and said: "I will not go, I will never go to him again." K. wanted to object, he wanted to urge her to go to Klamm, and began to gather what was left of her blouse, but he couldn't speak, for he was all too happy having Frieda in his arms, all too anxiously happy, since it seemed to him that if Frieda abandoned him all he possessed would abandon him too. And as though Frieda had been fortified by K.'s consent, she clenched her fist, knocked on the door, and cried: "I'm with the surveyor. I'm with the surveyor." Klamm now fell silent. Yet K. rose, knelt beside Frieda, and looked about in the dull early-morning light. What had happened? Where were his hopes? What could he expect from Frieda, now that all was betrayed. Instead of advancing with utmost caution in a manner befitting the size of the enemy and the goal, he had rolled about all night in the beer puddles, which now gave off an overpowering smell. "What have you done?" he said to himself. "We are lost, the two of us." "No," said Frieda, "only I am lost, but I have won you. And hush now. But look at the way those two are laughing." "Who?" asked K., turning around. Sitting on the counter were his two assistants, they were somewhat tired from lack of sleep, but cheerful, it was the kind of cheerfulness that comes from the faithful fulfillment of duty. "What do you want here?" K. shouted as though they were to blame for everything, he looked about for the whip that Frieda had in the evening. "We had to come looking for you," said the assistants, "you never came back down to the taproom, so we looked for you at Barnabas's and finally found you here. We've been sitting here all night. This isn't easy work, that's for sure." "I need you by day, not at night," said K., "go away!" "Well, it is day now," they said, without moving. It was indeed day, the gate to the courtyard opened, the peasants poured in, also Olga, whom K. had completely forgotten; Olga was as lively as last evening despite the disheveled state of her clothes and hair; from the doorway her eyes sought K. "Why didn't you go home with me," she said, almost in tears. "For the sake of a woman like that," she said, and then repeated the remark several times. Frieda, who had gone away for a moment, came back with a small bundle of clothes. Sadly, Olga moved aside. "Now we can go," said Frieda, obviously meaning that they should go to the inn by the bridge. K. walked with

Frieda, the assistants followed, that was the procession; the peasants were showing great contempt for Frieda, this was understandable, for she had handled them strictly up to now; one of them even took a stick and held it out as if he wouldn't let her go until she had jumped over it, but the look in her eyes was enough to drive him away. Outside in the snow K. breathed somewhat more easily, this time the joy of being outside made it easier to bear the difficulties along the way; if K. had been on his own, he could have made even better progress. At the inn he went straight to his room and lay down on the bed, Frieda arranged a place to sleep for herself on the floor beside it, the assistants had pushed their way into the room and were driven out, but they came back in through the window. K. was too tired to drive them out again. The landlady came up for the sole purpose of greeting Frieda, who called her "little mother"; the greetings that followed were incomprehensibly effusive, with kisses and long embraces. And in any case there wasn't much peace to be had in that little room, the maids in their men's boots often came clattering in, bringing things or removing them. Whenever they needed something from the bed, which was crammed with various objects, they inconsiderately pulled it out from under K. Frieda, though, they greeted as one of their own. Despite this commotion, K. stayed in bed all day and all night. Frieda did some small chores for him. Next morning, when he finally got up, feeling greatly refreshed, it was already the fourth day of his stay in the village.

IV.

FIRST CONVERSATION WITH THE LANDLADY

He would have liked to have a confidential conversation with Frieda, but the assistants, with whom Frieda even joked and laughed every now and then, prevented this through their intrusive presence. Otherwise they weren't demanding, they had settled down in a corner of the floor on two old skirts; their goal, which they often discussed with Frieda, was to avoid disturbing the surveyor and to take up as little room as possible, they made various attempts to bring that about, always to the accompaniment of whispers and giggles, by drawing in their arms and legs and huddling together, all one could see in their corner in the twilight was a large knot. Still, certain experiences in broad daylight had, alas, made it clear that they were attentive observers, they were constantly staring over at K., playing seemingly childish games, using their hands as telescopes and resorting to other such antics, or simply blinking at him while appearing to be engaged chiefly in tending their beards, which they set great store on and compared on countless occasions for length and thickness, letting Frieda be the judge. From his bed K. often watched the antics of the three of them with utter indifference.

Now when he felt strong enough to get up out of bed, they all rushed over to serve him. Yet he still wasn't strong enough to resist their offers, he saw that in this way he was becoming somewhat dependent on them, which could have negative consequences, but he simply had to let it happen. Besides, it wasn't so terribly unpleasant, sitting at the table drinking the good coffee Frieda had brought, warming himself at the stove Frieda had stoked, having the assistants run up and down the stairs ten times in their clumsy eagerness to bring him soap, water, a comb, a mirror, and finally, since K. had softly uttered a wish that could be interpreted that way, a little glass of rum.

Amid all this ordering and serving, more out of good cheer than in hope of success, K. said: "Now go away, you two, I have no further wishes for the present, and I want to speak to Miss Frieda alone," and since he saw no outright protest in their faces, he added by way of amends: "And then the three of us will go to the council chairman, wait for me downstairs in the taproom." Oddly enough, they complied, except for saying before they left: "We could also wait here," to which K. responded: "I know, but I don't want that."

K. was annoyed but in a certain sense glad too, when Frieda, who had sat down on his lap once the assistants had left, said: "What have you got against the assistants, darling? We needn't keep secrets from them. They are loyal." "Loyal," said K., "they're constantly lying in wait for me, it is senseless and also quite repulsive!" "I think I know what you mean," she said, clasping his neck and attempting to say something else, but she couldn't go on, and since the chair stood by the bed they stumbled over it and fell down. They lay there, but without abandoning themselves as fully as that time at night. She sought something and he sought something, in a fury, grimacing, they sought with their heads boring into each other's breasts; their embraces and arched bodies, far from making them forget, reminded them of their duty to keep searching, like dogs desperately pawing at the earth they pawed at each other's bodies, and then, helpless and disappointed, in an effort to catch one last bit of happiness, their tongues occasionally ran all over each other's faces. Only weariness made them lie still and be grateful to each other. Then the maids came up, "Look at the way they're lying there," one of them said, and out of pity she threw a sheet over them.

Later, when K. extricated himself from the sheet and looked about, the two assistants were back in their corner—this didn't surprise him—warning each other to be serious by pointing at K. and saluting—but in addition to that, the landlady was sitting by the bed, knitting a sock, a small task ill-suited to her huge frame, which almost darkened the room. "I've been waiting a long time," she said, lifting her wide face, which was criss-crossed and lined with age but for all its massiveness it was still smooth and had perhaps once been beautiful. Her words sounded like a reproach, an inappropriate one, for K. certainly hadn't asked that she come. So he merely acknowledged her words with a nod and sat up, Frieda, too, stood up, but she moved away from K. and leaned against the landlady's chair. "Landlady," K. said distractedly, "could you postpone whatever you want to tell me until I get back from the council chairman's? I have an important meeting there." "Believe me, Surveyor, this is a more important matter," said the landlady, "that is probably only about some work, while this is about a human being, about Frieda, my dear girl." "Oh, I see," said K., "then, yes indeed, though I don't understand why you cannot leave this up to us." "Out of love, out of concern," said the landlady, and she drew Frieda's head toward her; standing, Frieda only came up to the shoulder of the seated landlady. "If Frieda has such confidence in you," said K., "so must I. Only a moment ago Frieda called my assistants loyal, so we're among friends. And I can therefore tell you, Landlady, that I think it best that Frieda and I should marry, and very soon at that. Certainly, it's unfortunate, most unfortunate, that I cannot replace what Frieda has lost through me, her position at the Gentlemen's Inn and her friendship with Klamm." Frieda raised her face, her eyes were full of tears, they did not seem at all triumphant. "Why me? Why was I chosen for this?" "What?" K. and the landlady asked with one voice. "She's confused, the poor child," said the landlady, "confused because of the coming together of so much happiness and misfortune." And as if to confirm this, Frieda threw herself at K., kissed him wildly, and then, crying and embracing him as if there were nobody else in the room, fell on her knees before him. As he stroked Frieda's hair with both hands, K. said to the landlady: "You seem to agree with me?" "You're a man of honor," said the landlady, who, even though her voice was tearful and she looked somewhat decrepit and had trouble breathing, still found the strength to say: "The only issue now is what kind of assurances you will have to give Frieda, for no matter how much I respect you you're still a stranger, you cannot give references, we here know nothing about your domestic situation, so assurances are needed, but you, dear sir, can understand this, since it was, after all, you who pointed out how much Frieda is losing through this connection with you." "Certainly, assurances, of course," said K., "those are probably best given at the notary's, though some other authorities of the Count may also start meddling with this. By the way, there's something I absolutely must do before the wedding. I must speak with Klamm." "That's impossible," said Frieda, rising slightly and pressing against K., "what an idea!" "I must," said K., "and if I don't succeed, you must." "I cannot, K., I cannot," said Frieda, "Klamm will never speak to you. How can you believe that Klamm will speak to you?" "But he would speak to you?" asked K. "No, that isn't so," said Frieda, "not to me, not to you, those are utter impossibilities." She turned to the landlady, extending her arms: "Landlady, just see what he's asking for." "You're odd, Surveyor," said the landlady, who looked frightening now that she was sitting more upright, with her legs spread apart and her powerful knees pressing up through her thin skirt, "you're asking for the impossible." "Why is it impossible?" asked K. "I shall explain it to you," the landlady said in a voice that sounded as though the explanation were not a final favor but the first in a series of punishments that she was handing out, "I shall gladly explain that to you. True, I don't belong to the Castle and am only a woman and am only the landlady in one of the lowest-ranking inns—no, not the lowest-ranking, though not far from it—and so you may not attach any weight to my explanation, but I have gone through life with my eyes open and have come to know many different people and have had to carry the entire weight of the inn alone, for though my husband is a good lad all right, he isn't a landlord and will never understand the meaning of responsibility. For instance, it's only through his negligence—I was about to collapse that evening from exhaustion—that you are here in the village and can sit there on the bed in peace and comfort." "What?" K. asked, awakening from a certain distraction, roused more by curiosity than by anger. "It's only thanks to his negligence," cried the landlady again, pointing at K. with her raised forefinger. Frieda tried to calm her. "What is it you want," said the landlady, turning her entire body in one quick motion, "the surveyor has asked me and I must answer him. Otherwise, how can he possibly understand something that is absolutely self-evident to us, namely, that Mr. Klamm will never speak to him—why am I saying 'will'—can never speak to him. Listen here, Surveyor!, Mr. Klamm is a gentleman from the Castle, and that signifies in and of itself, even leaving aside Klamm's other position, a very high rank, but what are you? You, the very person whom we are so humbly imploring that he might deign to consider marriage. You're not from the Castle, you're not from the village, you are nothing. Unfortunately, though, you are something, a stranger, one who is superfluous and gets in the way everywhere, one who is a constant source of trouble and who, for instance, makes it necessary for us to dislodge the maids, one who seduces our dearest little Frieda, one whose intentions are utterly unknown here, but who is unfortunately the very person to whom we must give her away. On the whole, though, I'm not blaming you for all this; I have already seen too much in life not to be able to bear this sight as well. But stop for a moment to consider the nature of your request. You expect a man like Klamm to speak to you. It pained me to hear that Frieda let you look through the peephole, in doing so, she was already seduced. But tell me, how could you bear the sight of Klamm? You needn't say a word, I know, you had little difficulty bearing it. Indeed you cannot really see Klamm at all, and this isn't arrogance on my part, for neither can I. You expect Klamm to speak to you, but he doesn't even speak to people from the village, has never spoken to anyone from the village. It certainly was a great distinction for Frieda, a distinction that I, too, shall be proud of until the end of my days, that he would at least call her name and she could speak to him whenever she wished and was allowed to use the peephole, and yet he never spoke to her. And as for his calling Frieda now and then, that isn't necessarily as significant as one might care to think, he merely called Frieda's name—who knows what his intentions are?—and Frieda's decision to rush over was naturally her own business and the fact that she was admitted without difficulty is simply due to the goodness of Klamm, but nobody can claim that he actually called her. And now all that, such as it was, is finished for all time. Klamm may still call Frieda's name, that may be so, but a girl of that sort, who has consorted with you, will certainly never be admitted again. And there's one thing, one thing this little head of mine cannot understand, how could a girl whom some people call Klamm's mistress—and by the way I consider that a rather exaggerated term—even let you touch her?"

"It's certainly odd," said K., and he took Frieda on his lap; she yielded right away, though with her head down, "but it shows, I think, that everything isn't quite as you think. For instance, you're certainly right to say I am nothing in Klamm's eyes, and even if I insist on speaking to Klamm and refuse to let your explanations deter me, this doesn't mean I could bear the sight of Klamm if there weren't a door separating us, or wouldn't run from the room the moment he appeared. But such fears, even if they're justified, are still no reason for me not to risk going ahead. Yet if I can stand up to him, he needn't even speak to me, I'll be sufficiently gratified on seeing the effect my words have on him, and if they have none, or if he doesn't hear a word I say, I will still have gained something from the chance to speak frankly to a person with power. But you, Landlady, with your wide experience of life and people, and Frieda, who as of yesterday was still Klamm's mistress—I don't see why I should drop the term—can no doubt easily arrange for me to talk to Klamm; if there's no other way, then at the Gentlemen's Inn, perhaps he's still there today as well."

"That's impossible," said the landlady, "and I can see you're incapable of understanding this. But anyhow, tell me, what do you want to talk to Klamm about?"

"About Frieda, of course," said K.

"About Frieda?" asked the landlady, baffled, turning to Frieda. "Do you hear, Frieda, he, he wants to talk about you to Klamm, to Klamm."

"Oh, Landlady," said K., "you're such a clever woman, so worthy of respect and yet you're frightened by every little thing. Well, I want to talk to him about Frieda, there's nothing monstrous about that, it's only natural. For you're certainly mistaken again if you think Frieda lost all meaning for Klamm from the very moment I arrived. If that's what you think, you're underestimating him. I have the distinct feeling that it's presumptuous of me to lecture you on the subject, but I simply cannot avoid it. Nothing can have changed in Klamm's relationship to Frieda because of me. Either there was no significant relationship—and that's precisely what those who deprive Frieda of her honorable title as mistress are suggesting—in which case it doesn't exist today, or else there was one, but then how could it have been disturbed by me, by someone who, as you rightly said, is a mere nothing in Klamm's eyes? One believes such things in the first moment of fright, but a little thought ought to straighten it out. By the way, we should let Frieda say what she thinks."

Looking into the distance, her cheek resting on K.'s chest, Frieda said: "It's certainly as Mother says: Klamm doesn't want to have anything more to do with me. But certainly not because you came here, darling, nothing like that could ever shake him. But I believe it was through Klamm's work that we found each other under the counter, blessed, not accursed, be the hour!"

"If that's so," said K. slowly, for Frieda's words were sweet, he closed his eyes for several seconds to let the words permeate him, "if that's so, then there's even less reason to fear an interview with Klamm."

"Frankly," said the landlady, gazing down from her height at K., "you sometimes remind me of my husband, you're just as stubborn and childlike as he. You've been in the village a few days and already think you know everything better than everyone here, better than me, an old woman, and better than Frieda, who has heard and seen so much at the Gentlemen's Inn. I'm not denying it's possible to accomplish something that runs absolutely counter to the rules and the old traditions, I myself have never experienced anything of the sort, but such instances are said to occur, this may be so, but they certainly don't occur the way you go about it, simply by saying 'no, no' all the time and by swearing to do what you think and by ignoring the most well-meant advice. Do you really think I'm concerned about you? Did I do anything for you while you were still on your own? Although that wouldn't have been such a bad thing and might have prevented certain incidents. All I said to my husband about you then was: 'Stay away from him.' That would also be the case with me now if Frieda hadn't become entangled in your fate. It is to her—whether you like it or not—that you owe my care and even my respect. And you cannot simply turn me away, for I'm the only person who watches over little Frieda with motherly concern, and I hold you strictly accountable. Perhaps Frieda is right and everything that has happened is the will of Klamm, but now I know nothing about Klamm, I shall never again speak to him, he's completely beyond my reach, but you sit here, keep my

Frieda, and are in turn—why shouldn't I say this?—kept by me. Yes, kept by me, young man, for if I ever threw you out, just try to find lodgings anywhere in the village, even in a doghouse!"

"Thanks," said K., "you've spoken frankly and I believe you entirely. So my position is that uncertain, and in connection with that, Frieda's position, too!"

"No," the landlady broke in furiously, "in that respect Frieda's position has nothing whatsoever to do with yours. Frieda belongs in my house, and nobody has any right to call her position here uncertain."

"Fine, fine," said K., "I'll concede you're right this time, too, especially since Frieda—for reasons unknown to me—seems too afraid of you to get involved. So, for now, let's just stick to me. My position is utterly uncertain, you're not denying that, but rather struggling to prove it. As in everything you say, that's mostly right, but not entirely so. Just one instance, I do know of a good night's lodging that I can use."

"Where? Where?" Frieda and the landlady cried eagerly, almost in one voice, as if both had the same reason for asking.

"At Barnabas's," said K.

"That riffraff," cried the landlady, "that slippery riffraff! At Barnabas's! Do you hear—"and she turned toward the assistants' corner, but they had come out quite a while ago and now stood arm in arm behind the landlady, who, as if needing support, seized one by the hand, "do you hear where the gentleman hangs out, at Barnabas's! He's sure to find lodgings there, oh, if only he had liked it better there than at the Gentlemen's Inn! But where have the two of you been?"

"Landlady," said K. before the assistants could answer, "those are my assistants, but you treat them as if they were your assistants and my warders. On every other subject I'm at least willing to engage in a polite discussion of your opinions, but not concerning my assistants, for that's an absolutely clear cut affair. So I request that you not speak to my assistants, and if my request should not suffice, I shall forbid my assistants to answer you."

"So I'm not allowed to speak to you," said the landlady, and all three laughed, the landlady derisively but more softly than K. had expected, the assistants in their usual way, meaning everything and nothing, disclaiming all responsibility.

"Now don't get angry," said Frieda, "you must try to understand why we're so upset. One could say that it's solely thanks to Barnabas that the two of us are together now. When I first caught sight of you in the taproom—you came in arm in arm with Olga—I did already know a few things about you, but on the whole I felt completely indifferent about you. Yet you weren't the only one, I felt indifferent about almost everything, almost everything. Indeed, I felt dissatisfied then about many things and annoyed by many more, but what an odd sort of dissatisfaction and annoyance it was. If someone insulted me, say one of the guests in the taproom—they were always after me, you saw those fellows there, but others came who were far worse, Klamm's servants weren't the worst—if one of them insulted me, what difference did that make to me? I felt as if the incident had happened many years before or as if it hadn't happened to me or as if I had only heard people speak of it or as if I myself had forgotten it. But I cannot describe it, I cannot even imagine it anymore, that's how much everything has changed since Klamm abandoned me—"

And Frieda broke off her story, lowered her head sadly, and folded her hands in her lap.

"Look," cried the landlady, sounding as though she herself weren't speaking but werc lending Frieda her voice, she moved closer as well and was now sitting beside Frieda, "Surveyor, look at the results of your actions, and your assistants too—but then of course I'm not supposed to speak to them—may watch and learn a lesson from this. You wrenched Frieda out of the happiest state ever granted her, and could do so largely because Frieda herself, owing to her childlike, exaggerated sense of compassion, couldn't bear to see you hanging on Olga's arm and thus seemingly at the mercy of Barnabas's family. She rescued you and sacrificed herself. And now that this has happened and Frieda has given up all she had in exchange for the happiness of sitting on your knee, you come and pass off as your greatest trump card the fact that you once had the opportunity to spend the night at Barnabas's. You're probably trying to prove you're not dependent on me. Certainly, if you really had spent the night at Barnabas's, you would be so little dependent on me that you would have to leave my house at once, and double-quick, too."

"I don't know the sins of the Barnabas family," said K., carefully lifting Frieda, who seemed lifeless, placing her on the bed, and getting up again, "perhaps you're right in this case, though I was certainly right when I requested that you leave our affairs, Frieda's and mine, in our hands. You said something about love and concern, I haven't noticed much of that, but I have noticed great hatred and contempt and talk of banishment from the house. If your goal was to get Frieda to leave me or me to leave Frieda, then you went about this quite cleverly, but I don't think you'll succeed, and if you do—and now for a change let me be the one to give you a dark warning—you'll regret it bitterly. As for the lodgings you're providing me with—you must mean this awful hole—it isn't at all clear that this is a voluntary offer on your part, it seems more likely that the Count's authorities have issued a directive to this effect. I shall report now that I was given notice here, and if they assign other lodgings to me, you may well breathe more easily, but I'll certainly breathe more deeply. And now I'm going to see the council chairman about this and several other matters. You could at least take care of Frieda, whom you've seriously harmed with those so-called motherly talks of yours."

Then he turned to the assistants. "Come," he said, then he took Klamm's letter from the hook and was about to go. Although the landlady had watched him silently, his hand was already on the latch before she spoke: "Surveyor, I have a parting thought for you, for no matter what you say or how many insults you heap on an old woman like me, you are still the future husband of Frieda. And that's the only reason why I even bother telling you that you're dreadfully ignorant about the situation here, one's head buzzes from listening to you and from comparing your opinions and ideas with the real situation. Your ignorance cannot be remedied all at once, and perhaps not at all, but many things can get better if you would only show a little faith in me and always keep in mind how ignorant you are. And then you will, say, become less unjust toward me and begin to sense how shocked I was—I still haven't recovered from the shock—when I noticed that my dearest little one has, so to speak, abandoned the eagle to unite with a blindworm, but the actual relationship is worse still, and I'm constantly trying to forget all about it, because otherwise I couldn't speak calmly to you at all. Oh, now you're angry at me again! No, don't go yet, you must first listen to my final request: Wherever you go, keep in mind that you're the most ignorant person here and be careful; here with us you'll be out of harm's way with Frieda present, so you may chatter to your heart's content, you can even show us how you plan to talk to Klamm, but in reality, in reality . . . please, oh please don't do it."

She stood up, swaying somewhat with excitement, approached K., took his hand, and looked at him pleadingly. "Landlady," said K., "I cannot understand why you humiliate yourself over such a trifling matter by pleading with me like this. If, as you say, it's impossible for me to speak to Klamm, then I won't succeed whether you plead with me or not. If it were actually possible, though, why shouldn't I do it, especially since, after your main objection has fallen by the wayside, your other fears will be very doubtful. Certainly, I am ignorant, that at least is true, sadly enough for me, but the advantage here is that those who are ignorant take greater risks, and so I'll gladly put up with my deficient knowledge and its undoubtedly serious consequences for a little while, for as long as my energy holds out. But those consequences essentially concern only me, and so, particularly for that reason, I cannot understand why you are pleading with me. After all, you will certainly always take care of Frieda, and if I ever vanished from Frieda's sight, that would inevitably be good news for you. So what are you afraid of? Surely you aren't afraid—those who are ignorant naturally consider everything possible"—here K. opened the door—"surely you aren't afraid for Klamm's sake?" The landlady looked after him in silence as he hurried down the stairs followed by the assistants.

V.

AT THE CHAIRMAN'S

The meeting with the chairman caused K. little concern, almost to his own surprise. He sought to explain this to himself on the grounds that, judging by his previous experiences, dealing with the Count's authorities was very simple for him. On one hand, this was due to their having issued for his affairs, apparently once and for all, a definite ruling that was outwardly very much in his favor, and on the other, to the admirable consistency of the service, which was, one suspected, especially perfect on occasions when it appeared to be missing. Sometimes when thinking of such matters K. almost concluded that his situation was quite satisfactory, though he always told himself quickly after such fits of satisfaction that this is precisely where the danger lay. Dealing directly with the authorities wasn't all that difficult, for no matter how well organized they were, they only had to defend distant and invisible causes on behalf of remote and invisible gentlemen, whereas he, K., was fighting for something vitally close, for himself, and what's more of his own free will, initially at least, for he was the assailant, and he was not struggling for himself on his own, there were also other forces, which he knew nothing of, but could believe in because of the measures adopted by the authorities. By mostly obliging him from the start in some of the more trivial matters—and no more had been at stake until now—the authorities were depriving him not only of the chance to gain a few easy little victories but also of the corresponding satisfaction and the resulting well-founded confidence for other, greater battles. Instead they let K. wander about as he wished, even if only in the village, spoiling and weakening him, barred all fighting here, and dispatched him to this extra-official, completely unclear, dull, and strange life. If this went on, if he weren't always on guard, he might one day, despite the friendly attitude of the authorities, despite his meticulous fulfillment of his exaggeratedly light official duties, be deceived by the favor seemingly granted him and lead the rest of his life so imprudently that he would fall to pieces, and the authorities, gentle and friendly as ever, would have to come, as though against their will but actually at the behest of some official ordinance of which he knew nothing, in order to clear him out of the way. And what did that actually amount to here, the other part of his life? Nowhere else had K. ever seen one's official position and one's life so intertwined as they were here, so intertwined that it sometimes seemed as though office and life had switched places. How great, say, was the power Klamm wielded over K.'s service, which up to now had been no more than a formality, compared with the power Klamm possessed in actual fact in K.'s bedroom. That's why a slightly more frivolous approach, a certain easing of tension, was appropriate only when dealing directly with the authorities, whereas otherwise you always had to exercise great caution and look about on all sides before each step you took.

K. initially found his view of the local authorities very much confirmed at the chairman's. A friendly fat clean-shaven man, the chairman was ill, he had a severe attack of gout and received K. in bed. "So you must be our surveyor," he said, intending to sit up and greet K., but he couldn't manage it and, pointing apologetically to his legs, threw himself back down on the pillows. A woman, quite still, almost shadowlike in the dimly lit room, whose small curtained windows made it even darker, brought K. a chair and put it by the bed. "Sit down, sit down, Surveyor," said the chairman, "and tell me what you want." K. read Klamm's letter aloud and then added a few comments. Again he thought he felt the extraordinary ease of dealing with the authorities. They bore the whole burden, quite literally, you could leave everything up to them and remain free and untouched yourself. As though sensing this in his own way, the chairman stirred uneasily in his bed. Finally he said: "Surveyor, as you've noticed, I knew about the entire affair. The reason I haven't seen to it yet is, first, I have been ill, and then you took so long to come I thought you had given up the affair. But now that you're so kind as to call on me, I must of course let you know the entire unpleasant truth. You were, as you say, taken on as a surveyor, but we don't need a surveyor. There wouldn't be the least bit of work for a person like that. The boundaries of our small holdings have been marked out, everything has been duly registered, the properties themselves rarely change hands, and whatever small boundary disputes arise, we settle ourselves. So why should we have any need for a surveyor?" K., despite having never really thought about this before, was convinced deep down that he had been expecting some such communication. For that very reason he was immediately able to say: "I find this most surprising. It upsets all my plans. I can only hope there's been a misunderstanding." "Unfortunately not," said the chairman, "it is as I say." "But how is that possible?" cried K. "After all, I didn't set out on this endless journey only to be sent back now." "That is a different matter," said the chairman, "and one that's not for me to decide, though I can explain how this misunderstanding was possible. In an administration as large as the Count's, it can happen at some point that one department issues an order, another a second, neither department knows of the other, the higher-ranking control agency is indeed extremely precise, but by nature it intervenes too late, and so a little confusion can nonetheless arise. Of course, this happens only in the tiniest matters, such as yours, in a large affair I have never heard of an error, but even the small cases are often quite embarrassing. Now, as for your case, without turning this into an official secret—I'm simply not enough of an official for that, I'm only a peasant, and that's good enough for me—I want to give you a frank description of what happened. A long time ago, I had only been chairman for a few months, a decree came—I cannot recall from which department—stating in the categorical manner so typical of the gentlemen up there that a surveyor would be summoned and instructing the local council to be ready with all the plans and records needed for his work. This decree obviously cannot have been about you, for that was many years ago, and I wouldn't even have thought of it if I weren't ill in bed with all the time in the world to think about the silliest matters. Mizzi," he said, suddenly interrupting his account, to the woman, who was still flitting about the room on some incomprehensible errand, "please look in the cabinet, perhaps you'll find the decree. You see," he told K. by way of explanation, "it's from the early days when I still kept everything." The woman opened the cabinet right away, K. and the chairman watched. The cabinet was crammed with papers; once it was open, two large packs of files tied together in a bundle like firewood came rolling out, the woman started and jumped aside. "Down below, it should be down below," said the chairman, directing from his bed. After obediently gathering the files in both arms so as to reach the papers underneath, the woman threw out the entire contents of the cabinet. The papers already covered half the room. "We've certainly accomplished a great deal," said the chairman, nodding, "and that's only a small part of it. I stored the bulk of it in the barn, but most of it got lost. Who could keep all that together! But there is still a great deal left in the barn. You think you can find the decree?" he said, turning again to his wife, "You should look for a file with the word 'surveyor' underlined in blue." "It's too dark here, I'll get a candle," said the woman, walking on the papers as she went to the door. "My wife," said the chairman, "she's such a great help in carrying out this difficult official work, which is only part-time, I have one other aide, the teacher, for written work, but it's still impossible to finish everything, a large portion never gets done, but we have put that away in the cabinet there," and he pointed to another cabinet. "And especially now that I am ill, everything is quite out of hand," he said, lying down again, tired yet proud. "Well," K. said, the woman had come back with the candle and was on her knees looking for the decree, "couldn't I help your wife look?" The chairman shook his head and smiled: "As I said, I'm not keeping official secrets from you, but to let you look through the files would be going too far." There was now silence in the room, all one could hear was the rustling of papers, perhaps the chairman was dozing off. A light knock at the door made K. turn around. The assistants, of course. Still, they had picked up some manners, didn't barge into the room right away, but whispered first through the slightly open door: "It's too cold outside." "Who is it?" asked the chairman, starting. "Only my assistants," said K., "I'm not sure where I should get them to wait for me, it's too cold outside, and they're a nuisance here." "They won't bother me," said the chairman agreeably, "let them in. Incidentally, I know them. Old acquaintances." "But they do bother me," said K. frankly, letting his eyes wander from the assistants to the chairman and back again to the assistants; he found the smiles of all three indistinguishable. "Well, now that you're here," he added as a test, "stay and help the chairman's wife look for a file with the word 'surveyor' underlined in blue." The chairman did not object to this; what K. was not permitted, the assistants were now being permitted; they immediately threw themselves on the papers, but instead of searching, they merely rummaged about in the pile, and each time one of them spelled out the words on a file, the other tore the file from his hand. But the woman was still kneeling in front of the empty cabinet, she seemed to have stopped looking altogether, the candle was now some distance from her.

"The assistants," said the chairman with a self-satisfied smile, as though he himself had arranged all this without anybody else's knowledge, "so they bother you. But they're your own assistants." "No," said K. coolly, "they simply ran up to me here." "Why 'ran up'?" he said. "You must mean 'were assigned.'" "Fine, 'were assigned' then," said K., "but they could just as easily have fallen like snowflakes, given how little thought went into assigning them." "Nothing ever happens here without due thought," said the chairman, who even forgot about the pain in his foot and sat up. "Nothing," said K., "and what about my being summoned here?" "Even the decision to summon you was carefully considered," said the chairman, "but a few minor details introduced some confusion, I can prove this through the files." "Well, the files won't be found," said K. "Won't be found?" cried the chairman, "Mizzi, do hurry a bit with your search! I can first tell you the story, though, even without the files. We responded to the decree I mentioned earlier by pointing out gratefully that we don't need a surveyor. However, this reply seems never to have reached the first department—which I shall call A—and went by error to another department, B. So Department A was left without an answer, and unfortunately B didn't receive our entire answer; either because the contents of the file never left us, or because the file itself got lost on the way—though certainly not in the department itself, I'll vouch for that—all that came to Department B in any case was the file folder, which simply had on it a note saying that the enclosed, though in reality unfortunately missing, file dealt with the summoning of a surveyor. Meanwhile, Department A was waiting for our answer, they had preliminary notes on the affair, but as often happens, and this is quite understandable and even justifiable given the precision with which such matters must be handled, the designated official was expecting that we would answer and he would then summon a surveyor or, if need be, engage us in further correspondence about the matter. As a result he paid no attention to his preliminary notes and the entire matter slipped his mind. In Department B the folder reached a functionary famous for his conscientiousness, Sordini is his name, an Italian, even an insider such as myself cannot understand how a man of his abilities can be kept in what is virtually the lowest position of all. Now this Sordini did of course return the empty folder to us for completion. But by now many months, if not years, had passed since we had received the message from Department A, understandably, for when, as is the rule, a file heads the right way, it arrives at its department in one day at the latest and is dealt with that same day, but should it ever lose its way, the excellence of the organization is such that the file must zealously seek the wrong way, for otherwise it won't find it, and then it does indeed take a long time. So when we got Sordini's memorandum, we had only the vaguest memories of the affair, there were only two of us then for all this work, Mizzi and I, the teacher hadn't been assigned yet, and we kept copies only in the most important cases—in short, we could answer only vaguely to the effect that we knew of no such summons and that there was no need for a surveyor here.

"But," said the chairman, interrupting himself as if he had gone too far in his eagerness to tell the story, or as if it were at least possible that he had gone too far, "does the story bore you?"

"No," said K., "it amuses me."

At that, the chairman said: "I am not telling you this for your amusement."

"It amuses me," said K., "only because it gives me some insight into the ridiculous tangle that may under certain circumstances determine a person's life."

"You still haven't gained any insight," the chairman said gravely, "and so I can go on. Well of course our answer couldn't satisfy a Sordini. I admire the man, even though he torments me. You see, he distrusts everyone, even if for instance on countless occasions he finds that someone is a most trustworthy person, on the very next occasion he mistrusts him, as if he didn't know him or, more precisely, as if he knew him to be a rascal. I think that is right, that's how an official must behave, unfortunately by nature I cannot follow that precept myself, you can see how I'm telling all this openly to you, a stranger, I simply cannot help it. But Sordini immediately distrusted our answer. A lengthy correspondence came about. Sordini asked why I had suddenly realized that a surveyor shouldn't be summoned; with the help of Mizzi's excellent memory I answered that the initial proposal had come from his own office (that a different office had been involved we had of course long since forgotten), and then Sordini said: why was I mentioning this official memorandum only now; I: because I had only just recalled it; Sordini: that was quite odd; I: it wasn't odd in a long-drawn-out affair like this; Sordini: it *certainly* was odd, for the memorandum that I recalled did not exist; I: of course it didn't exist, since the whole file had been lost; Sordini: still, there should be a preliminary note concerning that first memorandum, but there was none. Then I faltered, for I was not so daring as to claim, or even to think, that Sordini's department had made a mistake. Surveyor, in your thoughts you may be reproaching Sordini for not having been prompted by my claim to make inquiries about the matter in other departments. But that would have been wrong, and I want this man cleared of all blame even in your thoughts. One of the operating principles of the authorities is that the possibility of error is simply not taken into account. This principle is justified by the excellence of the entire organization and is also necessary if matters are to be discharged with the utmost rapidity. So Sordini couldn't inquire in other departments, besides those departments wouldn't have answered, since they would have noticed right away that he was investigating the possibility of an error."

"Chairman, allow me to interrupt you with a question," said K., "didn't you mention a control agency? As you describe it, the organization is such that the very thought that the control agency might fail to materialize is enough to make one ill."

"You're very severe," said the chairman, "but multiply your severity by a thousand and it will still be as nothing compared with the severity that the authorities show toward themselves. Only a total stranger could ask such a question. Are there control agencies? There are only control agencies. Of course they aren't meant to find errors, in the vulgar sense of that term, since no errors occur, and even if an error does occur, as in your case, who can finally say that it is an error."

"That would be something completely new," cried K.

"It's very old as far as I'm concerned," said the chairman. "Not altogether unlike you, I'm convinced that there has been an error, that Sordini became seriously ill out of despair over this, and that the first control agencies, to which we owe the discovery of the source of the error, also recognize the error here. But who can claim that the second control agencies will judge likewise and the third, and so on?"

"Perhaps," said K., "but I would rather not start interfering with considerations like that yet, and also this is the first I have heard of these control agencies, and so naturally I can't understand them yet. Still, I think two things must be distinguished here, first, what happens inside the offices, which can then be officially interpreted this way or that, and second, the actual person, me, who stands outside those offices and is threatened by those offices with a restriction that would be so senseless that I still cannot believe in the gravity of the danger. Chairman, as regards the former, the matters you have just spoken of with such admirably uncommon expertise are probably valid, but I should also like to hear a few words about me."

"I'm getting there," said the chairman, "but you wouldn't be able to understand it if I didn't say a few other things first. Even my mentioning of the control agencies just now was premature. So I'm going back to the differences with Sordini. As I said, my defenses gradually weakened. But if Sordini has even the slightest advantage over a person, then he has already won, for this sharpens his attention, energy, and wits, and for those under attack he is a terrible sight, but a splendid one for the enemies of the person under attack. Only because I experienced the latter in other cases can I speak of him as I do. By the way, I have never yet succeeded in setting eyes on him, he cannot come down, he's overburdened with work, I was once told that the walls in his room are hidden behind columns of large bundles of files piled on top of one another, those are only the files Sordini is working on just then, and since files arc constantly being taken from and added to the bundles, all this at great speed, the stacks are constantly falling down, and it's precisely those endless thuds in rapid succession that have come to seem typical of Sordini's study. Well, Sordini is indeed a worker and pays as much attention to the smallest case as to the biggest."

"Chairman," said K., "you're always calling my case one of the smallest and yet it has kept many officials very busy and, even if it was perhaps quite small at first, it has through the zeal of officials of the same type as Mr. Sordini become a big case. Unfortunately and very much against my will; for my ambition is not to have big stacks of files concerning me piling up and then crashing down, but to work quietly as a little surveyor at his little drawing board."

"No," said the chairman, "it isn't a big case, you have no cause for complaint in that respect, it's one of the smallest of the small cases. It's not the amount of work that determines the rank of a case, you're still far from an understanding of the authorities if you believe that. But even if the amount of work were decisive, your case would still be one of the least significant; the ordinary cases, that is, those without so-called errors, create a far greater quantity of admittedly much more productive work. Incidentally, you still have no idea of the actual work caused by your case, so I want to tell you about that first. Initially, Sordini left me out of it, but his officials came, every day formal hearings were held at the Gentlemen's Inn with respected members of the community. Most stood by me, but a few became suspicious, land surveying is an issue that deeply affects peasants, they scented some sort of secret deals and injustice, they also found a leader, and Sordini had to conclude from their presentations that if I had raised the matter at the local council not everybody would have opposed the summoning of a surveyor. And so this perfectly obvious point—namely, that there's no need for a surveyor—was at the very least made to seem problematic. In all this a certain Brunswick played a prominent role, you probably don't know him, perhaps he isn't bad, just stupid and given to fantasy, he's the brother-in-law of Lasemann."

"Of the master tanner?" asked K., and he described the man with the full beard whom he had seen at Lasemann's.

"Yes, that's he," said the chairman.

"I know his wife too," K. said, just on an off-chance.

"That's possible," the chairman said, and he fell silent.

"She's beautiful," said K., "though rather pale and sickly. She probably comes from the Castle?" this was said half as a question.

The chairman glanced at the clock, poured medicine into a spoon, and swallowed it quickly.

"So you are merely acquainted with the office furnishings at the Castle?" K. asked rudely.

"Yes," said the chairman, with an ironic and yet grateful smile, "they're the most important thing about it. As for Brunswick: if we could expel him from the community, virtually everyone would be happy, Lasemann not least of all. But Brunswick gained some influence at that time, he's not a speaker but a shouter, and that's good enough for some. And so I was forced to lay the matter before the council, which by the way was Brunswick's only success at first, since the council naturally decided by a large majority to have nothing to do with the surveyor. That too was years ago, but the matter still hasn't died down, partly through the conscientiousness of Sordini, who tried to probe the motives of both majority and opposition by means of the most meticulous inquiries, partly through the stupidity and ambition of Brunswick, who has various personal contacts with the authorities that he was able to bring into play thanks to his boundless imagination. Sordini, though, didn't let himself be duped by Brunswick—how could Brunswick dupe Sordini?—but precisely so as not to be duped, he had to set up new inquiries, but before they had ended Brunswick had already thought up something else, he's actually quite quick, that's one form his stupidity takes. And now I'm going to talk about a special feature of our official apparatus. In keeping with its precision it is extremely sensitive. When a matter has been deliberated on at great length, it can happen, even before the deliberations have ended, that suddenly, like lightning, in some unforeseeable place, which cannot be located later on, a directive is issued that usually justly, but nonetheless arbitrarily, brings the matter to a close. It's as if the official apparatus could no longer bear the tension and irritation stemming year in year out from the same perhaps inherently trivial affair and had all by itself, without help from the officials, made the decision. Of course, there was no miracle and some official or other certainly wrote the directive or reached an unwritten decision, at any rate one cannot determine from down here, or indeed even from the administrative offices, which official reached the decision in this case and on what grounds. This is only determined much later by the control agencies, and so we never get to hear any more about it, and anyhow by then the matter would scarcely interest anybody. Now, as I said, it's precisely these decisions that are mostly excellent, the only disturbing thing is that one only gets to hear about them when it's too late, for one is still passionately discussing a matter that has long since been resolved. I don't know whether such a decision was reached in your case—there is evidence both for and against—but if that had happened, they would have sent for you and you would have set off on that long journey, which would have taken time, while Sordini would have been working on the same case to the point of exhaustion, Brunswick would have kept up his intrigues, and I would have been tormented by both. I'm only suggesting this as a possibility, but the following I know for sure: A control agency discovered meanwhile that many years previously Department A had sent the local council an inquiry concerning a surveyor, but still hadn't received a reply. Recently they sent me an inquiry that actually resolved the entire matter, Department A was satisfied with my reply stating that no surveyor was needed, Sordini had to acknowledge that he wasn't responsible for the case and that he had—though of course through no fault of his own—gone to a great deal of useless, nerve-wracking trouble. If new work hadn't come pouring in as usual from all sides, and if your case hadn't been only a very minor case—the most minor of minor cases, one could almost say—we would all have breathed sighs of relief, even Sordini would, I believe, have done so, Brunswick was the only one who muttered about it, but that was quite ridiculous. And just imagine how disappointed I was, Surveyor, after the happy conclusion of the entire affair—and a great deal of time has gone by since then—when suddenly you appear and it seems as if everything is about to begin all over again. That I want to prevent this from happening, insofar as it lies in my power, is something you'll surely understand, won't you?"

"Certainly," said K., "but I have an even better understanding of the dreadful mistreatment that I, and perhaps the laws as well, are being subjected to here. I, for one, know how to combat this."

"How do you plan to do so?" asked the chairman.

"I cannot give that away," said K.

"I don't want to intrude," said the chairman, "but keep in mind that you have in me—I don't want to say a friend, since we're actually total strangers—a business acquaintance, as it were. The only thing I shall not permit is your being taken on as a surveyor, but otherwise you can always approach me with confidence, though only within the limits of my power, which isn't great."

"You're always saying that I am going to be taken on as surveyor," said K., "but I have already been taken on, here's Klamm's letter."

"Klamm's letter," said the chairman, "well, it is valuable and even venerable because of Klamm's signature, which appears to be genuine, but otherwise—still, I wouldn't risk saying anything about it on my own. Mizzi!" he called, adding: "But what are you doing?"

The assistants, who had been left unobserved for such a long time, and Mizzi, had evidently not found the file they were looking for and had then tried to lock everything up in the cabinet again, but the jumble of files was so large that they hadn't succeeded. Then it had surely been the assistants who had hit upon the idea that they were now carrying out. They had put the cabinet on the floor, stuffed all the files in, then sat down with Mizzi on the cabinet door and were now trying to force it down slowly.

"So the file hasn't been found," said the chairman, "a pity, but of course you already know the story, we no longer need the file, besides it'll turn up, it must be at the teacher's, he has many more files. But come here with the candle, Mizzi, so you can read the letter with me."

Mizzi came over, she looked even more insignificant and gray sitting on the edge of the bed and clasping her strong and vigorous husband, who had his arm around her. All one could make out in the candlelight was her small face with its distinct stern lines, softened only by the decay of age. She had barely looked at the letter when she clasped her hands lightly, "From Klamm," she said. They read the letter together, whispering to each other from time to time, and finally, as the assistants shouted "Hurrah," for they had finally pushed the cabinet door shut, and Mizzi watched them in silent gratitude, the chairman said:

"Mizzi agrees with me completely, and now I can probably risk saying what I think. This letter isn't an official letter but rather a private one. That is already clearly apparent from the heading 'My dear Sir!' Besides, it doesn't say a word about your having been taken on as surveyor, rather it refers only in general terms to the lordly services, and even then the phrasing isn't binding, since you have merely been taken on 'as you know,' in other words, the burden of proving that you've been taken on rests with you. Lastly, you're referred exclusively to me, the chairman, who, as your immediate superior, will provide you with all further particulars, and that has, of course, already been largely taken care of. All this is utterly clear to anyone who is capable of reading official letters and therefore better still at reading unofficial ones; that you, a stranger, cannot make this out doesn't surprise me. All in all, the letter merely means that Klamm intends to look after you personally, should you be accepted into the lordly services."

"Chairman," said K., "you interpret the letter so well that all that's finally left is a signature on a blank sheet of paper. Can't you see how you're disparaging the name of Klamm, which you pretend to respect."

"That is a misunderstanding," said the chairman, "the significance of the letter hasn't escaped me, nor am I disparaging it with my interpretation, quite the contrary. A private letter from Klamm has far greater significance than would an official letter, but not the significance *you* give it."

"You know Schwarzer?" asked K.

"No," said the chairman, "perhaps you do, Mizzi? You don't either. No, we don't know him."

"That's odd," said K., "he is the son of a substeward."

"Dear Surveyor," said the chairman, "how am I supposed to know all the sons of all the substewards?"

"Fine," said K., "then you have to believe me when I say it's he. The day I came, I had an annoying encounter with this Schwarzer. He then made inquiries by telephone, spoke to a substeward called Fritz, and was told they had taken me on as surveyor. How do you explain that, Chairman?"

"Quite simple," said the chairman, "you haven't ever really come into contact with our authorities. All those contacts are merely apparent, but in your case, because of your ignorance of the situation here, you think they're real. As for the telephone: look, in my own house, though I certainly deal often enough with the authorities, there's no telephone. At inns and in places like that it may serve a useful purpose, along the lines, say, of an automated phonograph, but that's all. Have you ever telephoned here, you have? Well then, perhaps you can understand me. At the Castle the telephone seems to work extremely well; I've been told the telephones up there are in constant use, which of course greatly speeds up the work. Here on our local telephones we hear that constant telephoning as a murmuring and singing, you must have heard it too. Well, this murmuring and singing is the only true and reliable thing that the local telephones convey to us, everything else is deceptive. There is no separate telephone connection to the Castle and no switchboard to forward our calls; when anyone here calls the Castle, all the telephones in the lowest-level departments ring, or all would ring if the ringing mechanism on nearly all of them were not, and I know this for certain, disconnected. Now and then, though, an overtired official needs some diversion—especially late in the evening or at night—and turns on the ringing mechanism, then we get an answer, though an answer that's no more than a joke. That's certainly quite understandable. For who can claim to have the right, simply because of some petty personal concerns, to ring during the most important work, conducted, as always, at a furious pace? Nor can I understand how even a stranger can believe that if he calls Sordini, for instance, it really is Sordini who answers. Quite the contrary, it's probably a lowly filing clerk from an entirely different department. But it can also happen, if only at the most auspicious moment, that someone telephones the lowly filing clerk and Sordini himself answers. Then of course it's best to run from the telephone before hearing a sound."

"But that isn't how I saw it," said K. "I couldn't have known the details, but I had little confidence in those telephone conversations and always knew that the only things that are of any real significance are those one discovers or accomplishes at the Castle itself."

"No," said the chairman, seizing one phrase, "those telephone answers are of 'real significance,' how could it be otherwise? How could the information supplied by a Castle official be meaningless? I said so already in relation to Klamm's letter. All these statements have no official meaning; if you attach official meaning to them, you're quite mistaken, though their private meaning as expressions of friendship or hostility is very great, usually greater than any official meaning could ever be."

"Fine," said K., "if all that is indeed so, then I must have plenty of good friends at the Castle; on closer inspection the idea the department had many years ago of possibly sending for a surveyor at some point was a friendly gesture toward me, and from then on there was one such gesture after the other until it came to a bad end with my being enticed here and threatened with being thrown out."

"There is some truth in your view," said the chairman, "you're right that the Castle's statements shouldn't be taken literally. Still, caution is always necessary, not only here, and the more important the statement, the greater the need for caution. But what you then say about your being enticed here I find incomprehensible. If you had paid closer attention to my observations, you would know that the question of your being summoned here is far too difficult to be dealt with in one little conversation."

"Well, then," said K., "the only possible conclusion is that everything is very unclear and insoluble except for my being thrown out."

"Who would dare to throw you out, Surveyor," said the chairman, "it's precisely the lack of clarity in the preliminary questions that guarantees you the most courteous treatment, only it seems that you are too sensitive. Nobody is keeping you here, but that still doesn't mean you're being thrown out."

"Oh, Chairman," said K., "now it's once again you who is seeing certain matters far too clearly. I shall list for you certain things that keep me here: the sacrifices I had to make to get away from home, the long difficult journey, the reasonable hopes I held out for myself of being taken on here, my complete lack of fortune, the impossibility of finding suitable work at home, and finally, my fiancée, who comes from here."

"Oh, Frieda!" said the chairman, not at all surprised. "I know. But Frieda would follow you anywhere. As for the rest, though, certain considerations must indeed be taken into account and I shall report this to the Castle. If a decision comes or if it's necessary to question you again, I shall send for you. Do you approve of this?"

"No, absolutely not," said K., "what I want from the Castle is not charity, but my rights."

"Mizzi," said the chairman to his wife, who still sat pressed up against him, dreamily playing with Klamm's letter, which she had turned into a little boat; startled, K. now took it away from her, "Mizzi, my leg is beginning to hurt again, we'll have to change the compress."

K. rose, "Then I shall take my leave," he said. "Yes," said Mizzi, who was already preparing some ointment, "besides, it's too drafty." K. turned around; upon hearing K.'s comment the assistants had in their usual misplaced zeal immediately opened both door panels. Obliged to shield the sickroom from the powerful blast of cold air, K. was only able to bow quickly to the chairman. Then, dragging the assistants along, he ran from the room, quickly closing the door.

VI.

SECOND CONVERSATION WITH THE LANDLADY

Waiting for him in front of the inn was the landlord. Without being asked, he wouldn't have dared to speak, so K. asked what he wanted. "Have you found new housing?" the landlord asked, looking at the ground. "You're asking on your wife's instructions," said K., "you're probably quite dependent on her?" "No," said the landlord, "I'm not asking on her instructions. But she's very upset and unhappy because of you, cannot work, is always lying in bed, sighing and complaining." "Should I go to her?" asked K. "Please do," said the landlord, "I tried to get hold of you at the chairman's, I listened at the door, but the two of you were talking, I didn't want to interrupt, besides I was worried because of my wife, ran back, but she wouldn't let me in, so I had no choice but to wait for you." "Then come quickly," said K.,

"I'll soon calm her down." "If only that were possible," said the landlord.

They went through the bright kitchen, where three or four maids, scattered about doing odd chores, literally froze at the sight of K. Even in the kitchen one could already hear the landlady sighing. She lay in a windowless alcove separated from the kitchen by a light wooden partition. There was room only for a large double bed and a wardrobe. The bed was so positioned that one could see the whole kitchen and supervise the work from it. But from here in the kitchen one could barely see anything in the alcove, it was quite dark there, only the white and red bedclothes shimmered through a little. Not until one had gone in and one's eyes had adjusted could one make out the details.

"So you've finally come," the landlady said feebly. She lay stretched out on her back, evidently had trouble breathing, and had thrown back the down quilt. In bed she looked much younger than in her usual clothes, but the little nightcap of delicate lacework that she wore, though too small and swaying back and forth on her hair, made the decay of her face seem pitiable. "How could I have come?" said K. gently, "after all, you never sent for me." "You shouldn't have kept me waiting so long," said the landlady with an invalid's stubbornness. "Sit down," she said, pointing to the edge of the bed, "but the rest of you go away." Besides the assistants, the maids too had meanwhile pushed their way in. "I should go away, too, Gardena?" said the landlord, K. was hearing the woman's name for the first time. "Of course," she said slowly, and as though she had other thoughts on her mind, she added absentmindedly: "Why should you of all people stay?" Yet once all of them had withdrawn to the kitchen—this time even the assistants followed immediately, but then they were after a maid—Gardena showed enough presence of mind to realize one could hear everything that was said here from the kitchen, for the alcove had no door, and so she ordered them all to leave the kitchen. This happened at once.

"Please, Surveyor," said Gardena, "right inside the wardrobe there's a shawl, hand it to me, I want to pull it up over me, I cannot stand the down quilt, it's so hard to breathe." And once K. had given her the shawl, she said: "Look, it's a beautiful shawl, isn't it?" To K. it seemed like an ordinary woolen shawl, he felt it once again merely to be obliging, but said nothing. "Yes, it's a beautiful shawl," Gardena said, and covered herself up with it. She was now lying there quietly, all her ailments seemed to have vanished; she even remembered her hair, which was disheveled from lying in bed, sat up a moment and adjusted her hairdo slightly round her nightcap. She had a full head of hair.

K. became impatient and said: "Landlady, you made someone ask me whether I had found new housing." "I made someone ask you?" the landlady said. "No, that's wrong." "Your husband asked me about it just now." "I can believe that," said the landlady, "I had a fight with him. When I didn't want you here, he kept you here, now that I'm happy you're living here, he drives you away. He's always doing this kind of thing." "So," said K., "you've changed your opinion of me that much? In an hour or two?" "I haven't changed my opinion," the landlady said, more feebly again. "Give me your hand. That's it. And now promise me you'll be absolutely honest, which is exactly how I'll be with you." "Fine," said K., "but who goes first?" "Me," said the landlady; it didn't seem as though she were trying to be accommodating toward K. but rather as though she were eager to speak first.

She pulled a photograph from under the pillow and handed it to K. "Look at this picture," she asked. So as to see better, K. took one step back into the kitchen, but even there it wasn't easy to make anything out in the picture, for it was faded with age, broken in several places, crushed, and stained. "It's not in very good shape," said K. "Alas, alas," said the landlady, "that's what happens when one keeps carrying it around for years. But if you look at it closely, you'll surely be able to make everything out. Besides, I can help you, tell me, what do you see, I like hearing things about the picture. So what is it?" "A young man," said K. "Right," said the landlady, "and what's he doing?" "He's lying down, I think, on a board, stretching and yawning." The landlady laughed. “That’s quite wrong,” she said. “But here’s the board, and he’s lying here,” said K., insisting on his point of view. “But take a closer look,” said the landlady in annoyance, “now then, is he really lying there?” “No,” K. now said, “he isn’t lying there, he’s hovering, and now I can see that it’s not a board but most likely a rope, and the young man is doing a high jump.” “That’s it,” said the landlady, delighted, “he’s jumping, that’s how the official messengers practice; well, I knew you would make it out. Can you see his face, too?” “I can’t see much of his face,” said K., “he’s obviously making quite an effort, his mouth is open, his eyes are screwed up, and his hair is blowing about.” “Very good,” said the landlady appreciatively, “that’s all anybody who hasn’t seen him in person could possibly make out. But he was a handsome youth, I caught only one fleeting glimpse of him and yet I shall never forget him.” “So who was it?” asked K. “The messenger,” said the landlady, “the messenger Klamm first summoned me with.”

K. found it impossible to listen closely, he was distracted by rattling glass. He immediately found the cause of the disturbance. The assistants were standing outside in the courtyard, hopping from one foot to the other in the snow. They acted as if they were happy to see K. again, out of happiness they pointed him out to each other by tapping on the kitchen window. At a threatening gesture from K. they stopped right away and each tried to push the other back, but one of them slipped past the other and now they were back at the window again. K. rushed into the alcove, where the assistants couldn’t see him and he didn’t have to see them. But there, too, the faint and as if imploring rattle of the windowpanes pursued him for quite a while.

“Those assistants again,” he said to the landlady, so as to excuse himself, pointing out the window. But she was paying no attention to him, she had taken the picture from him, looked at it, smoothed it out and pushed it back under the pillow. Her movements had become slower not out of weariness but under the burden of memory. She had wanted to tell K. something and had forgotten him because of the story. She played with the fringe of her shawl. Not until a little while later did she look up, brush her eyes with her hand, and say: "This shawl comes from Klamm. And the nightcap, too. The picture, the shawl, and the nightcap, those are my three mementos of him. I'm not young like Frieda, I'm not as ambitious as she nor as sensitive, she's very sensitive, in short I know how to adjust to life, but I must admit that without these three items I wouldn't have lasted so long here, indeed I probably wouldn't have lasted a day. To you, these three mementos may seem trivial, but, you see, Frieda, who consorted for so long with Klamm, hasn't a single memento, I asked her, she's too effusive and too demanding, but I, who was only with Klamm three times—later on he never sent for me again, I don't know why—as if sensing the shortness of my time there, I took these mementos along. Of course, one has to do it oneself, Klamm himself never gives one anything, but if one sees anything suitable lying about, one can ask him for it."

K. felt uncomfortable about these stories, however much they concerned him. "How long ago was that," he asked, sighing.

"Over twenty years ago," said the landlady, "well over twenty years ago."

"So one stays faithful to Klamm that long," said K. "Landlady, do you realize that you're causing me great concern, when I think of my own future marriage?"

The landlady considered it unseemly that K. wanted to barge in at this point with his own affairs, and gave him an irritated side-glance.

"Not so angry, Landlady," said K., "I'm certainly not saying a word against Klamm, but through force of circumstances I have entered into certain relations with Klamm; this is something not even Klamm's greatest admirer could deny. And so, as a result, whenever Klamm is mentioned I must also think of myself, that cannot be helped. Besides, Landlady"—here K. seized her hesitant hand—"remember the bad way our last conversation ended and that this time we want to part in peace."

"You're right," the landlady said, bowing her head, "but spare me. I'm no more sensitive than anyone else, on the contrary, everybody has sensitive spots, I have only this one."

"Unfortunately I have the same one," said K., "but I shall certainly restrain myself; now, Landlady, tell me how I should endure this dreadful fidelity to Klamm in my own marriage, assuming Frieda is like you in this respect."

"Dreadful fidelity," the landlady repeated sullenly. "Well, is it fidelity? I'm faithful to my husband, but to Klamm? Klamm once made me his mistress, can I ever lose that distinction? And you ask how you should endure this with Frieda? Oh, Surveyor, who are you who dare to ask such a thing?"

"Landlady!" said K. admonishingly.

"I know," said the landlady, yielding, "but my husband never asked questions like that. I don't know who should be considered more unfortunate, me then or Frieda now. Frieda, who willfully left Klamm, or me, whom he never sent for again. Perhaps it is after all Frieda, though she does not yet seem to realize the full extent of this. My thoughts dwelt exclusively on my misfortune, though, for I had to ask myself, and indeed essentially still have to ask myself: Why did it happen? Three times Klamm sent for you, but not a fourth time, never a fourth time! And what could have concerned me more then? What else could I talk about with my husband, whom I married shortly afterwards? By day we had no time, we acquired the inn in a miserable condition and had to try to bring it up to standard, but at night? For years our nighttime conversations circled around Klamm and the reasons for his change of mind. And when my husband fell asleep during these conversations, I woke him up and we went on talking."

"Now, if you will permit me," said K., "I will ask you a rather rude question."

The landlady remained silent.

"So I may not ask," said K., "that's enough for me, too."

"Oh, of course," said the landlady, "that's enough for you, that especially. You misinterpret everything, even the silence. You simply cannot help it. I do give you permission to ask."

"If I'm misinterpreting everything," said K., "then perhaps I'm also misinterpreting my own question, perhaps it isn't all that rude. I simply wanted to know how you met your husband and how this inn came into your hands."

The landlady frowned, but said calmly: "It's a very simple story. My father was a blacksmith, and Hans, who is now my husband, and who was then a stable boy for a large farmer, often came to see my father. This was just after my last encounter with Klamm, I was very unhappy and actually shouldn't have been, since everything followed the correct procedure, and the fact that I was no longer allowed to go to Klamm was Klamm's decision, so it was correct, but the reasons were obscure, I was allowed to probe those reasons but shouldn't have been unhappy, well, I was all the same, and couldn't work and sat in our little front garden all day. Hans saw me there, sometimes sat down with me, I never complained to him, but he knew what it was about and, being a good lad, sometimes wept with me. And when the then landlord—whose wife had died and who for that reason had to give up the trade, and anyhow he was already an old man—passed by our little garden and saw us sitting there, he stopped and on the spot offered to lease us the inn, and, since he trusted us, he didn't want any money in advance and arranged cheap terms for the lease. I didn't want to become a burden to my father and couldn't care about everything else, so, thinking of the inn and all the new work, which might make me forget a little, I gave Hans my hand. That's the story."

For a little while there was silence, then K. said: "The landlord's conduct was fine, but imprudent too, or had he particular reasons for trusting you two?"

"He knew Hans well," said the landlady, "he was Hans's uncle."

"No wonder then," said K., "so Hans's family was evidently very interested in the connection with you?"

"Perhaps," said the landlady, "I don't know, I never worried about that."

"Still, that's how it must have been," said K., "if the family was ready to make such sacrifices and simply place the inn in your hands without any security."

"It wasn't imprudent, as became clear later," said the landlady. "I threw myself into the work, I was strong, a blacksmith's daughter, I didn't need a maid or a servant, I was everywhere, in the taproom, in the kitchen, in the stables, in the courtyard, my cooking was so good I even drew guests from the Gentlemen's Inn, you have not as yet been in the inn at noon, you don't know our luncheon guests, there were even more of them then, but in the meantime many have drifted away. And as a result we were not only able to pay the lease on time but after a few years to buy the whole place, and now it's almost free of debt. The other result, though, was that I ruined myself, had heart problems, and now I am an old woman. You may think I'm much older than Hans, but actually he's only two or three years younger and will never get any older, for his work—smoking a pipe, listening to the guests, emptying his pipe, and getting a glass of beer every now and then—such work doesn't make anyone older."

"Your achievements are admirable," said K., "no doubt about that, but we were talking about the time before your marriage, and at that time it would have been strange if Hans's family, under great financial sacrifice, or at least having taken on the great risk involved in giving up the inn, had actually pressed for marriage, for they could only put their hopes in your ability to work, which of course they didn't know anything about yet, and in Hans's, which, as they must already have discovered, was nonexistent."

"Well, yes," the landlady said wearily, "I do know what you're getting at and how mistaken you are. There was no trace of Klamm in all this. Why should he have cared about me, or rather: how could he have cared about me? For by then he had forgotten all about me. That he hadn't called me was a sign he had forgotten me. Anyone whom he no longer summons he forgets entirely. I didn't want to speak of this in front of Frieda. But it isn't simply that he forgets, it's more than that. If you forget someone, you can of course get to know that person again. With

Klamm that is not possible. Anyone whom he no longer summons, he forgets, not only for the past but literally for all time. If I make an effort, I can even think my way into your thoughts, which make no sense here, but are perhaps valid in the foreign lands you come from. Perhaps you're so madly presumptuous as to think that Klamm gave me a husband like Hans so that almost nothing could prevent me from coming to him, should he ever call me in the future. Well, there could be nothing crazier than that! Where is the man who could prevent me from running to Klamm if Klamm gives me a sign? What nonsense, what utter nonsense, one merely makes oneself all confused by toying with such nonsense."

"No," said K., "we certainly don't want to make ourselves all confused, my thoughts hadn't gone as far as you think, but to tell the truth, they were heading in that direction. For the time being, though, I was merely surprised that the relatives had such high hopes for your marriage and that these hopes were indeed realized, if at some risk to your heart, to your health. The thought that there was a connection between all this and Klamm did occur to me, but not, or not yet, in the crude manner you implied, evidently only so you can shout at me again, for this clearly gives you pleasure. Well, have your pleasure! But these were my thoughts: First, Klamm is obviously the cause of your marriage. Without Klamm you wouldn't have been unhappy, wouldn't have sat idly in your little front garden, without Klamm Hans wouldn't have seen you there, without your sadness the shy Hans would never have dared speak to you, without Klamm you would never have found yourself in tears with Hans, without Klamm your dear old uncle-landlord wouldn't have seen Hans and yourself sitting there peacefully, without Klamm you wouldn't have felt so indifferent about life, and so you wouldn't have married Hans. Well, that is surely enough Klamm, I should say. But there is more. If you hadn't been trying to forget, you certainly wouldn't have worked so recklessly and brought the inn up to such a high standard. So there's also some Klamm there. But even leaving that aside, Klamm is the cause of your illness since even before your marriage your heart was drained by that unfortunate passion. The only question left is why Hans's relatives found the marriage so appealing. You yourself once mentioned that being Klamm's mistress is an increase in stature that cannot be lost, so perhaps that is what attracted them. But I believe they were also hoping that the lucky star which led you to Klamm—assuming it was indeed a lucky star, but you claim it was—belonged to you and would remain yours and would not, say, abandon you as quickly or as suddenly as Klamm did."

"Do you mean all of this seriously?" asked the landlady.

"Very seriously," said K. quickly, "only I think that the hopes of Hans's relatives were neither completely justified nor completely unjustified, and I also think I recognize the mistake you've made. Outwardly, everything does seem to have worked out, Hans is well provided for, has an imposing wife, enjoys great esteem, the inn is free of debt. But everything didn't actually work out; with a simple girl, whose first great love he would have been, Hans would certainly have been far happier; if he sometimes stands about the inn as if lost, as you chide him for doing, that's because he truly does feel lost—not that this makes him unhappy, that's for sure, I know him well enough by now to be able to say so—but it's equally certain that this handsome, sensible lad would have been happier with another wife, and by 'happier' I mean more independent, more diligent, and more manly. And, after all, you yourself certainly aren't happy, and, as you yourself said, without those three mementos you wouldn't want to go on living, and you also have a weak heart. So was it wrong of his relatives to hope? I don't think so. There were blessings above you, but nobody knew how to get them down."

"And what was it we failed to do?" asked the landlady. She was now lying stretched out on her back, gazing up at the ceiling.

"Ask Klamm," said K.

"So we're back to you," said the landlady.

"Or to you," said K., "our concerns overlap."

"So what do you want from Klamm?" said the landlady. She had sat up straight, shaken out the pillows so she could lean on them as she sat, and now looked K. directly in the eye. "I've told you openly about my own case, which you could learn something from. Tell me just as openly what you want to ask Klamm. I had difficulty persuading Frieda to go to her room and stay there, I was afraid you wouldn't speak openly enough with her here."

"I have nothing to hide," said K. "But first I must point out one thing. Klamm forgets at once, you said. Well, first, I find that highly improbable, and second, it cannot be proved, it's obviously nothing but a legend, concocted in the girlish minds of those who just happened to be in Klamm's good graces. I'm surprised you believe in such a trite fabrication."

"It is not a legend," said the landlady, "but comes from general experience."

"So it can be refuted by new experiences," said K. "But then there is one other difference between your case and Frieda's. As for Klamm's not having called Frieda again, in a sense no such thing happened, he called her, but she didn't comply. It's even possible he's still waiting for her."

The landlady remained silent, merely observing K. from head to toe. Then she said: "I want to listen quietly to all you have to say. It's better if you speak openly and don't spare my feelings. I have only one request. Do not use Klamm's name. Call him 'he' or something else, but not by his name."

"Gladly," said K., "but it's difficult to say what I want from him. First, I want to see him close-up, then I want to hear his voice, then I want him to tell me where he stands concerning our marriage; whatever other requests I make will depend on how the conversation goes. A number of subjects may come up, but for me the most important thing is simply to be standing there opposite him. I have not yet spoken directly to a real official, you see. That seems harder to achieve than I had thought. But now I have an obligation to speak with Klamm, the private individual, and to my mind that is much easier to accomplish; I can only speak with the official in his perhaps inaccessible office at the Castle or, and this is already quite dubious, at the Gentlemen's Inn, but I can speak with the private individual at the inn, on the street, anywhere I manage to meet him. The chance of having the official face to face as well is something I shall gladly accept, but that isn't my primary goal."

"Fine," said the landlady, pressing her face into the pillows as if she were saying something shameful, "if I succeed through my connections in getting your request for a conversation forwarded to Klamm, promise me you won't try anything on your own initiative until an answer comes down."

"That I cannot promise," said K., "much as I would like to grant your request, or whim. This is urgent, you see, especially after the unfavorable outcome of my meeting with the chairman."

"That objection isn't applicable," said the landlady, "the chairman is utterly insignificant. So you never noticed? He wouldn't last a day in his position were it not for his wife, who runs everything."

"Mizzi?" asked K. The landlady nodded. "She was there," said K.

"Did she express an opinion?" asked the landlady.

"No," said K., "but I did not get the impression that she was capable of that."

"That's it," said the landlady, "that's how wrongly you view everything here. Besides: the chairman's decision concerning you has no significance, and I shall certainly speak with his wife at some point. And if I now promise you that Klamm's reply will arrive a week from now at the latest, then you will surely not keep on coming up with new reasons for not giving in to me."

"None of that is decisive," said K., "my decision stands, and I would try to carry it out even if the answer that arrived were negative. But since this has been my intention from the start, I obviously cannot request an interview in advance. What remains in the absence of that request a daring but well-meant venture would after an adverse answer be open rebellion. And that of course would be far worse."

"Worse?" said the landlady. "It's rebelliousness anyhow. And now do as you like. Hand me my skirt."

Showing no consideration for K., she pulled on her skirt and hurried to the kitchen. For some time now a commotion had been audible from the parlor. Someone was knocking on the spy window. The assistants had at one point opened it and shouted in that they were hungry. Other faces had appeared there, too. Even a song, faint but in several parts, could be heard.

K.'s conversation with the landlady had naturally very much delayed the cooking of lunch; it was not yet ready, but the guests were assembled; still nobody had dared to defy the landlady's prohibition by entering the kitchen. But now when the observers at the spy window announced that the landlady was coming, the maids immediately ran into the kitchen, and when K. entered the parlor an amazingly large company, more than twenty, men and women, dressed provincially though not like peasants, poured from the spy window, where they had gathered, to the tables, in order to secure places for themselves. Only at one small table in the corner was a couple already seated with several children, the man, a friendly blue-eyed gentleman with tousled gray hair and a beard, was bending down to the children and beating time with a knife for their song, which he kept trying to quiet down. Perhaps he wanted to make them forget their hunger by getting them to sing. The landlady excused herself before the company with a few casually spoken words, nobody reproached her for this. She looked around for the landlord, who had surely fled the difficult situation some time ago. Then she went slowly into the kitchen; for K., who was hurrying to Frieda in his room, she hadn't a glance to spare.

VII.

THE TEACHER

Upstairs K. met the teacher. The room was fortunately almost unrecognizable, so diligent had Frieda been. It had been given a good airing, the stove was lit, the floor had been scrubbed, the bed straightened out, the maids' things, all that disgusting rubbish, including their pictures, had vanished, and the table, which used to stare at you with its dirt-encrusted top no matter which way you turned, had been covered with a crocheted white cloth. Now you could receive guests; that K.'s small batch of laundry, which Frieda had obviously washed this morning, hung by the stove to dry, barely spoiled the effect. The teacher and Frieda had been sitting at the table, they rose as K. entered, Frieda greeted K. with a kiss, the teacher bowed slightly. K., still distracted and uneasy after the conversation with the landlady, began to excuse himself for not having visited the teacher; it was as if he assumed that the teacher had become impatient over his failure to appear and had now called on him instead. In his measured way the teacher seemed only gradually to recall that he and K. had once spoken about a possible visit. "Surveyor," he said slowly, "you are indeed the stranger I spoke to in the church square a few days ago." "Yes," said K. curtly; the sort of thing he had put up with earlier in his isolation, he no longer had to tolerate in his own room. He turned to Frieda and mentioned an important visit he had to make at once and needed to be as well dressed as possible for. Immediately, without asking for an explanation, Frieda called the assistants, who were busy inspecting the new tablecloth, and ordered them down to the courtyard to clean with great care K.'s clothes and shoes, which he had already begun to remove. She herself took a shirt from the line and ran down to the kitchen to iron it.

Now K. was alone with the teacher, who again sat at the table in silence, K. made him wait a little longer, took off his shirt and began to wash at the basin. Only then, with his back to the teacher, did K. ask why he had come. "I have come on instructions from the chairman," he said. K. was prepared to listen to the instructions. But since K.'s words were difficult to understand with all the splashing, the teacher had to come closer, and he leaned against the wall next to K. K. excused his washing and his agitation by mentioning the urgency of the planned visit. Ignoring this, the teacher said: "You were impolite to the council chairman, that worthy, experienced, and venerable old man." "I'm not aware of having been impolite," said K., drying himself, "though you're quite right that I have more important things to worry about than fancy manners, for what was at stake was my livelihood, which has been jeopardized by the ignominious machinations of officialdom, the details of which I needn't fill you in on, since you yourself are an active part of that official apparatus. Has the council chairman ever complained about me?" "Whom do you think he could complain to?" said the teacher, "and even if there were such a person, do you think he would ever complain? I simply took down from his dictation a short deposition concerning that meeting, and this has given me insight into the kindness of the chairman and the quality of your answers." As K. looked for his comb, which Frieda must have tidied away somewhere, he said: "What? A deposition? Taken down afterwards, in my absence, by someone who wasn't even present at the meeting. Not bad at all. But why a deposition? Was it official business?" "No," said the teacher, "it was semiofficial, the deposition itself is only semiofficial and was only drawn up because everything must be kept strictly in order here. Anyhow it's finished, and reflects badly on your honor." K., who had finally found the comb, which had slipped between the covers of the bed, said more calmly: "Well then, let it be finished. And you've come here to inform me of that?" "No," said the teacher, "but I'm not an automaton and had to tell you what I think. The chairman's instructions, on the other hand, offer further proof of his kindness; I would like to stress that I find his kindness incomprehensible and am carrying out his instructions only as an official duty and out of respect for the chairman." Washed and combed, K. sat at the table waiting for his shirt and clothes, he had little interest in the message the teacher had brought; besides, he was influenced by the landlady's low opinion of the chairman. "It must already be past twelve?" he asked, thinking of the way he wanted to go, but then on second thoughts he added: "You were about to give me some message from the chairman." "Oh yes," the teacher said with a shrug, as though shaking off all responsibility. "The chairman fears that if the decision in your case takes too long, you will take the initiative and do something rash. As for me, I don't know why he fears that, for to my mind it would be best if you did as you pleased. We are not your guardian angels and don't have to follow you down every single byway. Well, all right. The chairman thinks differently. Of course the actual decision, which is handled by the Count's authorities, is not something he can speed up. But within his sphere of influence he seems to want to arrive at a truly generous temporary settlement, which you are free to accept or to reject, he is offering you temporarily the post of school janitor." At first K. almost ignored the offer he had been made, but the very fact of his being offered something was, it seemed to him, not without significance. It showed that the chairman thought him capable of carrying out acts in his own defense that would even justify certain expenses by the community so as to protect itself. And how seriously they were taking the whole thing. The teacher, who had already been waiting here a while and had prepared the deposition beforehand, must have been literally chased over by the chairman.

When the teacher saw that he had finally made K. stop and reflect, he went on: "I stated my objections. I pointed out that we had managed without a school janitor up to now, the wife of the sexton tidies up now and then, and her work is supervised by the schoolmistress, Miss Gisa, I already have enough torment with the children, I don't want the added bother of a janitor. The chairman countered that the schoolhouse was actually very dirty. I replied, truthfully, that it wasn't so bad. And besides, I added, would things get any better if we took that man on as janitor? Certainly not. Quite apart from his ignorance of that kind of work, the schoolhouse has only two large classrooms, without any small adjoining rooms, so the janitor and his family must live, sleep, and perhaps even cook in one of the classrooms, and of course this will hardly enhance the general cleanliness. The chairman, though, declared that the position would assist you in time of need and that you would therefore discharge your duties well, with great energy; besides, the chairman said that we would, in addition to you, gain the services of your wife and assistants, and that the school and the garden, too, could be kept in impeccable condition. I rebutted all this easily. Finally, the chairman, unable to come up with anything else in your favor, laughed and said that you were a surveyor so you should be able to lay out marvelously straight flowerbeds. Well, there's no point objecting to a joke, so I brought you the message." "Teacher, you needn't worry about that," said K., "I would not even consider accepting the post." "Splendid," said the teacher, "splendid, you decline, and unconditionally at that," and, picking up his hat, he bowed and left.

Immediately thereafter Frieda came up, her face was distraught, she still hadn't ironed the shirt she was carrying and did not respond to questions; in order to distract her a little, K. told her about the teacher and his offer; no sooner had she heard it than she threw the shirt on the bed and ran off again. She was soon back, though this time with the teacher, who looked annoyed and didn't even greet K. Frieda asked him to be patient for a while—she had obviously done so several times on the way here—then pulled K. through a side door he hadn't noticed into the neighboring attic, where, excited and breathless, she finally told him what had happened. The landlady, incensed at having humiliated herself by making certain confessions to K. and, worse still, at having given way over an interview between Klamm and K.—for she had gained nothing, so she said, but a cold and, what's more, insincere rebuff—was determined not to tolerate K.'s presence in her house any longer; if he had any connections with the Castle, then he should take advantage of them right away, for he must leave the inn today, this instant, and she would take him back only if expressly ordered or compelled to do so by the authorities, but she hoped this would never happen, for she too had connections with the Castle, and would know how to make use of them. Incidentally, he had been admitted to the inn only through the negligence of the landlord, besides he was in no real need, for even this morning he had boasted about other lodgings that were available to him. Of course Frieda should stay; if Frieda moved out with K., she, the landlady, would be deeply unhappy; she, a poor woman with a weak heart, had already collapsed in tears downstairs by the stove in the kitchen at the mere thought of it, but how could she respond any differently, for at least in her opinion the honor of Klamm's memory was at stake. That's how the landlady feels. Frieda would certainly follow him, K., wherever he wanted to go, in the snow and ice, and no more need be said on that score; anyhow, the situation was quite serious for both of them, which is why she had responded with such enthusiasm to the chairman's offer; even if the post was unsuitable for K., it was, after all—and the chairman had singled this out for special emphasis—only a temporary one, and in that way they could gain some time and easily find other opportunities, even if the final decision proved unfavorable. "And if need be," cried Frieda, who had already put her arms round K.'s neck, "we shall go abroad, what keeps us here in the village? Temporarily, though, we accept the offer, don't we, dearest, I've brought the teacher back, you just have to say 'agreed,' that's all, and then we'll move into the schoolhouse."

"That's terrible," said K., though without really meaning it seriously, for their housing was of little concern to him, besides he was freezing in his underwear here in the attic, which, lacking both wall and window on two sides, was swept by a cold sharp wind, "now that you've done up the room so beautifully, we're supposed to move out. I have little desire, very little desire, to take on the post, that one brief moment of humiliation in front of this little teacher is already embarrassing enough, and now he's even supposed to be my superior. If only we could stay a little longer, my situation might well change by this afternoon. Or at least if you stayed here on your own, we could wait and simply give the teacher some vague answer. I can always find a night's lodging, if need be at Bar—" with her hand Frieda sealed his lips. "Don't," she said anxiously, "please don't say that again. But otherwise I'll do everything you want. If you want, I'll stay here alone, though that would make me sad. If you want, we'll reject the offer, but I think that would be wrong. For look, if you actually find another opportunity for us, possibly even this afternoon, we'll immediately give up the post in the school, nobody will try to stop us. And as for your being humiliated in front of the teacher, I'll make sure that doesn't happen. I'll speak to him, you need only be present, you don't have to say a word, and it will always be this way, you will never have to speak to him yourself, unless you want to, indeed I'm the only one who will be his subordinate, and even I shall be no such thing, for I know his weaknesses. And therefore we won't lose anything if we accept the post, but a great deal if we turn it down; above all else, if you don't get anything from the Castle today, you will certainly never find any lodgings here in the village—even for you alone—lodgings that I, as your future wife, wouldn't have to feel ashamed of. And then when you fail to find lodgings, I suppose you'll even expect me to sleep here in this warm room, knowing that you're outside wandering about in the dark and cold." K., who had crossed his arms on his chest and was slapping himself on the back in an effort to warm up a little, said: "Then we have no choice but to accept, come!"

Once in the room he rushed straight to the stove, ignoring the teacher; the latter, who was seated at the table, pulled out his watch and said: "It's gotten late." "Yes, Teacher, but the two of us agree now," said Frieda, "we accept the post." "Fine," said the teacher, "but the post was offered to the surveyor, he has to say what he thinks." Frieda helped K. out, "Of course," she said, "he accepts the post, don't you, K.?" K. could therefore confine himself to a simple "Yes" that was addressed not to the teacher but to Frieda. "Well then," said the teacher, "all I have to do now is point out your official duties, that way we will have agreed upon this once and for all: Surveyor, you must clean and heat both schoolrooms on a daily basis, assume responsibility for all minor repairs to the building, as well as to the school and gymnastic equipment, keep the garden path clear of snow, run messages for myself and the schoolmistress, and in the milder seasons do all the gardening. In exchange you may live in whichever schoolroom you choose; if the two rooms are not both being used simultaneously for instruction and you happen to live in a room in which instruction is to take place, you must of course move into the other room. You may not cook in the schoolhouse, but in return you and your dependents will receive free board at the inn at the community's expense. That your conduct must remain in keeping with the dignity of the school and that the children especially must not witness any disagreeable domestic scenes, particularly during class, I mention only in passing, for this is of course something that you, an educated person, must already know. In this regard I would also point out that we must insist that you legalize your relations with Miss Frieda as soon as possible. To cover these issues and a few other minor points there will be an employment contract, which you must sign on moving into the schoolhouse." All this seemed unimportant to K., as if it didn't apply to him or at least weren't binding on him, but annoyed by the teacher's self-importance, he said casually: "Oh yes, simply the usual commitments." In an effort to cover up that comment, Frieda inquired about the salary. "The payment of a salary," said the teacher, "will only be considered after a one-month probationary period." "But that will make it hard for us," said Frieda, "we are supposed to get married on almost no money and set up a household with nothing. Teacher, couldn't we petition the council for a small salary right away? Would you recommend this?" "No," said the teacher, addressing his remarks as always to K. alone. "Such a petition would be approved only if I recommended it, and I would not do so. You're being awarded this post as a favor, and if one remains conscious of one's official responsibilities one shouldn't push such favors too far." Now, however, K. broke in, almost against his will. "Teacher, as far as the favor goes," he said, "I believe you are mistaken. The favor may be more on my side." "No," said the teacher, smiling now that he had actually forced K. to speak, "I have precise information about this. Our need for a janitor is about as urgent as our need for a surveyor. Janitor and surveyor, that's a weight round our necks. I must think long and hard about how to justify this expense to the council, but the best and most honest course would simply be to throw the demand down on the table without any attempt to justify it." "That's just what I mean," said K., "even against your will you must take me on, no matter how serious the concerns this raises for you, you must still take me on. And when someone is obliged to take a person on and that person lets himself be taken on, then he's the one doing the favor." "Odd!" said the teacher, "what could possibly compel us to take you on, it's the chairman's kind heart, his excessively kind heart that compels us to do so. Surveyor, I see clearly now that you will have to give up many fantasies before you can become a decent janitor. And as for the eventual award of a salary, such comments naturally don't help to create the right atmosphere for that. And I see, too, that your conduct will unfortunately cause me a lot of other trouble as well, you have all this time been negotiating with me, I keep staring and can hardly believe it, in your shirt and underpants." "Yes," K. exclaimed, laughing and clapping his hands, "but those dreadful assistants, what's keeping them?" Frieda hurried to the door; the teacher, who noticed that K. was no longer paying any attention to him, asked Frieda when they would move into the schoolhouse. "Today," said Frieda. "Well then, tomorrow morning I shall come to check," said the teacher, waving goodbye; he was about to pass through the door, which Frieda had opened for herself, when he collided with the maids, who were already carrying in their things so that they could settle back into their room; blocked by the maids, who would never step aside for anyone, he had to slip between them, followed by Frieda. "You're certainly in a hurry," said K., very pleased with them now, "you come barging in even though we're still here?" They didn't answer, in their embarrassment they merely twisted the bundles with the all-too-familiar dirty rags sticking out. "You've probably never washed your things," K. said, not so much out of malice as with a certain affection. They noticed it, opened their severe mouths, showed their beautiful strong animal-like teeth, and laughed silently. "Well, do come in," said K., "settle down; it is after all your own room." Yet since they hesitated—the changes in the room must have taken them aback—K. took one of them by the arm to lead her in. But he immediately let her go, so startled was the identical stare that after a brief exchange of glances they fixed on K. "But you've been staring at me long enough," said K., and, fending off a certain unpleasant sensation, he picked up his clothes and shoes, which Frieda—with the assistants following timidly behind—had just brought in, and dressed. He had always found

Frieda's patience with the assistants incomprehensible, and this was once again so. After a long search she had discovered that the two of them, who ought to have been brushing the clothes in the courtyard, were quietly eating lunch downstairs, the still unbrushed clothes lay crumpled on their laps; then she was obliged to brush them herself, but though she certainly knew how to keep common people in check, she did nothing to rebuke the assistants, treated their utterly negligent behavior as a little joke, and even tapped one of them lightly, and as if affectionately, upon the cheek. K. wanted to rebuke her later for this. But now it was high time to leave. "The assistants will stay behind to help you move," said K. Yet they weren't willing to accept this; well-fed and cheerful as they were now, they would have liked a little exercise. Only when Frieda said "You are staying here" did they fall in line. "Do you know where I'm going?" asked K. "Yes," said Frieda. "So you're no longer keeping me here?" asked K. "You'll run into so many obstacles," she said, "and then what would my words mean?" She kissed K. goodbye and, since he hadn't eaten at noon, gave him a small package with bread and sausage, which she had brought up from the kitchen, reminded him that he should not come here but rather straight to the school, and accompanied him, with her hand on his shoulder, to the door.

VIII.

WAITING FOR KLAMM

At first K. was glad to have escaped the crush of maids and assistants in that warm room. Besides, it was almost freezing, the snow was firmer, the walking easier. Only it was getting darker, and he hastened his step.

The Castle, whose contours were already beginning to dissolve, lay still as ever, K. had never seen the slightest sign of life up there, perhaps it wasn't even possible to distinguish anything from this distance, and yet his eyes demanded it and refused to tolerate the stillness. When K. looked at the Castle, it was at times as if he were watching someone who sat there calmly, gazing into space, not lost in thought and therefore cut off from everything, but free and untroubled; as if he were alone, unobserved; and yet it could not have escaped him that someone was observing him, but this didn't disturb his composure and indeed—one could not tell whether through cause or effect—the observer's gaze could not remain fixed there, and slid off. Today this impression was further reinforced by the early darkness, the longer he looked, the less he could make out, and the deeper everything sank into the twilight.

Just as K. reached the Gentlemen's Inn, which was still dark, a window opened on the second floor, and a fat clean-shaven young gentleman in a fur coat leaned out, then stood by the window, and didn't seem to respond with even the slightest nod to K.'s greeting. K. did not encounter anybody in the corridor or the taproom; the smell of stale beer in the taproom was even worse than of late, this sort of thing surely never happened at the inn by the bridge. K. immediately went to the door through which he had recently observed Klamm, pressed the handle cautiously, but the door was locked; he felt about for the peephole, but the catch was no doubt so evenly inset that he couldn't find the spot, so he lit a match. At that, he was startled by a shout. In the corner between the door and the sideboard near the stove cowered a young girl in the light of the flaring match and stared at him with laboriously opened, sleep-filled eyes. This was obviously Frieda's successor. Quickly she recovered her composure, turned on the electric light, an angry expression still on her face, then recognized K. "Oh, the surveyor," she said smiling, and she held out her hand to him and introduced herself, "my name is Pepi." She was small, rosy, and healthy; her plentiful reddish-blond hair was plaited in a thick braid, and it curled about her face; she wore a dress of shiny gray material that scarcely suited her, hung straight down, and was gathered below in a clumsy, childlike manner by a silk band ending in a bow, so that it restricted her movements. She asked about Frieda, whether she would be back soon. The question almost verged on malice. "I was summoned at once," she then said, "urgently, when Frieda left, because after all they can't use just any old person in this position, I was a chambermaid until then, but this hasn't been a good exchange for me.

There's a great deal of evening and night work here, it's very tiring, I shall probably find it unbearable, it doesn't surprise me that Frieda gave it up." "Frieda was always very satisfied here," said K., in order to finally alert Pepi to the difference that existed between Frieda and herself and that she failed to take into account. "Don't believe her," said Pepi, "Frieda can control herself in a way almost nobody else can. If she doesn't want to confess something, she simply doesn't confess it, so nobody even knows she has something to confess. But I have been in service with her here for several years, we have always slept together in the same bed, but I'm not all that close to her, and she certainly never even thinks of me now. Her only friend perhaps is the old landlady from the Bridge Inn, but that too is indicative." "Frieda is my fiancée," said K., as he attempted to find the peephole in the door. "I know," said Pepi, "that's why I'm telling you this. Otherwise it would be of no importance to you." "I understand," said K., "you mean I can be proud of having won myself such a reserved girl." "Yes," she said, laughing happily, as though she had gained K.'s complicity in a furtive agreement concerning Frieda.

Yet it was not actually the words that bothered K. and distracted him slightly from his search but rather her appearance and her presence in this place. Of course, she was indeed considerably younger than Frieda, almost childlike, and her clothes were ridiculous, for she had obviously dressed in a manner that reflected her exaggerated notions of a barmaid's importance. And in a way these notions of hers were even justified, for she had probably been granted the position, for which she was still altogether unsuited, unexpectedly, without merit, and only temporarily, for she hadn't even been entrusted with the small leather bag that Frieda always wore on her belt. And as for her supposed dissatisfaction with the position, that was nothing but arrogance. And yet despite her childish lack of common sense, even she probably had connections with the Castle; she had, unless she was lying, been a chambermaid; without any knowledge of what she possessed, she dozed away her days here, and though one couldn't snatch the possession from her by embracing this small, fat, slightly round-backed body, one could touch it and cheer oneself up for the difficult path ahead. So this was perhaps no different than with Frieda? Oh yes, it was different. One only had to think of the look on Frieda's face to understand this. K. would never have touched Pepi. Still, for a moment he had to cover his eyes, so lecherously was he staring at her.

"There's no need for the light," said Pepi, switching it off again, "I only turned it on because you gave me such a fright. What are you doing here? Has Frieda forgotten something?" "Yes," said K., pointing to the door, "right next door, a tablecloth, a crocheted white tablecloth." "Oh yes, her tablecloth," said Pepi, "I remember, a beautiful piece, I even helped her with it, but it's hardly in that room." "Frieda thinks so. Anyhow, who lives there?" asked K. "Nobody," said Pepi, "it's the gentlemen's room, that's where the gentlemen eat and drink, or rather it is meant for their use, but most gentlemen stay upstairs in their rooms." "If I knew," said K., "that there was nobody next door, I'd gladly go in to look for the tablecloth. But one cannot be certain of that; Klamm, for instance, likes to sit there." "Klamm is certainly not there now," said Pepi, "indeed he's about to leave, the sleigh is already waiting in the courtyard."

Immediately, without a word of explanation, K. left the taproom and once in the corridor turned, not toward the exit, but toward the interior of the house, and in just a few steps reached the courtyard. How still and beautiful it was here! A four-sided courtyard closed off on three sides by the building and toward the street—a side street unfamiliar to K.—by a high white wall with a large, heavy, and now open gate. Here, on the side facing the courtyard, the building seemed taller than in front, or at least the second floor had been fully finished and seemed bigger, for it was surrounded by a wooden gallery, entirely closed except for a narrow opening at eye level. Diagonally opposite K., still in the central section but right in the corner, where it joined the sidewing opposite, was an open entrance to the house with no door. Before it stood a dark, closed sleigh, to which two horses were harnessed. Except for the coachman, whose presence at this distance in the twilight K. suspected rather than perceived, there wasn't a soul in sight.

Hands in his pockets, looking about carefully, K. went around two sides of the courtyard, staying close to the wall until he reached the sleigh. Sunk in his fur coat, the coachman—one of the peasants who had been in the taproom the other evening—had watched K. approach, impassively, as one follows the progress of a cat. Even when K. came and stood next to him, greeting him, and the horses grew somewhat restless because of the man appearing out of the dark, he remained entirely unconcerned. This was agreeable to K. Leaning against the wall, he unpacked his food, thought gratefully of Frieda, who had been so solicitous, and peered into the interior of the house. A stairway turning at a right angle led downward and was crossed at the bottom by a low but seemingly deep passageway, everything was clean, whitewashed, set off sharply and evenly.

The wait took longer than K. had expected. He had long since finished the food, it was bitterly cold, the twilight had already yielded to complete darkness, and yet there was still no sign of Klamm. "It can take a lot longer," said a coarse voice all of a sudden, so close to K. that he started. It was the coachman, who, as if awakening, stretched and yawned loudly. "What can take a lot longer?" asked K., pleased by the interruption, for the constant stillness and tension had grown irksome. "Till you leave," said the coachman. K. did not understand him, but asked no more questions, he believed this was the best way to get this arrogant person to speak. Not answering here in the dark was already incitement enough. And indeed a moment later the coachman asked: "Would you like some cognac?" "Yes," said K. without thinking, all too tempted by the offer, for he was shivering. "Then open the sleigh," said the coachman, "there are a few bottles in the side pocket, take one, have a drink, and then hand it to me. It's too awkward getting down with this fur coat on." K. was annoyed at having to lend a hand, but seeing as he was already mixed up with the coachman, he obeyed, even at the risk of having someone like Klamm, say, catch him in the sleigh. He opened the wide door and could easily have pulled the bottle out of the bag fixed to the inner door, but now that the door was open he had such an urge to enter the sleigh that he could not resist, he would only sit there a moment. He slipped in. How extraordinarily warm it was in the sleigh, and it didn't cool off, even though the door, which K. did not dare close, was wide open. And there wasn't even any way of knowing if one was sitting on a bench, there were so many blankets, cushions, and furs; on each side one could turn and stretch in every direction and always sink down soft and warm. With his arms extended, his head supported by the abundant supply of cushions, K. gazed from the sleigh into the dark house. Why was it taking Klamm so long to come down? As if dazed by the warmth after having stood so long in the snow, K. wished that Klamm would finally come. The thought that he would rather not be seen by Klamm occurred to him only vaguely, as a slight distraction. His forgetfulness was reinforced by the conduct of the coachman, who must have known that he was in the sleigh, but left him here without even asking for the cognac. That was considerate, but of course K. wanted to do him a service; cumbersomely, without changing position, he reached over to the side pocket, not to the one on the open door, that was too far, but to the one on the closed door behind him; but it didn't matter, there were bottles here too. He took one out, unscrewed the cap, smelled it, and then had to smile involuntarily; the smell was so sweet, so pleasing, so much like praise and kind words from someone whom you're very fond of, though you don't quite know what it is all about and do not want to know either and are simply happy in the knowledge that it is he who is saying such things. "And this is supposed to be cognac?" K. asked dubiously, trying it out of curiosity. But it was indeed cognac, oddly enough, warm and burning. How it changed as one drank, from something that was virtually no more than a bearer of sweet fragrance into a drink fit for a coachman. "Can it be?" K. asked as though reproaching himself, and drank again.

At that—just as K. was engaged in taking a long sip—it

became bright, the electric light came on, not only inside, on the stairs, in the passage, and in the corridor, but outside above the entrance. Footsteps could be heard descending the stairs, the bottle fell from K.'s hand, cognac spilled onto a fur, K. jumped from the sleigh, he had no sooner slammed the door with a thud than a gentleman came slowly out of the house. The only consolation, it seemed, was that it wasn't Klamm, or was that actually cause for regret? It was the gentleman whom K. had already seen at the second-floor window. A young gentleman, extremely good-looking, pale and reddish, but quite grave. K. gave him a gloomy look as well, but it was really aimed at himself. It would after all have been better to have sent the assistants here, for even they would have been capable of conducting themselves as he had done. The gentleman opposite still hadn't spoken, as if there weren't enough breath in his extremely broad chest for the words about to be spoken. "This is really terrible," he then said, pushing his hat off his forehead a little. What? Though the gentleman didn't know about K.'s having been in the sleigh, he already thought something was terrible? That K. had, say, penetrated into the courtyard? "Now how did you get here?" the gentleman asked, more softly, already exhaling, reconciled to the inevitable. What questions! What answers! Perhaps he should assure the gentleman that the path on which he had set out with such hope had led nowhere? Instead of answering him, K. turned to the sleigh, opened the door, and retrieved his cap, which he had left inside. With discomfort he noticed that the cognac was dripping onto the footboard.

Then he turned toward the gentleman again; he was no longer hesitant to reveal that he had been in the sleigh, that wasn't the worst part; if he were asked, but only then, he would certainly not refrain from saying that the coachman himself had given the order, at least the one to open the sleigh. Actually, the worst part was that the gentleman had surprised him and that there hadn't been enough time to hide from him and to wait undisturbed for Klamm, or rather, that he hadn't shown sufficient presence of mind to stay in the sleigh, close the door, and wait there on the fur blankets for Klamm, or at the very least to stay there while the gentleman was still around. True, he couldn't have known whether Klamm himself might not come now, in which case it would naturally have been better not to greet him outside. Yes, several things ought to have been taken into consideration here, but not now, for it was all over.

"Come with me," said the gentleman, not quite as an order, and yet it was an order, not so much in the words as in the accompanying gesture, a short and deliberately indifferent wave. "I'm waiting here for someone," K. said, no longer in hope of success, but simply as a matter of principle. "Come," the gentleman repeated, not in the least deterred, as if he wanted to show that he had never doubted that K. was waiting for somebody. "But then I'll miss the person I'm waiting for," said K., flinching. Regardless of everything that had happened, he had the feeling that what he had achieved here was a kind of possession, which he only apparently retained but that needn't be surrendered simply upon some arbitrary command. "You'll miss him whether you wait or go," said the gentleman, whose opinion certainly was dismissive but also showed remarkable indulgence for K.'s train of thought: "Then I would rather miss him as I wait," said K. defiantly, it would take more than mere words from this young gentleman to drive him away. At that the gentleman, with a superior expression on his tilted face, closed his eyes for a moment, as though he wanted to leave K.'s unreasonableness behind and resume his own reasoning, ran the tip of his tongue over the lips of his barely open mouth, and said to the coachman: "Unharness the horses!"

The coachman, submissive toward the gentleman but with an angry side-glance at K., finally had to climb down in his fur coat, and then, very hesitantly, as though he did not so much expect the gentleman to rescind his order as K. to change his mind, began to draw the horses and sleigh backwards to the side wing, in which, apparently behind a large gate, the stable with the carriage shed was to be found. K. saw himself being left alone, on one side the sleigh was retreating, as was also, on the other, along the very path K. himself had taken, the young gentleman, though both went quite slowly, as though wanting to show K. that it was still in his power to call them back.

Perhaps he had that power, but it would have done him no good; to call the sleigh back would be to drive himself away. So he stood still, the only one who had held his ground, but it was a victory that gave no joy. He looked at the gentleman and then at the coachman. The gentleman had already reached the door through which K. had first entered the courtyard, he glanced back again, K. thought he could see him shake his head over such stubbornness, and then in a resolute, brief, final motion, he turned around and entered the corridor, where he immediately disappeared. The coachman remained in the courtyard, the sleigh gave him a great deal of work to do, he had to open the heavy stable door, drive the sleigh in backwards, unharness the horses, and lead them to their stalls, he did all this gravely, lost in thought, having given up all hope of an excursion; the man's silent bustle without even a glance in his direction seemed to K. a far harsher reproach than the conduct of the gentleman. And now when after finishing his work in the stable the coachman walked straight across the courtyard with his slow swaying gait, closed the large gate, then came back, all this slowly and meticulously focusing only on his own tracks in the snow, then locked the stable behind him and all the electric lights went out—for whom should they have shone?—and only the opening above in the wooden gallery remained bright and briefly arrested one's wandering gaze, it seemed to K. as if they had broken off all contact with him, but as if he were freer than ever and could wait as long as he wanted here in this place where he was generally not allowed, and as if he had fought for this freedom for himself in a manner nobody else could have done and as if nobody could touch him or drive him away, or even speak to him, yet—and this conviction was at least equally strong—as if there were nothing more senseless, nothing more desperate, than this freedom, this waiting, this invulnerability.

IX.

THE STRUGGLE AGAINST THE INTERROGATION

And he tore himself away and went back toward the house, this time not along the wall but straight through the snow, in the corridor he met the landlord, who greeted him silently and pointed to the taproom door, he followed his gesture because he was cold and because he wanted to see people, but was very disappointed when he saw the young gentleman sitting at a little table, which had surely been put there specifically for that pur pose since they usually made do with barrels, and standing in front of him—an oppressive sight for K.—the landlady from the Bridge Inn. Pepi, proud, with her head thrown back, always the same smile, unshakably conscious of her dignity, swinging her braid at every turn, hurried to and fro, brought beer and then a pen and ink, for the gentleman had spread papers out in front of him and was comparing figures, which he found, now in this paper, now in another at the far end of the table, and was about to start writing. From her full height the landlady gazed down in silence at the gentleman and his papers, her lips slightly pursed, as though she had said all that was necessary and it had been well received. "The surveyor, finally," said the gentleman, glancing up as K. entered, then burying himself once again in his papers. The landlady, too, only looked at K. indifferently, not at all surprised. Pepi, though, seemed to notice K. only when he went up to the counter and ordered a cognac.

K. leaned on it, put his hand over his eyes, and ignored everything else. Then he sipped some of the cognac and pushed it away, saying it was undrinkable. "All of the gentlemen drink it," Pepi said curtly, poured out the rest, washed the small glass, and put it on the shelf. "The gentlemen have something better than this," said K. "Possibly," said Pepi, "but I don't," and at that she had finished with K. and was again at the service of the gentleman, who did not require anything, though, and so she merely walked from one side to the other behind him, deferentially attempting to look over his shoulder at the papers, yet this was nothing but idle curiosity and boastfulness, which even the landlady criticized by knitting her eyebrows.

Yet all of a sudden the landlady pricked up her ears and, listening intently, stared into space. K. turned around, he heard nothing out of the ordinary, the others apparently hadn't heard anything either, but the landlady, with long strides and on tiptoe, ran to the rear door, which led to the courtyard, looked through the keyhole, turned to the others with wide-open eyes and a flushed face, beckoning them with her finger; and each one looked through, the landlady got the most turns, but Pepi was not left out either, the gentleman being the most indifferent of the three. Pepi and the gentleman soon came back, now only the landlady was still straining to see, bending over, almost kneeling, you almost had the impression she was pleading with the keyhole to let her through, for there had probably been nothing to see for some time now. Yet when she finally stood up, passed her hands over her face, fixed her hair, took a deep breath, was evidently obliged to readjust her eyes to the room and to the people here, which she reluctantly did, K. said, not so as to confirm what he already knew but to ward off an attack that he almost feared, so vulnerable was he now: "So Klamm is already gone?" The landlady walked past him in silence, but from his little table the gentleman said: "Yes, certainly. Once you gave up your sentry post, Klamm was naturally able to leave. But it's wonderful how sensitive the gentleman is! Landlady, did you notice how uneasily Klamm looked about him?" The landlady appeared not to have noticed it, but the gentleman went on: "Well, fortunately there was no longer anything to be seen, the coachman had smoothed out the footprints in the snow with a broom." "The landlady didn't notice anything," said K., not in hope of success but simply irritated by the gentleman's assertion, which had been made to sound so conclusive and irreversible. "Perhaps I wasn't at the keyhole just then," the landlady said, coming to the gentleman's defense, but then, wanting to give Klamm his due, she added: "Still, I don't believe in this great sensitivity of Klamm's. We are indeed concerned about him, we try to protect him, on the assumption that Klamm is extremely sensitive. That is fine and certainly the will of Klamm. How the situation is in reality, though, we don't know. Certainly, Klamm will never speak to anyone he doesn't want to speak to, no matter how strenuously a certain individual exerts himself and no matter how insufferably he pushes himself to the fore, but this fact alone, that Klamm will never speak to him, will never allow him to come face to face with him, is already quite enough, for in reality why shouldn't he be capable of enduring the sight of anybody whomsoever. This cannot be proved, for it'll never come to a test." The gentleman nodded eagerly. "I am of course of the same opinion," he said, "if I put the matter a little differently just now, it was only so as to make it comprehensible for the surveyor. It's correct, though, that after coming outside, Klamm did look around repeatedly in a half circle." "Perhaps he was looking for me," said K. "Possibly," said the gentleman, "that never occurred to me." Everybody laughed, Pepi, who barely understood any of this, the loudest.

"Since we're all so cheerfully assembled," said the gentleman, "I would ask, sir, that you give me some information to complete my files." "A lot of writing goes on here," said K., looking from a distance at the files. "Yes, a bad habit," said the gentleman, laughing again, "but perhaps you still don't know who I am. I am Momus, Klamm's village secretary." After those words were spoken, the entire room became serious; although the landlady and Pepi clearly knew the gentleman well, they still seemed upset by the reference to his name and title. And even the gentleman himself, as though what he had said exceeded his own comprehension, and as if he wanted to flee all traces of the solemnity his words had subsequently acquired, buried himself in his files and began to write, and then there was not a sound in the room save for his pen. "And so what is that: village secretary?" K. asked after a little while. The landlady, speaking on behalf of Momus, who, now that he had introduced himself, considered it inappropriate to offer any further explanation, said: "Mr. Momus is Klamm's secretary, just like any of Klamm's secretaries, but his office, and also, if I'm not mistaken, his jurisdiction—" Momus shook his head vigorously as he wrote and the landlady corrected herself, "so it's only his official seat, not his official jurisdiction, that is confined to the village. Mr. Momus handles all of Klamm's written work in the village and is first to receive all petitions sent to Klamm from the village." Since K., still little affected by these matters, was gazing at her blankly, she added in a half-embarrassed voice: "That's the arrangement, all of the gentlemen from the Castle have their own village secretaries." Momus, who had followed everything more closely than had K., elaborated for the benefit of the landlady: "Most village secretaries work only for a single gentleman, but I work for two, for Klamm and for Vallabene." "Yes," said the landlady, in turn recalling that this was indeed so and turning to K., "Mr. Momus works for two gentlemen, for Klamm and for Vallabene, so he is a village secretary twice over." "Twice over, indeed!" said K., nodding at Momus, who was almost leaning forward and gazing straight up at K., just as one nods at a child whom one has just heard being praised in one's presence. If there was a certain contempt in K.'s remark, it either passed unnoticed or was exactly what they wanted. For they were discussing the merits of a man from Klamm's immediate entourage in front of K., who wasn't even sufficiently worthy to be seen by Klamm, not even by chance, and they did so with the unconcealed intention of provoking K.'s recognition and praise. And yet K. didn't truly feel so inclined; striving as he was with all his might to gain a glimpse of Klamm, he had little respect for the post of a Momus, who was allowed to live in sight of Klamm; far be it from him to feel admiration or even envy since it was not the closeness to Klamm in itself that was worth striving for but rather that he, K., and he alone, not anybody else with his wishes, or anybody else's, should approach Klamm, and approach him not so as to rest there with him but to get past him and go on into the Castle.

And he looked at his watch and said: "But I must go home now." Immediately the relationship changed in Momus's favor. "Why, of course," said Momus, "your janitorial duties beckon. But you must give me another moment. Just a few short questions." "I don't feel like it," said K., and he started toward the door. Slamming a file on the table, Momus stood up: "In the name of Klamm, I call upon you to answer my questions." "In the name of Klamm?" K. repeated. "Is he concerned about my affairs, then?" "That," said Momus, "is something I have no opinion about and you surely even less so; so the two of us need have no qualms in leaving the matter to him. Nevertheless, by virtue of the position bestowed upon me by Klamm, I call upon you to stay and answer." "Surveyor," the landlady broke in, "I'll be careful not to give you any more advice, my previous suggestions, the most well-meant suggestions conceivable, were turned down in a most disgraceful way, and I came here to the secretary—I have nothing to hide—only so as to notify the administration of your conduct and intentions in an appropriate manner and to guard against the possibility of your ever being lodged with me again, that's how things stand between the two of us and this isn't likely to change, and so if I give you my opinion, I do so not to help you but to ease somewhat the difficult task of the secretary, who has to deal with a person such as you. Still—and it's only by being frank that I can associate with you at all, and then only with great reluctance—you can profit from what I say; you need only have the desire to do so. And just in case you do, I should like to draw your attention to the following; in your case the only path leading to Klamm passes through the secretary's depositions. But I don't wish to exaggerate, perhaps this path doesn't lead to Klamm, perhaps it ends long before it reaches him; that decision is made by the secretary at his own discretion. Anyhow, for you this is the only path that does at least lead in Klamm's direction. And you want to give up the only path, for no reason other than contrariness?" "Oh, Landlady," said K., "it is not the only path leading to Klamm, nor is it of greater value than the others. And it is you, Mr. Secretary, who decides whether or not anything I might say here will reach Klamm." "Certainly," said Momus, lowering his eyes with pride and gazing right and left, where there was nothing to be seen, "why else would I be secretary?" "You see, Landlady," said K., "it's not to Klamm that I need a path, but first to the secretary." "That's the path I wanted to open up for you," said the landlady, "didn't I offer this morning to forward your request to Klamm? That would have happened through the secretary. But you rejected the offer, and now you have no alternative. Of course, after your performance today, after your attempt to waylay Klamm, you'll have even less prospect of success. But this final, tiniest, vanishing, even nonexistent hope is your only hope." "How is it, Landlady," said K., "that you initially tried so hard to prevent me from pressing on to Klamm, and now take my request so seriously and seem to think I'm lost, as it were, if my plans fail? If it at one point was possible to advise me sincerely from the bottom of one's heart against any attempt to reach Klamm, how can one now with seemingly equal sincerity almost push me along the path to Klamm, which of course may never lead to him." "So I'm pushing you, am I?" said the landlady. "Do you mean that I'm pushing you when I call your attempts hopeless? Now, that truly would be the height of audacity, if in this way you were trying to shift your own responsibility for yourself onto me. Might it be the presence of the secretary that prompts you to do so? No, Surveyor, I'm certainly not pushing you to do anything at all. I have only one thing to confess, that when I first saw you, I may have overestimated you a little. Your quick victory over Frieda frightened me, I didn't know what you might still be capable of, I wanted to ward off additional misfortunes and thought the only way I could bring this about was by shocking you with pleas and threats. Meanwhile I have learned to think about everything more calmly. You may do exactly as you like. In the snow outside in the courtyard your deeds will perhaps leave deep footprints, but that's all." "I don't think the contradiction is entirely resolved," said K., "but I'm satisfied now that I have alerted you to it. But, Secretary, I would ask you to tell me whether the landlady's opinion is correct, namely, whether the deposition you want to take from me could lead to my being allowed to appear before Klamm. If that is so, then I'm ready to answer all questions right away. In that respect I am certainly ready for everything." "No," said Momus, "there are no such connections. I'm simply interested in getting a precise description of this afternoon for Klamm's village registry. The description is ready, you need only fill in two or three gaps, simply as a matter of form, there is no other objective and none can be attained." K. looked in silence at the landlady. "Why are you looking at me," the landlady asked, "isn't that exactly what I told you? He's always like this, Secretary, he's always like this. Distorts the information given to him, then claims he's been given the wrong information. I have been telling him for ever and ever, and once again today, that there isn't the slightest chance of his being received by Klamm; now if there is no such chance, he won't get it through this deposition either. Could anything be clearer than that? Besides, I've been telling him that this deposition is the only truly official connection that he can have with Klamm, but this too is altogether clear and indubitable. But if he doesn't believe me, and constantly hopes—I don't know why and to what end—to be able to reach Klamm, then his sole hope, if one keeps to his train of thought, lies in the only truly official connection that he has with Klamm, namely, in this deposition. That's all I have said, and anyone who says otherwise is twisting my words maliciously." "Landlady, if that is so," said K., "then please excuse me, for I have indeed misunderstood you; I gathered from your earlier remarks, mistakenly as it now turns out, that there is the tiniest hope for me." "Certainly," said the landlady, "I think so, but now you're twisting my words again, only this time the other way around. I think there is some such hope for you, but it is based solely on this deposition. Yet the situation isn't such that you can simply attack the secretary with the question: 'Will I be allowed to see Klamm if I answer the questions.' When a child asks in such a way, one laughs, when an adult does so, it's an insult to the office, only the secretary has graciously concealed this through the delicacy of his reply. But the hope I have in mind has to do with your possessing through the deposition a kind of connection, perhaps a kind of connection, with Klamm. Isn't that hope enough? If you were asked about the accomplishments that make you worthy of the gift of such hope, could you come up with anything at all? Of course, one cannot speak more precisely about this hope, and in his official capacity the secretary in particular would not be able to give even the slightest hint of this. For him it is, as he said, only a matter of getting a description of this afternoon, simply as a matter of form, he will say no more, even if you were to question him right now about my statements." "So then, Secretary," asked K., "will Klamm read this deposition?" "No," said Momus, "why should he? After all, Klamm cannot read every deposition, and indeed he reads none: 'Don't come anywhere near me with those depositions!' he often says." "Surveyor," the landlady complained, "you exhaust me by asking such questions. For is it truly necessary, let alone desirable, that Klamm should read this deposition and get to know the trifling details of your life, word for word, wouldn't you prefer to request most humbly that the report be hidden from Klamm, a request by the way that would be just as foolish as your previous one, for who can hide anything from Klamm, but one that would nonetheless reveal a more sympathetic character. And is this necessary for what you call your hope? Didn't you yourself state that you'd be satisfied if you could only have an opportunity to speak in the presence of Klamm, even if he neither looked at you nor listened to you? And through this deposition won't you obtain at least that much, and perhaps far more?" "Far more?" asked K., "in what way?" "If only you didn't always, like a child, insist on having everything served up right away in edible form," cried the landlady. "For who can come up with answers to such questions? The deposition goes into Klamm's village registry, this you have already heard and no more can be said with any certainty. But can you truly grasp the full meaning of the deposition, of the secretary, of the village registry? Do you know what it means to be interrogated by the secretary? This is something that he himself may not, or probably doesn't, know. He sits quietly here doing his duty, simply as a matter of form, as he said. But remember that he was appointed by Klamm, that he works in Klamm's name, that everything he does, even if Klamm never hears about it, still has Klamm's approval from the outset. And how can anything have Klamm's approval that isn't filled with his spirit? Far be it from me to want to flatter the secretary blatantly, he himself would even forbid this, but I'm not talking about his personality as an independent individual but rather about what he is when he has Klamm's approval, as he does now, for instance. Then he is an instrument upon which Klamm's hand lies, and woe betide anybody who will not submit to him."

The landlady's threats did not frighten K., the hopes with which she sought to trap him wearied him. Klamm was remote, the landlady had once compared Klamm to an eagle and that had seemed ridiculous to K., but no longer, he considered Klamm's remoteness, his impregnable abode, his muteness, broken perhaps only by shouts the likes of which K. had never heard before, his piercing downturned gaze, which could never be proved, never be refuted, and his, from K.'s position below, indestructible circles, which he was describing up there in accordance with incomprehensible laws, visible only for seconds—all this Klamm and the eagle had in common. But it certainly had nothing to do with the deposition, over which just now Momus broke a salted pretzel, which he enjoyed with his beer, sprinkling all his papers with salt and caraway seeds.

"Good night," said K., "I have an aversion to all manner of interrogations," and now he actually did go to the door. "So he is indeed leaving," said Momus to the landlady, almost anxiously. "He wouldn't dare," said the landlady, K. heard no more, he was already in the corridor. It was cold, there was a strong wind blowing. From a door opposite came the landlord, he seemed to have been observing the corridor from behind a peephole. He had to tie his coattails around his body, so strongly did the wind pull at them even here in the corridor. "Surveyor, you're already leaving?" he said. "That surprises you?" asked K. "Yes," said the landlord, "were you not interrogated, then?" "No," said K., "I did not submit to the interrogation." "Why not?" asked the landlord. "It is unclear to me," said K., "why I should let myself be interrogated, why I should subject myself to a prank or an official whim. Perhaps I would have done so another time also as a joke or whim, but not today." "To be sure," said the landlord, but his assent was merely polite, not convinced. "But now I must let the servants into the taproom," he said, "their allotted time began quite a while ago. Only I didn't want to interrupt the interrogation." "So you thought it that important?" asked K. "Oh, yes," said the landlord. "So I ought not to have refused?" asked K. "No," said the landlord, "you ought not to have done so." Since K. remained silent, he added, either to console K. or to hasten his own departure: "There, there, this doesn't mean that sulphur will come raining down right away from the heavens." "No," said K., "not by the looks of the weather." And they parted, laughing.

X.

ON THE STREET

K. stepped out on the wild blustery steps and gazed into the darkness. Nasty, nasty weather. Somehow in connection with this, he thought of how the landlady had endeavored to make him amenable to the deposition and how he had held his ground. It was not a candid effort, though, for she had at the same time furtively dragged him away from the deposition, and ultimately one couldn't tell whether one had held one's ground or given way. An intriguer by nature, operating like the wind, seemingly to no end, upon remote alien instructions that one never got to see.

No sooner had he taken a few steps along the main road than he saw two wavering lights in the distance; this sign of life pleased him and he hurried toward them and they in turn glided toward him. He had no idea why he was so greatly disappointed on seeing the assistants, it was indeed they coming toward him, probably sent by Frieda, and the lanterns that rescued him from the darkness, in which there were noises all around him, were his all right, but he was disappointed, he had expected strangers, not these old acquaintances, who were a burden to him. But it wasn't just the assistants, out of the dark between them stepped Barnabas. "Barnabas," cried K., extending his hand, "you've come to see me?" The surprise at seeing him made K. initially forget all the trouble Barnabas had caused him. "Yes, to see you," said Barnabas, as cordially as ever, "with a letter from Klamm." "A letter from Klamm!" said K., throwing his head back and taking the letter quickly from Barnabas's hand. "Give me some light!" he told the assistants, who drew close on either side, raising their lanterns. K. had to fold the large sheet up tiny in order to shield it from the wind. Then he read: "To the Land Surveyor at the Bridge Inn! The surveying work that you have carried out so far meets with my approval. The assistants' work is also praiseworthy; you really know how to induce them to work. Do not relax your exertions! Carry your work to a successful conclusion! Any interruption would embitter me. But rest assured, the question of remuneration will soon be resolved. I will keep you in mind." K. looked up from the letter only when the assistants, who read much more slowly than he, gave three loud hurrahs in celebration of the good news and swung the lanterns. "Be quiet," he said, and then to Barnabas: "It's a misunderstanding." Barnabas did not understand him. "It's a misunderstanding," K. repeated, and the weariness brought on by the afternoon came over him again, the school was still such a long way off, and behind him seemed to loom up the entire Barnabas family; the assistants still clung to K., so he elbowed them aside; why had Frieda sent them out to meet him when he had expressly ordered that they should stay with her. Besides, he certainly would have found the way home alone, and it would have been easier alone than in such company. And now, to crown it all, one of them had wrapped about his neck a scarf with loose ends flapping in the wind that had already hit K. several times in the face, and though the other assistant had always lifted the scarf off K.'s face right away with his long, pointed, continually fidgeting fingers, this hadn't improved matters. Both of them even seemed to have enjoyed the to-and-fro, just as the wind and the unruly night excited them. "Go away," K. shouted, "since you insisted on coming, why didn't you bring my walking stick? And now what can I use to drive you home?" They ducked behind Barnabas, but their fear did not prevent the two of them, one on either side, from placing their lanterns on the shoulders of their defender, but of course he shook them off right away. "Barnabas," said K., and it weighed upon his heart that Barnabas obviously couldn't understand him, that though his jacket gave off a brilliant sheen in times that were calm, when the situation became serious Barnabas was no help at all, he simply resorted to a kind of silent resistance that was impossible to overcome, for he was quite defenseless, all that glittered at such moments was his smile, but it was about as effective as the stars above against the gale down here. "Look what the gentleman wrote," K. said, holding the letter up to his face. "The gentleman is ill-informed. For I am not doing any work as surveyor, and as for the assistants, you can see what they are worth. And work I am not doing, I obviously cannot interrupt; I cannot even arouse the gentleman's bitterness, so how could I earn his recognition! And I will never be able to rest assured." "I'll deliver the message," said Barnabas, who had been looking past the letter, which in any case he couldn't have read for he had put it right next to his face. "Oh," said K., "you promise to deliver it, but can I really believe you? I need a trustworthy messenger so badly, now more than ever!" K. bit his lips in impatience. "Sir," said Barnabas, bending his head gently—K. almost let this seduce him again into believing Barnabas—"I'll certainly deliver it, and the other message you gave me recently, I'll certainly deliver that, too." "What!" cried K., "you mean you haven't delivered it yet? Didn't you go to the Castle the following day?" "No," said Barnabas, "my dear father is old—well, you saw him—and just then there was a great deal of work, I had to help him, but I'll soon be going up to the Castle again." "But what are you doing, you incomprehensible person, you?" cried K., slapping himself on the forehead, "don't Klamm's affairs take precedence over everything else? You have the high position of messenger, yet you discharge it so shamefully? Who cares about your father's work? Klamm is waiting for news, but instead of rushing there head over heels, you spend your time carting dung from the cowshed." "My father is a shoemaker," Barnabas said, undeterred, "he had orders from Brunswick, and I am Father's apprentice." "Shoemaker—orders—Brunswick," K. cried bitterly, as if trying to make each word forever unusable. "And who needs shoes here on these everlastingly empty paths? And why should I care about shoemaking, I entrusted a message to you not so you would forget it or garble it on your cobbler's bench but so you would take it to the gentleman right away." K. now calmed down somewhat on realizing that all this time Klamm had probably not been at the Castle but rather at the Gentlemen's Inn, yet Barnabas annoyed him again, for in an effort to prove that he had memorized K.'s first message, he began reciting it. "That's enough, I don't want to hear it," said K. "Don't be angry at me, sir," said Barnabas, and then, as if unconsciously wanting to punish K., he withdrew his gaze and lowered his eyes, but probably only in dismay over K.'s raised voice. "I'm not angry at you," said K., and now he himself was overcome by uneasiness, "no, not at you, though it's very bad for me to have only a messenger like this for important business." "Look," said Barnabas, and it seemed as if, in an attempt to defend his honor as a messenger, he was saying more than he ought, "Klamm doesn't wait for the news, he even gets annoyed when I come, 'More fresh news,' he once said, and he usually stands up on seeing me come from afar, goes into the next room, and doesn't receive me. Besides, it hasn't been stipulated that I should take every message there at once; had it been stipulated, I would naturally go at once, but it wasn't stipulated, and if I never went, nobody would admonish me because of that. Whenever I take a message, I do so voluntarily." "Fine," said K., observing Barnabas and studiously looking away from the assistants, who took turns slowly rising up from behind Barnabas's shoulders, as if through a trapdoor, and then quickly, whistling a little in imitation of the wind as if frightened by the sight of K., they disappeared again, amusing themselves at length in this way, "how it is at Klamm's I don't know, but I doubt that you can distinguish everything clearly there, and even if you could, we couldn't bring about any improvement. But you can take a message and that's what I ask of you. An extremely short message. Can you deliver it tomorrow right away and give me the answer tomorrow right away, or at least let me know how you were received? Can you and will you? That would be very valuable for me. And perhaps I will still get an opportunity to thank you fittingly, or perhaps you already have a wish that I can grant you." "Certainly I shall carry out the assignment," said Barnabas. "And will you endeavor to carry it out as well as possible and to deliver it to Klamm himself, to get the answer from Klamm himself, very soon, and to do all this immediately, tomorrow, tomorrow morning, will you?" "I'll do my best," said Barnabas, "but then I always do." "Let's stop fighting about this," said K., "here is the assignment: The surveyor K. asks the director for permission to call on him in person and accepts in advance all stipulations that might be attached to any such permission. He is obliged to make this request because all previous intermediaries have utterly failed, as proof of which he adduces the fact that he has done no surveying so far and, judging by the council chairman's statement, will never do so; it was therefore with a desperate feeling of shame that he read the director's last letter and the only thing that can help here is a personal interview with the director. The surveyor realizes the burdensome nature of this request, but he will try to minimize any disruption to the director, he submits to all restrictions as regards time, including, for example, a restriction on the number of words he may use during the interview, he believes that he could even make do with ten words. With deep reverence and extreme impatience he awaits the decision." K. had spoken in utter self-forgetfulness, as though he stood at Klamm's door and spoke with the doorkeeper. "It's become much longer than I expected," he then said, "but you must nonetheless deliver it orally, I don't want to write a letter, for it would once again travel along the endless path of the files." It was only for Barnabas's sake that K. scribbled down the message on a piece of paper on one assistant's back while the other shone the light, but K. was already able to take it down right away from the dictation of Barnabas, who had retained everything and recited it with a schoolchild's precision, disregarding the false clues given by the assistants. "You have an extraordinary memory," said K., handing him the paper, "and now please show that you're extraordinary in other ways, too. And what about your wishes? Have you none? Indeed, to be frank, I would be somewhat reassured about the fate of my message if you had some." At first Barnabas kept silent, and then he said: "My sisters send you their regards." "Your sisters," said K., "yes, those big strong girls." "Both send their regards, but especially Amalia," said Barnabas, "today she gave me this letter for you from the Castle." Latching on to that particular communication, K. asked: "Couldn't she also take my message to the Castle? Or couldn't both of you go and each of you try your luck?" "Amalia isn't allowed into the offices," said Barnabas, "otherwise she would certainly be glad to do so." "I shall, perhaps, come to see you tomorrow," said K., "but do come here first with the answer. I shall wait for you at the school. My regards to your sisters, too." K.'s promise seemed to have made Barnabas quite happy, he not only gave K. a parting handshake but touched him lightly on the shoulder. As though everything were once more as it had been when Barnabas in his radiance first came among the peasants in the taproom, K., though smiling, regarded Barnabas's gesture as a distinction. Having mellowed, on the way back he let the assistants do as they pleased.

XI.

IN THE SCHOOLHOUSE

He arrived home completely frozen, it was dark everywhere, the candles in the lanterns had burned down, and, led by the assistants, who already knew their way around, he groped his way through a schoolroom—"Your first praiseworthy deed," he said, recalling Klamm's letter—from a corner, Frieda, still half asleep, cried: "Let K. sleep! Don't disturb him!" so preoccupied was she with thoughts of K., even though, overcome by sleepiness, she hadn't been able to wait up for him. Then the lamp was lit, but it couldn't be turned up all that high since there wasn't much kerosene left. This new household still had a number of deficiencies. True, the stove was lit, but the large room, which was also used for gymnastics—the equipment lay on the floor and hung from the ceiling—had used up the entire supply of wood and though it had been pleasantly warm, so K. was assured, in the meantime it had, alas, cooled down again. Though there was a large supply of wood in a shed, the shed was locked and the key with the teacher, who permitted wood to be removed only for heating during school hours. This would have been tolerable had there been beds to take refuge in. But there was nothing of the sort, except for a straw mattress covered with commendable cleanliness by a woolen shawl of Frieda's, but there was no eiderdown and only two stiff coarse blankets, which barely gave off any warmth. And now the assistants greedily eyed this miserable straw mattress, though naturally without hope of ever lying on it. Anxiously, Frieda looked at K.; she had shown at the Bridge Inn that she could take any room, no matter how miserable, and make it comfortable to live in, but she couldn't have done anything more here, completely without means as she was. "Our only decoration is the gymnastic equipment," she said, smiling with difficulty under her tears. But as for the main deficiencies, the inadequate sleeping arrangements and the heating, she would definitely see to them tomorrow and was only asking K. to be patient till then. There was not a word, a hint, a sign to suggest that she bore K. the slightest bitterness in her heart, though he had torn her, not only from the Gentlemen's Inn, but now, as he had to admit to himself, from the Bridge Inn too. But that is why he was making an effort to find all of this bearable, which was not all that difficult, for in thought he was walking alongside Barnabas, repeating the message word for word, not as he had told it to Barnabas but as he thought it would sound in front of Klamm. Still, he was genuinely looking forward to the coffee Frieda had made for him on a kerosene burner and, leaning on the now almost cold stove, he followed the quick and experienced movements with which she spread the inevitable white cloth on the teacher's desk, put out a flowered coffee cup along with some bread and bacon, and even a tin of sardines. Everything was ready, Frieda hadn't eaten either, but had waited for K. There were two chairs at hand, K. and Frieda sat down at the table, the assistants at their feet on the podium, but they wouldn't stay quiet and even created a disturbance during the meal; though they had plenty of everything and were still nowhere near finished, now and then they got up to ascertain how much food was still left on the table and whether they could expect any more. K. was not in the least concerned about the assistants and took notice of them only when Frieda laughed. Then he covered her hand cajolingly with his and asked softly why she treated them so leniently and tolerated their misconduct. That was certainly no way to get rid of them, but if you dealt with them very firmly, as became their conduct, you could rein them in or—and this was not only more likely but also better still—make their position so unpleasant that they would finally run away. It looked as if their stay in the school wouldn't be particularly pleasant, and of course it wouldn't last, but they would barely notice all the deficiencies if the assistants left and the two of them were alone in the silent building. Didn't she notice too that the assistants were getting cheekier each day, as though they were encouraged by Frieda's presence and the hope that, with Frieda there, K. wouldn't deal as vigorously with them as he would otherwise have done. Incidentally, there might be some extremely simple measures for getting rid of them at once, without fuss, and perhaps Frieda even knew of some, given her intimate knowledge of local affairs. And one would probably only be doing the assistants a favor by driving them away, for the life they led here could scarcely be called luxurious, and they would have to cease lounging about, or at least do less of that, since they would have to work, whereas Frieda needed to go easy on herself after the excitement of the last few days, and he, K., would be busy seeking a way out of their predicament. Still, if the assistants left, he would feel so relieved that he could easily take care of all the janitorial work in addition to everything else.

Frieda, who had listened carefully, stroked his arm slowly and said she fully agreed with him, though he had perhaps exaggerated the assistants' misconduct, they were young lads, cheerful and somewhat simple-minded, serving a stranger for the first time, newly freed from the severity of Castle discipline, and therefore always a little excited and bewildered and in that state apt to get up to silly mischief, and though it was quite natural to get annoyed at this, the more sensible approach would be to laugh. There were times when she herself simply couldn't keep from laughing. Still, she fully agreed with K. that it would be best to send them away and be all on their own here together. She drew closer to K. and hid her face on his shoulder. And in that position, speaking so incomprehensibly that K. had to bend down to her, she said that she knew of no measure that could be taken against the assistants and feared that everything K. had suggested would be futile. To the best of her knowledge, it was K. who requested them and now he had them and must keep them. It would be best to accept them lightheartedly as the lighthearted sort they were; that was the easiest way to put up with them.

K. was dissatisfied with this answer, half in jest and half seriously he said that she seemed to be in league with them or was at least very fond of them; well, they were handsome lads all right, but there was nobody who couldn't somehow be got rid of, given a bit of good will, and he would demonstrate this to her with the assistants.

Frieda said she would be most grateful to him if he succeeded. Besides, from now on she wouldn't laugh at them or speak to them, except when necessary. She no longer considered them funny; it wasn't a trifling matter being constantly observed by two men, she had learned to see them through his eyes. And she really did recoil a little when the assistants got up again, partly to check the provisions, partly to investigate the constant whispering.

K. took advantage of this to turn Frieda against the assistants, he drew Frieda toward him and, seated close together, they finished the meal. It was certainly time for bed, and indeed everyone was tired, one of the assistants had even fallen asleep over his meal, much to the amusement of the other, who tried to persuade his masters to come and look at the silly face of the sleeping assistant, but to no avail; on the chairs above, K. and Frieda remained seated, dismissively. The cold having become increasingly unbearable, they were hesitant to go to bed, so in the end K. declared that they had to light the stove, otherwise they wouldn't get any sleep. He looked around for an axe, the assistants knew of one and brought it over, they set off for the woodshed. In no time the light door was broken down; delighted, as if they had never before experienced anything so wonderful, chasing and pushing each other, they began to carry wood into the schoolroom, where there was soon a large pile, they lit the stove and everybody installed themselves around it, the assistants were given a blanket to wrap themselves in, that was adequate for them, since it had been agreed they would take turns staying awake to keep the stove going, soon it was so warm by the stove that the blankets were no longer required, the lamp was extinguished, and, pleased with the warmth and quiet, K. and Frieda stretched out to sleep.

Awakened at night by some noise, K. first groped about drowsily for Frieda before noticing that it was not Frieda who lay beside him but one of the assistants. No doubt because of his irritation on being suddenly awakened, this came as the greatest shock he had experienced in the village up to now. With a shout he half rose and, without stopping to think, struck the assistant so hard with his fist that he began to cry. But the matter was soon resolved. Frieda had also been awakened—at least this is how it seemed to her—when some large animal, possibly a cat, had jumped onto her chest and then immediately run off. She had risen and gone through the room, candle in hand, looking for the animal. The assistant had seized the chance to sample the pleasure afforded by the straw mattress, for which he was now paying a bitter price. Unable to find anything, perhaps it had all been an illusion, Frieda returned to K., but on the way, as though she had forgotten all about the conversation earlier that afternoon, she stroked the hair of the crouching, whimpering assistant in order to console him. K. didn't say a word about this, he simply ordered the assistants to stop stoking the fire, since, with the expenditure of almost the entire pile of wood, the room was already much too hot.

Next morning none of them woke up until after the first

schoolchildren had come and gathered eagerly around their bed. This was unpleasant, for, owing to the intense heat, which had in any case yielded to bitter cold toward morning, they had all stripped to their undershirts, and just as they were beginning to get dressed, Gisa, the schoolmistress, a tall blond beautiful, if rather stiff, girl, appeared in the doorway. She was clearly prepared to deal with the new janitor, having perhaps been briefed by the teacher, for, while still on the threshold, she said: "I simply cannot tolerate this. What a fine state of affairs that would be. You merely have permission to sleep in the schoolroom, I'm not obliged to teach in your bedroom. A janitor's family lounging about in bed till late morning. Ugh!" Well, you could object to some of that, especially about the family and the beds, thought K., as he and Frieda—the assistants could not be used for this; lying on the floor, they were staring in wonder at the schoolmistress and the children—in great haste dragged over the parallel bars and the horse, threw the blankets on them, creating a little room where one could at least dress, shielded from the children's stares. Still, there wasn't a moment's peace, the schoolmistress was already scolding him because there was no fresh water in the washbasin—K. had just been thinking of bringing over the washbasin for Frieda and himself, but he abandoned the thought for now, so as not to needlessly annoy the schoolmistress, but the sacrifice was futile, for just then there was a loud crash, unfortunately they had forgotten to clear the remnants of the evening meal from the teacher's desk, the schoolmistress removed all of it with the ruler, everything was sent flying to the floor; and anyhow the schoolmistress didn't have to worry about the spilled sardine oil and coffee dregs and the smashed coffee pot, the janitor would of course tidy up right away. Not yet fully clothed, K. and Frieda leaned upon the parallel bars, watching the destruction of their few belongings; the assistants, who clearly hadn't the slightest intention of getting dressed, peeped out through the blankets below, much to the children's delight. Frieda was, of course, most upset by the loss of the coffee pot; only when K., in an effort to console her, assured her that he would go to the council chairman at once to demand and, what's more, obtain compensation, did she compose herself sufficiently to run out of the enclosure, dressed only in a chemise and slip, so as to fetch the tablecloth and prevent its getting dirtier. She succeeded, even though the schoolmistress, in an effort to frighten her off, kept slamming the ruler down nerve-wrackingly on the table. After K. and Frieda put on their clothes, they found it necessary to prod the assistants, who seemed dazed by all this, to get dressed, ordering them, pushing them, and to some extent even dressing them themselves. Then when everybody was ready, K. assigned the next tasks; the assistants should get wood and light the stove, but first in the other schoolroom, where great danger lurked, for the teacher was probably already there, Frieda was to wash the floor while K. went for water and did a general tidying-up, there could be no thought of breakfast for now. K. wanted to be first outside, so as to ascertain the teacher's mood; the others should follow when he called, he gave this order, on one hand, because he wanted to ensure that the stupid antics of the assistants didn't make matters worse from the start and, on the other, because he wanted to spare Frieda as much as possible, for she had ambition, he had none, she was sensitive, he was not, her thoughts centered exclusively on the minor abominations of the present, his on Barnabas and the future. Frieda listened carefully to his instructions and barely took her eyes off him. No sooner had he stepped outside than the schoolmistress cried amid the children's laughter, which from then on simply would not end: "Well, are you quite rested now?" and when, instead of answering, for this was hardly a question, K. headed toward the wash stand, the schoolmistress asked: "But what have you done to my kitty?" A large heavy old cat lay sprawled lazily on the table, the schoolmistress was examining one of its paws, which was evidently slightly injured. So Frieda was right; this cat certainly hadn't jumped on her, for she was surely no longer capable of jumping, though she had indeed crawled over her, and then, shocked to find people in the usually empty building, quickly hidden, injuring herself in her unaccustomed haste. K. tried to explain this calmly to the schoolmistress but, ignoring everything except the result, she said: "Yes, you certainly have injured her, what a marvelous way of introducing yourselves here! Look," and calling K. to the teacher's desk, she showed him the paw, and, before he knew what was happening, scratched the back of his hand with the claws; though the claws were already blunt, the schoolmistress, who no longer showed the slightest concern for the cat, pressed down so firmly that they nonetheless left bloody welts. "And now get back to work," she said impatiently, bending over the cat again. Frieda, who had been watching from behind the parallel bars with the assistants, screamed at the sight of the blood. K. showed his hand to the children and said: "Look what an evil cunning cat has done." He wasn't saying this for the children, their screaming and laughter had already taken on such a life of its own that it needed no further motive or provocation and couldn't be pierced or influenced in any way by words. But since the schoolmistress merely responded to the insult with a sidelong glance and for the rest remained intent on her cat, her initial fury evidently sated by the bloody punishment, K. called Frieda and the assistants, and they set to work.

After K. had taken out the bucket with the dirty water, brought in fresh water, and begun to sweep the schoolroom, a boy of about twelve stepped out from a bench, touched K.'s hand, and said something that was incomprehensible in the noise. Suddenly the noise ceased. K. turned around. His greatest fear all morning had come about. Standing in the doorway was the teacher; in each hand the little man held an assistant by the collar. He had probably caught them while they were getting wood, for in a powerful voice he shouted, pausing after each word: "Who dared to break into the woodshed? Tell me where the fellow is so I can tear him to bits." Then Frieda got up from the floor, which she had been laboriously washing at the feet of the schoolmistress, looked at K., as if trying to summon strength, and then, with some of her former superiority in gaze and bearing, said: "I did it, Teacher. I could think of no other solution. The stoves in the schoolrooms had to be lit by morning, so someone had to open the shed, I didn't dare go to get the key from your house at night, my fiancé was at the Gentlemen's Inn and might conceivably have spent the night there, so I had to make the decision on my own. If what I did was wrong, excuse my inexperience, my fiancé gave me quite a scolding when he saw what had happened. He even forbade me to light the stoves earlier, for he thought you had indicated by locking the shed that you didn't want the stoves lit before you came. So it's his fault the stoves weren't lit and mine the shed was broken into." "Who broke open the door?" the teacher asked the assistants, who were still vainly attempting to shake off his grip. "The gentleman," both said at once, and to exclude all doubt, they pointed at K. Laughing in a manner that seemed even more conclusive than her words, Frieda began to wring into the bucket the rag she had used to wash the floor, as if her explanation had terminated the matter and the assistants' explanation were only a belated joke, she was already on her knees and about to begin work when she said: "Our assistants are still children who, despite their years, still belong on these school benches. For it was I who opened the door with the axe myself, it was very easy, I didn't need the assistants, they would merely have been in the way. But then at night when my fiancé got back and went out to inspect and possibly repair the damage, the assistants ran after him, probably because they were afraid of being left here alone, they saw my fiancé working on the torn-off door, which is why they now say—well, they are children." Yet the assistants shook their heads repeatedly during Frieda's explanation, pointed again at K., and attempted through silent mimicry to get Frieda to change her mind, it was to no avail, though, and so they finally gave up, accepted Frieda's words as an order, and on being asked again by the teacher, refused to answer. "Oh," said the teacher, "so you lied? Or at least accused the janitor on frivolous grounds?" They remained silent, but their trembling, frightened glances appeared to suggest guilt. "Then I will give you a good beating this instant," the teacher said, and sent a child to the other room for the cane. Then, as he raised the cane, Frieda cried: "The assistants were telling the truth," and in desperation she threw the rag into the bucket with such force that the water splashed out, and ran behind the parallel bars, where she hid herself. "A pack of liars," said the schoolmistress, who had finished bandaging the paw and took the creature onto her lap, for which it was almost too wide.

"So that leaves the janitor here," said the teacher, pushing the assistants aside and turning to K., who had listened all along, resting on his broom: "This janitor, who out of sheer cowardice openly admits that others are being wrongly accused of his dirty tricks." "Now," said K., realizing that Frieda's intervention had softened the teacher's initially unrestrained outburst of anger, "I wouldn't have been sorry if the assistants had received a little beating, they were let off scot-free on ten just occasions and can certainly atone for it on a single unjust one. But, Teacher, in other ways too I would have preferred to avoid an outright confrontation between us, and you might have preferred that, too. However, since Frieda has sacrificed me to the assistants"—here K. paused, Frieda's sobs came from behind the blanket—"we must naturally straighten all this out." "Outrageous," said the schoolmistress. "I agree with you entirely, Miss Gisa," said the teacher, "you, Janitor, are of course dismissed on the spot owing to this disgraceful dereliction of duty, I reserve the right to impose further punishment, but get out of this building now with all your things. For us this is truly a great relief, classes can finally begin. Quick now!" "I'm not moving," said K., "you certainly are my superior, but not the person who granted me this position, that was the council chairman, and he's the only one from whom I shall accept notification of dismissal. Now he hardly gave me this position so that I and these people of mine should freeze here but rather—as you yourself said—to prevent me from engaging in rash acts of despair. Letting me go now would be directly contrary to his intentions, and I refuse to believe it till I hear the opposite from his own lips. It is decidedly in your interest that I should refuse to accept such a frivolous dismissal." "So you refuse?" asked the teacher. K. shook his head. "Think this over carefully," said the teacher, "you don't always make the wisest decisions, just recall, for instance, your refusal to submit to questioning yesterday afternoon." "Why do you bring that up now?" asked K. "Because I'm so inclined," said the teacher, "and I'm telling you this now for the last time: get out!" But since this had no effect, the teacher went to the desk and spoke softly to the schoolmistress; she said something about the police, but the teacher dismissed this, and they finally agreed on a solution; the teacher told the children to go to his classroom, where they would receive instruction with the other children, this diversion pleased all, the room emptied amid laughter and shouting, with the teacher and schoolmistress following behind. The schoolmistress carried the class register on which lay the amply proportioned and utterly indifferent cat. The teacher would have rather left the cat there, but the schoolmistress rejected a suggestion along those lines with a vehement allusion to K.'s cruelty; so on top of all the other irritations K. was now burdening the teacher with the cat. This surely left its mark on the last words spoken by the teacher, which he addressed to K. from the doorway: "The lady has no choice but to leave this room with the children, since you refuse in a refractory manner to accept my notification of dismissal, and since nobody can expect a young girl like her to impart lessons amidst your dirty family shambles. So you'll stay here on your own, and since you'll no longer have the revulsion of decent onlookers to contend with, you may stretch out as you please. But it won't last long, I can guarantee that." Then he slammed the door.

XII.

THE ASSISTANTS

No sooner had they all left than K. said to the assistants: "Go away!" Baffled by this unexpected command, they complied, but when K. locked the door behind them, they immediately tried to come back in and began whimpering and knocking on the door. "You're dismissed," K. cried, "I will never employ you in my service again." They weren't willing to accept this, though, and hammered with their hands and feet on the door. "Let us come back to you, sir," they cried, as if K. were the land and they were about to sink in the floods. But K. had no sympathy for them, he waited impatiently for the moment when the unbearable noise would force the teacher to intervene. This soon happened. "Let those damned assistants of yours in!" he shouted. "I've dismissed them!" K. shouted back; this had the undesired side-effect of showing the teacher what happened when one actually had the strength not only to give notice of dismissal but to enforce the dismissal. The teacher now attempted in an amicable way to soothe the assistants, they need only wait here calmly, for K. would finally have to let them back in again. Then he left. And the situation would have remained quiet if K. hadn't begun shouting to them that they were dismissed and hadn't the slightest hope of reinstatement. At that, they began to make as much noise as before. The teacher came back, but he would no longer negotiate with them and instead drove them, evidently with his greatly feared cane, from the school.

Before long they appeared at the windows of the gymnasium, knocking on the panes and shouting, but their words were no longer audible. Yet they didn't stay there long either, in the deep snow they couldn't jump about as much as their restlessness demanded. So they rushed to the fence of the school garden, jumped up on the stone base, where, though only from afar, they could get a better view of the room, there they ran up and down, holding on to the fence, then halted, and stretched their clasped hands beseechingly toward K. They kept this up a long time, despite the futility of their efforts; it was as if they were blind, and they probably didn't even stop when K. lowered the curtains to get them out of his sight.

In the now dusky room K. went to the parallel bars to see about Frieda. At a glance from him she got up, tidied her hair, dried her face, and silently set about making coffee. Although she already knew about all this, K. nonetheless gave her formal notice of his dismissal of the assistants. She merely nodded. K. sat down on a school bench and observed her weary movements. It had always been her freshness and resolve that had lent her paltry body a certain beauty, but now that beauty was gone. It had taken only a few days of living with K. to bring this about. The work in the taproom hadn't been easy, but it probably suited her better. Or was the distance from Klamm the real reason for her decline? Klamm's proximity had made her so madly enticing, in that enticement K. had seized her, but now she was wilting in his arms.

"Frieda," said K. She put the coffee mill down at once and came to K. on the bench. "You're angry at me?" she asked. "No," said K., "I think you cannot help it. You were quite content living at the Gentlemen's Inn. I should have left you there." "Yes," said Frieda, gazing sadly into space, "you should have left me there. I'm not worthy enough to live with you. Freed of me, you could perhaps achieve everything you want. Out of concern for me you submit to that tyrannical teacher, take on this miserable post, and now you are making a painstaking application for an interview with Klamm. All for me, but I give you little in return." "No," said K., putting his arm around her consolingly, "those are merely trifles that don't hurt me, and it isn't just for you that I want to go to Klamm. And then there's everything that you have done for me! Before getting to know you, I was very much adrift here. Nobody took me in and anybody I thrust myself upon soon made me leave. And even if I could have found peace with certain people, it could only have been with those I ought to have fled from, like Barnabas's family—" "You fled from them? Isn't that so? Darling!" Frieda broke in quite animatedly, and then, after a hesitant "Yes" from K., fell back into her weariness. By now, though, K. was no longer so determined to explain how everything had taken a turn for the better for him through the alliance with Frieda. Slowly he took his arm away, they sat a moment in silence, and then, as if K.'s hand had supplied her with a warmth that she now found indispensable, she said: "I cannot stand this life here. If you want to hold on to me, we must leave and go somewhere else, to southern France, or to Spain." "I cannot go abroad," said K., "I came here in order to stay here. I will stay here." And in a contradiction he didn't bother to explain, he added as if speaking to himself: "Now what could have attracted me to this desolate land other than the desire to stay?" Then he said: "But you too want to stay here, it is your country. All you miss is Klamm and that prompts such desperate thoughts." "So I miss Klamm?" said Frieda, "there's surely an abundance of Klamm here, too much Klamm; it's so as to escape from him that I want to get away. It isn't Klamm that I miss, but you. It's for your sake that I want to leave; because I cannot get enough of you here, where everybody is constantly tearing at me. Better to have this pretty mask torn off, better to have this body made ugly, so that I can live with you in peace." K. noted only one thing: "So Klamm is still in touch with you?" he asked at once, "he calls you?" "I know nothing about Klamm," said Frieda, "I'm talking about others, for instance, the assistants." "Oh, the assistants," K. said in astonishment, "they follow you?" "Did you never notice it, then?" asked Frieda. "No," said K., vainly trying to recall some details, "they surely are intrusive, lecherous young lads, but I never noticed their having the audacity to go near you." "You never did?" said Frieda, "you never noticed how impossible it was to get them out of our room at the Bridge Inn, how jealously they observed our relations, how one of them lay in my place on the straw mattress, how they testified against you so as to drive you away, ruin you, and have me to themselves. You didn't notice any of that?" K. looked at Frieda without answering. These charges against the assistants were surely true, but they could also be interpreted much more innocently as a reflection of the assistants' ridiculous, childish, unstable, uncontrollable nature. And wasn't it further proof against the accusation that they should have always endeavored to go with K. instead of staying behind with Frieda? K. mentioned something of the sort. "Hypocrisy," said Frieda. "You didn't see through it? Then why did you drive them away, if not for those reasons?" And she went to the window, pulled the curtain slightly to one side, looked out, and called to K. The assistants were still outside at the fence; visibly tired though they were, summoning all their energy, they extended their arms beseechingly every now and then toward the schoolhouse. One of them, in order to avoid having to keep holding on, impaled the back of his coat on the fence.

"Poor things! Poor things!" said Frieda. "You asked me why I drove them away?" K. asked. "You're directly to blame for that." "Me?" Frieda asked, without taking her eyes from the window. "You were all too friendly toward the assistants," said K., "you tolerated their bad habits, laughed at them, stroked their hair, pitied them constantly, 'poor things, poor things,' you've just said so again, and then finally that last incident, since you believed I wasn't too high a price to pay for getting the assistants out of a beating." "That's just it," said Frieda, "that's what I'm talking about, that's exactly what makes me so unhappy, what keeps me from you, even though I know of no greater happiness than to be with you, constantly, without interruption, without end, but in the dreams I dream there's no tranquil place on earth for our love in the village or anywhere else, so I picture a deep and narrow grave where we embrace each other as if with clamps, I hide my face in you, you hide yours in me, and nobody will ever see us again. But then—look at those assistants! It isn't you they are thinking of when they clasp their hands like that, but me." "And it's not me who is watching them," said K., "but you." "Of course it's me," said Frieda almost angrily, "but that's what I have been telling you all along; why else would the assistants be pursuing me, even if they are the emissaries of Klamm—" "The emissaries of Klamm," said K., for though the term immediately seemed quite natural to him, it still came as a big surprise. "Yes, of course, Klamm's emissaries," said Frieda, "but even if they are, they're still clumsy youths whose education could profit from a beating. What ugly, swarthy youths, and how repulsive the contrast between their faces, which make one see them as adults, or almost as students, and their childish, silly behavior. Do you think I can't see this? I am ashamed of them. But that's exactly it, they don't repel me, I'm ashamed of them. I can't stop looking at them. When one ought to get annoyed at them, I can only laugh. When one ought to strike them, I can only stroke their hair. When I lie beside you at night, unable to sleep, I cannot help looking across you and observing one of them sleeping tightly rolled up in the blanket and the other kneeling by the open oven door stoking the fire and I must bend so far forward that I almost wake you. And it isn't the cat that frightens me—oh, I know all about cats and I know all about those uneasy, constantly interrupted naps in the taproom—it's not the cat that frightens me, but I who give myself a fright. And it doesn't take that monster of a cat, for I jump at the least noise. One moment I'm afraid you'll wake up and it'll be all over and the next I'm jumping up to light the candle so you'll wake up quickly and protect me." "I had no idea about any of those things," said K., "though in an inkling of it I drove them away, but now that they're gone perhaps everything will be fine." "Yes, they're finally gone," said Frieda, though her face was tormented rather than joyful, "but we don't know who they are. Klamm's emissaries, that's what I call them in my thoughts, just playfully, but perhaps that is what they really are. Their eyes, those naive but sparkling eyes, somehow remind me of Klamm's eyes, yes, that's it, Klamm's glance sometimes leaps from their eyes and goes straight through me. And so it was wrong of me to have said that I'm ashamed of them. I only wish that were so! Though I realize that in other places and with other people this same conduct would be stupid and offensive, with them it isn't, I watch their silly antics with admiration and respect. But if they are Klamm's emissaries, who will free us from them, and would it even be good to be freed from them? Wouldn't you have to bring them back in at once and be happy if they actually came?" "You want me to let them back in?" K. asked. "No, no," said Frieda, "nothing could be further from my wishes. The sight of them if they were to burst in now, their delight in seeing me again, their hopping about like children and their stretching out their arms like men, I might not be able to bear that. But then when I think that if you keep treating them this harshly you may be denying Klamm access to you, I want to save you from the repercussions of that. Then I want you to let them in. So quickly let them in. Don't worry about me, what difference do I make. I will defend myself for as long as I can, but if I lose, well then I lose, but with the awareness that this, too, was for your sake." "You're only reinforcing my opinion about the assistants," said K., "they will never come in here again with my permission. The fact that I got them out shows that under certain circumstances it is indeed possible to curb them and that they have no significant business with Klamm. Only yesterday evening I got a letter from Klamm from which it emerges that Klamm has been completely misinformed about the assistants, and the only conclusion this permits is that he is utterly indifferent to them, for if this weren't so he could certainly have obtained precise information about them. The fact that you see Klamm in the assistants proves nothing, for unfortunately you're still influenced by the landlady and see Klamm everywhere. You're still Klamm's mistress and not my wife yet by any means. This sometimes makes me feel quite dismal, then it's as if I had lost everything, then I have the feeling I have just arrived in the village, not full of hope, as I truly was then, but aware that nothing but disappointments lie ahead and that I will have to drink each one down to the dregs. But still that's only sometimes," K. added, smiling, when he saw Frieda sag under his words, "besides, it does underline something positive, namely, what you mean to me. And if you call upon me to choose between you and the assistants, then the assistants have already lost. What an idea, to choose between you and the assistants. Now I want to get rid of them, once and for all. Who knows, perhaps the weakness that came over the two of us simply comes from our not having had breakfast yet." "Possibly," said Frieda, smiling wearily, and she set to work. K., too, picked up his broom again.

XIII.

HANS

A little while later there was a light knock. "Barnabas!" K. shouted, threw down the broom, and in a few bounds was at the door. Frieda, startled more by the name than by anything else, looked at him. With his unsteady hands K. couldn't immediately open the old lock. "I'm opening it," he kept repeating, instead of asking who was knocking. And then he had to watch entering through the now wide-open front door, not Barnabas but the small boy who had once wanted to speak to K. But K. had no desire to remember him. "Well, what are you doing here?" he said, "classes are next door." "I came from there," said the boy, looking up at K. with large brown eyes, erect, his arms close to his body. "So what do you want? Quick!" said K., bending down a little, for the boy spoke softly. "Can I help you?" asked the boy. "He wants to help us," K. said to Frieda, and then to the boy: "So what's your name?" "Hans Brunswick," said the boy, "fourth grade, son of Otto Brunswick, master shoemaker, Madeleine Street." "Well then, your name is Brunswick," said K., who now became friendlier. It turned out that Hans had become so upset over the bloody welts the schoolmistress had raised on K.'s hand that he then had decided to help him. Without asking, he had at the risk of severe punishment crept from the other classroom like a deserter. He was no doubt largely driven by such boyish notions. They were matched by the earnestness evident in everything he did. Only initially hampered by shyness, he soon got used to K. and Frieda, and on being given good hot coffee to drink he grew lively and confiding and his questions eager and insistent, as if he wanted to ascertain the essential as quickly as possible in order to be able to make decisions for K. and Frieda on his own. There was also a certain imperiousness in his nature, but mixed with childish innocence so that you were glad to submit to him, half sincerely, half jokingly. In any case he monopolized everybody's attention, all work had ceased, breakfast was dragging on. Although he was seated on a bench, K. above at the teacher's table, and Frieda on a nearby chair, it looked as if Hans were the teacher, as if he were examining them and judging their answers, a faint smile around his soft mouth seemed to suggest he knew very well that this was merely a game, but this only made him concentrate all the more intently, perhaps it wasn't so much a smile as the happiness of childhood that played about his lips. It took him a remarkably long time to admit that he knew K. from the time he had come by Lasemann's. This pleased K. "You were playing at the woman's feet?" K. asked. "Yes," said Hans, "that was my mother." And now he had to speak about his mother, but he did so only hesitantly, after repeated requests, it became clear, though, that he was indeed a young boy, from whom, especially when he was asking questions, there seemed to issue a voice, perhaps in a premonition of the future, but perhaps this was merely a sensory illusion on the part of the uneasy tense listener, the voice of an almost energetic, clever man with foresight, but then without transition he was once again a schoolboy who was incapable of understanding certain questions and misinterpreted others and spoke too softly, with a childish inconsiderateness, even though this failing was repeatedly pointed out to him, and then, faced with some especially penetrating questions, he fell quite silent, as though out of stubbornness, and also without the slightest embarrassment, in a way no adult could have done. Indeed it seemed as if he thought that he alone was permitted to ask questions and that questions from the others would only break some rule and waste time. He could sit there quietly for a long time, body erect, head lowered, lower lip pouting. This so pleased Frieda that she often asked him questions in the hope that they would silence him in this way. Sometimes she even succeeded, but this annoyed K. On the whole one didn't learn much, Hans's mother was rather sickly, but the exact nature of the illness was still unclear, the child that Frau Brunswick had been holding on her lap was Hans's sister and was called Frieda (Hans wasn't pleased to discover that the woman questioning him had the same name), they all lived in the village, though not at Lasemann's, they had only gone there for a bath since Lasemann had the large tub in which the small children—Hans no longer counted as such—loved to bathe and frolic; Hans spoke of his father with reverence or fear, but only when there was no mention of his mother; when set against his mother, his father evidently counted for little; incidentally, no matter how you questioned him about his family life, he never responded, all you learned about his father's trade was that he was the largest shoemaker in the village, nobody else came near, as Hans repeated often enough in response to entirely unrelated questions; the father even gave out work to other shoemakers, such as Barnabas's father, but in that particular case Brunswick must have done so as a special favor, as indicated by the proud way Hans tossed his head, which made Frieda jump down and kiss him. Asked whether he had ever been at the Castle, he answered only after repeated questioning, and what's more with a "No"; when asked the same question concerning his mother he simply did not answer. K. finally wearied of this, the questioning seemed useless even to him, for in that respect he agreed with the boy, there was also something rather shameful about this effort to probe family secrets in a roundabout way through an innocent child, and indeed doubly so if you couldn't even come up with anything. And finally, when K. asked the boy how he proposed to help, he was no longer surprised to learn that Hans merely wanted to help them with their tasks so as to ensure that the teacher and schoolmistress ceased scolding K. K. explained to Hans that no such help was needed, it was probably in the teacher's nature to be a scold, and one could scarcely escape this even through the most meticulous work, the work itself wasn't that difficult and only because of certain chance events had he fallen behind today, and in any case this scolding didn't affect K. as it would a pupil, he simply shook it off, it meant almost nothing to him, and he hoped to escape soon from the teacher. Since this merely concerned help against the teacher, K. thanked him very much and said he could go back now, he hoped he wouldn't be punished. Although K. never emphasized this and only intimated it involuntarily, it was only the help against the teacher that he didn't need, whereas he wasn't ruling out the possibility of another sort of help, Hans clearly took note of this and asked whether K. needed help of some other kind, he would be very glad to help him, and if he couldn't, he would ask his mother to do so, and then success would be assured. Besides, when Father had worries he also asked Mother for help. And Mother had once even asked about K., she hardly ever left the house, her presence that day at Lasemann's was exceptional, but he, Hans, often went there to play with Lasemann's children, and Mother had once asked him whether the surveyor had ever come back. Well, one shouldn't ask Mother needless questions, for she was weak and ill, and so he had simply told her that he hadn't seen the surveyor there, and nothing more was said; on finding K. here in the school, though, he had to speak to him so that he could inform his mother. For Mother liked it best if you carried out her wishes without explicit orders. At that, after a moment's reflection, K. said he didn't need help, he had everything he needed, but it was very kind of Hans to want to help him and he thanked him for his good intentions, it was certainly possible he might need something later, then he would turn to him, he did have his address. But this time maybe he, K., could be of some help, he was sorry that Hans's mother was ailing and that nobody here evidently understood her illness; in a case as badly neglected as this, even illnesses that are quite minor in and of themselves can become quite serious. Well, he, K., not only had some medical knowledge but also, and this was even more valuable, experience treating patients. There were cases where doctors had failed and he had succeeded. At home, on account of his healing powers, they always called him "the bitter herb." Anyhow, he would like to take a look at Hans's mother and talk to her. Perhaps he could give some good advice, he would gladly do so, even if only for Hans's sake. At first Hans's eyes lit up at this offer, tempting K. to become even more insistent, though the result was unsatisfactory, for in answer to repeated questions and without even expressing regret Hans said that no strangers were allowed to visit Mother since she needed constant care; though K. had barely spoken to her that one time, she had had to spend a few days in bed afterwards, but this was a frequent occurrence. Father had become very angry at K. and would certainly never allow K. to come and visit Mother, indeed he had actually wanted to go and see K. in order to punish him for his behavior, only Mother had dissuaded him. But above all Mother herself generally didn't want to speak to anyone and her question about K. was no exception to that rule, on the contrary, in mentioning him she could have said that she wished to see him, but she had not done so, and had thus made her intentions plain. She only wanted to hear about K. and didn't want to speak to him. By the way it wasn't actually an illness she suffered from, she was fully aware of the cause of her condition and sometimes hinted as much, it was probably the air here that didn't agree with her, but then again because of Father and the children she didn't want to leave the village, and also her condition was much better than it had been. And this is all K. learned; Hans's powers of reasoning had noticeably improved now that he had to shield his mother from K., the very person whom he supposedly wanted to help; indeed, in the good cause of keeping K. from his mother, he even contradicted some of his own previous statements, those, for instance, concerning her illness. Nonetheless, K. could now see too that Hans still viewed him favorably, only he forgot everything else because of his mother; anybody one happened to mention in the same breath as his mother immediately got put in the wrong, just now it was K. but it could just as easily be someone like, say, his father. K. wanted to test that last notion and said that it was certainly very sensible of Hans's father to shield his mother from all disturbances and if he, K., had had even the slightest inkling of that, he certainly wouldn't have risked speaking to his mother and so he was asking Hans to convey his belated apologies to the family. Still, he couldn't quite understand why, if the causes of the illness were so clearly established, his father was preventing his mother from recovering in the air someplace else; one had to say that his father was preventing her since it was only for his sake and the children's that she didn't go away, but she could take the children with her, she certainly needn't go away for long, nor very far either; for up on the Castle hill the air was entirely different. His father needn't fear the cost of such an excursion, he was after all the largest shoemaker in the village, and he or his mother surely had relatives or acquaintances at the Castle who would gladly take her in. Why wouldn't he let her go? He shouldn't underestimate an ailment of that sort, K. had caught only a glimpse of his mother, but it was her striking paleness and infirmity that had prompted him to speak to her, and even then he had been surprised that Hans's father had left that sick woman in the bad air of a room used for communal bathing and washing and hadn't tempered his own loud voice either. His father probably didn't know what was at stake, it could be that the ailment had improved of late, that sort of ailment is fickle, but in the end if you don't fight it, it gathers force and comes back, and nothing more can be done. Well, if K. couldn't speak to Hans's mother, it would perhaps be a good idea to speak with his father and make him aware of all this.

Hans had listened intently, understood most, and strongly sensed the threat in the remainder, which he found incomprehensible. Nonetheless, he said that K. couldn't speak to Father, Father disliked him and would surely treat him as the teacher had done. All smiles and shyness when talking about K., he was all bitterness and grief whenever he mentioned his father. Yet he added that K. could perhaps speak to Mother, but only without Father's knowledge. After reflecting for a moment with a fixed gaze, like a woman who wants to do something forbidden and seeks a way to carry it out with impunity, Hans said that it would perhaps be possible the day after tomorrow; in the evenings Father went to the Gentlemen's Inn, he had meetings there, and so in the evening he, Hans, would come and lead K. to Mother, but only if Mother agreed, which was still quite unlikely. Above all else she never did anything contrary to Father's will, submitted to him in everything, including matters whose unreasonableness even he, Hans, could clearly recognize. In reality Hans was looking for K.'s help against his father, it was as if he had deceived himself, for he had thought that he wanted to help K. whereas what he had truly wanted, since nobody in their old circle could help them, was to determine whether this stranger, whose sudden appearance even Mother had noted, might perhaps be able to help them. How unintentionally reserved and almost underhanded the boy was, one couldn't have gathered this from his appearance or his speech, only through the rather belated confessions extracted from him by chance or design. And now in long conversations with K. he considered what difficulties had to be overcome, even with the best intentions of Hans these difficulties were almost insurmountable; lost in thought but also seeking help, he stared the whole time with uneasily twinkling eyes at K. Until Father left, he couldn't say anything to Mother, otherwise Father would find out and it would be all over, so he could only mention it later, but even then out of consideration for his mother he would have to ask her consent, not quickly and all of a sudden but slowly and on some suitable occasion, and only then could he come to get K., but wouldn't that be too late, wouldn't his father's return be already dangerously imminent? Indeed, it couldn't be done. But K. showed that it could be done. There was no reason to fear there not being enough time, a short conversation, a short meeting would be enough, and Hans needn't come for K. K. would wait in hiding somewhere near the house and at a sign from Hans he would come at once. No, said Hans, K. shouldn't wait near the house—once again it was his sensitivity about his mother that ruled him—without Mother's knowledge K. shouldn't set out on his way, he, Hans, shouldn't enter into any such secret agreement which left out Mother, he must come and get K. from the school, but not before Mother knew of it and gave her permission. Fine, said K., then it was really dangerous, for it was conceivable that Hans's father would catch him in the house and, even if this didn't happen, his mother would fear as much and wouldn't let Hans go, and so the whole plan would fail because of his father. Here again Hans objected, and in this way the argument went back and forth. Some time ago K. had called over Hans, who was seated in the bench, to the teacher's desk, pulled him between his knees, and patted him soothingly a few times. And despite some resistance from Hans, this closeness actually helped them come to an understanding. They finally agreed to the following: Hans would first tell his mother the whole truth, but to make it easier for her to give her consent he would add that K. also wanted to speak with Brunswick himself, not about Hans's mother but about his own affairs. That was true, too; during the conversation it had occurred to K. that Brunswick, no matter how dangerous and evil a person he was in other respects, couldn't really be his adversary, for he was after all, at least according to the council chairman's report, the leader of the faction that had, even if merely on political grounds, demanded the summoning of a surveyor. So Brunswick must have welcomed K.'s arrival in the village; but then the irritated greeting from him that first day and the dislike of which Hans had spoken were almost incomprehensible, but perhaps Brunswick felt hurt precisely because K. hadn't turned first to him for help, perhaps there was some other misunderstanding that could be resolved in a few words. Once that was done, though, K. could surely count on Brunswick for support against the teacher, and even against the council chairman; all the official chicanery—what else could you call it?—with which the council chairman and the teacher kept him from the Castle authorities and forced him to take the janitorial post could be exposed, and if it soon came to a fight between Brunswick and the council chairman over K., then Brunswick would have to take K. on his side, K. would be a guest in Brunswick's house, Brunswick's means of combat would be placed at his disposal in defiance of the council chairman, who knows how far he would get in this way, and in any case he would often be near the woman—thus he played with his dreams and they with him, while Hans, thinking only of his mother, observed K.'s silence with concern, just as one does with a doctor who is lost in thought in an effort to find a cure for a serious case. K.'s proposal to speak to Brunswick about the surveyor position met with Hans's approval, though only because it ensured his mother some protection from his father and, besides, merely concerned an emergency situation that would hopefully never come about. Hans simply asked how K. would explain the late hour of his visit to his father, and finally contented himself, if with a slightly glum face, with K.'s statement that the unbearable janitorial post and dishonorable treatment by the teacher had in a sudden attack of despair made him lose all sense of consideration.

Then, when everything had been thus considered, insofar as one could see, and the possibility of success could at least no longer be ruled out, Hans, relieved of his burdensome reflections, became more cheerful, chattered childishly for a while, first with K. and then also with Frieda, who had sat there a long time, as though thinking of entirely different matters, and only now began to take part in the conversation again. Among other things she asked him what he wanted to be, he didn't think for long before saying that he wanted to be a man like K. Then, when asked why, he naturally couldn't answer, and the question whether he wanted to be a janitor, for instance, he answered with an emphatic "No." It was only after further questioning that one noticed in what a roundabout way he had obtained his wish. K.'s current situation was not so much enviable as sad and contemptible; Hans, too, saw this clearly himself and didn't have to observe others to make it out, he would have dearly liked to preserve his mother from every look and every word of K.'s. Nevertheless, he came to K. and asked him for help and would be happy if K. agreed to this, in others too he detected something similar, and his mother especially had spoken of K. This contradiction led him to believe that K., low and frightening though he was right now, would, if only in the almost inconceivably distant future, outstrip everyone else. And it was precisely this absolutely foolish distance, and the proud development it was supposed to usher in, that tempted Hans; to gain this prize he was even prepared to make allowances for K. as he currently was. What was so especially childish and precocious about this wish was that Hans looked down on K. as though on a younger child whose future extended beyond his own, the future of a small boy. And it was with an almost bleak gravity, after insistent questioning by Frieda, that he spoke of these matters. It took K. to cheer him up by saying that he knew what it was Hans envied him for, namely, K.'s beautiful knobby walking stick, which lay on the table and which Hans had absentmindedly played with during the conversation. Well, K. knew how to make walking sticks like that, and once their plan had worked, he would make an even more beautiful one for Hans. It was no longer entirely clear that Hans hadn't simply been thinking of the walking stick, so pleased was he with K.'s promise, and he cheerfully took his leave, though not before pressing K.'s hand firmly and saying: "So the day after tomorrow, then."

XIV.

Frieda's Reproach

It was high time Hans left, for before long the teacher flung open the door and, on seeing K. and Frieda sitting quietly at the table, shouted: "Excuse the disturbance! But tell me, when are you finally going to tidy up in here. We must sit packed together next door, it's bad for the teaching, but you lie about and stretch out in the big gymnasium, and to make even more room for yourselves you have even sent away the assistants. The least you can do now is stand up and get a move on!" And to K. alone: "And you, bring me my luncheon from the Bridge Inn." He had shouted all this angrily, but the words themselves were relatively mild, even the rather crude form of address. Though K. was instantly ready to comply, simply in order to sound out the teacher he said: "But I'm dismissed." "Dismissed or not dismissed, bring me my luncheon," said the teacher. "Dismissed or not dismissed, that's precisely what I want to know," said K. "What are you talking about?" said the teacher, "You never accepted the dismissal." "So that's enough to set it aside?" asked K. "Not for me," said the teacher, "believe me when I say so, though it is enough for the council chairman, quite incomprehensibly so. But now run along, otherwise you'll really end up being thrown out." K. was satisfied, so in the meantime the teacher had spoken to the council chairman, or could it be that he hadn't even spoken to him but had simply adopted the chairman's probable opinion, which was in K.'s favor. Now K. wanted to rush out at once for the luncheon, but the teacher called him back from the corridor, either because he had merely wanted to test K.'s willingness to carry out his duty by giving this special order, in order to be able to respond accordingly in the future, or because he once again felt like giving orders, for he liked making K. run off at an order from him and then wheel about just as quickly, like a waiter. K., for his part, knew that by giving in too much he would turn himself into the teacher's slave and whipping boy, but he intended to accept the teacher's moods, patiently, up to a certain point, for if the teacher couldn't legally dismiss him, as had just become clear, then he could certainly make the position unbearably excruciating. But this position meant more to K. now than it had before. The conversation with Hans had given him new, admittedly unlikely, entirely baseless but no longer forgettable hopes, they even half-obscured Barnabas. If he tried to pursue them, and he had no other choice, then he would have to gather all his strength and not worry about anything else, about food, housing, the village authorities, not even about Frieda, and this was essentially all about Frieda, because everything else mattered to him only with regard to her. So he would have to try to hold on to this position which gave Frieda some security, and he ought not to regret that with this goal in mind he would have to put up with more of the teacher than he could have forced himself to put up with otherwise. All this wasn't too painful, it was part of the series of life's endless little sufferings, it was nothing in comparison with what

K. was striving for, he had not come here in order to lead a life in honor and peace.

And so just as he had immediately wanted to run to the inn, on hearing the new order he was immediately ready to tidy up the room so that the schoolmistress could come over again with her class. But everything had to be tidied up quickly since K. was then supposed to fetch the luncheon and the teacher was already quite hungry and thirsty. K. assured him that everything would be done exactly as he had wished; for a moment the teacher watched as K. rushed about, putting away the bedding, straightening out the gymnastic equipment, sweeping up quickly while Frieda washed and scrubbed the podium. This eagerness seemed to satisfy the teacher, he pointed out that outside the door there was a pile of firewood for the stove—he was probably determined not to let K. set foot in the shed again—and then, after threatening that he would be back soon to check, he went over to the children.

After working in silence for a while, Frieda asked K. why he was giving in so much to the teacher. This was probably a concerned and compassionate question, but K., who was thinking of how poorly—given her original promise—Frieda had succeeded in shielding him from the imperiousness and aggression of the teacher, simply said curtly that now, since he had become a janitor, he would have to carry out the duties of the post. Then there was silence again until K., reminded by this brief exchange that Frieda had been lost in anxious thought for some time now, especially during almost the entire conversation with Hans, asked her openly, as he was carrying in the wood, what she was worried about. She answered, raising her face slowly toward him, that it was nothing in particular, she was simply thinking of the landlady and of the truth of certain things she had said. Only at K.'s insistence, after refusing several times, did she answer in greater detail, but without interrupting her work, not out of diligence, for the work wasn't advancing at all, but only so that she wouldn't be obliged to look at K. And now she described how at first she had listened calmly to K.'s conversation with Hans, but then, startled by certain words of K.'s, she had begun to get a clearer sense of the meaning of his words and how from then on she couldn't avoid hearing in K.'s words the confirmation of a warning she had the landlady to thank for, though she certainly hadn't wanted to admit it was justified. Annoyed by these vague generalities and more irritated than moved by Frieda's tearfully plaintive voice—especially since the landlady was again interfering in his life, by means of memories at any rate, for until now she hadn't had much success in person—K. threw the wood he was holding in his arms on the floor, sat down on it, and asked gravely for clarification. "Quite often," Frieda began, "right from the start the landlady tried to make me doubt you, she didn't claim that you're lying, on the contrary, she said you are childishly open but by nature so different from us that even when you're speaking openly we can barely bring ourselves to believe you, and if a certain good friend of ours doesn't rescue us first, we will have to find out how true this is through bitter experience. Despite her keen eye for people, even she has gone through something similar. But after her last conversation with you at the Bridge Inn—and I'm simply repeating her malicious words—she caught on to you, then you couldn't deceive her anymore even though you made a great effort to hide your intentions. 'But he's not hiding anything,' she said again and again and then she added: 'Do make an effort sometime to listen to him properly, not just superficially, no, really listen to him.' That's all she had done and she had been able to make out something like the following concerning me: You cozied up to me—she actually used that shameful expression—simply because I happened to cross your path, wasn't exactly displeasing to you, and because you quite mistakenly think that a barmaid is preordained to be the victim of every guest who reaches out a hand. Besides, as the landlady learned from the landlord at the Gentlemen's Inn, for some reason you were determined to spend the night at the Gentlemen's Inn and yet the only way that could be accomplished was through me. Now all this would have been a sufficiently good reason to take you as my lover for that one night, but if more was to come of it, more was needed, and that more was Klamm. The landlady doesn't claim to know what it is you want from Klamm, she merely claims that before getting to know me you sought to reach Klamm just as eagerly as you've been doing ever since. The only difference was that back then you had no hope while now you thought that in me you had a reliable means of really penetrating through to Klamm, without delay, and even with a certain amount of superiority. How startled I was—but only for a moment and without having any particularly deep reason—when at one point today you said that before getting to know me you were adrift here. Those are perhaps the same words the landlady used, she too says it's only since getting to know me that you have become conscious of your goal. That was because you believed that in me you had conquered a mistress of Klamm's and thus had a pawn that could be redeemed only at the highest price. Negotiating about this price with Klamm was your sole aim. Since I mean nothing to you and the price everything, you're ready for every compromise concerning me, but remain stubborn concerning the price. So you couldn't care less about my loss of the position at the Gentlemen's Inn, couldn't care less about my having to leave the Bridge Inn, couldn't care less about all the heavy janitorial work that I will have to do, you have no tenderness, let alone time for me, you leave me to the assistants, you don't feel jealous, the only value I have in your eyes is that I was Klamm's mistress, in your ignorance you try to ensure that I do not forget Klamm, so that in the end I don't put up too much resistance when the decisive moment arrives, but you also fight with the landlady, the only person you think capable of tearing me from you, and that's why you carry the fight with her to such extremes, in order to make it necessary for you to leave the Bridge Inn with me; you have absolutely no doubt that I myself am—insofar as it's simply a question of me and no matter what happens—your property. You think of the interview with Klamm as a business, cash for cash. You're counting on every possibility; you're ready to do anything provided you get your price; if

Klamm wants me, you'll give me back to him, if he wants you to stay with me, you'll stay, if he wants you to cast me out, you'll cast me out, but you're also prepared to put on a comedy, and if it's to your advantage, you'll pretend to love me, you'll try to combat his indifference by stressing your own insignificance and by shaming him with the fact that you're his successor or with tales of my confessions of love for him, which I did indeed make, and you'll ask him to take me back, but only on payment of your price; and if nothing else works, then you'll simply beg on behalf of the married couple, the K.'s. And then, the landlady said in conclusion, if you see that you've been wrong about everything, about your assumptions, your hopes, your notion of Klamm and of his relations with me, then my true hell will begin, then, even more than before, I shall be your only possession, on which you are dependent, but at the same time a possession that has proved to be worthless and that you'll treat accordingly, since the only feeling you have for me is as the proprietor."

Intently, with compressed lips, K. had listened, the logs beneath him had begun to roll, he had almost slipped onto the floor, had paid no attention to that and only now got up, sat on the podium, took Frieda's hand, which she feebly attempted to withdraw, and said: "In the account you gave I couldn't always distinguish your opinion from the landlady's." "It was only the landlady's opinion," said Frieda, "I listened to it all because I admire the landlady, but it was the first time in my life that I utterly rejected her opinion. Everything she said seemed so pathetic to me, so far removed from any real understanding of how things were with the two of us. The complete opposite of what she said seemed more likely to me. I thought of the bleak morning after our first night. How you knelt beside me looking as though everything were already lost. And how eventually, no matter how hard I tried, I wasn't helping you but rather hindering you. It was because of me that the landlady became your enemy, a powerful enemy, whom you still underestimate; it was for my sake, because I was in your care, that you had to fight for your position, that you were at a disadvantage in your dealings with the council chairman, that you had to submit to the teacher, that you were at the assistants' mercy, but worst of all: it was for my sake that you may have committed an offense against Klamm. Your constant efforts to reach Klamm were nothing but an ineffectual striving to appease him in some way. And I told myself that the landlady, who surely knew far more about this than I did, was merely attempting with her blandishments to ensure that I didn't reproach myself too seriously. A well-meant but superfluous effort. My love for you would have helped me to overcome everything, and in the end would also have taken you further, if not in the village, then somewhere else; it had of course already demonstrated its strength, it saved you from the Barnabas family." "So that was your objection then," said K., "and in the meantime what has changed?" "I don't know," Frieda said and she glanced at K.'s hand, which was holding hers, "perhaps nothing has changed; when you're so close to me and you ask so quietly, then I think nothing has changed. But in reality—" she withdrew her hand from K., sat erect across from him, and wept without covering her face; spontaneously she turned her tear-streaked face toward him not as though she were weeping about herself and therefore had nothing to hide but rather as if she were weeping about K.'s betrayal and he therefore deserved the miserable look on her face—"but in reality everything has changed from the moment I heard you talking to the boy. How innocently you began, you asked about the situation at home, about this person and that, it seemed to me as though you had just come to the inn, you were so affectionate, so open-hearted, and sought my eye with such childlike eagerness. It was just the way it used to be, and all I wished was that the landlady were here, listening to you and still trying to stick to her opinion. But then all of a sudden, I don't know how it happened, I understood what your intention was in speaking to the boy. With your sympathetic words you gained his confidence, which isn't easy to do, so that you could quietly pursue your goal, which had become increasingly clear to me. That woman was your goal. The only thing that emerged clearly from your remarks, seemingly so full of concern for her, was your devotion to your own affairs. You deceived that woman even before you won her. In your words I heard not only my past but also my future, I felt as though the landlady were sitting beside me explaining everything and I were trying with all my strength to push her away, but now I see clearly the hopelessness of such efforts, and indeed it was no longer I who was being deceived, I wasn't even being deceived, but rather that strange woman. And then when I pulled myself together and asked Hans what he wanted to be and he said he wanted to be like you, and was therefore already entirely yours, what was the big difference between him, the good boy who was mistreated here, and me then, at the inn?"

"Everything," said K., who, in becoming accustomed to the reproach, had pulled himself together, "everything you say is in a sense right, it is not wrong, only it is hostile. Those are the landlady's thoughts, those of my enemy, even if you think they're your own, which I find reassuring. But they are instructive, the landlady is still capable of teaching one a thing or two. She didn't tell me this directly, though she certainly hasn't spared me in other ways, she obviously entrusted this weapon to you in hopes that you would make use of it at a particularly bad or decisive hour; if I mistreat you, then she mistreats you in the same way. But Frieda, just think: Even if everything were exactly as the landlady says, that would be terrible only in one case, namely, if you're not fond of me. Then, well then it would really be true that I won you by means of calculation and wiles, so that I would make a huge profit from this possession. So perhaps it was even part of my plan that I came before you arm in arm with Olga in order to arouse your pity, and that the landlady simply forgot to include this in her tally of my guilt. Yet, if it isn't such a dreadful case and a sly beast of prey didn't drag you away but instead you came toward me as I came toward you and in this way we found each other, both oblivious to everything else, tell me, Frieda, what then? Then I am after all not only furthering my own cause but yours too, there's no difference between them, and only a certain enemy of ours can distinguish between them. This is true everywhere, even with Hans. Besides, with your delicacy of feeling you exaggerate greatly in assessing the conversation with Hans, for if Hans's intentions and mine don't entirely coincide, that still doesn't mean there's a contradiction between them, besides our disagreement wasn't lost on Hans, if you thought so, you would be seriously underestimating that cautious little fellow, and even if everything remained hidden from him, it still wouldn't do anybody any harm, I hope."

"It's so difficult, K., to get one's bearings," said Frieda, sighing, "I certainly don't distrust you, and if anything of that sort has come down to me from the landlady, I shall gladly cast it off and kneel down to beg your forgiveness, as I'm actually doing the whole time, even if I do say such dreadful things. It's true, though, that you keep many secrets from me; you come and you go, I don't know where from and where to. When Hans knocked, you even called out Barnabas's name. If only you had called me even once as lovingly as you did then, for reasons I couldn't understand, called that hated name. If you have no faith in me, why shouldn't I become distrustful, for then I'm completely dependent on the landlady, and your conduct merely confirms her opinion. Not in everything, I'm not claiming you confirm everything she says since you did drive away the assistants for my sake, didn't you? Oh, if only you knew the longing with which I search for a decent core for myself in everything you do and say, even if it torments me." "First of all, Frieda," said K., "I'm not hiding the slightest thing from you. How the landlady hates me, and how she tries to wrench you away from me with such despicable methods, and how you give in to her, Frieda, oh how you give in to her. But tell me, what is it I am hiding from you? I want to reach Klamm, this you know, you cannot help me achieve this and I must therefore take matters into my own hands, this you also know, I still haven't had any success, this you can see. Should I now in describing my useless efforts, which in reality are already sufficiently humiliating, humiliate myself twice over? Should I, say, brag about having waited in vain an entire afternoon, freezing, at the door of Klamm's sleigh? Delighted that I no longer had to think of such things, I hurried over to you, only to have to listen to all these threats from you. And Barnabas? Certainly, I am expecting him. He is Klamm's messenger, I didn't appoint him." "Barnabas again," cried Frieda, "I cannot believe that he is a good messenger." "Perhaps you're right," said K., "but he's the only messenger who is sent to me." "Too bad," said Frieda, "then you should be all the more wary of him." "Unfortunately, he has given me no cause for that," said K. smiling, "he rarely comes and what he brings is insignificant; it's valuable only because it comes directly from Klamm." "But look," said Frieda, "you're no longer even aiming for Klamm, perhaps that's what upsets me most; it was bad enough that you were always pushing past me to Klamm, but that you now seem to be turning away from Klamm is far worse, it's something not even the landlady could have foreseen. According to the landlady, my happiness, my questionable but nonetheless very real happiness, would end on the day you finally realized that your hope for Klamm was futile. But now you're no longer even waiting for that day, all of a sudden a little boy comes in and you start fighting with him over his mother, as if you were fighting for the air you need to live." "You've understood my conversation with Hans correctly," said K., "that's how it was. But do you think your entire earlier life is so submerged (except of course for the landlady, who won't let herself be forced down with it) that you no longer know how hard one must fight to get ahead, especially if one is coming up from the depths? How one must use everything that can somehow give one hope? And this woman comes from the Castle, she herself told me so when I wandered into Lasemann's that first day. What was more natural than to ask her for advice or even for help; if the landlady only knows the obstacles that keep one from Klamm, then this woman probably knows the way, for that's how she herself came down." "The way to Klamm?" Frieda asked. "To Klamm, of course, where else," said K. Then he jumped up: "But now it's high time to get that luncheon." Urgently, more insistently than was called for, Frieda asked him to stay, as though all the consoling things he had said to her would be confirmed only if he stayed. But K. reminded her about the teacher, pointed to the door, which at any moment could burst open with a sound like thunder, and also promised he would soon be back, she needn't even light the stove, he would see to it himself. Finally, Frieda submitted silently. Once K. was outside trudging through the snow—the path should have been cleared long ago, strange how slowly the work was going—he saw one of the assistants, dead tired, clinging to the fence. Only one, where was the other? Had K. at least exhausted the staying power of one of them? The fellow still left certainly had lost none of his zeal, one could see this when, animated by K.'s gaze, he immediately began to stretch out his arms and roll his eyes longingly. "His stubbornness is exemplary," K. said to himself, though he had to add: "still, it's making him freeze at the fence." Outwardly, all K. had for the assistant was a raised, threatening fist, which prevented any approach, indeed the assistant anxiously backed off a considerable distance. Just then Frieda opened a window, as had been agreed upon with K., in order to air the place before lighting the stove. Instantly the assistant stopped bothering K. and then, irresistibly attracted, crept toward the window. With a face contorted by friendliness toward the assistants and pleading helplessness toward K., she gave a little wave from the upstairs window, it wasn't even clear whether this was a dismissal or a greeting, the assistant did not let it deter him from approaching. Then Frieda hastily closed the outer window, but remained behind it, with her hand on the latch, head turned sideways, eyes wide-open and a fixed smile. Did she realize that she was luring the assistant rather than frightening him away? But K. didn't look around again, he wanted to hurry as much as possible and come back soon.

XV.

AT AMALIA'S

*F*inally—it was already dark, late afternoon—K. had cleared the garden path, piled the snow on both sides, beaten it down, and was now finished with the day's work. He stood at the garden gate, the only person anywhere around. He had driven away the assistant hours ago, chased him a great distance, then the assistant had hidden himself somewhere between the little garden and the sheds, simply wasn't to be found and hadn't come out since. Frieda was at home, already washing the clothes or still at work on Gisa's cat; it was a sign of great trust on Gisa's part that she had turned this task over to Frieda, an unappetizing and unsuitable task, and K. certainly wouldn't have tolerated Frieda's undertaking it had it not been quite advisable, after their various derelictions of duty, to use every opportunity to make Gisa feel obliged to them. Gisa had watched with pleasure as K. carried the small children's tub down from the attic, as water was warmed up and as, finally, with great care, they lifted the cat into the tub. And then Gisa had even left the cat entirely in Frieda's care, since Schwarzer, K.'s acquaintance from the first evening, had appeared, greeted K. with a mixture of diffidence—for which the foundation had been laid that evening—and the unbridled contempt that befits a mere janitor, and then gone into the other schoolroom with Gisa. The two of them were still there. According to what K. had been told at the Bridge Inn, Schwarzer, who was after all the son of a steward, had, out of love for Gisa, been living for some time now in the village and had succeeded through his connections in getting the council to appoint him to the post of assistant teacher but had chiefly discharged those duties by almost never missing Gisa's classes, where he sat on a bench between the children or, preferably, on the podium at Gisa's feet. This was no longer a distraction, the children had long since grown used to it, perhaps all the more readily given that Schwarzer showed no affection for, nor understanding of, children, barely spoke to them, having merely taken over Gisa's gymnastics class and being otherwise content to live in the proximity, the air, the warmth of Gisa. His greatest pleasure was to sit next to Gisa, correcting copybooks with her. Today too they were busy with the same task, Schwarzer had brought along a large pile of copybooks, the teacher always gave them his, too, and while it was still light outside K. had seen the two of them working over a small table, their heads close together, immobile, all one could see there now were two flickering candles. It was a serious, silent love that united the two, its tone in fact set by Gisa, whose lethargic being sometimes went wild and broke all bounds but who on any other occasion would never have tolerated anything of the sort from others, and so even the lively Schwarzer was obliged to comply and to walk slowly, speak slowly, be silent much of the time; but for all this he was, as one could see, amply rewarded with Gisa's simple calm presence. At the same time Gisa may not have loved him at all, at any rate her round and literally unblinking gray eyes, in which only the pupils seemed to move, gave no answer to such questions; though one could see that she tolerated Schwarzer without protest, she certainly didn't know how to appreciate the honor of being loved by the son of a steward and always carried her full, voluptuous body in the same quiet manner, whether Schwarzer was following her with his eyes or not. Schwarzer, on the other hand, constantly made for her the sacrifice of remaining in the village; the messengers from his father who often came to pick him up he dismissed with great anger, as if such brief reminders of the Castle and of his duty as a son were seriously, irreparably compromising his happiness. And yet he actually had a great deal of free time, for Gisa generally let him see her only during classes and copybook corrections, though not out of calculation but simply because she particularly valued comfort and thus solitude and was probably happiest at home, completely free, stretched out on the settee with the cat, which wouldn't disturb her, for it could now barely move. And so Schwarzer wandered about most of the day with nothing to do, but he liked that too, since it gave him an opportunity, which he often took advantage of, to go to Lion Street where Gisa lived, to climb the stairs to her small attic room, to listen at her always locked door, and then to leave, having always noticed in the room the most perfect inexplicable silence. Still, even in him the consequences of this kind of life occasionally manifested themselves, though never in Gisa's presence, in the form of briefly rekindled, ridiculous outbursts of official arrogance, which were not exactly suited to his present position; and then things certainly didn't turn out well, as K. knew from experience.

The only astonishing thing was that people, at least those at the Bridge Inn, still spoke of Schwarzer with a certain respect, even concerning matters that were more ridiculous than significant, and this respect also extended to Gisa. But still it was wrong that Schwarzer should think that he, an assistant teacher, was greatly superior to K., there was no such superiority, a janitor is an important person for the teaching staff, even for a teacher such as Schwarzer, and if one cannot avoid despising him for reasons of social class, then one should at least make one's disdain more tolerable by providing him with something suitable in return. K. intended to think about this some other time; besides, Schwarzer was indebted to him since that first evening, and the fact that the following few days had justified Schwarzer's reception of him didn't lessen that debt. For the thing to remember here was that his reception may have set the course for all subsequent events. Because of Schwarzer the full attention of the authorities had focused on K. right away in that first hour, rather absurdly so, for he was a complete stranger then in the village, without acquaintances, without a refuge, exhausted after the long walk, lying utterly helpless on the straw mattress, at the mercy of each official intervention. Had it been only one night later, everything would have happened differently, smoothly, virtually out of sight. In any case nobody would have known about him and they wouldn't have become suspicious or hesitated before letting him spend a day here as a journeyman, they would have noticed his usefulness and reliability, the news about him would have spread throughout the neighborhood, and he would probably have soon found a place somewhere as a farmhand. Of course he would not have evaded the authorities. But there was a great difference between the main office, or whoever came to the telephone there, being aroused in the middle of the night and pressured into making an immediate decision, yes, pressured, seemingly with humility but actually with annoying persistence—by none other than Schwarzer, who was probably unpopular up at the Castle—a great difference between that and K. himself knocking on the door at the council chairman's during office hours the following day and registering as a foreign journeyman who had already found a place to sleep at a local citizen's and would probably continue his journey next day, unless, and this was most unlikely, he found work here, but then only for a few days, since he hadn't the slightest intention of staying longer. This is what would have happened, or something of that sort, had it not been for Schwarzer. The authorities would have gone on dealing with the matter, but calmly through official channels, unruffled by the impatience of the individual party, whom they probably considered especially repugnant. Well of course K. was innocent in all this, the guilt lay with Schwarzer, but Schwarzer was the son of a steward, and outwardly he had indeed behaved correctly so they could make K. alone pay for it. And what was the ridiculous reason for all this? Perhaps a bad-tempered mood of Gisa's that day, owing to which Schwarzer couldn't sleep and roamed about at night before finally taking out his woes on K. Of course from another point of view you could argue that K. owed a great deal to Schwarzer's behavior. Only in that way had something become possible that K. would never have achieved on his own, would never have dared to attempt and that the authorities for their part would scarcely have admitted, namely, he had approached the authorities without making any shady moves, face to face, openly, insofar as this was at all possible with them. But that was a terrible gift; true, it spared K. a great many lies and deceptions, but it also deprived him of almost all his defenses, hampered him in the struggle and would have made him despair if he had not been obliged to tell himself that the difference between himself and the authorities in terms of power was so enormous that all the lies and cunning he would have been capable of wouldn't have produced any significant reduction of that difference to his advantage and would necessarily have had to remain more or less negligible. But this was merely a thought with which K. was consoling himself, Schwarzer nevertheless owed him a favor; if he had harmed K. earlier, perhaps he could help in the near future, K. would continue to need help with the most trivial tasks, with the very first preconditions, since even Barnabas seemed to have failed. For Frieda's sake, K. been reluctant to call at Barnabas's to make inquiries; so as not to have to receive him in front of Frieda, he had worked outside and had stayed on here after work, waiting for Barnabas, but Barnabas hadn't come. Well, the only course left was to go to the sisters, but only for a little while, he would simply ask them from the threshold, he would be back before long. And he rammed the shovel into the snow and ran. Breathless he arrived at Barnabas's house, knocked quickly, flung open the door, and, without glancing around the room, asked: "Hasn't Barnabas come?" It was only then he noticed that Olga wasn't there, that the two old people were once again sitting half-asleep at a far-off table, that they hadn't realized yet what happened at the door and were slow to turn their heads, and, finally, that Amalia lay on the bench by the stove covered with a few blankets and, in her initial fright at K.'s appearance, started and put her hand on her forehead in order to pull herself together. Had Olga been here, she would have answered immediately and K. could have left, but now he had to take those few steps over to Amalia, hold out his hand, which she silently pressed, and ask that she prevent her startled parents from wandering about, which she did with a couple of words. K. learned that Olga was chopping wood in the courtyard, and that Amalia, who was exhausted—she didn't say why—had had to lie down a short while ago and, though Barnabas still hadn't come, he would have to come soon, for he never stayed overnight at the Castle. K. thanked her for the information, now he could go; but Amalia asked whether he would wait a moment for Olga, unfortunately he no longer had time, and then Amalia asked whether he had already talked to Olga today, he said no in astonishment and asked whether Olga had anything special to tell him, Amalia screwed up her mouth as though she were slightly annoyed, nodded silently to K.—this was clearly a signal for him to leave—and lay back down again. From her reclining position she scrutinized him, as though surprised he was still there. Her gaze was cold, clear, as immobile as ever, it wasn't directly fixed on what she was observing, but instead—and this was unsettling—went past it, only slightly, ever so imperceptibly, but undeniably so; it didn't seem to be weakness, embarrassment, or dishonesty that caused this but rather a constant desire for solitude that dominated all other feelings and that she herself had perhaps only become conscious of in this way. K. thought he recalled that he had already been preoccupied by that gaze the first evening and that the disagreeable impression this family had instantly created was probably due to that gaze, which was not inherently disagreeable but rather proud and honest in its reserve. "You're always so sad, Amalia," said K., "is there something tormenting you? Can't you tell me what it is? I have never seen a country girl like you. This has only just occurred to me today, right now. Are you from the village? Were you born here?" Amalia said yes, as if K. had asked only the second question, and then she said: "So you will wait for Olga?" "I don't know why you keep asking me the same question," said K. "I cannot stay because my fiancée is waiting for me at home." Amalia was leaning on her elbow, she had never heard of his fiancée. K. mentioned her name, Amalia did not know her. She asked whether Olga knew of the engagement, K. thought she probably knew, Olga had actually seen him with Frieda; besides, news like that spread quickly in the village. But Amalia assured him that Olga knew nothing of this and that it would make her very unhappy since she seemed to be in love with K. She hadn't spoken openly about this, for she was quite reserved, but then love always betrays itself involuntarily. K. said he was convinced that Amalia was mistaken. Amalia smiled, and her smile, sad though it was, brightened her bleak, drawn face, made her silence eloquent and her strangeness familiar, it was the surrender of a secret, the surrender of some hitherto closely guarded possession that could be reclaimed, but never fully. Amalia said she certainly wasn't mistaken, she knew even more than that, she knew, for instance, that K. was also fond of Olga and that his visits, supposedly for some messages of Barnabas's, were actually intended for Olga alone. But now that Amalia knew everything, he needn't be so strict and could come by often. That's all she had wanted to tell him. K. shook his head and reminded her of the engagement. Amalia didn't seem to waste much thought on the engagement; the immediate impression of K. standing alone there was decisive for her, she merely asked when K. had met the girl, for he had been in the village only a few days. K. mentioned his going that evening to the Gentlemen's Inn, upon which Amalia merely said curtly that she was very much against his being taken to the Gentlemen's Inn. Turning to Olga, who came in just then with an armful of wood, she asked for confirmation; Olga, refreshed and fortified by the cold air, seemed vigorous and energetic as if transformed by work very different in nature from her usual lethargic standing about in this room. She threw down the wood, greeted K. boldly, and immediately asked about Frieda. K. gave Amalia a meaningful look, but she did not seem to think that her opinion had been refuted. A little irritated about this, K. spoke of Frieda in greater detail than he might otherwise have done, described the difficult conditions under which she had successfully run a household of sorts in the schoolhouse, and became so carried away in his haste to finish his account—he really wanted to go home at once—that by way of saying goodbye he invited the sisters to visit him sometime. But here he started and faltered, while Amalia immediately announced, without letting him say a word, that she would accept the invitation, Olga also had to go along with this, and did so. Yet K., hard-pressed because of the need to leave quickly and also uneasy under Amalia's scrutiny, did not hesitate to admit without further embroidery that the invitation was ill-considered, having been prompted solely by personal sentiments, and that unfortunately he couldn't honor it because of the great enmity between Frieda and the Barnabas household, which he found incomprehensible. "It isn't enmity," said Amalia, getting up from the bench and throwing the blanket down behind her, "it's nothing that significant, only a slavish repetition of common opinion. And so go now, go to your fiancée, I can see you're in a hurry. Besides, you needn't fear our coming to visit, I first said yes, but only as a joke, out of malice. But you can come to see us often, there's surely nothing to prevent that, and you can always use Barnabas's messages as a pretext. I will make this even easier for you by telling you that even if Barnabas does bring you a message from the Castle he can no longer take it all the way to the school. He cannot run about so much, poor boy, his duties are wearing him out, you will have to come yourself to pick up your messages." K. had never heard Amalia speak continuously at such length, it even sounded different from her normal speech, for it had a certain majesty, which was felt not only by K. but apparently also by Olga, her sister, who was after all well used to her;

she stood a little to the side, hands in her lap, once again in her usual posture, legs apart, slightly stooped, keeping her eyes fixed on Amalia, who was looking only at K. "It's a mistake," said K., "a great mistake if you think I'm not serious about waiting for Barnabas; my greatest and indeed my only wish is to settle my affairs with the authorities. And Barnabas should help me to accomplish this, many of my hopes lie with him. True, he has disappointed me greatly, but that was more my fault than his. In the confusion of the first few hours I thought I could accomplish everything by means of a short evening walk, and when the impossible proved impossible I blamed him for it. It even affected my opinion of your family and of you. But that's over, I think I can understand you better now, you're even—" K. was searching for the right word, but couldn't find it right away and made do with a rough equivalent—"perhaps you're more good-natured than any of the other villagers, more so at least than the ones I have met so far. But Amalia, you're putting me off again by belittling, if not your brother's service, then what he means to me. Perhaps you aren't initiated into Barnabas's affairs, and that's good, I am therefore willing to let the matter rest, but perhaps you are initiated—this seems more likely to me—and that's bad, for it would mean that your brother is deceiving me." "Calm down," said Amalia, "I'm not initiated, nothing could persuade me to let myself be initiated, not even consideration for you, and I would do quite a lot for you, for we are, as you said, good-natured. But my brother's affairs are his own concern, I know nothing about them other than what I get to hear by chance now and then, against my will. But Olga can give you the full story since she is his confidante." And Amalia left, going first to her parents, with whom she exchanged whispers, and then to the kitchen; she had gone away without taking leave of K., as though she knew that he would stay a long time and that there was no need to say goodbye.

XVI.

K. stayed behind, a rather astonished look on his face, Olga laughed at him, drew him over to the bench by the stove, she seemed really happy that she could sit here with him on her own, but it was a peaceful happiness, certainly not marred by jealousy. And precisely this absence of jealousy and thus of any trace of severity did K. good, he liked looking into those blue, not enticing, not domineering, but shyly tranquil, shyly steadfast eyes. It was as if the warnings of Frieda and the landlady had not made him more receptive to everything here but rather more alert and resourceful. And he laughed with Olga when she expressed surprise at his having called Amalia, of all people, good-natured, for though Amalia was any number of things, she was not really good-natured. At that, K. explained that the praise had actually been meant for her, Olga, but Amalia was so domineering that she not only appropriated everything said in her presence but that one was even willing to let her have all of it. “That’s true,” said Olga, becoming more serious, “truer than you think. Amalia is younger than me, younger than Barnabas too, but she’s the one who decides everything in the family, the good and the bad, and of course she also shoulders more than everyone else, both good and bad.” K. thought this exaggerated, Amalia had just said that she didn’t look after her brother’s business, for instance, whereas Olga knew everything about it. “How should I explain this?” said Olga, “Amalia doesn’t look after Barnabas or me, she doesn’t look after anybody except for our parents, whom she cares for day and night, just now she asked again if they needed anything and went into the kitchen to cook for them, forcing herself to get up because of them, for she’s been unwell since noon and has been lying here on the bench. But though she doesn’t look after us, we depend on her as if she were the eldest, and if she gave us advice about our affairs we would certainly follow it, but she doesn’t, to her we are strangers. But you have great knowledge of people, you come from abroad, doesn’t she seem especially clever to you too?” “To me she seems especially unhappy,” said K., “but how can you reconcile your respect for her, say, with Barnabas’s duties as a messenger, which Amalia disapproves of and may even despise.” “If he knew of something else he could do, he would immediately leave the messenger service, which doesn’t satisfy him at all.” “Didn’t he complete his apprenticeship as a shoemaker?” asked K. “Certainly,” said Olga, “indeed he also works on the side for Brunswick and, if he wanted to, he could have work both day and night and good pay too.” “Well, then,” said K., “in that case he’d have something as a replacement for the messenger service.” “The messenger service?” Olga asked in astonishment, “so he took it on for the income?” “Possibly,” said K., “but you did mention that he’s dissatisfied with it.” “He’s dissatisfied with it for several reasons,” said Olga, “but it’s still Castle work, well, a certain kind of Castle work, or at least one ought to think so.” “What?” said K., “do you people even have doubts about that?” “Well,” said Olga, “not really, Barnabas goes into the offices, deals with the servants on an equal footing, gets to see individual officials from a distance, receives relatively important letters, even ones that have to be delivered orally; that is quite a lot, and indeed we could be proud that he has accomplished so much at such a young age." K. nodded, he was no longer thinking of going home. "He also has his own livery?" he asked. "The jacket, you mean?" said Olga, "no, Amalia made it for him before he became a messenger. But now you're getting to the sore point. What he should have received from the offices a long time ago is not a livery, there are none at the Castle, but a suit, it has even been promised to him, but in this respect they're very slow at the Castle and the terrible thing is that one never knows for sure what this slowness means; it can mean that the official procedure has begun, but it can also mean that the official procedure has not yet even begun, that, for instance, they first want to continue testing Barnabas, but finally, it can even mean that the official procedure is already over, that for some reason the promise has been withdrawn and Barnabas will never get his suit. One hears nothing more precise than this, or only after a long time. There's an expression here, perhaps you know it: 'Official decisions are as shy as young girls.'" "That's a good observation," said K., taking it even more seriously than Olga did, "a good observation, and the decisions may have other traits in common with girls." "Perhaps," said Olga, "I really don't know how you mean that. Perhaps you even mean it as praise. But, as for the official clothing, this is one of Barnabas's concerns and, since we share those concerns, also mine. Why doesn't he receive an official suit, we vainly ask ourselves. Well, this entire affair is not exactly simple. The officials, for instance, don't seem to have any official clothing; so far as we villagers know and so far as Barnabas tells us, the officials go around in ordinary, though certainly beautiful, clothing. Besides, you have seen Klamm. Now Barnabas is of course not an official, not even an official of the lowest rank, nor is he so presumptuous as to want to become one. But even the higher servants, whom we admittedly never get to see here in the village, do not, according to Barnabas, have an official suit; there's some consolation in this, or one might initially be tempted to think so, but that is misleading, for is Barnabas a higher servant? No, even if one is very favorably disposed toward him, one cannot say so, his coming to the village and even living here is already proof of the opposite, the higher servants are even more reserved than the officials, perhaps justifiably so, perhaps they're even higher than certain officials, there is some evidence to this effect, they work less and, according to Barnabas, it's a wonderful sight to watch these exquisitely tall strong men go through the corridors, Barnabas always sneaks around them. In short, there can be no question of Barnabas's being a higher servant. He could therefore be one of the lesser servants, but they wear official suits, at least whenever they come down to the village, it's not a real livery, there are many variations, but still one can immediately recognize a Castle servant by his clothes, and anyhow you've seen such people at the Gentlemen's Inn. The most striking thing about their clothes is that they're usually tight-fitting, a suit like that would be of no use to a farmer or a tradesman. Well, Barnabas does not have this suit, that is not only, let's say, shameful or demeaning, that one could tolerate, but it causes Barnabas and me—especially in bleak hours, which we do have now and then, and not all that infrequently—to despair about everything. Is it even Castle work that Barnabas is doing, we then ask; he certainly does go into the offices, but are the offices actually the Castle? And even if the Castle does have offices, are they the offices Barnabas is permitted to enter? He enters offices, but those are only a portion of the total, then there are barriers and behind them still more offices. He has not been altogether prohibited from going farther, but he certainly cannot go farther once he has found his superiors and they have dealt with him and sent him away. One is always under observation up there, or at least one thinks so. And even if he went farther, what good would that do if he had no official duties up there and were merely an intruder. You shouldn't imagine these barriers as a fixed boundary, Barnabas is constantly pointing this out to me. There are also barriers in the offices that he enters, those are the barriers he crosses, and yet they look no different from the ones he has not yet crossed, so one shouldn't assume from the outset that the offices behind those other barriers differ significantly from the ones Barnabas has already been in. It is only during those bleak hours that one thinks so. And then one's doubts increase, one is defenseless against them. Barnabas speaks to officials, Barnabas receives messages. But what kind of officials, what kind of messages are they? Now he has been assigned to Klamm, he tells us, and receives instruction from him personally. Well, that would indeed be quite a lot, even higher servants never get that far, it would almost be too much, that's what is so frightening about it. Just think, to be directly assigned to Klamm, to speak with him face to face. But is it really so? Well yes, it is indeed so, but then why does Barnabas doubt that the official identified there as Klamm really is Klamm?" "But Olga," said K., "surely you don't mean to turn this into a joke; how can there be any doubt about Klamm's appearance, his appearance is well known, I've seen him myself." "Certainly not, K.," said Olga, "this isn't a joke, it's my gravest concern. But I'm telling it to you not to ease my heart and perhaps weigh down yours but because you asked about Barnabas, because Amalia instructed me to tell you, and because I believe that it's also useful for you to know more about this. I'm also doing it because of Barnabas, so that you do not put excessive hope in him and he does not disappoint you and then have to suffer because of your disappointment. He is very sensitive; he didn't sleep last night, for instance, because you were dissatisfied with him yesterday afternoon and apparently said that it's very bad to have 'only' a messenger like Barnabas. Those words deprived him of his sleep, you yourself probably saw little of his agitation, Castle messengers have to keep themselves very much under control. But it isn't easy for him, even with you. To your mind, you're certainly not asking too much of him, you came here with definite ideas about the messenger service and base your demands on them. But at the Castle they have different ideas about the messenger service, these cannot be reconciled with yours even if Barnabas were to sacrifice himself entirely to the service, which he unfortunately sometimes seems prepared to do. One would certainly have to accept this, couldn't say anything against it, were it not for the question whether it is really messenger work that he is doing. Of course he cannot disclose his doubts about this to you; to do so would be to undermine his own existence and blatantly violate the laws he thinks he lives under, he doesn't even speak openly to me, I have to coax his doubts out of him through flattery and kisses, and even then he finds it difficult to admit to himself that his doubts are indeed doubts. He has something of Amalia in his blood. And he certainly doesn't tell me everything, though I'm his only confidante. But sometimes we do speak about Klamm, I still haven't seen Klamm; you know, Frieda has little love for me and would never have let me take a look, but his appearance is of course well known in the village, some have actually seen him, everyone has heard of him, and what emerges from this mixture of sightings, rumors, and distorting ulterior motives is a picture of Klamm that is probably correct in its essential features. But only in its essential features. Otherwise it is variable and perhaps not even as variable as Klamm's real appearance. They say he looks completely different when he comes into the village and different when he leaves it, different before he has had a beer, different afterwards, different awake, different asleep, different alone, different in a conversation, and, quite understandably after all this, almost utterly different up there at the Castle. And even within the village there are some rather significant differences in the reports, differences in size, posture, corpulence, beard, and only concerning the coat do the reports happily agree, he always wears the same coat, a black morning coat with long tails. Now all these discrepancies did not of course come about by magic but are quite understandable, they are a product of the momentary mood, the degree of excitement, the countless gradations of hope or despair in which the observer, who in any case is at most allowed to see Klamm only briefly, happens to find himself, I repeat all this to you just as Barnabas often explained it to me, and in general, if one is not personally, directly involved in the affair, one can calm oneself down with such thoughts. We cannot do so; for Barnabas this is a vital matter, whether or not he actually speaks to Klamm." "No less so for me," said K., and they drew even closer on the bench by the stove. K. was indeed affected by Olga's unfavorable news, but he thought that this was largely offset by the encounter with these people here, who were at least outwardly more or less in the same situation as he himself and with whom he could therefore ally himself, whom he could agree with on many things, and not only on some as with Frieda. True, he was gradually losing hope that Barnabas's messages would accomplish anything, but the worse everything went for Barnabas up there, the closer he felt to him down here, K. would never have thought that an endeavor as ill-fated as the one launched by Barnabas and his sister could have come from the village itself. This was not yet entirely clear and the opposite could eventually prove true, you had to be careful not to let Olga's undoubtedly innocent nature seduce you into believing in Barnabas's honesty. "As for the reports of Klamm's appearance," Olga went on, "Barnabas knows them well, he has gathered and compared many of them, perhaps too many, he himself once saw Klamm through a carriage window, or thought he saw him, and was therefore quite ready to recognize him, and yet—how can you explain this to yourself?—when he came to an office at the Castle and an official standing with several others was pointed out to him and identified as Klamm, he did not recognize him and for a long time afterward couldn't get used to that man's supposedly being Klamm. But if you ask Barnabas how that man differs from the usual notion one has of Klamm, he cannot answer, or rather he answers by describing the official at the Castle, yet his description tallies exactly with the description of Klamm as we already know it. 'Look, Barnabas,' I say, 'why do you doubt it, why are you tormenting yourself.' And then, clearly distressed, he begins to list the Castle official's traits, which he seems to be inventing rather than actually describing, and anyhow they are so trivial—they include, for instance, a particular way of nodding his head or even just an unbuttoned vest—that one cannot possibly take them seriously. Even more important, it seems to me, is the way Klamm deals with Barnabas. Barnabas described this often to me, and even drew it. He is usually taken into a large office chamber, but it is not Klamm's office, nor indeed that of any particular individual. Lengthwise the room is divided in two by a single high desk, which reaches from one side wall to the other, a narrow section in which two persons could barely get past each other, that's the space for the officials, and a wide section, the space for the individual parties, the spectators, the servants, the messengers. Lying open on the desk are large books, one next to the other, with officials standing over most of them, reading. Yet they do not always stay at the same book, and exchange not books but rather places, Barnabas is most astonished by the way they must squeeze past one another while switching places owing to the tightness of the space. At the front near the high desk are tiny low tables, where sit the copyists, who, if the officials so wish, write from their dictation. Barnabas always wonders how this is done. The official doesn't give any explicit order, there's no loud dictation to be heard, one barely notices that someone is dictating; on the contrary, the official seems to continue reading, only he begins to whisper and the copyist hears it. Often the official dictates so softly that the copyist cannot hear it sitting down, he must constantly jump up, catch the dictation, sit down and make a note of it, jump back up, and so on. It's so strange! It's almost incomprehensible. Of course Barnabas has sufficient time to observe all this since he stands there in the spectators' room for hours and sometimes days before Klamm's gaze falls on him. And even when Klamm has seen him and Barnabas comes to attention, nothing decisive has happened since Klamm can turn away from him again and go back to his book and forget him, that's what often happens. But what sort of messenger service can it be if it's so insignificant? I become melancholy when Barnabas says in the morning that he will go to the Castle. That probably entirely useless path, that probably lost day, that probably futile hope. What's the point of it all? And here there's shoemaker's work piled up that nobody does and Brunswick keeps demanding it be finished." "All right," said K., "Barnabas has to wait a long time before he gets an assignment. That is understandable, there certainly seem to be more than enough employees here, it's not possible for everybody to get an assignment every day, you shouldn't complain about this, it surely applies to everybody. But in the end surely even Barnabas gets assignments, he has already brought me two letters." "Well," said Olga, "it is of course possible that it's wrong for us to complain, especially since I know all this only from hearsay and, as a girl, cannot understand it as well as Barnabas, who does keep certain things to himself. But now listen to how matters stand with the letters, with your letters, for instance. These letters he receives not directly from Klamm but from the copyist. On any day, at any hour—and for that reason the service, easy though it seems, is actually very tiring, since Barnabas has to be constantly alert—the copyist can remember him and signal to him. Klamm wouldn't appear to be behind this, he is still quietly reading his book, but sometimes, though this often happens on other occasions too, he's busy cleaning his pince-nez when Barnabas arrives, and perhaps Klamm looks at him, assuming that he can see at all without his pince-nez, Barnabas doubts it, at such moments Klamm's eyes are almost closed, he seems to be asleep and to be cleaning his pince-nez merely in a dream. Meanwhile the copyist searches through the many files and correspondences that he keeps under the table for a letter to you, it's therefore not a letter he has just written, but more likely by the looks of the envelope a very old letter that was lying there for a long time. But if it's an old letter, why did they make Barnabas wait so long? And you too, no doubt? And finally the letter as well, for it's probably already outdated. And this gives Barnabas a reputation as a bad, slow messenger. The copyist certainly makes things easy for himself, gives Barnabas the letter, says: 'From Klamm to K.,' whereupon Barnabas is dismissed. Then Barnabas comes home, breathless, with the letter that he has finally managed to get hold of under his shirt on his bare skin, and we sit on this bench, like the two of us now, and he talks, and then we examine everything in detail and estimate what he has accomplished and decide in the end that it's very little and that little questionable and Barnabas puts away the letter and doesn't feel like delivering it but doesn't feel like going to bed either so he picks up his shoemaker's work and spends the night sitting there on his shoemaker's stool. That's it, K., those are my secrets, and surely you're no longer surprised that Amalia will have nothing to do with it." "And the letter?" K. asked. "The letter?" said Olga, "well, some time later, once I have put sufficient pressure on Barnabas, days or weeks may have passed, he takes the letter and goes off to deliver it. In trivial things like that he's very dependent on me. I can always pull myself together after I recover from my first impression of his story, but he cannot, probably because he actually does know more. And I am therefore able to tell him over and over again: 'What is it you really want, Barnabas? What sort of career, what sort of goal is it you dream of? Perhaps you want to get so far ahead that you'll have to leave me behind completely, leave me for good? Might this be your goal? Don't I have to believe it, for otherwise your great dissatisfaction with your accomplishment would seem incomprehensible? Just take a look, though, and see whether any of our neighbors have come this far. True, their situation differs from ours and they have no reason for striving to reach beyond their own households, but even without such comparisons one has to recognize that in your case everything is going extremely well for you. There are obstacles, questionable matters, disappointments, but this merely shows, as we already knew, that nothing is given to you on a platter, that you yourself have to fight for every trifle, another reason for being proud, not dejected. Besides, aren't you fighting for us too? Does that mean nothing to you? Doesn't it give you new strength? And my happiness, almost haughtiness, at having a brother like you, doesn't that give you some security? Truly, it's not what you've accomplished at the Castle that disappoints me, but what I have accomplished with you. You're allowed into the Castle, you're a constant visitor in the offices, you spend entire days in the same room as Klamm, you are an officially recognized messenger, you're entitled to official clothing, you are entrusted with the delivery of important correspondences, you are all these things, you're actually allowed to do all these things, and you come down and instead of our crying for joy in each other's arms, you seem to lose all courage as soon as you see me and have doubts about everything, only the shoemaker's iron tempts you, but the letter, this guarantee of our future, you set aside.' That's how I talk to him, and after I have kept repeating it for days on end he picks up the letter with a sigh and goes off. But this probably isn't even due to the impact of my words, he's simply compelled to go to the Castle, and without having first carried out the instruction he would not dare to go there." "But everything you're saying to him is absolutely correct," said K., "you have summed things up in an admirably correct fashion. Your thinking is astonishingly clear!" "No," said Olga, "it's deceiving you, and this may also be how I deceived him. So what has he accomplished? He can enter an office, though it doesn't even seem to be an office but rather an anteroom to the offices, and perhaps not even that, perhaps it's a room intended for all those who aren't allowed into the real offices. He speaks to Klamm, but is it Klamm? Isn't it rather someone who merely resembles Klamm? Perhaps at the very most a secretary who is a little like Klamm and goes to great lengths to be even more like him and tries to seem important by affecting Klamm's drowsy, dreamlike manner. That part of his being is easiest to imitate, many try to do so; as for the rest of his being, though, they wisely steer clear of it. And a man such as Klamm, who is so often the object of yearning and yet so rarely attained, easily takes on a variety of shapes in the imaginations of people. For instance, Klamm has a village secretary here called Momus. Really? You know him? He too keeps to himself but I have seen him a couple of times. A powerful young gentleman, isn't he? And so he probably doesn't look at all like Klamm? And yet you can find people in the village who would swear that Momus is Klamm and none other than he. That's how people create confusion for themselves. And why should it be any different at the Castle? Somebody told Barnabas that the official is Klamm, and there actually is a resemblance between the two of them, but it's a resemblance that Barnabas himself has always doubted. And everything supports his doubts. Klamm is supposed to squeeze between other officials in a public room, with a pencil stuck behind his ear? But that is highly unlikely. Barnabas often says rather childishly, though only when he's in a confident mood: 'That official certainly looks very like Klamm, and if he were sitting in his own office, at his own desk, and his name were on the door, I would no longer doubt it.' That's childish, but it does make sense. But it would make far more sense if Barnabas, when he's up there, would ask several people about the real state of affairs, for according to him there are enough people standing about in that room. And even if their reports weren't much more reliable than the report of the man who, without even being asked, showed him Klamm, then at least some reference points, some points of comparison, might emerge from the diversity of opinion. This isn't my idea, it's Barnabas's idea, but he won't dare try it out; out of fear of possibly losing his position by inadvertently breaking some unknown rules, he won't dare speak to anyone; that's how insecure he feels; to my mind this truly pitiful insecurity sheds more light on his position than all of his reports. How suspicious and threatening everything must seem to him there if he doesn't even dare to open his mouth to ask an innocent question. Whenever I reflect on this I accuse myself of leaving him alone in those unknown rooms where the things that go on are such that even he, who is timid rather than cowardly, surely trembles with fear."

"Here, I think, you're coming to the decisive point," said K. "That's it. After hearing all you've said, I think that now I can see clearly. Barnabas is too young for this task. Nothing that he says about what happens up there can be taken seriously. Since he's always dying of fear up there, he cannot make observations, and if one makes him talk about it here, all one hears are confused fairy tales. It doesn't surprise me. Respect for the authorities is innate here, and then it's instilled in you throughout your lives in many different ways and from all sides, and you yourselves help this along as best you can. Still, on the whole, I'm not saying anything against that; if an authority is good, then why shouldn't one respect it? But then one shouldn't all of a sudden dispatch to the Castle an uninformed youth like Barnabas, who has never gone beyond the village surroundings, and then expect faithful reports from him and scrutinize his every word as though it were a word from Revelations and make one's own happiness in life depend on the interpretation. Nothing can be more mistaken. True, I too, not unlike you, let him lead me astray, put my hopes in him and also suffered disappointments through him that were based on his words alone, and thus on next to nothing." Olga remained silent. "It won't be easy for me," said K., "to shake your trust in your brother, for I can see now how much you love him and what you expect of him. But it has to happen and not least because of your love and your expectations. For look here, there's always something preventing you—I don't know what it is—from fully recognizing not so much what Barnabas has accomplished as what has been given to him. He is allowed into the offices or, if you prefer, into an anteroom, all right then it's an anteroom, but there are doors there that lead farther, barriers one can cross if one has the skill to do so. In my case, for instance, that anteroom is, at least for now, completely inaccessible. Who Barnabas speaks to there I don't know, perhaps that copyist is the lowest of the servants, but even if he is the lowest he can lead you to the next highest and if he cannot lead you to him, then he can at least name him and if he cannot name him then he can after all point out someone who will be able to name him. That so-called Klamm may not have anything at all in common with the real one, the similarity may exist only in Barnabas's eyes, which are blind from excitement, he may be the lowest of the officials, perhaps he is not even an official, but some task or other does keep him busy at his desk, he reads something in his large book, whispers something to the copyist, thinks of something when, after a long interval, his eye falls on Barnabas, and even if all of this isn't true and his actions are quite insignificant, then at least somebody put him there and did so with some purpose in mind. By all this I simply want to say that something is there, that Barnabas is being offered something, and that it is only Barnabas's fault if he can achieve nothing with that other than doubt, fear, and hopelessness. And as a starting point I always took the least favorable case, which is actually quite unlikely. For we do have the letters in hand, which I certainly don't trust much, though far more so than the words of Barnabas. Even if they are old worthless letters pulled out indiscriminately from a pile of equally worthless letters, indiscriminately, and with no more sense than that employed by canaries at fairs who pick somebody's fortune out of a pile, even if that is so, then at least these letters bear some relation to my work, are clearly intended for me, though perhaps not for my use, and, as the council chairman and his wife have testified, were personally signed by Klamm, and have, once again according to the council chairman, a significance that, while merely private and scarcely transparent, is nevertheless quite considerable." "Did the council chairman say so?" Olga asked. "Yes, he said so," K. answered. "I'll tell Barnabas," Olga said quickly, "that will greatly encourage him." "But he needs no encouragement," said K., "encouraging him now means telling him that he's right, that he need only carry on in the same way as before, but that way he'll never accomplish anything; no matter how much you keep encouraging someone who is blindfolded to stare through the cloth, he still won't see a thing; it's only when you take off the blindfold that he can see. It is help that Barnabas needs, not encouragement. But bear this in mind: up there are the authorities in their inextricable greatness—I thought I had an approximate conception of them before coming here, how childish all that was—up there, therefore, are the authorities, and Barnabas approaches them, nobody else, only he, pitiably alone, he would be too greatly honored if he doesn't spend the rest of his life lost in a dark corner of the office." "Don't imagine, K.," said Olga, "that we underestimate the difficulty of the task that Barnabas has taken on. And we do not lack respect for the authorities, you yourself said so." "But it's misguided respect," said K., "it's respect that is addressed to the wrong place, that kind of respect demeans its object. Can one still call it respect when Barnabas misuses the gift of entry to those rooms in order to while away his days idly there or when he comes down and discredits and belittles those whom he has just trembled before or when out of despair or weariness he fails to deliver the letters and messages that are entrusted to him? That is hardly respect. But the reproach goes even further, goes against you as well, Olga, I cannot spare you this, for though you think you respect the authorities, you sent Barnabas, young, weak, and isolated as he is, to the Castle, or at any rate never kept him from going."

"The reproach you're making," said Olga, "is one I have always leveled against myself. In any case what I should be reproached for is not that I sent Barnabas to the Castle, I didn't send him, he went on his own, but rather that I should have kept him from going by every means, through persuasion, through cunning, and through force. I ought to have kept him from going, but if this were that day again, that day of decision, and I felt the plight of Barnabas, the plight of our family, as I did then and do now, and if Barnabas himself, fully conscious of all the responsibility and danger, were to free himself from me consciously, with a smile, gently, in order to leave, even today I wouldn't keep him from going, despite all my experiences in the meantime, and I believe that in my place you couldn't help doing likewise. You don't know our plight, so you treat all of us, but Barnabas in particular, unjustly. We had more hope then than we do today, but at the time our hope was not great either, what was great was our plight, and that is still so. Hasn't Frieda told you anything about us?" "Only a few hints," said K., "nothing definite, but the mere mention of your name irritates her." "And the landlady didn't tell you anything either?" "No, nothing." "And nobody else either?" "Nobody." "Of course how could anybody tell you anything! Everybody knows something about us, either the truth, insofar as people have access to it, or at least a rumor, picked up somewhere or mostly fabricated outright, and everybody thinks about us more than they ought, but nobody will go so far as to tell you, because they're afraid to let such things cross their lips.

And they're right about that. It's difficult to bring this up even with you, K., for isn't it possible that after you've heard it you'll go away and will want to have nothing more to do with us, little enough though this seems to affect you. Then we will have lost you, a person who, I must confess, almost means more to me than does the entire previous Castle service of Barnabas. And yet—this contradiction has been tormenting me all evening—this is something that you must hear, for otherwise you won't get an overall picture of our situation, and would continue—this would be especially hurtful to me—being unjust toward Barnabas, for the complete agreement that is necessary would be missing, and you couldn't help us or accept our help, our unofficial help. But there is one other question still: Do you even want to know?" "Why do you ask that?" said K., "if it is necessary, I want to know, but why do you ask like that?" "Out of superstition," said Olga, "You will be drawn into our affairs, innocently, not much guiltier than Barnabas." "Tell me quickly," said K., "I'm not afraid. Besides, you're making things worse with your woman's fears."

XVII.

AMALIA'S SECRET

"Judge for yourself," said Olga, "in any case it sounds quite simple, one doesn't immediately understand how it can be so important. There's an official at the Castle called Sortini." "I've heard of him," said K., "he was involved in summoning me." "I don't think so," said Olga, "Sortini hardly ever appears in public. Aren't you mistaking him for Sordini, written with a 'd'?" "You're right," said K., "it was Sordini." "Yes," said Olga, "Sordini is quite well known, one of the most industrious officials, he's often mentioned, Sortini by contrast is very retiring and little known. Three years ago I saw him for the first and last time. It was on the third of July at a festival of the Firemen's Association, the Castle had participated by donating a new fire engine. Sortini, who is said to deal partly with fire department matters but may only have been present as a substitute—usually the officials fill in for one another and so it's difficult to determine the responsibility of this or that official—Sortini took part in the handing over of the engine, others too had of course come from the Castle, officials and servants, and Sortini, as befits his character, remained in the background. He's a small, frail, pensive gentleman, what struck everyone who even noticed him was the way he wrinkled his forehead, all his wrinkles—and there were a lot, though he could hardly be over forty—spread out in fanlike fashion straight across his forehead and down to the bridge of his nose, I have never seen anything like it. And so this was the festival. We, Amalia and I, had been looking forward to it for weeks, our Sunday clothes had been made to seem almost like new again, Amalia's dress was very beautiful, her white blouse was billowing at the top with row upon row of lace, Mother had lent her all her lace, I was jealous then, and before the festival I wept half the night. It was only when the landlady from the Bridge Inn came to inspect us in the morning—" "The landlady from the Bridge Inn?" asked K. "Yes," said Olga, "she was a good friend of ours, she came and had to admit that Amalia had an advantage over me, and then, to calm me down, she lent me her own necklace of Bohemian garnets. But just when we were ready to leave, Amalia was standing in front of me, we were all admiring her, and Father was saying: "Today, mark my words, Amalia will find a fiancé," just then, I don't know why, I took off the necklace, my pride, and, no longer jealous, put it around Amalia's neck. I simply bowed down before her victory and thought that everyone else would also have to bow down before her; perhaps we were surprised that she looked different than usual, for she certainly wasn't beautiful, but her bleak gaze, which has been the same ever since, went high up over our heads, so that we, quite involuntarily and almost literally, bowed down before her. Everybody noticed it, even Lasemann and his wife, who came to fetch us." "Lasemann?" asked K. "Yes, Lasemann," said Olga, "we were held in great esteem and the festival, for instance, couldn't really have started without us, since Father was third drillmaster in the fire company." "So your father was still that robust?"

asked K. "Father?" asked Olga, as though she didn't quite understand, "three years ago he was still more or less a young man and, during a fire at the Gentlemen's Inn, for instance, he sprinted out with an official, the heavyset Galater, on his back. I was there myself, there was certainly no danger of fire, only some dry wood by a stove had started smoldering, but Galater became frightened, he called out the window for help, the firemen came and my father had to carry him out, though the fire had already been put out. Well, Galater finds it difficult to move and has to be cautious in situations like that. I'm only telling you this because of Father, that's little more than three years ago and now look at how he is sitting there." Only now did K. notice that Amalia was back in the room, but she was far off at her parents' table, feeding her mother, who couldn't move her rheumatic arms, and encouraging her father to be a little more patient about his meal, saying she'd be over soon to feed him. But her rebuke had little effect, since her father, ravenous for his soup, overcame his physical weakness, attempted to slurp the soup out of the spoon and then to drink it straight from the soup plate, muttering angrily each time over his lack of success; the spoon, empty long before it reached his mouth, which he was trying to dip into the soup, got only so far as his drooping mustache, which was dripping and splashing soup everywhere except into his mouth. "That's what those three years have done to him?" K. asked, but he still had no pity for these old people, he had nothing but distaste for that entire corner with the family table. "Those three years," said Olga slowly, "or to be precise, a couple of hours at a festival. The festival was held on a meadow outside the village at the brook, it was already packed when we arrived, many people had come from the neighboring villages as well, the din left us quite confused. First Father led us to the fire engine, he laughed with joy when he saw it, a new engine made him happy, he began to touch it and to explain it to us, he would tolerate no argument or contradiction from the others; if something had to be inspected under the engine, all of us had to bend down and virtually crawl under the engine, Barnabas, who put up some resistance, got blows.

Only Amalia ignored the engine, she was standing upright in her beautiful dress, nobody dared say a word to her, I occasionally ran over to her and took her by the arm, but she remained silent. Even today I cannot explain to myself how we could have kept standing there in front of that engine for so long, and only when Father freed himself from it did we notice Sortini, who evidently had been behind the fire engine the whole time, leaning against one of its levers. True, there was a dreadful din at the time, and not just the usual sort of thing at festivals; the Castle had also donated a few trumpets to the fire company, special instruments on which a person, even a child, could without the slightest effort produce the wildest sounds; on hearing them, one would think the Turks were coming, and one could never get used to it, at each blast one jumped. And since they were new trumpets, everyone wanted to try them out, and since it was after all a public festival, permission was given. Standing around us, perhaps they had been attracted by Amalia, were a few such trumpeters, it was difficult to keep our wits about us, and then when in addition on Father's orders we were obliged to watch the engine, we were absolutely stretched to the limit, which is why Sortini, whom we had never seen before, escaped our attention so long. 'There's Sortini,' Lasemann finally said—I was standing next to him—in a whisper to Father. Father bowed low and, very excitedly, motioned for us to bow too. Although Father had never before met Sortini, he had always had great respect for his expertise in fire company matters and had often spoken of him at home, and so it was extremely surprising and significant to see Sortini in person. But Sortini paid no attention to us, that wasn't an idiosyncrasy of Sortini's, in public most officials seem indifferent, besides he was tired, only his official duties kept him down here, those officials who find these representational duties particularly oppressive aren't the worst sort, the other officials and servants mingled with the ordinary people now that they had actually come, but he remained beside the engine, anybody who attempted to approach him with requests or flattery he drove away with his silence. And this explains why he noticed us even later than we noticed him. Only when we bowed respectfully and Father attempted to apologize for us did he glance over at us, glancing wearily from one to the other, as if sighing over the fact that behind each person there was always another, until he fixed on Amalia, whom he had to look up at since she was much taller than he. He gave a start, then jumped over the shaft in order to be close to Amalia, we misunderstood this at first and all of us tried to approach him with Father in the lead, but he kept us away by raising his hand and then motioned for us to leave. That's all that happened. We teased Amalia a great deal about having actually found a fiancé and in our foolishness were quite cheerful all afternoon, but Amalia was more silent than ever, 'She's utterly, madly in love with Sortini,' said Brunswick, who's always quite coarse and cannot understand people with natures such as Amalia's, but this time his comment seemed to us almost justified, that day we were quite silly and all of us, except for Amalia, seemed in a daze from the sweet Castle wine when we arrived home after midnight." "And Sortini?" asked K. "Oh, Sortini," said Olga, "I saw Sortini several times during the festival, he was sitting on the shaft with his arms crossed over his chest and stayed like that until the carriage from the Castle came to pick him up. He didn't even go to the fire drills, in the course of which Father, precisely in hopes of being seen by Sortini, stood out from the other men his age." "And did you never hear from him again?" asked K. "You seem to have great admiration for Sortini." "Yes, admiration," said Olga, "and yes, we did hear from him again. Next morning we were awakened from our wine-induced sleep by Amalia's screams, the others immediately sank back on their beds, but I was fully awake and ran to Amalia, she stood by the window holding a letter which had just been handed in the window by a man who was still waiting for an answer. Amalia had already read the letter—it was brief—and she held it in her hand, which hung limply by her side; how I always loved her when she was tired. I knelt down beside her and read the letter. I had barely finished when Amalia, after a quick glance at me, picked it up and, unable to force herself to read it again, tore it up, threw the scraps in the face of the man outside, and shut the window. And so that was the decisive morning. I call it decisive, but every moment of the previous afternoon was just as decisive." "And what was in the letter?" asked K. "Oh yes, I haven't told you yet," said Olga, "the letter came from Sortini and was addressed to the girl with the garnet necklace. I cannot repeat the whole thing. It was a demand that Amalia should come to him at the Gentlemen's Inn and, to be precise, that she should come at once since Sortini had to leave in half an hour. The letter made use of the most vulgar expressions, I had never heard the likes of them before and from the context could only half-guess their meaning. Anybody who did not know Amalia and who had read only this letter would have to think that a girl to whom someone had dared to address such a letter was dishonored, even if she had not been touched. And it wasn't a love letter, it contained no flattery; on the contrary, Sortini was obviously annoyed that the sight of Amalia had moved him and kept him from his work. The way we explained it later to ourselves was that Sortini had probably wanted to go to the Castle that evening, had stayed behind only because of Amalia, and then, furious next morning at not having succeeded in forgetting Amalia at night, had written the letter. Even the most cold-blooded person couldn't help being outraged by the letter, but then in anyone other than Amalia fear of the malicious, threatening tone would have gained the upper hand; in Amalia's case, it went further than outrage, she simply knows no fear, neither for herself nor for others. And then as I crawled back to bed, repeating the fragmentary final sentence: 'So come at once, or else—!' Amalia stayed on the window sill, gazing out as if she were waiting for further messengers and were determined to treat each one just like the first." "Those then are the officials," K. said hesitantly, "there are even types like that among them. And what did your father do? I hope he lodged a forceful complaint about Sortini with the proper office, unless he chose to take the shorter, more certain path to the Gentlemen's Inn. What's most dreadful about the story is of course not the insult to Amalia, that could have been easily remedied, I cannot understand why you insist on attaching such disproportionate importance to that; why should Sortini have permanently disgraced Amalia with such a letter, that is the conclusion which could be drawn from your story, but that's actually quite impossible, Amalia would have been easily satisfied and in a few days the incident would have been forgotten, Sortini did not show Amalia up but rather himself. I recoil from Sortini and the possibility of such abuse of power. The approach that failed in this case because it was stated clearly and bluntly and encountered in Amalia a superior opponent can succeed completely in thousands of other cases in circumstances that are only slightly more unfavorable and cannot be seen by anybody, even by the mistreated person." "Hush," said Olga, "Amalia is looking over." Amalia had finished feeding her parents and was about to undress her mother, she had just untied her skirt, put her mother's arms around her neck, raised her slightly, took off her skirt, and laid her gently down. The father, constantly impatient that the mother was being taken care of first, though this obviously had happened only because the mother was even more helpless than he, attempted, perhaps in order to punish his daughter for her supposed slowness, to undress himself, but even though he had begun with the least necessary and easiest part, the enormous slippers in which his feet were flopping about, he had absolutely no success in slipping them off; breathing hoarsely, he soon had to give up and to lean back stiffly on his chair. "You missed the decisive point," said Olga, "everything you say may be true, but the decisive point was that Amalia wouldn't go to the Gentlemen's Inn; her treatment of the messenger could have been let slip, could have been hushed up; but because of her refusal to go, the curse was placed on our family and then the treatment of the messenger came to be seen as unpardonable, and was even thrust to the forefront of public attention." "What!" cried K., and instantly lowered his voice since Olga was raising her hands pleadingly, "You, Amalia's sister, surely don't mean she should have obeyed Sortini and rushed to the Gentlemen's Inn?" "No," said Olga, "spare me your suspicions, how can you believe such a thing? I don't know anybody who's so firmly in the right in all she does as Amalia. Had she gone to the Gentlemen's Inn, I would of course have thought she was right, but her not going was heroic. As for me, I will openly admit to you that if I had received a letter like that I would have gone. I couldn't have endured the anxiety about what might happen, only Amalia could have done so. Well, there were several ways around this, another woman might for instance have dressed very beautifully, which would have taken time, and then gone to the Gentlemen's Inn and found out that Sortini had already left, perhaps that he had left immediately after sending the messenger, something that is indeed quite likely since the gentlemen's whims are short-lived. But Amalia didn't do that or anything of the sort, she was too deeply insulted and could not restrain herself. If only she had somehow made a show of obeying, simply stepped over the threshold of the Gentlemen's Inn, then the disaster could have been averted, we have very clever lawyers here who know how to transform a mere trifle into anything one cares for it to be, but in this case there wasn't even a favorable trifle; on the contrary, there was only the degradation of Sortini's letter and the insult to the messenger." "But what kind of disaster is this," said K., "what kind of lawyers are they? They couldn't accuse, let alone punish Amalia because of Sortini's criminal behavior?" "Oh yes they could," said Olga, "though not after a regular trial, and they didn't punish her directly either, but they certainly punished her in another way, her and our entire family, and surely you're beginning to understand the severity of this punishment. To you, it seems unjust and monstrous, but in the village that is an extremely rare opinion, it's very favorable to us and should console us, as indeed it would if it weren't clearly attributable to certain mistakes. I can easily prove this to you, pardon me if I mention Frieda here, but what happened between Frieda and Klamm is actually, except for the form it ultimately took, extremely similar to what happened between Amalia and Sortini, and yet, however shocked you may initially have been, you now think it's a good thing. And that isn't simply habit, habit doesn't dull one's perceptions in that manner, if one simply has to arrive at some judgment; it's just a casting off of error." "No, Olga," said K., "I don't know why you're bringing Frieda into this, her case was entirely different, don't get such completely different things mixed up, go on." "Please," said Olga, "don't take it amiss if I insist on comparing them, you're still mistaken concerning Frieda if you think you have to defend her against such a comparison. She doesn't need to be defended, simply praised. In comparing the two cases I don't mean to say that they're identical, they are to each each other as white is to black, and Frieda is white. If worst comes to worst, one can always laugh at Frieda, as I so rudely did in the taproom—I very much regretted it later—but even then the person who laughs is merely malicious or envious; still, one can laugh whereas for Amalia all one can have, if one is not a blood relative of hers, is contempt. So they certainly are, as you say, entirely different cases, but they're similar too." "They are not similar either," said K., shaking his head in anger, "leave Frieda out of this. Frieda didn't get a nice fine letter like Amalia's from Sortini, and Frieda truly loved Klamm, anyone who doubts this can ask her, she still loves him." "But are those such big differences?" asked Olga. "Do you think Klamm couldn't have written to Frieda in the same manner? That's how the gentlemen are when they stand up from their desks; they cannot get their bearings in the world; in their absentmindedness they say the coarsest things, not everyone does, but many do. The letter to Amalia may well have been dashed off while deep in thought, without any regard whatsoever for what was actually being written. What do we know about the gentlemen's thoughts! Have you not heard anything yourself, or found out through anybody else, about the tone in which Klamm consorted with Frieda? Klamm is known to be very vulgar, supposedly he doesn't say a word for hours and then suddenly he says something so vulgar that one can only shudder. Sortini isn't particularly known for that, indeed he is entirely unknown. Actually, all that's known about him is that his name is similar to Sordini's, and if it weren't for the similarity of their names, people would probably not even know him. Even as an expert in fire company matters he is probably confused with Sordini, the real expert, who uses the similarity of the two names to shift his representational duties onto Sortini so that he isn't interrupted at work. When a man so unfamiliar with the ways of the world as Sortini is overcome by love for a village girl, this naturally takes on a very different shape from the love affair of the cabinet-maker's apprentice next door. Nor should one forget the great distance between an official and a shoemaker's daughter, which must somehow be bridged, this is how Sortini went about it, another person might do so differently. True, they say that all of us belong to the Castle and that there's no distance between them and us, and that there's nothing to bridge, and in general this may indeed be so, but unfortunately we had a chance to see that when everything is at stake it isn't that way at all. Anyhow, after all this, Sortini's behavior will at least seem more understandable and slightly less outrageous to you, and indeed, compared with Klamm's behavior, it's far more understandable and, even if one happens to be directly involved, far more tolerable. A tender letter from Klamm is more painfully embarrassing than the most vulgar letter from Sortini. Don't misunderstand me, I wouldn't dare to pronounce judgment on Klamm, I'm comparing them only because you resist the comparison. But Klamm is like a commandant over women, he commands this one here and that one there to come to him, but doesn't tolerate any one of them for long and just as he commands them to come, so too does he command them to go. Oh! Klamm wouldn't even go to the trouble of writing a letter first. And by contrast does it still seem so outrageous that Sortini, who leads a completely retiring existence and whose relationships with women are at the very least unknown, should one day sit down and in his beautiful official's script write a truly repulsive letter. And if this doesn't yield a difference that is favorable to Klamm but rather the opposite, could Frieda's love possibly do so? Believe me, the relationship between women and officials is very difficult, or rather always very easy, to determine. Love is never lacking here. In the case of the officials there is no unhappy love. So in this regard it is not praise when one says of a girl—and I'm certainly not talking about Frieda alone—that it was only out of love that she gave herself to the official. She loved him and gave herself to him, that's how it was, but there's nothing praiseworthy about that. But Amalia didn't love Sortini, you want to object. All right, so she didn't love him, but then again perhaps she did love him, who can tell? Not even she is capable of that. How can she think she loved him when she rejected him more forcefully than any official was probably ever rejected. Barnabas says that even now she sometimes still trembles from the emotion with which she slammed that window three years ago. That is indeed true, so one cannot ask her about it; she's finished with Sortini and that's all she knows; she does not know whether she loves him. But we know that women cannot help loving officials when the officials approach them, and indeed even beforehand they're in love with the officials, no matter how strongly they attempt to deny it, and Sortini not only approached Amalia, on seeing Amalia he even jumped over the shaft, with legs stiff from desk work he jumped over the shaft. But, you will say, Amalia is an exception. Yes, she is, she proved that when she refused to go to Sortini, and that's already enough of an exception; but as for her not having loved Sortini, that would be almost too much of an exception, it would be utterly incomprehensible. That afternoon certainly we were blinded, but our very belief that we could see through all that fog some sign of Amalia's being in love surely shows some awareness. But if one pieces all this together, what difference does that leave between Frieda and Amalia? The only difference is that Frieda did what Amalia refused to do." "Maybe so," said K., "but to me the main difference is that Frieda is my fiancée whereas Amalia fundamentally concerns me only inasmuch as she is the sister of Barnabas the Castle messenger, and her fate is perhaps bound up with Barnabas's service. Had an official done her such a screaming injustice as I initially thought after hearing your story, then I would have worried about it a great deal, but more as a matter of public concern than as Amalia's private sorrow. Now after your story the picture changes in a way that I find less than comprehensible, but since you are the one telling it, it's credible enough, and so I shall be quite happy to disregard the matter entirely, I am not a fireman, why should I care about Sortini? But I do care about Frieda and therefore find it strange that you, whom I trusted completely and shall always be willing to trust, are constantly attempting through the roundabout means of Amalia to attack Frieda and to make me suspicious of her. I'm not assuming you do so intentionally, let alone with bad intentions, for if that were so I would long since have been obliged to leave, you're not doing so intentionally, the circumstances lead you to do so, out of love for Amalia you want to set her above all other women and, since you cannot find enough to praise in Amalia even for that purpose, you help yourself out by belittling other women. Amalia's deed is odd, but the more you speak of the deed, the harder it is to decide whether it was great or small, clever or foolish, heroic or cowardly, Amalia keeps her motives sealed within her breast, nobody can drag them from her. Frieda, on the other hand, hasn't acted strangely but simply followed her heart, as is clear to anyone willing to occupy himself with this, anyone can check for himself, there is no cause for gossip. And I have no desire to belittle Amalia nor to defend Frieda, I simply want to explain how I stand with regard to Frieda and to show that all attacks against Frieda are at the same time attacks against my existence. I came here voluntarily and have tied myself down here voluntarily, but everything that happened in between, and especially my future prospects—bleak though they are, they do exist—I owe to Frieda, that simply cannot be denied. I was indeed taken on here as a surveyor, but only in appearance, they played games with me, drove me out of every house, and even today they're still playing games with me, but now it's all much more complicated, I have in a sense increased in girth and that already says something; trivial though all this is, I do after all have a home, a position, and real work, I have a fiancée who takes over my professional work whenever I have other business to attend to, I shall marry her and join the community; I also have, besides an official connection to Klamm, a personal one which I have admittedly not yet been able to take advantage of. Now surely this is more than a little? And when I come to you, whom do you greet? In whom do you confide your family's story? From whom do you expect a chance, be it even the tiniest most improbable chance, of some help? Surely it's not from me, the surveyor, who for instance only a week ago was forcibly ejected by Lasemann and Brunswick from their house, but rather you expect this from the man who already has some means of power, yet it is precisely to Frieda that I owe these means of power, to Frieda, who is so modest that were you to ask her anything of that nature she would certainly say she didn't know the slightest thing about it. And nonetheless after all this it seems as if Frieda in her innocence has done more than Amalia in all her arrogance, for look, I have the impression that you're seeking help for Amalia. And from whom? Well, in reality from none other than Frieda." "Did I really say such nasty things about Frieda?" said Olga, "I certainly had no intention of doing so and do not believe I did, but that's possible, the situation is such that we have fallen out with absolutely everyone and once we start complaining we get carried away and don't know where we will end up. You're right again, there is a big difference now between Frieda and us, and it's good to emphasize that for a change. Three years ago we were middle-class girls and Frieda, the orphan, was a maid in the Bridge Inn, we went past her without even glancing at her, we were probably too arrogant, but that is how we were brought up. Yet that evening at the Gentlemen's Inn, you may have noticed the present situation: Frieda with whip in hand and me among the bunch of servants. But of course it is even worse. Frieda may despise us, that is only fitting in her position, the existing circumstances dictate it. But who does not despise us! Anybody who decides to despise us immediately joins the biggest circle of all. You know Frieda's successor? Pepi is her name. I met her only two evenings ago, she used to be a chambermaid. Her contempt for me surpasses even Frieda's. On catching sight of me through the window when I came for beer, she ran to the door and locked it, I had to plead for a long time and it wasn't until I promised her the ribbon I wore in my hair that she finally opened up for me. But when I handed it to her, she simply threw it in a corner. Well, she's entitled to despise me, I'm partly dependent on her goodwill and she is after all a barmaid at the Gentlemen's Inn, but she is only temporary and certainly doesn't have the qualities that are needed to obtain a permanent position there. One need only listen to how the landlord speaks to Pepi and compare it with how he spoke to Frieda. But that doesn't stop Pepi from despising Amalia, Amalia, whose very expression would be enough to whisk tiny little Pepi with all her braids and bows from the room at a speed that, if she had been exclusively dependent on her own fat little legs, she could never have managed. What outrageous chatter about Amalia I had to put up with yesterday again until the guests finally took my side, but only in the way you yourself once saw." "How frightened you are," said K., "all I did was give Frieda her rightful place, I didn't want to disparage you, as you now make out. Besides, your family means something to me, I never concealed that; how this specialness could be a reason for contempt I cannot understand." "Oh, K.," said Olga, "even you will eventually understand it, I fear; that Amalia's conduct toward Sortini was the original reason for the contempt, is there no way you can understand that?" "But that would be too odd," said K., "one could either admire or condemn Amalia for that reason, but despise her? And if on the strength of a feeling that I find quite incomprehensible they actually despise Amalia, why do they extend that contempt to you, the innocent family? It's a little much that Pepi, say, despises you, and next time I go by the Gentlemen's Inn I intend to make her pay for it." "K.," said Olga, "if you wanted to win over everyone who despises us it would be hard work since all of this comes from the Castle. I still have a distinct recollection of the next morning. Brunswick, our assistant at the time, had arrived as he did each day, Father had given him some work and sent him home, then we sat down to breakfast, everyone except Amalia and myself was quite lively, Father kept talking about the festival, he had various plans concerning the fire company; the Castle, you see, has its own fire company, which had also sent a delegation to the festival, with whom there had been several discussions, the gentlemen from the Castle who were present had seen the performance of our fire company, had spoken quite favorably of them, and had compared them with the performance of the Castle fire company, the outcome was in our favor, they spoke of the need to reorganize the Castle fire company, instructors from the village were needed for that, there were several possible contenders, but Father hoped that the choice would fall on him. He now spoke about this, and being in the rather endearing habit of spreading himself out rather wide at table, he sat there, clasping half the table with his arms and looking out the open window toward the sky, his face so young and so joyously hopeful, I would never again see him like that. Then Amalia said, with a sovereignty we had never noticed in her before, that one shouldn't put one's trust in speeches like that from the gentlemen, for on such occasions the gentlemen liked to say agreeable things, but they had little or no significance and, once uttered, they were forgotten for all time, but, admittedly, on the very next occasion one got caught again in their trap. Mother forbade her to speak like that, Father simply laughed at her precociousness and experienced airs, but then gave a start, seemed to look about for something he had just noticed was missing, but nothing was missing, and said that Brunswick had told a story about a messenger and a torn-up letter, he asked whether we knew anything about it, whom it concerned, and what the situation was in that regard. We remained silent; Barnabas, still young as a little lamb, said something particularly stupid or cheeky, we spoke about something else and the affair was forgotten."

XVIII.

AMALIA'S PUNISHMENT

"But a little while after that we were inundated from all sides with questions about the letter affair; friends and enemies, acquaintances and strangers came, our best friends were quickest to leave, Lasemann, usually slow and dignified, came in looking as though he merely wanted to check the dimensions of the room, one look around and he was finished, it looked like some awful children's game as Lasemann ran off and Father freed himself from several others and ran after him as far as the threshold of the house and then gave up, Brunswick came and gave Father notice, he wanted to set up his own shop, he said this quite honestly, a clever man, who knew how to seize the moment, the customers came and began to search through Father's storeroom for the boots they had brought for repair, Father first tried to change the customers' minds—all of us helped as best we could—then gave up and quietly helped people look, line after line in the order book was crossed out, the leather supplies that had been left with us were returned, debts were paid, all this was done without the slightest quarrel, people were happy to be able to break off the connection with us quickly, completely, even at some loss to themselves, that wasn't an issue. And then, finally, as might have been expected, Seemann, chief of the fire company, came, I can still see the scene before my eyes, Seemann, tall and strong, but somewhat stooped and tubercular, always serious—he is quite incapable of laughter—stands before my father, whom he admired and to whom once in a cordial moment he held out the prospect of a post as a deputy chief, but now he's supposed to inform Father of his dismissal by the association and request the return of his diploma. The customers in the house just then dropped what they were doing and gathered in a tight circle round the two men. Seemann cannot speak, keeps tapping Father on the shoulder as though determined to tap from him the words that he himself ought to say but cannot find. He laughs the whole time, probably trying to calm himself and everyone else somewhat, but since he cannot laugh and since nobody has ever heard him laugh, nobody realizes that it is actually laughter. But from this day on Father is too tired and despondent to be able to help Seemann, he even seems too tired to try to understand what's happening. Indeed, we were all despondent, but since we were young we couldn't imagine such a total collapse, we kept thinking that somewhere in the long line of visitors someone would finally come and get it all to stop, make everything go back to the way it was. In our foolishness we considered Seemann just the right person for this. We waited in suspense for a clear statement to emerge from the constant laughter. What was so funny anyhow, surely only the stupid injustice being inflicted on us. Chief, Chief, go and finally tell these people, we thought as we pressed around him, but this merely elicited the oddest gestures from him. Finally, responding not to our secret wishes but to encouraging or annoyed shouts from the customers, he did begin to speak. But we still had hope. He began with great praise for Father. Called him a jewel of the association, an unsurpassable model for the new recruits, an indispensable member whose departure would almost destroy the association. All this was quite fine, had he only ended there. But he went on. If the association had nevertheless resolved to ask Father for his resignation, though only provisionally, the seriousness of the reasons forcing this step on the association should be easily discernible. Perhaps things wouldn't necessarily have gone so far had it not been for Father's brilliant achievements at the previous day's festival, and yet it was precisely those achievements that had attracted official attention, the association was in the spotlight and had to be even more concerned about its purity than before. And then when the messenger was insulted, the association could find no other way out, and he, Seemann, had undertaken the difficult task of reporting it. Father shouldn't make this even more difficult for him. How glad Seemann was to have finally come out with this, indeed so satisfied that he was no longer exaggeratedly considerate, and simply pointed to the diploma hanging on the wall, waving his finger. Father nodded and went to get it, but with his shaking fingers he couldn't lift it off the hook, I climbed on a chair to help. And that was that, he did not even take the diploma from the frame but gave it to Seemann as it was. Then he sat down in a corner, not moving, no longer speaking to anyone, we ourselves had to deal with the customers as best we could." "And where in all this do you see the influence of the Castle?" K. asked. "It doesn't seem to have intervened yet. What you have told me up to now is nothing more than the mindless timidity of the people, their delight in someone else's plight, their fickleness in friendship, exactly the sort of thing one finds everywhere, and then in your father's case—or so it seems to me—there is a certain pettiness, for, after all, what did the diploma amount to? Confirmation of his talents, but those he kept; if they made him indispensable, then so much the better, for the only way he could really have made things difficult for the chief would have been to throw the diploma at his feet before he could say another word. It seems significant to me that you haven't mentioned Amalia;

Amalia, the one to blame for all this, probably stood quietly in the background, observing the havoc." "No, no," said Olga, "nobody should be blamed for this, nobody could behave any differently, it was all due to the influence of the Castle." "The influence of the Castle," repeated Amalia, who had entered unobserved from the courtyard, their parents had long since gone to bed, "telling Castle stories? Still sitting here together? But you wanted to leave right away, K., and now it's almost ten. Do you even care about such stories? There are people here who feed on such stories, they sit together as you sit here, regaling one another, but you do not strike me as one of them." "Yes I am," said K., "I am indeed one of them, whereas I am not greatly taken by those who do not concern themselves with such stories and simply make others concern themselves with them." "Well, yes," said Amalia, "but people are interested in different ways, I once heard of a young man whose mind was taken up day and night with thoughts of the Castle, he neglected everything else, people feared for his ordinary faculty of reason since all his faculties were always up at the Castle, but in the end it turned out that it wasn't actually the Castle he was thinking of but only the daughter of a scullery maid at the offices, he got her, and then all was fine again." "I would like that man, I think," said K. "As for your liking that man," said Amalia, "I'm not so sure about that, but you might like his wife. Now don't let me disturb you, but I am going to bed and have to extinguish the lights because of our parents, they fall fast asleep right away, but in an hour their real sleep is over and then even the slightest glimmer will disturb them. Good night." And indeed everything went dark right away, Amalia was most likely arranging a place to sleep on the floor by her parents' bed. "Who is this young man she spoke of," K. asked. "I don't know," said Olga, "perhaps Brunswick, though it doesn't quite fit him, or perhaps someone else. It isn't easy to understand exactly what she is saying, for one doesn't know whether she is speaking ironically or seriously, it's mostly serious, but sounds ironic." "Stop interpreting everything!" said K. "How did you grow so heavily dependent on her, then? Was this already the case before the great misfortune? Or only afterwards? And don't you ever wish you were independent of her? And are there any rational reasons for your dependence on her? She is the youngest, and as such she must obey. She is the one, whether guilty or innocent, who brought the misfortune on the family. Instead of begging each of you all over again for forgiveness every day, she carries her head higher than everybody else, doesn't look after anything other than your parents—and then only barely, as an act of mercy—refuses to be initiated into anything, as she herself puts it, and when she finally does speak to you, she is 'mostly serious, but sounds ironic.' Or perhaps she rules through the beauty you sometimes mention. Well, you three greatly resemble one another, but the trait that distinguishes her from the two of you certainly isn't to her advantage, and even on first seeing her I was scared off by the blank loveless look in her eyes. And though she is indeed the youngest, not a trace of it can be detected in her outward appearance, she has the ageless look of women who scarcely age, but who were scarcely ever young either. You see her every day, you don't even notice the severity of her features. That's why I too, if I think about it, cannot take Sortini's affection seriously, perhaps he merely wanted to punish her with the letter rather than actually summon her." "I don't want to talk about Sortini," said Olga, "anything is possible with those gentlemen from the Castle, no matter how beautiful or ugly the particular girl happens to be. But as for the rest, you're completely mistaken about Amalia. Look, I have no particular reason for winning you over to Amalia's side, and if I try to do so, it's only for your sake. Amalia somehow was the cause of our misfortune, that is certain, but even Father, who was after all most seriously affected by the misfortune and could never keep his language under control, especially at home, even Father never spoke a word of reproach to Amalia, not even in the worst of times. And that wasn't, say, because he approved of Amalia's action; how could he, an admirer of Sortini's, approve of it, let alone show the slightest understanding, for he would surely have been glad to sacrifice himself and all his possessions for Sortini, though not in the way it had actually happened, namely, on account of Sortini's likely anger. His likely anger, for we heard no more from Sortini; if until then he had been withdrawn, from now on it was as if he didn't exist anymore. And you should have seen Amalia then! We all knew that there would be no express punishment. People simply withdrew. The people here as well as at the Castle. While we did of course notice the villagers' withdrawal, there was no noticeable reaction from the Castle. We hadn't noticed the Castle's caring beforehand, so how could we now notice a complete change. The silence was the worst. And by no means the villagers' withdrawal, which had not been undertaken out of any particular conviction, they probably had no serious reservations about us, their present contempt had not yet emerged, it was only out of fear that they had done so, and then they simply waited to see how matters would turn out. We still had no fear of hardship either, all the debtors had paid, the settlements had been favorable, relatives secretly supplied the food we lacked, that was easy, it was harvest time, but we had no fields and nobody would give us work anywhere, and so for the first time in our lives we were virtually condemned to idleness. And then we sat together behind closed windows in the July and August heat. Nothing happened. No summons, no news, no visitors, nothing." "Well," said K., "since nothing happened and no express punishment was to be expected, what did you fear? What sort of people are you at all!" "How should I explain this to you?" said Olga. "We weren't afraid of anything to come, we were only suffering from present circumstances and were in the middle of being punished. The villagers even expected that we would come back, that Father would reopen his workshop, and that Amalia, who could sew extremely beautiful clothes, if only for the most genteel, would come to take new orders, and indeed all of the villagers regretted what they had done; when a respected family in the village is suddenly cut off completely, that is to everyone's disadvantage in some way or other; they broke with us, they thought they were only doing their duty, and in their place we would have behaved no differently. And they didn't really know what it was all about, all they knew was that the messenger had gone back to the Gentlemen's Inn, his hand filled with scraps of paper, Frieda had seen him go out and come back, had exchanged a few words with him and immediately spread what she discovered, but she certainly didn't do so out of hostility toward us but simply out of duty, a duty that under similar circumstances anyone else would have had to assume too. And of course, as I said, the villagers would have greatly favored a happy solution to the entire affair. If we had suddenly appeared with the news that all was now fine again, that the affair had, say, simply been a misunderstanding which had been completely cleared up, or that it was indeed an offense but had through its very commission been rectified, or that we had through our connections at the Castle succeeded in having the affair dismissed—even this would have been enough for the villagers—they would definitely have received us again with open arms, there would have been kissing, embracing, celebrations, I have sometimes seen that kind of thing with other people. But it wouldn't even have been necessary to have such news; if we had only gone and presented ourselves of our own accord, taken up our old connections again without wasting a word about the letter affair, that would have been enough, everyone would have gladly stopped talking about the matter, for in addition to fear it was the painful embarrassment of the matter that had made them break with us, simply so that they would no longer have to hear anything about the matter or speak about it or think of it or be in any way touched by it. If Frieda had disclosed the matter, she had done so not because she took pleasure in it but in order to protect herself and everyone else from it, to notify the community that a certain incident had taken place in our house which one should be most careful to stay away from. The issue here was not us as a family but rather the actual affair, and we came into it only because of the affair in which we had become involved. So if we had simply come out again, let the past rest, shown through our behavior that we had overcome the matter, regardless of how, and if the public had been thus persuaded that whatever the entire matter might have been about, it would never be discussed again, even then everything would have been fine, we would have encountered the same old helpfulness everywhere; even if we had only partly forgotten the matter, they would have understood this and helped us to forget it entirely. Instead we sat at home. I'm not sure what we were waiting for, probably for Amalia's decision, she had that morning seized the leadership of the family and kept a tight grip on it. Without recourse to special actions, orders, or pleas, almost solely by means of silence. The rest of us, though, had much to discuss, there was ceaseless whispering from morning until evening, and sometimes Father in a sudden attack of fright called me and I spent half the night by his bedside. Or sometimes we sat together, myself and Barnabas, who at first showed little understanding of the entire matter and ardently demanded explanations, always the same ones, he must have known that the untroubled years expected by others of his age no longer existed for him, we sat together, K., like the two of us now, and forgot that night had come and morning again. Mother was the weakest of us, no doubt because she had endured not only our shared sorrows but each individual sorrow, and so with horror we observed in her changes which, we suspected, awaited our entire family. Her favorite spot was the corner of a settee, we no longer have it, it's in Brunswick's large parlor, she sat there, either—one couldn't tell which it was—dozing or, as her moving lips seemed to suggest, conducting lengthy conversations with herself. So it was only natural that we should have gone on discussing the letter affair from all angles, in all its certain details and uncertain possibilities, constantly outdoing ourselves in an effort to devise ways to achieve a favorable solution, this was all quite natural and unavoidable, but not good, and indeed we kept getting more and more mired in the very thing we wanted to escape from. And however excellent these ideas, what use were they, none could be carried out without Amalia, they were only preliminary deliberations, meaningless because the results never even reached Amalia, and if they had, they would have met with nothing but silence. Well, fortunately I understand Amalia better now than I did then. She bore more than the rest of us, it's incomprehensible that she bore it and is still living among us today. Mother did perhaps bear all our sufferings, but she bore them because they had befallen her and didn't bear them for long; one cannot say that she still somehow bears these sorrows today, and even then her mind was confused. But Amalia not only bore the sorrow, she also had the sense to see through it, we saw only the consequences, she saw the cause, we hoped for some little remedy or other, she knew everything had already been decided, we had to whisper, she merely had to keep silent, she stood face to face with the truth and lived and endured this life then as now. How much better things were for us in all our misery than for her. Still, we had to leave our house, Brunswick moved in, they allotted us this cottage, and in several trips we brought our property here in a handcart, Barnabas and myself pulling, Father and Amalia helping out behind, Mother, whom we had brought here first, always greeted us, sitting on a crate, with low wails. But I remember that even during those strenuous journeys—which were humiliating, since we often met harvest wagons whose occupants fell silent on seeing us and looked away—we, Barnabas and I, couldn't refrain from discussing our worries and our plans, sometimes we came to a stop as we spoke and it took Father's 'Hey' to remind us of our duty. But even after the move all those discussions did not change our life except that we now gradually began to feel the poverty. The subsidies from our relatives ceased, our means were almost exhausted, and just then the contempt, as you know it, began to develop. People noticed that we hadn't the strength to extricate ourselves from the letter affair and held this very much against us, it wasn't that they underestimated the grave nature of our fate, although they did not know exactly what it was; if we had overcome this they would certainly have honored us accordingly, but since we hadn't succeeded, they made definitive what they had done only temporarily till then, they banished us from all circles, knowing that they themselves probably wouldn't have withstood the test any better, but that it was all the more necessary to make a complete break with us. Then they no longer spoke of us as people, our family name never came up again; if they had to talk about us they called us after Barnabas, the most innocent among us; even our cottage fell into disrepute, and if you examine yourself you'll have to admit that on first arriving here you too thought that you noticed the justification for this contempt; later when people began coming to see us again, they turned up their noses at the most trivial things, for instance that the little oil lamp was hanging over the table. Where else should it hang if not over the table, but to them that was intolerable. Yet if we hung the lamp elsewhere, it still didn't lessen their aversion. Everything that we were and possessed met with the same contempt."

XIX.

PETITIONING

"And what did we do meanwhile? The worst we could have done, something that would have provided better justification for their contempt than did the actual cause—we betrayed Amalia, we tore ourselves away from her silent command, we couldn't keep living like that, we couldn't live completely without hope, and in our own way each of us began to beg or to storm the Castle in an effort to make it forgive us. But we knew that we couldn't make amends, we also knew that the only hopeful connection we had with the Castle, namely, through Sortini, the official who had a fondness for Father, had been blocked for us precisely through these events, nevertheless we set to work. Father began, there began the senseless petitions to the chairman, secretaries, lawyers, clerks, generally he was not admitted, and if by means of deception or chance he actually was admitted—how we cheered and rubbed our hands at such news—then he was dismissed with extreme speed and never admitted again. Besides, it was so easy to answer him, the Castle always had an easy time of it. What did he want? What had happened to him? What did he want to be pardoned for? When, and by whom, had a finger ever been raised against him at the Castle? He was indeed impoverished, having lost his customers and so on, but this had to do with everyday life, with trade matters and the marketplace, and was the Castle supposed to take care of everything? But in reality it did take care of everything, yet it couldn't crudely intervene in developments for no reason other than to serve the interests of one individual. Should it, say, send out its officials and have them pursue Father's customers and lead them back to him by force? But, Father then objected—we carefully discussed all these matters at home beforehand and afterward, squeezed into a corner as though hiding from Amalia, who noticed everything but let us carry on—but, Father then objected, he wasn't actually complaining because of his impoverishment, everything he had lost here, he would easily make up for again, all this would be beside the point if they would only forgive him. But what should he be forgiven, they said, no complaint had been filed, at least there was no mention of it in the depositions, or at least not in the depositions open to the legal community, and consequently, insofar as could be determined, no action had been taken against him nor was there one under way. Perhaps he could name an official decree issued against him? Father could not. Or had an official organ intervened? Father knew nothing of that. Well, if he knew nothing and nothing had happened, what did he want? What could one forgive him? At most that he was now senselessly pestering the offices, but that's precisely what was so unforgivable. Father wouldn't give up, he was still very strong then and had plenty of time because of his enforced idleness. 'I shall restore Amalia's honor, it won't take much longer,' he would tell Barnabas and myself several times a day, but only softly, for Amalia wasn't supposed to hear this; nevertheless, it was said merely for Amalia's benefit, for in reality he was not at all thinking of winning back her honor but only of securing forgiveness for her. But to obtain pardon, he first had to establish guilt, and that's precisely what they denied him at the offices. He hit on the idea—and this showed that his mind had grown feeble—that they were concealing his guilt because he wasn't paying enough; till then he had paid only the fixed fees, which were very high, at least for our circumstances. But he thought that he had to pay more, and that was certainly wrong because even though bribes are indeed accepted in our offices for the sake of simplicity and to avoid needless talk, they don't get you anywhere. But if that was Father's hope, then we had no wish to upset it. We sold what we still had—almost everything was indispensable—to provide Father with the means to pursue his inquiries, and then for a long time we had each morning the satisfaction of knowing that when Father set off in the morning there were at least a few coins in his pocket for him to jingle. Of course we were hungry all day, whereas all we achieved with the money was to keep Father in a certain state of joyous hope. But this was hardly an advantage. He tormented himself on his rounds, and so what would have come to a well-deserved end, had it not been for the money, dragged on in this way. Since in reality they could not offer us anything special for the overpayments, a clerk occasionally tried to do something for us, at least ostensibly, promising investigations and hinting that certain leads had been found that would be pursued not out of duty but merely as a favor to Father—instead of becoming more skeptical, Father became ever more gullible. He came back with a clearly meaningless promise, as though he were restoring the full blessing to our house, and it was painful to see him standing behind Amalia's back with his contorted smile and wide-open eyes, gesturing toward her to indicate to us that the rescue of Amalia, which would surprise nobody more than Amalia herself, was, thanks to his efforts, imminent, but that all of this was still a secret, which we should keep strictly in confidence. This would certainly have gone on for a long time if we hadn't discovered that we could no longer provide Father with money. Barnabas had been taken on as an assistant by

Brunswick after much pleading, but only in such a way that each evening he collected the orders in the dark and delivered the finished work in the dark—it is true, for our sake Brunswick had exposed his business to certain risks, but he paid Barnabas very little for that and Barnabas's work is flawless—yet the pay was barely enough to save us from real hunger. With much care and after a great deal of preparation we announced to Father that our financial assistance had been terminated, but he took this calmly. His powers of reason were now such that he could no longer understand the futility of his interventions, but he had grown weary of the continual disappointments. Although he said—he no longer spoke as clearly as before, he used to speak almost too clearly—that he would have needed very little more money, because tomorrow or even today he would have found out everything, but now everything had been in vain, and it was only because of the money that it had come to naught and so on, his tone of voice indicated that he didn't believe a word of this. And then suddenly he had new plans. Since he hadn't succeeded in establishing guilt and therefore couldn't get any further through official channels either, he would have to resort exclusively to begging and approach the officials in person. Surely there were some among them who had good, compassionate hearts, which they admittedly could not give in to at the office, but outside the office they could if you surprised them at the right moment."

At this, K., who had been absorbed in listening to Olga, interrupted the story by asking: "And you think that's mistaken?" True, the rest of the story would have to give him the answer to this, but he wanted to know at once.

"No," said Olga, "there can be no talk of compassion and the like. Young and inexperienced as we were, we knew this, and Father also knew it of course, but he had forgotten it, this and most other things. He had prepared a plan to post himself on the main road near the Castle where the officials' carriages went by and then, if at all possible, to present his appeal for forgiveness. Frankly, it was a plan quite devoid of reason even if the impossible had come about and the appeal had actually reached the ear of an official. For is an individual official capable of granting pardon? At best this might be a matter for the administration as a whole, but even it is incapable of granting forgiveness, it can only judge. But even if an official wanted to give in and deal with the affair, could he form an impression based on what Father, the poor, weary, aged man, muttered to him? The officials are highly educated, but only one-sidedly so, in his own area an official can on hearing a single word dart at once through complete trains of thought, but if someone explains cases from another department to him for hours on end, he may nod politely, but he won't understand a word. Well, all this is obvious, just try to understand the minor official affairs concerning you, the tiniest things, which an official settles with a shrug, just try to understand them fully and you'll be busy all your life and never get to the end. But even if Father had managed to find an authorized official, the latter cannot settle anything without the preliminary files, and certainly not out on the road; in other words, he cannot forgive, he can only dispatch matters officially, and to this end can only refer back to official channels, but Father's attempts to achieve anything in that way had already ended in utter failure. How far downhill things must have gone for Father if he thought he could get anywhere with this new plan. Had there been even the remotest possibility of the sort, the road would be teeming with petitioners, but since this was a sheer impossibility, as even the most elementary schooling ought to make one realize, the road is completely empty. Perhaps this, too, strengthened Father's hope, he found nourishment for it everywhere. There was a great need for that too, for a healthy mind wouldn't have to get involved in such lengthy reflections; from the most superficial details it would recognize the sheer impossibility of the endeavor. When the officials drive to the village or back to the Castle, it isn't really a pleasure trip, work awaits them in the village and at the Castle, which is why they drive at top speed. Nor does it occur to them to look out the carriage window to search for supplicants, the carriages are crammed with files, which the officials are busy studying."

"Still," said K., "I have seen the inside of an official's sleigh, and there were no files there." The world unfolding to him in Olga's story was so large, almost unbelievably so, that he couldn't refrain from touching it with his meager experience in order to persuade himself more clearly of its existence as well as of his own.

"That is possible," said Olga, "but then it's even worse since the official has such important concerns that the files are too valuable or too voluminous to be taken along, such officials give orders to drive at a gallop. In any case nobody has time to spare for Father. And besides: There are several approaches to the Castle. At times this one is fashionable and most drive there, at others that one and everyone rushes in that direction. The rules according to which these changes take place are still unknown. At eight o'clock in the morning all of them may be traveling on a certain road, half an hour later all are on a different one, ten minutes later on a third, half an hour later back on the first, which they then remain on all day, but at any moment this may change. True, all approach roads merge near the village, but by then all carriages are speeding along, whereas near the Castle the pace is somewhat more moderate. But just as the sequence of departures in relation to the roads is irregular and inscrutable, so too is the number of carriages. Indeed, there are often days when there's not a single carriage to be seen, but there soon are throngs of them out driving again. And just think of Father having to cope with all this. In his best suit, soon his only one, he sets off each morning from the house accompanied by our blessings. He takes along a small fire company badge, which he has kept illicitly, so that he can pin it on outside the village, he's afraid to show it in the village itself, though it's so small you can barely see it two paces away, and yet to Father's mind it's even supposed to be able to draw the attention of passing officials. Not far from the entrance to the Castle is a market garden, it belongs to one Bertuch who supplies the Castle with vegetables, there on the narrow stone pedestal of the garden fence Father selected a place for himself. Bertuch tolerated that because he had been friends with

Father and had been one of his most faithful customers; he has a rather crippled foot, you see, and believed that only Father was capable of making him a boot that fit. Father sat there day after day, it was a bleak rainy fall but he was utterly indifferent to the weather, each morning at a certain hour he put his hand on the latch and waved goodbye; in the evening—each day he seemed more stooped—he returned completely soaked and threw himself in a corner. First he described his little experiences, for instance, that Bertuch had thrown him a blanket over the fence out of compassion or old friendship, or that he thought he had recognized one or other official in a passing carriage, or that a coachman would recognize him from time to time and jokingly flick him with his whip. Later he stopped telling us these things, he had obviously given up hope of accomplishing anything there, he merely considered it his duty, his dreary vocation, to go and spend the day there. That was when he started getting rheumatic pains, winter was coming, snow fell early, the winters here begin very early, anyhow he sat there, first on the rain-drenched stones, then in the snow. At night he gasped with pain, in the morning there were times when he wasn't sure whether he should go, but then he overcame his reluctance and went. Mother clung to him and did not want to let him go, so probably out of anxiety over his no longer compliant limbs he let her go with him, and then before long Mother too was racked with the same pains. We often went to see them, brought them food or simply visited them or tried to persuade them to return home, how often we found them there, slumped on their narrow seat, leaning on each other, crouched in a thin blanket that barely covered them, with only the gray of snow and mist for surroundings and no person or carriage anywhere about, what a sight, K., what a sight! Until one morning Father could no longer get his stiff legs out of bed; he was inconsolable, in the delirium of a light fever he thought that he saw a carriage halt up at Bertuch's, an official get down, look for Father at the fence, shake his head angrily, and go back to the carriage. Meanwhile, Father let out screams as if he were determined to make the official up there notice him so that he could explain the blamelessness of his absence. And it turned into a long absence, he never went back, for weeks he had to remain in bed. Amalia took over all care, services, treatment, everything, and indeed, with a few breaks, she has kept it up to this day. She knows medicinal herbs that ease the pains, needs almost no sleep, is never startled, fears nothing, never becomes impatient, she did all the work for our parents; whereas we were unable to do anything to help and fluttered about uneasily, she remained cool and calm throughout. But when the worst was over and Father was able to work his way out of bed, carefully, supported on both sides, Amalia immediately withdrew and left him to us."

XX.

OLGA'S PLANS

"Then we had to find some occupation for Father that he could still do, anything that would at least support him in his belief that his work served to shift the guilt away from the family. Finding something like that wasn't difficult, for anything, essentially, could match the effectiveness of sitting outside Bertuch's garden, yet I found something that gave hope even to me. Each time the question of our guilt was raised in offices, by clerks, or elsewhere, there was only talk of the insult to Sortini's messenger, nobody dared to probe any further. Well, I said to myself, if people in general know only of the insult to the messenger, even if only seemingly so, then it would be possible, again even if only seemingly so, to make amends for everything if we succeeded in appeasing the messenger. Of course no complaint arrived, as has been stated, nor has the matter been taken up by any agency, and so the messenger is, in his capacity as an individual—and that's all that matters here—free to forgive. All of this couldn't possibly be of decisive importance, was merely an illusion, might once again lead nowhere, but still it would please Father, and in this way one might almost manage, perhaps even to his satisfaction, to drive into a corner the numerous information givers who had tormented him. But first, of course, the messenger had to be found. When I told Father of my plan, at first he became very annoyed; you see, he had become extremely stubborn, partly in the belief, which had come to him during his illness, that we had always prevented him from obtaining final victory, first by ending his subsidy and then by keeping him in bed, and partly because he was no longer capable of grasping the ideas of anybody else. I had not even come to the end of my story when my plan was rejected; he believed that he had to continue waiting at Bertuch's garden and that we should take him there in the handcart because he would no longer be able to climb up there every day. But I didn't relent and gradually he became reconciled to the idea, all that disturbed him was his complete dependence upon me, since I was the only one who had seen the messenger at the time, Father didn't know him. Of course one servant resembles the next, and even I wasn't entirely sure that I could recognize that one. Then we began to go to the Gentlemen's Inn to look among the servants there. True, he had been a servant of Sortini's and Sortini no longer came to the village, but the gentlemen often switch servants, we could surely find him in some other gentleman's group, and even if we didn't find him we might be able to gather information about him from the other servants. To that end we would have to spend every evening at the Gentlemen's Inn, and we weren't particularly welcome anywhere, especially not in a place of that sort, and of course it wasn't possible for us to go there as paying guests. But as it turned out, they actually were able to find some use for us, I'm sure you know what a torment the servants were for Frieda, mostly they are on the whole quiet people, the easy work makes them spoiled and ponderous, 'May you fare like a servant' is how officials wish somebody well, and it's said that when it comes to the good life the servants are the true masters at the Castle; they certainly do know how to appreciate that and while at the Castle, where they must move about under its laws, they are calm and dignified, I have heard various reports confirming this, and even among the servants here you find traces of it, but only traces, because in the village the laws of the Castle are no longer entirely applicable to them, they seem transformed, having turned into a wild, unruly horde, governed not by the laws but by their insatiable drives. Their shamelessness knows no bounds, it's lucky for the village that they can leave the Gentlemen's Inn only upon orders, but at the Gentlemen's Inn itself one has to try to get along with them; well, Frieda found that very difficult so she was very glad she could use me to calm the servants; for over two years now I have spent the night in the stable with the servants, at least twice a week. Earlier, when Father was still able to go to the Gentlemen's Inn he slept somewhere in the taproom waiting for the news that I used to bring in the morning. It was little enough. To this day we haven't found the messenger we sought, they say he's still working for Sortini, who has high regard for him, the messenger must have followed Sortini when he withdrew to more distant offices. The servants haven't seen him any more recently than we have, and if one of them insists that he has, then it's probably a mistake. So my plan might seem to have failed, but that isn't quite so, we haven't actually found the messenger, and the treks to the Gentlemen's Inn and the nights spent there, and perhaps even his compassion for me, if he's still capable of any such thing, have unfortunately almost finished off Father, and he has been in the condition in which you saw him for almost two years, but he may be faring better than Mother, whose end we expect each day, for it's been postponed only thanks to the superhuman efforts of Amalia. But what I did manage to do at the Gentlemen's Inn was establish a certain connection with the Castle; don't despise me if I say that I don't regret having acted as I did. But what could that important connection to the Castle possibly be, you may be asking yourself. And you're right, it certainly isn't an important connection. But I have come to know many servants, the servants of almost all the gentlemen who have come to the village over the last few years, and if I do reach the Castle someday, I won't be a stranger there. Of course, that was only the servants in the village, they're completely different at the Castle and probably wouldn't even recognize anyone anymore, especially not someone they have associated with in the village, even if they had sworn a hundred times in the stable that they were eagerly anticipating a reunion at the Castle. Besides, I know from experience how little all such promises mean. But that certainly isn't the most important thing. It's not only through the servants themselves that I have a connection with the Castle but perhaps also hopefully in such a way that whoever is observing me and my actions from up there—and managing the large staff of servants is of course an extremely important and vexatious part of official work—that the person observing me in that manner will perhaps reach a milder verdict about me than anyone else would, perhaps he will recognize that I too am fighting, no matter how miserably, for the sake of our family, and am continuing Father's efforts. If that is how they see things, then perhaps I will also be forgiven for accepting money from the servants and for using it for our family. And I accomplished something else, though you blame me for this too. I found out from the domestics that it is possible, for instance, in roundabout ways, without difficult official application proceedings, to enter the Castle services, but then you're not an official employee, only a secret semi-probationer, you don't have rights or duties, it's harder not having duties, though you do have some since you're close to everything and can notice favorable opportunities and take advantage of them, you aren't an employee, but then by chance some kind of work can turn up; just then there's no employee around, someone cries, you hurry over and the very thing that a moment ago you were not, namely an employee, you then become. But when can such opportunities be found? Sometimes right away, you have barely entered, barely looked around, and the opportunity is already at hand, but it is not everyone who already has, as a novice, enough presence of mind to immediately seize the chance, at other times this takes years longer than the proceedings for public admission, and for such semi-probationers there's no possibility whatsoever of a regular public admission. So a good many doubts arise; but they become moot since the candidates for public admission are most painstakingly selected, and any member of a family found to be in any way disreputable is immediately rejected; if such a person subjects himself to this proceeding, for instance, and spends years trembling about the outcome, everyone will ask in astonishment how he could dare to attempt anything so pointless, but he does have hope, for otherwise how could he live, though after many years, perhaps as an old man, he learns that he was rejected, finds out that all is lost and that his life was in vain. Of course here too there are exceptions, which is why one is so easily tempted. It sometimes happens that it's precisely those disreputable people who are finally accepted, there are some officials who very much against their own will love the smell of that sort of wild game, and during admission exams they sniff the air, twist their mouths, roll their eyes, men like that somehow seem to stir their appetite, and they must cling to the law books in order to be able to resist. But sometimes that doesn't help the man gain admission but only endlessly prolongs the admission proceedings, which are not terminated but simply broken off after the man dies. Thus both the legal admission and the other kind are full of open and hidden difficulties, and it certainly makes sense to weigh everything carefully before getting mixed up in anything of that sort. Well, we did not fail to do so, Barnabas and I. Each time I came from the Gentlemen's Inn we sat down together, I talked about my latest discovery, we discussed it for days, and it wasn't good that the work in Barnabas's hands went untouched for so long. And here I may be at fault from your point of view. After all, I knew the domestics' stories weren't very reliable. I knew that they never had the slightest desire to tell me about the Castle and always diverted attention elsewhere, they made us beg for each word, but of course once they got going, they let rip, talked gibberish, bragged, outdid one another with exaggerations and fabrications, so that the constant shouting everybody took turns at inside the dark stable must have obviously at best contained only a few meager hints of the truth. I told all this to Barnabas, just as I had seen it, and he, who was still utterly incapable of separating truth from lies and, because of our family circumstances, almost thirsted with longing for these matters, drank everything in, and glowed with fervor for more. And my new plan did indeed rely on Barnabas. No more could be accomplished through the domestics. Sortini's messenger was not to be found and would never be found; Sortini, and therefore his messenger too, seemed to have receded ever farther, people had often forgotten their appearance and their names, so I often had to describe them at length, with no result other than that they remembered them with great difficulty, but that's all they could say about them. And as far as my life with the domestics was concerned, I had no say of course in how they pronounced judgment on it, and could only hope that they would take that episode in the spirit in which it had been engaged in and therefore deduct a small part of our family's guilt, but I got no outward signs of that. Still, I kept it up since I could see no other possibility of our accomplishing anything at the Castle. For Barnabas, though, I could see a possibility of that sort. From the domestics' stories I could deduce, if I wanted to, as I certainly do, that anyone who is admitted to the Castle services can accomplish a great deal for his family. But then, of course, how credible were these stories? That was impossible to determine, but I knew it was little enough. For if, say, I was solemnly assured by a domestic, whom I would never see again or would hardly recognize even if I did, that he would help my brother find a position at the Castle, or at least support him if Barnabas were somehow to enter the Castle, say by providing him with refreshment, for according to the stories the domestics tell, in the course of the excessively long waiting periods it does happen that applicants for positions faint or become confused and then they are lost, unless their friends watch out for them—when these warnings alerted me to such matters and much else besides, they were probably justified, but the promises accompanying them were absolutely empty. But not for Barnabas, whom I cautioned against believing in such promises, but even the mere mention of them won him over to my plans. The examples I gave didn't greatly impress him, he was far more impressed with the stories of the domestics. And so I was actually thrown back on my own resources, no one except for Amalia could get through to our parents, the more I pursued Father's old plans in my own way, the more Amalia cut herself off from me; she still speaks to me in front of you and others, but not when the two of us are alone; for the domestics at the Gentlemen's Inn I was a plaything, which they kept trying to break; throughout those two years I have never said an intimate word to any of them, nothing but dissimulation, lies, or craziness, so I had only Barnabas to turn to, and Barnabas was still very young. While informing him of all this, I noticed the gleam in his eyes, which he still has; I was startled but didn't give up, for I thought the stakes were too high. True, I didn't have the great if empty plans of my father, and I also lacked the determination that men possess, I stuck to the task of making amends for the insult to the messenger and even wanted to get credit for my modesty. But what I had failed to do alone I now wanted to achieve through Barnabas in a different and more secure way. After we had insulted a messenger and driven him from the front offices, we took what was surely the most natural step and offered them a new messenger in the shape of Barnabas, who would carry out the duties of the insulted messenger and thus make it possible for the insulted party to bide his time quietly someplace, at some remove, for as long as he wanted, for as long as he needed to forget the insult. But I fully realized that, for all its modesty, this plan wasn't lacking in presumption, for it might seem as though we wanted to dictate to the authorities how they should settle personnel matters or as if we doubted that the authorities were capable of arranging everything in the best way through their own devices and had even made arrangements long before it dawned on us that anything could be done here. But then again I thought it impossible that the authorities should misunderstand me in that way or, even if they did, that they would do so intentionally, that they would in other words reject everything I do from the outset, without further scrutiny. So I didn't relent, and Barnabas's ambition took care of the rest. During the preparations Barnabas became so arrogant that he began to feel that a shoemaker's job was too dirty for a future office employee like him, and on those rare occasions when Amalia spoke to him he even had the audacity to contradict her outright. I didn't begrudge him this short-lived joy, for, as could easily have been foreseen, on the very first day he went to the Castle his joy and his arrogance instantly disappeared. It was the start of that apparent service I've already told you about. It was astonishing that Barnabas had no difficulty entering the Castle, or rather the office which has become his workplace, as it were. This success almost made me go mad, the moment Barnabas whispered me news of it when he came home I ran to Amalia, grabbed her, pressed her into a corner, and kissed her with lips and teeth, causing her to weep in pain and fright. I was so agitated I couldn't say a word, besides we hadn't spoken to each other in a long time, I therefore put off the conversation for a few days. But of course over the next few days there was no reason to talk. After those rapid gains, that was it. And then for two years Barnabas led that monotonous wrenching life. The domestics let us down completely; I gave Barnabas a short letter to take along, commending him to the care of the domestics, whom I at the same time reminded of their promises, and whenever Barnabas saw a domestic he pulled out the letter and held it up in front of his eyes, and though he had probably come across domestics who didn't know me, and though his way of showing the letter without saying a word—he doesn't dare to speak up there—irritated my acquaintances, all the same it was shameful that nobody helped him, and it was a deliverance, which we admittedly could have brought about a long time ago on our own, when a domestic, who may have several times had the letter thrust at him, crumpled it up and threw it into a wastebasket. It even occurred to me that he could almost have said: 'After all, you treat letters the same way too.' But, however fruitless this entire period, it had a positive effect on Barnabas, if one wants to describe as positive his aging before his time and prematurely becoming a man, in some ways earnest and insightful beyond manhood itself. It often saddens me to look at him and to compare him with the youth he was even two years ago. And yet I do not get from him any of the consolation and support that he might be able to give me as a man. Without me, he would hardly have got into the Castle, but ever since going up there he has become independent of me. I'm the only one he confides in, but he probably tells me only a fraction of what he has on his mind. He tells me a great deal about the Castle, but from his stories, from the little facts he discloses, it's impossible to gather how this can have so greatly transformed him. It is especially difficult to understand why up there, as a man, he has so completely lost the courage which, when he was a boy, was enough to drive us to despair. Of course this futile standing around, this waiting around over and over again for days on end without any prospect of change, is wearying and fills you with despair and finally even makes you unable to do anything better than stand around in desperation. But why didn't he resist earlier? Especially since he soon noticed that I had been right and that there was nothing there to further his goal, though one could probably take advantage of certain things to improve our family's lot. For up there everything, except for the whims of the servants, is quite modest, and since ambition seeks fulfillment in work and the task itself becomes paramount, eventually all ambition disappears; there is no reason to indulge in childish wishes there. Still, Barnabas was convinced, he told me, that he could clearly see how power and knowledge were wielded even by those rather dubious officials whose rooms he could enter. How they dictated, quickly, with half-closed eyes and brief gestures; how, only with their index finger, wordlessly, they dispatched the surly servants who, breathing heavily at such moments, smiled happily, or how they found an important passage in their books, pounded on it, and the others, insofar as this was possible in the confined space, ran up and stretched their necks out toward it. Such things gave Barnabas exalted ideas about these men and he had the impression that if he advanced far enough to be noticed and could exchange a few words with them not as a stranger but as an office colleague, if only of the most subordinate kind, then it would be possible to obtain unforeseen benefits for our family. But things have simply not yet gone that far, and Barnabas doesn't dare to undertake anything that might take him closer to that goal, though he is keenly aware that within the family, because of the unfortunate circumstances and despite his youth, he has moved up and taken on the heavy responsibility of acting as head of the family. And there's one other thing I must confess: It has been a week now since you arrived. I heard someone say so at the Gentlemen's Inn but paid no attention to it; a land surveyor had come, I didn't even know what that was. But the following evening Barnabas comes home earlier than usual—at a set time I used to go to meet him partway—and seeing Amalia in the room, he pulls me out onto the street, presses his face down on my shoulder, and weeps for several minutes. He has again become the little boy he once was. Something has happened to him, and he's clearly no match for it. It's as if a completely new world has opened up before him and he cannot stand the happiness and worries stemming from the novelty of it all. And yet all that happened to him was that he received a letter to deliver to you. Still, it is the first letter, the first task he has ever been given."

Olga broke off. It was quiet except for her parents' heavy and at times rattlelike breathing. K. said casually, as if elaborating on Olga's story: "You put on a show for my benefit. Like an old, harried messenger Barnabas delivered the letter, and you as well as Amalia, who for once sided with you, pretended that the messenger service and the letters were simply something on the side." "You must distinguish between the two of us," said Olga, "those two letters made Barnabas a happy child again, despite all his doubts about his task. He confesses these doubts only to himself and to me, but he wants to find honor in your eyes by acting like a real messenger, the way he thinks real messengers act. And therefore, to give you one example, despite his increasing hope of obtaining an official suit, I had to tailor his trousers within two hours, so that they would at least resemble the tight-fitting trousers of the official clothing and he could pass muster in front of you, who in that respect are of course still quite easy to deceive. So much for Barnabas. But Amalia really despises the messenger service, and now that he's apparently had some minor success, which she can easily detect from the way Barnabas and I sit about whispering, she despises it even more than before. She is therefore telling the truth, don't ever fool yourself by doubting that. K., if I sometimes disparaged the messenger service, it was not with any intention of deceiving you but out of fear. The two letters that have passed through Barnabas's hands so far are the first, if still rather doubtful, signs of favor that our family has received in three years. This change, if it actually is a change in fortune rather than an illusion—illusions are more common than changes in fortune—is connected to your arrival here, our fate has become somewhat dependent on you, perhaps these two letters are only the beginning and Barnabas's occupation will soon go beyond delivering messages dealing with you—let's hope so, for as long as we can—but for now everything is aimed solely at you. Up there we have to be satisfied with whatever they assign us, but down here perhaps we can do something for ourselves as well, namely: assure ourselves of your favor or at least preserve ourselves from your dislike or, most important, protect you to the best of our ability and experience so that you don't end up losing your connection to the Castle, which we might be able to live on. What would be the best way to bring this about? So that you're not suspicious of us when we approach you, for you are a stranger here and are no doubt filled with suspicion about everything, filled with justified suspicion. Besides, people despise us, and you're influenced by that prevailing view, especially through your fiancée, so how should we get through to you without for example, however unintentionally, opposing your fiancée and hurting your feelings. And the messages, which I read carefully before you received them—Barnabas didn't read them, as a messenger he wouldn't allow himself to do so—first seemed quite unimportant, obsolete; they undermined their own importance by referring you to the council chairman. And how should we treat you in that regard? If we stressed their importance we would make people suspect that we were overrating something that was obviously so unimportant merely so as to recommend ourselves to you as the bearers of this news and to pursue our own ends instead of yours, and in the end we might even devalue the news in your eyes, and in that way, very much against our will, deceive you. But if we didn't attach much importance to the letters we should make ourselves just as suspect, for why were we taking the time to deliver these unimportant letters, why did our behavior contradict our words, why were we deceiving not only you, the addressee, but our employer, who certainly hadn't handed us the letters so that we would go and make statements that might lessen their value for the addressee. And staying in the middle between the exaggerations, that is, weighing the letters correctly is impossible, their value keeps changing, the thoughts that they prompt are endless and the point at which one happens to stop is determined only by accident and so the opinion one arrives at is just as accidental. And if fear for your sake comes into this too, then everything becomes confused; you shouldn't judge these words of mine too harshly. If, for instance, as actually happened once, Barnabas comes with the news that you're dissatisfied with his service as a messenger and that he himself has, in the initial shock and unfortunately not without showing some sign of a messenger's testiness, offered to resign from this service, then I could, in order to make amends for the error, deceive, lic, swindle, and do absolutely any bad thing if it would only help. But then I'm doing it, at least that's what I believe, as much for your sake as for ours."

Someone knocked. Olga ran to the door and unlocked it. A streak of light from a covered lantern breached the darkness. The belated visitor asked questions in a whisper and received answers in a whisper but wasn't satisfied with that and tried to force his way into the room. Olga evidently couldn't hold him back any longer and therefore called Amalia, obviously in hopes that

Amalia would, in an effort to protect her parents' sleep, do anything to get rid of the visitor. And she actually did hurry over, push Olga aside, step out into the street, and shut the door behind her. It took only a moment, she came back right away, having quickly accomplished what Olga had been unable to do.

K. then learned from Olga that the visit had been intended for him, it had been one of the assistants who had come to look for him on instructions from Frieda. Olga had tried to shield K. from the assistant; if K. wanted to confess his visit here to Frieda later on he was free to do so, but it shouldn't be discovered by the assistant; K. gave his approval. But he declined Olga's offer that he spend the night here waiting for Barnabas; he might have accepted this on its own merits, for it had already become quite late and it seemed to him that he was now so connected to this family, whether he wanted to be or not, that a night's lodgings here, though perhaps embarrassing for other reasons, would because of that connection be the most natural place in the entire village for him; nevertheless, he refused, the assistant's visit had startled him, it was incomprehensible to him that Frieda, who knew what he wanted, and the assistants, who had learned to fear him, should have teamed up again in such a way that Frieda even went so far as to send an assistant for him, but only one, the other must have stayed behind with her. He asked Olga whether she had a whip but she did not have one, though she had a good willow switch, which he took; then he asked whether there was any other exit from the house, there was one such exit through the courtyard, only then you had to clamber over the fence of the next-door garden and cross that garden before you came to the street. K. resolved to do so. While Olga was leading him across the courtyard to the fence, K. attempted to calm her worries by explaining that far from being angry at her because of the little tricks in her story he actually understood her quite well and wished to thank her for the confidence she had in him, which she had demonstrated through her story; he instructed her to send Barnabas back to the schoolhouse the moment he returned, even if it was still dark. Though Barnabas's messages weren't his only hope, otherwise he would be in a bad way, he certainly didn't want to give them up, he wanted to hold on to them without forgetting Olga; almost more important to him than the messages was Olga herself, her bravery, her prudence, her cleverness, and her sacrifices for her family. If given a choice between Olga and Amalia, it wouldn't take long to decide. And he pressed her hand warmly as he swung himself up onto the fence of the garden next door.

Once he stood out on the street he saw, insofar as he could see anything at all on this bleak night, the assistant walking back and forth up there outside Barnabas's house, sometimes coming to a halt in an effort to shine a light through a curtained window into the room. K. called out to him; without seeming at all startled, he gave up spying on the house and came toward K. "Who are you looking for?" asked K., testing the suppleness of the willow switch on his thigh. "You," said the assistant, coming closer. "Well, who are you?" K. suddenly said, since it did not seem to be the assistant. He seemed older, wearier, more wrinkled, but with a fuller face, even his gait was completely different from the assistants', which was nimble, as though their joints were electrified; he walked slowly, limping slightly, elegantly infirm. "You don't recognize me," said the man, "I'm Jeremias, your old assistant." "Oh?" said K., pulling out the willow switch, which he had hidden behind his back. "But you look quite different." "That's because I'm alone," said Jeremias. "When I'm alone, carefree youth is gone." "So where's Artur?" asked K. "Artur?" asked Jeremias, "the little darling? He has given up his duties. But you were a little too harsh with us. The delicate soul couldn't stand it. He went back to the Castle and is filing a complaint against you." "And you?" asked K. "I was able to stay," said Jeremias, "Artur is filing the complaint for me too." "What are you complaining about?" asked K. "We are complaining," said Jeremias, "that you cannot take a joke. Now then, what did we do? Joked a bit, laughed a bit, teased your fiancée a bit. And all this, by the way, in accordance with instructions. When Galater sent us to you—" "Galater?" asked K. "Yes, Galater," said Jeremias, "he was Klamm's substitute at the time. When he sent us to you, he said—I remember since that's what we're referring to—'You're being sent there as assistants of the surveyor.' We said: 'But we don't know anything about that kind of work.' At that he said: 'That isn't so important; if it becomes necessary he will teach you. But it's important that you should cheer him up a bit. From what I hear, he takes everything very seriously. He has come to the village and right away thinks this is some great event, but in reality it's nothing at all. You should teach him that.'" "Well," said K., "was Galater right and did you carry out your instructions?" "I don't know," said Jeremias, "in that short time it may not have been possible. All I know is that you were very crude and that's what we're complaining about. I don't understand how you, who are only an employee after all, and not even a Castle employee at that, can fail to see that this kind of duty is hard work and that it's very wrong to make the work even more difficult for the worker, in a willful, almost childish manner, as you have done. How thoughtless it was of you to leave us freezing at the fence, or again how, on the mattress, you struck Artur an almost mortal blow, Artur, someone who feels the pain of a cross word for days; how that afternoon you chased me back and forth in the snow in such a way that I needed an hour to recover from the mad rush. After all, I'm no longer young!" "Dear Jeremias," said K., "everything that you're saying is right, only you should raise this matter with Galater. He sent the two of you here of his own free will, I didn't request you from him. And since I didn't ask for you, I was free to send you back and would rather have done so peacefully than by use of force, but that's clearly how the two of you wanted it. By the way, when you first came to me, why didn't you speak as openly as you do now?" "Because I was on duty," said Jeremias, "but that goes without saying." "And you're no longer on duty?" asked K. "No longer," said Jeremias, "Artur has given notice at the Castle, or at least the procedure is under way and should free us at last." "But you're still looking for me as though you were on duty," said K. "No," said Jeremias. "I'm looking for you only to reassure

Frieda. When you left her because of the Barnabas girls she was very unhappy, not so much at the loss as at your having betrayed her, though she had seen it coming a long time and had already suffered a lot because of it. I had just come back to the schoolhouse window to see whether you mightn't have become more reasonable. But you weren't there, only Frieda was, sitting on a school bench, weeping. So I went up to her and we came to an understanding. And everything has already been taken care of. I'm a room waiter at the Gentlemen's Inn, at least while my case at the Castle remains unresolved, and Frieda is back in the taproom. It's certainly better for Frieda this way. It made no sense for her to become your wife. Besides, you could not appreciate the sacrifice she was willing to make for you. But the good woman is having second thoughts, perhaps she actually wronged you, perhaps you weren't really at Barnabas's. Even though there was of course no doubt at all as to your whereabouts, I came here to establish conclusively that that was indeed the case; for after all that great excitement Frieda finally deserves a good night's sleep, as do I. So I came here and not only found you but on the side also noticed the way those girls are at your beck and call. Especially the black-haired one, a real wildcat, put herself out for you. Well, each to his own taste. In any case there was no need for you to make that detour through the next-door garden, I know that path."

XXI.

Well, so it had actually happened, as one could have foreseen, but there was no way it could have been prevented. Frieda had abandoned him. This wouldn't have to be final, it wasn't that bad, Frieda could be won back, she was easily influenced by strangers, even by those assistants, who thought that Frieda's position resembled their own and who, since they had given notice, caused Frieda to do so too, but K. need only go up to her, remind her of everything that spoke in his favor, and she would once again be his, would even be full of remorse, especially if he could justify the visit to the girls with a success that he owed to them. But despite these thoughts with which he sought to calm himself with regard to Frieda, he was not calm. Just a little while ago he had boasted to Olga about Frieda, calling her his only support, well, it was not the most stable kind of support; stealing Frieda from K. did not require the intervention of some powerful figure, all it took was this not particularly appetizing assistant, whose flesh sometimes gave one the impression that it wasn't quite alive.

Jeremias had already begun to leave, K. called him back. "Jeremias," he said, "I want to be very open with you, and so do answer the question I have honestly asked. Our relationship is no longer that of master and servant, and I'm as pleased by that as you are, and so we don't have any reason to deceive each other. And now before your very eyes I will break this switch which was meant for you, for it wasn't out of fear of you that I chose the path through the garden but in order to surprise you and to take a few swipes at you with the switch. Well, don't hold it against me anymore, that's all over; if you weren't a servant imposed on me by the authorities but simply an acquaintance of mine we would certainly have got along extremely well, though your appearance sometimes bothers me a little. And we could certainly make up for all the things of that sort that we've neglected." "You think so?" said the assistant and, yawning, he rubbed his weary eyes, "well, I could tell you about it in greater detail, but I haven't time, I must go to Frieda, the dear child is waiting for me, she hasn't begun her duties yet, for at my request the landlord gave her a little time to recuperate—she wanted to throw herself into the work right away, no doubt so as to forget everything—and that time at least we want to spend together. As for your proposal, I certainly have no reason for lying to you, but just as little reason for confiding anything in you. You see, the situation is different for me than it is for you. As long as my relationship to you was an official one, you were of course a very important person to me, not because of your own qualities but because of my official instructions, and I would have done anything for you at the time, but now I couldn't care less about you. I'm not moved by your having broken the willow switch either, that only reminds me what a callous master I had, it's hardly likely to win me over." "You speak to me," said K., "as though it were very certain that you need never fear anything from me again. But that is not so. You're probably not rid of me yet, they don't reach decisions that quick here—" "Sometimes even quicker," Jeremias threw in. "Sometimes," said K., "but nothing points to that having happened this time, at any rate neither of us has a written decision. So the proceedings have only just begun, and I haven't even intervened in them yet with the help of my connections, but I will do so. If the results are not in your favor then you certainly won't have done much to predispose your master in your favor and perhaps there was no need for me to break the willow switch. True, you carried off Frieda, and that especially is what has given you a swollen head, but I must say, despite all my respect for you as a person, even if you no longer have any for me, that if I addressed a few words to Frieda it would be enough, I'm sure, to rip apart the lies with which you've ensnared her. And only lies could draw Frieda away from me." "Threats like that don't frighten me," said Jeremias, "you don't want me as an assistant, you even fear me as an assistant, you are particularly fearful of assistants, it was only out of fear that you hit dear Artur." "Perhaps," said K., "but did it hurt any less because of that? Perhaps I will often be able to show my fear of you in the same way. If I see that your assistantship isn't giving you much joy, I will, despite all that fear, take the greatest pleasure in forcing you to do your duty. And indeed this time I shall make a point of getting hold of you alone, without Artur, and then I can devote special attention to you." "Do you really think," said Jeremias, "that I have even the slightest fear of any of that?" "I certainly do," said K., "you certainly fear me a little, and, if you're clever, a great deal. If not, why haven't you gone to Frieda? Tell me, are you fond of her?" "Fond?" said Jeremias, "she's a good and also clever girl, a former mistress of Klamm's, so she's definitely respectable. And if she keeps asking me to rescue her from you, why shouldn't I oblige her, especially since it doesn't do any harm to you, who consoled yourself with the accursed Barnabases." "I see your fear now," said K., "what a miserable fear it is, you're trying to ensnare me with your lies. Frieda asked only one thing of me, that I should rescue her from those frenzied and doggishly licentious assistants, unfortunately I didn't have time to do all she asked and the consequences of my omission are now there."

"Surveyor! Surveyor!" someone was shouting up the street. It was Barnabas. He was out of breath but did not forget to bow before K. "I succeeded," he said. "What did you succeed in doing?" asked K. "You have presented my request to Klamm?" "There was no way that could be done," said Barnabas, "I tried very hard but it was impossible, I pushed my way forward, and, without being asked, spent all day standing so close to the desk that a clerk in whose light I was standing even pushed me away, each time Klamm looked up I announced my presence by raising my hand, even though that is forbidden, stayed in the office longest, was the only one left with the servants, had once again the pleasure of seeing Klamm return, but it wasn't for me, he merely wanted to check something else in a book quickly and then went away again at once, and in the end the servant, seeing that I still hadn't moved, took his broom and almost swept me out the door. I'm admitting all this so that you won't be dissatisfied with my accomplishments again." "Barnabas, what good is all your diligence to me," said K., "if you had no success at all." "But I did have some success," said Barnabas. "As I stepped from my office—I call it my office—I see a gentleman coming from the corridors deeper inside, the entire place was already empty, it was already very late, I decided to wait for him, it was a good opportunity to stay a bit longer there, besides I would rather have stayed there than bring you the bad news. But for other reasons too the gentleman was worth waiting for, it was Erlanger. You don't know him? He's one of the first secretaries of Klamm. A short, frail gentleman with a slight limp. He recognized me at once, he's well known for his memory and for his ability to judge people, he simply knits his brow, that's all it takes for him to recognize anyone, often even people whom he's never seen before, whom he has only heard or read about, and in my case, for instance, he could hardly have seen me before. But though he recognizes everyone right away, he asks first as though he were unsure: 'Aren't you Barnabas?' he said to me. And then he asked: 'You know the surveyor, don't you?' And then he said: 'That's convenient. I'm going to the Gentlemen's Inn. The surveyor should visit me there. I'm in room 15. But he would need to come at once. I have only a few meetings there and go back tomorrow morning at five. Tell him that I set great store on speaking to him.'"

Suddenly Jeremias took flight. Barnabas, who in his agitation had barely noticed him, asked: "What is Jeremias up to?" "Trying to beat me to Erlanger's," said K., who ran after Jeremias, caught up with him, took his arm, and said: "Was it the longing for Frieda that suddenly overcame you? It's no less strong in me, so we'll go there in step."

Standing in front of the dark Gentlemen's Inn was a small group of men, two or three were holding lanterns in such a way that some faces were recognizable. K. found only a single acquaintance, Gerstäcker the coachman. Gerstäcker greeted him with a question: "You're still in the village?" "Yes," said K., "I came here for good." "That's really no concern of mine," said Gerstäcker, coughing loudly, and he turned toward the others.

It became clear that they were all waiting for Erlanger. Erlanger had already come but was still negotiating with Momus before receiving the parties. The general tenor of the conversation concerned their not being allowed to wait in the building and having to stand outside in the snow. It wasn't very cold, to be sure, nevertheless it was inconsiderate to keep the parties standing in front of the house at night, perhaps for hours. That wasn't of course the fault of Erlanger, who was, on the contrary, most obliging, probably did not know about it, and would certainly have been quite annoyed had it been reported to him. It was the fault of the landlady at the Gentlemen's Inn, who in her already quite pathological striving for refinement couldn't bear to have a large number of parties coming into the Gentlemen's Inn at the same time. "If it's really necessary and they must come," she often said, "then for heaven's sake, always only one by one." And she had seen to it that the parties, who at first had simply waited in a corridor, later on the staircase, then in the corridor, and finally in the taproom, were ultimately pushed out onto the street. And even that wasn't enough to satisfy her. She found it unbearable being, as she put it, constantly "under siege" in her own house. She couldn't understand the point of holding office hours for the parties. "To dirty the front steps of the inn," an official had once said in response to a question from her, most likely in anger, but to her the remark seemed very convincing and she liked to quote it often. Her goal—and here her aspirations coincided with the wishes of the parties—was to see that a building was built across from the Gentlemen's Inn, where the parties could wait. She would have much preferred that the meetings with the parties and the interrogations be held outside the Gentlemen's Inn, but the officials opposed this idea, and anything that was seriously opposed by the officials was naturally unattainable for the landlady, though in minor issues she succeeded through her indefatigable but at the same time femininely delicate zeal in exercising a kind of minor tyranny. The landlady would probably have to continue to endure the meetings and interrogations at the Gentlemen's Inn, for while in the village the Castle officials refused to leave the Gentlemen's Inn on official business. They were always in a hurry, for it was only very much against their will that they were in the village, they hadn't the slightest desire to prolong their stay here beyond what was absolutely necessary, and so it wasn't reasonable to expect that they should, simply for the sake of ensuring peace and quiet at the Gentlemen's Inn, temporarily move into some house across the street with all their writings and thereby lose time. The officials far preferred to discharge their official business in the taproom or in their own rooms, if at all possible during a meal or from their beds before going to sleep, or in the morning when they were too tired to get up and wanted to stretch out in bed a little while longer. On the other hand, the question of whether to construct a building for the waiting parties seemed about to be resolved; still, it was quite a severe punishment for the landlady—people had a good little laugh over this—that the waiting-room issue required many meetings and that the corridors of the inn were rarely empty.

All these matters were discussed in a low voice by those waiting outside. K. found it remarkable that, though there was a great deal of dissatisfaction, nobody had any objection to Erlanger's summoning the parties in the middle of the night. He asked about this and was informed that one ought to be grateful to Erlanger for that. It's only his goodwill and the exalted idea that he has of his office that makes him come down to the village in the first place, for he certainly could, if he wanted to—and that might be more in accordance with the regulations—send some undersecretary and get him to take the depositions. But he usually refused to do that, he wanted to see and hear everything for himself, but was obliged to sacrifice his nights for that purpose, since no time was set aside in his official schedule for journeys to the village. K. objected that, after all, Klamm also came to the village during the day and even stayed for days at a time; was Erlanger, who after all was only a secretary, more indispensable up there? A few laughed good-naturedly, others remained silent out of embarrassment, the latter soon gained the upper hand, and K. barely received an answer. Only one of them responded hesitantly by saying that Klamm was naturally indispensable, in the Castle as well as in the village.

Then the front door opened and Momus appeared, flanked by two servants carrying lamps. "The first to be admitted to see Secretary Erlanger," he said, "are: Gerstäcker and K. Are those two here?" They answered, but Jeremias slipped ahead of them, saying "I work here as a room waiter," was greeted with a smile and a slap on the shoulder by Momus, and entered the house. "I must pay closer attention to Jeremias," K. told himself while remaining aware that Jeremias was probably far less dangerous than Artur, who was working against him at the Castle. Perhaps it was even wiser to let them torment him as his assistants rather than have them prowling about unchecked and freely engaging in intrigues, for which they seemed to have a special talent.

As K. went past, Momus pretended that he had only just noticed it was the surveyor. "Oh, if it isn't the surveyor!" he said, "the gentleman who so disliked being interrogated is now pushing his way in to an interrogation. It would have been far easier with me back then. But of course it's difficult to choose the right interrogations." K. was about to stop in response to this remark but Momus said: "Go! Go! Back then I could have used your answers, but not now." In spite of this, K., agitated by Momus's behavior, said: "You're thinking only of yourselves. Simply for the sake of the office I won't answer, neither then nor now." Momus said: "Well, whom else should we be thinking of? Who else is here? Do go!"

In the corridor they were received by a servant who led them along the path already known to K., across the courtyard and then through the gate into the low, slightly sloping passageway. The upper floors were evidently occupied only by the higher officials and this corridor here only by the secretaries, including Erlanger, though he was one of the highest-ranking in their midst. The servant put out his lantern, for there was bright electric lighting in here. Everything here was small, but delicately built. Full advantage had been taken of the space. The passage barely sufficed for walking upright. On the sides, one door came immediately after the next. The side walls didn't reach the ceiling; this was probably to ensure ventilation, for the little rooms in this deep cellarlike corridor surely had no windows. The drawback of these walls that didn't quite meet the ceiling was the noise in the corridor, and therefore, inevitably, in the rooms too. Many rooms seemed occupied, in several of them people were still awake, one could hear voices, hammer blows, clinking glasses. But this didn't leave one with the impression of great merriment. The voices were hushed, one could barely understand a word every now and then, but it didn't seem like conversation, it was probably only somebody dictating something, or reading something aloud, and it was precisely from those rooms giving off the sound of clinking glasses and plates that one couldn't hear a word, and the hammer blows reminded K. of something he had been told somewhere, namely, that in order to recuperate from the constant mental effort some officials occasionally took up cabinetmaking, precision toolmaking, and the like. The actual corridor itself was empty except for a spot by a door where sat a pale, slender, tall gentleman in a fur coat with his nightclothes showing underneath, the room had probably become too stuffy for him, so he had sat down outside, where he was reading a newspaper, though not attentively, he often gave up reading with a yawn, then leaned out and looked along the corridor, perhaps he was expecting a party whom he had summoned and who had failed to come. After they had passed him, the servant said to Gerstäcker concerning the gentleman: "Pinzgauer!" Gerstäcker nodded: "He hasn't been down in a long time," he said. "Not in a very long time," confirmed the servant.

Finally they came to a door no different from the others but behind which, so the servant reported, lived Erlanger. Having asked K. to lift him up on his shoulders, the servant looked in through the narrow opening on top. "He's lying on the bed," he said, climbing down, "he has his clothes on, but I think he's dozing. Sometimes he is quite overcome by weariness here in the village because the way of life is so different. We will have to wait. When he wakes up, he'll ring. There have been times when he has slept through his entire stay in the village, and then when he woke up he had to go back at once to the Castle. In any case it's voluntary, the work he does here." "If only he would choose to sleep through to the end," said Gerstäcker, "for when he wakes up again and finds he has little time to finish his work, he's quite indignant at having slept and tries to expedite everything in a hurry, and one can hardly discuss one's concerns." "You've come because of the assignment of haulage contracts for the building?" asked the servant. Gerstäcker nodded, pulled the servant aside, and spoke quietly to him, but the servant was barely listening, he was looking out over Gerstäcker, whom he towered over by more than a head, while earnestly, deliberately stroking his hair.

XXII.

At that moment K., who was looking around aimlessly, saw Frieda some distance away at a bend in the corridor; she pretended not to recognize him, merely fixed her gaze on him; in one hand she held a tray with empty dishes. He said to the servant, who did not pay the slightest attention to him—the more you spoke to the servant, the more absentminded he seemed to become—that he would be back at once, and ran to Frieda. When he reached her, he grabbed her by the shoulders as though seizing possession of her again, and asked some trivial questions while looking quizzically into her eyes. But her rigid posture scarcely relaxed; distractedly she tried to rearrange the dishes on the tray and said: "What is it you want from me? Just go to those—you know their names, you've just come from them, I can tell from the way you look." K. quickly changed the subject; that discussion shouldn't begin so suddenly nor with the worst matters, with those least favorable to him. "I thought you were in the taproom," he said. Frieda looked at him in astonishment, then ran her one free hand gently over his forehead and cheek. It was as if she had forgotten what he looked like and wanted to recall it that way, her eyes too had the blurred look of somebody trying with great difficulty to remember something. "I've been taken on for the taproom again," she said slowly, as if what she was saying was not important but beneath the words she was holding a conversation with K. and this was what was important, "this work doesn't suit me, anybody could do it, anybody who can make beds and put on a friendly face and does not fear being pestered by the guests but even invites it, any such person can be a chambermaid. But in the taproom it's somewhat different. I was immediately taken on in the taproom again, though I didn't leave it all that honorably earlier, but of course now I had patronage. But the landlord was glad that I had patronage, and that it was therefore easy for him to take me back. They even had to pressure me to accept the post; if you think about what the taproom reminds me of, you'll have no difficulty understanding that. In the end I accepted the position. But I'm only here temporarily. Pepi asked that she not be obliged to endure the disgrace of having to leave the taproom right away, and since she did her work diligently and saw to everything, to the extent that this was possible with her limited abilities, we have given her a twenty-four-hour extension." "That's a great arrangement," said K., "only you once left the taproom for my sake, and now, just before the wedding, you want to go back?" "There will be no wedding," said Frieda. "Because I was unfaithful?" asked K. Frieda nodded. "Look here, Frieda," said K., "we have often talked about this so-called infidelity and you always had to acknowledge in the end that the suspicion was unjust. Since then there has been no change on my side, everything is still as innocent as it was, and must always remain so. Something must therefore have changed on your side, through the insinuations of strangers or for other reasons. In any case you're treating me unjustly, for look, how do matters really stand with these two girls? One of them, the dark one—I'm almost ashamed at having to defend myself at such length, but you invited it—anyhow, the dark one is probably no less embarrassing to me than she is to you; whenever I can keep away from her somehow or other, I do so, and she even makes that easy, one cannot possibly be more reserved than she is." "Yes," cried Frieda, her words came out as though against her will; K. was glad to see her being distracted in this way; she was not what she wanted to be, "you may think she's reserved, you call the most shameless of them all reserved, and this, unbelievable as it is, is your honest opinion, you're not pretending, I know that. The landlady at the Bridge Inn says of you: I cannot stand him but cannot abandon him either, just as on seeing a little child who cannot quite walk venture off too far, one cannot restrain oneself, one must intervene." "You should accept her warning," said K., smiling, "but that girl, no matter how reserved or shameless she is, we can leave aside, I do not want to hear another word about her." "But why do you call her reserved?" Frieda asked implacably, K. interpreted this expression of interest as a sign favorable to him, "have you put it to the test or is this simply an attempt to disparage somebody else?" "Neither the one nor the other," said K., "I call her that out of gratitude, because she makes it easy for me to overlook her and because I couldn't get myself to go there again no matter how often she spoke to me, which would certainly be a great loss for me, since I must, as you know, go there for the sake of our common future. And that's another reason why I have to speak to the other girl, whom I respect for her diligence, prudence, and selflessness, but nobody can really claim that she is seductive." "The domestics don't agree," said Frieda. "In this and no doubt also in many other respects as well," said K. "Are you trying to draw conclusions about my unfaithfulness from the lusting of the domestics?" Frieda remained silent and allowed K. to take the tray from her hand, put it on the floor, slide his arm under hers, and walk slowly back and forth with her in the cramped space. "You have no idea what faithfulness is," she said, trying to fend off his closeness, "however you may have behaved with the girls, that's not the most important thing; that you should go there to that family at all and come back with the smell of their room in your clothes is already an unbearable disgrace for me. And you run out of the schoolhouse without saying a word. And you even spend half the night there. And when anyone asks whether you're there, you have those girls deny it, and deny it passionately they do, especially the one who is said to be uncommonly reserved. You sneak out of that house along a secret path, perhaps even to protect the reputation of those girls, the reputation of those girls! No, let's say no more about that." "No more about that," said K., "but rather about something else, Frieda. No more need be said about that. You know why I must go there. It won't be easy, but I will overcome my reluctance. You shouldn't make this more difficult for me than it is. All I intended to do today was to go there for a moment to ask them whether Barnabas, who should have brought me an important message long ago, had finally come. He hadn't, but he should be coming very soon, so they assured me, plausibly enough. I didn't want to let him follow me to the schoolhouse so that he wouldn't torment you with his presence. The hours went by, but unfortunately he didn't come. But another person came whom I despise. The idea of his spying on me didn't appeal to me, so I went through the next-door garden, but I had no intention of hiding from him either and, once outside on the street, went up to him openly, holding, I have to admit, a very supple willow switch. That's all, no more need be said about that, but rather about something else. What's the situation with the assistants, the mere mention of whom is almost as repulsive for me as the mentioning of that family is for you? Compare your relationship to them with how I relate to that family. I understand your dislike of that family and can certainly share it. I go there only because of this particular affair, and at times it almost seems to me as though I were doing them an injustice and exploiting them. But as for you and the assistants! You haven't even tried to deny that they pursue you and you've also admitted that you're attracted to them. I wasn't angry at you because of that, I realized you were no match for the forces at work here and was happy to see you were at least putting up a fight, I helped to defend you, and it was only because I failed to do so for an hour or two, trusting in your faithfulness and also in hopes that the building would inevitably be locked and the assistants finally put to flight—I still underestimate them, I fear—only because I failed to do so for an hour or two and because this Jeremias, who on closer inspection is a none-too-healthy, oldish fellow, had the cheek to come to the window, it's for those reasons alone that I must lose you, Frieda, and hear greetings such as: 'There will be no wedding.' Shouldn't I be the one to utter reproaches, but I do not, I still do not." And again K. thought it a good idea to distract Frieda, so he asked her to bring him something to eat, for he had not eaten anything since noon. Frieda, obviously relieved by the request, nodded and ran to get something, not farther along the corridor where K. assumed the kitchen was, but off to the side down a few steps. She soon brought a plate of cold meats and a bottle of wine, but these were evidently only the remnants of a meal, the individual slices had been quickly rearranged so that this could not be discerned, a few sausage skins had even been left lying there, and the bottle was three-quarters empty. But K. said nothing about this and with a good appetite set about eating. "You were in the kitchen?" he asked. "No, in my own room," she said, "I have a room downstairs." "If only you had taken me along," said K., "I'll go downstairs so that I can sit for a little while I eat." "I'll bring you a chair," said Frieda, who was already on her way. "No thanks," said K., holding her back, "I won't go and don't need a chair either." Defiantly, Frieda endured his grip, she had her head bent low and was biting her lips. "Well, he's downstairs," she said, "what else did you expect? He's lying in my bed, he caught a chill outside, he's shivering, and has barely eaten. Basically this is all your fault; if you had not chased away the assistants and run after those people, we could be sitting peacefully in the schoolhouse. You alone destroyed our happiness. Do you really think Jeremias would have dared to abduct me while he was still on duty? In that case you fail to appreciate the system of order here. He tried to approach me, tormented himself, lay in wait for me, but it was only a game, just as a hungry dog plays about without quite having the audacity to jump up on the table. And the same is true of me. I was drawn to him, he's my playmate from childhood days—we used to play with one another on the slope of the Castle hill, wonderful days, you've never once asked me about my past—but none of that was of any great moment while Jeremias's position was still holding him in check, for I knew my duty as your wife-to-be. But then you drove away the assistants, and still boast of that, as though you had achieved something for me; well, in a sense that's true. With Artur you attained your goal, though only temporarily, he's delicate, he lacks Jeremias's passion, which fears no obstacle, and also that night with your fist—that blow with your fist was also dealt against our happiness—you nearly destroyed him, he fled to the Castle to complain, and even if he comes back soon, he's gone right now. But Jeremias stayed. On duty he fears every twitch in his master's eye, but off-duty he fears nothing. He came and took me; abandoned by you, overpowered by him, my old friend, I couldn't hold out anymore. It was not I who unlocked the school door, he smashed the window and pulled me out. We flew here, the landlord respects him, and nothing could please the guests more than to have a room waiter like him, so we were taken on, he doesn't live in my room, but we have taken a room together." "In spite of everything," said K., "I don't regret having driven the assistants from my service. If the relationship was as you describe it, in other words if your faithfulness depended solely on the professional commitment of the assistants, then it was good that all this came to an end. The happiness of that marriage in between those two predators, who backed down only under the threat of a whipping, would not have been that great. So I too am grateful to that family, which inadvertently played a role in separating us." In silence they walked up and down, side by side, but now it was impossible to tell who had begun first. Frieda, who was beside K., seemed annoyed that he didn't take her by the arm again. "And then everything would be in order," K. went on, "we could take leave of each other, you could go to your master Jeremias, who probably still has a chill from the school garden and whom you have, under the circumstances, left alone for too long, and I could go on my own to the schoolhouse or, now that I have nothing to do there without you, anywhere I will be admitted. If I am nevertheless hesitant, it's because I still have good reason to doubt what you told me. I have the opposite impression of Jeremias. All the time he was on duty, he was pursuing you, and I cannot believe that his being on duty would ultimately have restrained him from assaulting you in earnest. But now, ever since he chose to regard his duties here with me as suspended, he is different. Forgive me if I explain it to myself this way: Ever since you ceased to be his master's fiancée, you are no longer the temptation you once were for him. You may be his friend from childhood, but in my opinion—and I know him only from a brief conversation I had with him tonight—he doesn't attach much importance to sentimental matters of that sort. I don't know why you consider him a passionate individual. On the contrary, I find his way of thinking remarkably cold. From Galater he received in my regard certain perhaps not very favorable instructions, he endeavors to carry them out, with, as I willingly admit, a certain passion for duty—it is not all that rare here—specifying that he should destroy our relationship; he may have attempted this in various ways, for instance, by trying to entice you with his lascivious longings, and also—the landlady supported him in this—by spinning yarns about my unfaithfulness; his attack was successful, some memory or other of Klamm that still clings to him may have been of some help here, he certainly lost his post, but perhaps precisely when he no longer needed it, now he reaps the fruits of his labor and pulls you through the school window, but with that his work is finished, and, abandoned by his passion for duty, he becomes tired and would prefer to take over from Artur, who is not complaining but picking up praise and new orders, yet someone has to stay to keep track of how things develop here. He regards it as a somewhat bothersome duty having to care for you. There is no love for you, he openly admitted that to me, but as the mistress of Klamm you are naturally somebody he respects, and it must make him feel very good to be able to settle down in your room and have for once the feeling of being like a little Klamm, but that's all, you yourself mean nothing to him now; placing you in a position in here was, in his opinion, simply an addition to his main work; in order not to unsettle you he himself remained here, but only temporarily, so long as he does not have any news from the Castle and you have not cured his cold for him." "How you slander him!" said Frieda, knocking her little fists together. "Slander him?" said K., "no, I don't want to slander him. Perhaps I'm doing him something of an injustice, that is of course possible. What I said about him doesn't lie openly on the surface, it can be interpreted differently. But slander? After all, the only purpose in slandering him would be to combat your love of him. Were that necessary and were slander a suitable means, I wouldn't hesitate to slander him. Nobody could condemn me for that, he has such a great advantage over me because of his patrons that I, thrown back as I am entirely on my own resources, should also be allowed to do a little slandering. That would be a relatively innocent and in the end also quite impotent means of defense. So drop your fists." And K. took Frieda's hand in his own; Frieda attempted to withdraw it, but smiling and without any great effort. "But I have no need to slander him," said K., "for you certainly don't love him, you only think you do, and you'll be grateful when I deliver you from that illusion. Look, if someone wanted to take you from me without resorting to force, in the most carefully calculated fashion, he would have to do so through the two assistants. They are seemingly good, childish, funny, irresponsible youths, blown in from high up, from the Castle, along with a few childhood memories, but all this is quite endearing, especially if I myself am the opposite, as it were, for I'm constantly running after things that aren't entirely comprehensible to you, that annoy you, that bring me together with people who seem despicable to you, and some of that gets carried over to me in all my innocence. All of this is simply a malicious, though certainly very clever, exploitation of the shortcomings in our relationship. Every relationship has its shortcomings, even ours; we came together, each of us from a completely different world, and ever since getting to know each other, each of our lives has taken a completely new path, we still feel uncertain, all of this is too new. I'm not talking about myself, that isn't so important, on the whole I have been constantly inundated with gifts ever since you first turned your eyes toward me, and of course it isn't all that difficult to get used to receiving gifts. But as for you, aside from everything else, you were torn from Klamm, I cannot gauge what that means, but I have gradually gained an idea of what that means, one staggers, one cannot find one's way, and, even if I was always prepared to take you in, I was not always there, and when I was there, you were sometimes detained by your daydreams or something even more alive, like, for instance, the landlady—in short, there were times when you looked away from me, you were yearning, poor child, for something that was only half-defined, and at moments like that all that was needed was that the right people be posted in the direction you were looking and you were lost to them, you succumbed to the illusion that all of this, which was nothing but moments, ghosts, old memories, mostly your past and constantly receding former life, was still your real life right then. A mistake, Frieda, nothing but the final, and, rightly considered, rather contemptible obstacle facing our ultimate union. Pull yourself together, compose yourself; even if you thought that the assistants were sent by Klamm—it isn't true, they come from Galater—and if with the help of this illusion they could so enchant you that you believed that even in their dirt and their lechery you could find traces of Klamm, like a person who thinks he is seeing a long-lost precious stone in a dung heap, whereas in reality he would be incapable of finding it even if it actually was there—they too are simply the same type of fellows as the domestics in the stable, only not as healthy, a little fresh air makes them ill and throws them into bed, which they admittedly go about choosing with the craftiness of a domestic." Frieda had leaned her head on K.'s shoulder; with their arms wrapped around each other they walked up and down in silence. "If only," said Frieda, slowly, calmly, almost contentedly, as though she knew that she had merely been granted a tiny little interlude of peace on K.'s shoulder but intended to enjoy it to the utmost, "if only we had gone abroad at once, that same night, we could be somewhere else, safe, always together, your hand always close enough for me to catch hold of; how I need your closeness; how lost I am ever since I came to know you without your closeness; believe me, your closeness is the only dream that I dream, none other."

At that, someone cried out from the side corridor, it was Jeremias, he stood on the bottom step, he had only a shirt on but had thrown one of Frieda's shawls around himself. Standing there like that with his tousled hair, thin and seemingly rain-soaked beard, his eyes strenuously, pleadingly, reproachfully open, his dark cheeks reddish but as if consisting of extremely loose flesh, his bare legs trembling from the cold and the long fringes of his shawl trembling along with them, he was like a patient who had escaped from a hospital, so that one's only thought was how to get him back to bed. That's also how Frieda saw the matter, she withdrew from K. and immediately joined Jeremias downstairs. Her closeness, the solicitous way she drew the shawl more tightly about him, and her haste, in trying to press him back into the room, already seemed to be fortifying him a bit, it was as if he only now recognized K., "Oh, it is the surveyor," he said, soothingly stroking the cheek of Frieda, who wanted to prevent all further discussion, "forgive the disturbance. I'm not feeling at all well, so I do have an excuse. I think I have a fever, I must have some tea and sweat it out. That damned fence in the school garden, it'll take me a long time to forget it, and then after catching cold I continued to run about during the night. Although one doesn't realize it at the time, one ends up sacrificing one's health for things that are truly not worth it. But, Surveyor, don't let me disturb you, join us in the room, pay a sick visit, and at the same time you can tell Frieda whatever still needs to be said. When two people who have become used to each other part, there is still so much to tell each other in the final moments that a third party, especially one lying in bed waiting for the tea he has been promised, cannot possibly understand what it's all about. Come right in, I shall be quite still." "Enough, enough," said Frieda, tugging at his arm, "he is feverish and has no idea what he's saying. But K., don't come with us, I beg you. The room is mine and Jeremias's, or rather just mine, I forbid you to enter. You're pursuing me, oh K., why are you pursuing me. I will never, never go back to you, the very thought of it makes me shudder. Do go to your girls; they're sitting in their chemises on the oven bench by your side, so I'm told, and when anybody comes for you they snarl at him. You must be at home there if you feel so strongly drawn to the place. I always held you back, without much success, still I did hold you back, but that's over now, you're free. You have a lovely life ahead of you, you may have to fight a little with the domestics over that first girl, but so far as the second is concerned, no one in heaven or on earth will begrudge you that one. The union is blessed from the start. Don't object, you can certainly contradict everything, but in the end nothing would be contradicted. Just imagine, Jeremias, he has contradicted everything!" They signaled to each other by nodding and smiling. "But," Frieda went on, "assuming that he contradicted everything, what good would that do, what concern is it of mine? What happens at their house is absolutely their own business, and also his, but not mine. Mine is to care for you until you become healthy again, the way you were before K. tormented you because of me." "So you're not coming, Surveyor?" asked Jeremias, but just then he was dragged away by Frieda, who did not even turn around to look at K. One could see a small door down there, even lower than the doors in this corridor; not only Jeremias but Frieda too had to bend down to go in, it seemed to be bright and warm inside, one could still hear some whispering, probably affectionate words coaxing Jeremias to go to bed, and then they closed the door.

XXIII.

It was only now that K. noticed how quiet it had become in the corridor, not only here in this part of the corridor, where he had been with Frieda and which seemed to belong to the public rooms, but also in the long corridor with the guest rooms that had been so animated earlier. So the gentlemen had finally fallen asleep. K., too, was very weary, perhaps it was out of weariness that he hadn't defended himself as much against Jeremias as he ought to have done. It might have been wiser to take a cue from Jeremias, who was clearly exaggerating his cold—his misery was not due to his cold but was innate in him and could not be chased away by any medicinal tea—and to make just as much of a show of one's truly great weariness, sinking down here in the corridor, which would already do some good, dozing off a bit and then maybe even getting taken care of a little. Except the result wouldn't have been as favorable as for Jeremias, who would certainly, and no doubt rightly, have been victorious in this competition for sympathy, and obviously in every other battle as well. K. was so weary that he thought of going into one of these rooms, some of which were certainly empty, and having a good sleep in a nice bed. This would, in his opinion, have compensated for a good deal. There was even a nightcap handy. On the tray that Frieda had left lying on the floor there had been a small carafe of rum. K. did not recoil from the effort of going back, and he emptied the little bottle.

He now felt at least strong enough to appear before Erlanger. He looked for Erlanger's door, but since there was no longer any trace of the servant or of Gerstäcker and all of the doors were identical, he was unable to find it. Yet he thought he recalled the spot in the corridor where the door had been, and decided to open the door that he considered most likely to be the one he sought. This experiment couldn't possibly prove all that dangerous; if it was Erlanger's room, then he would surely receive him, if it was someone else's, then he could still excuse himself and leave, and if the guest was sleeping, which was most likely, then K.'s visit wouldn't even be noticed, it would be unfortunate only if the room was empty, for then K. would scarcely be able to resist the temptation to lie down in bed and sleep endlessly. Again he looked right and left in the corridor to see whether anybody was coming who could give him information and make it unnecessary to take such a risk, but the long corridor was silent and empty. Then K. listened at the door, there was not a sound here either. He knocked so softly that the sound couldn't have woken up anyone who was asleep, and since there was no response even then, he opened the door with extreme caution. But he was now greeted by a low cry. It was a small room, more than half of it occupied by a wide bed, the electric lamp on the night table was still on, next to it was a travel bag. Lying in bed but completely hidden under the blanket, someone was stirring uneasily and whispering through an opening between the blanket and sheet: "Who is it?" K. couldn't leave that easily now; disgruntled, he gazed at the sumptuous but unfortunately not empty bed, remembered the question, and gave his name. That seemed to have a positive effect, the man in bed pushed the blanket off his face a little, but fearfully, prepared to cover himself immediately again if everything wasn't quite right outside. But then without hesitation he threw off the blanket and sat up. It certainly was not Erlanger. It was a short, good-looking gentleman, with a somewhat contradictory face, the cheeks round and childlike, the eyes cheerful and childlike, yet the high forehead, the pointed nose, and the narrow mouth with its barely closed lips and almost vanishing chin were by no means childlike but revealed a superior mind. It was probably his satisfaction with that, his satisfaction with himself, that had preserved a powerful remnant of healthy childlikeness in him. "Do you know Friedrich?" he asked. K. said no. "But he knows you," the gentleman said, smiling. K. nodded, there was no shortage of people who knew him, and this was even one of the main obstacles in his way. "I'm his secretary," said the gentleman, "my name is Bürgel." "Excuse me," said K., reaching for the door handle, "unfortunately I mistook your door for another one. I was actually summoned to Secretary Erlanger's." "What a pity!" said Bürgel. "Not that you've been summoned elsewhere but that you mistook the doors. You see, once I've been awakened, I certainly will not fall asleep again. Well, this shouldn't make you so gloomy, it is my personal misfortune. Why can't these doors be locked, isn't that it? Of course there is a reason for that. Because, according to an old saying, the doors of the secretaries should be open at all times. But there is no need to take that literally." Bürgel gave K. a quizzical, cheerful look; contrary to his complaint he seemed perfectly well rested; as tired as K. was now, Bürgel had probably never been. "So where do you want to go now?" asked Bürgel. "It's four o'clock. You would have to wake up anybody you wanted to see, not all are so used to disturbances as I am, not all will take it so patiently, the secretaries are a nervous bunch. So stay a while. At about five o'clock the people here start getting up, you will be best able to comply with your summons at that time. And please finally let go of that handle and take a seat somewhere, it's certainly cramped here, it would be best if you sat here on the edge of the bed. You're surprised that I haven't a chair or table here? Well, I had a choice—either a complete set of furniture with a narrow hotel bed, or this large bed with nothing but the washstand. I chose the large bed, for, after all, the main thing in a bedroom surely is the bed. Oh, for anyone who could stretch out and sleep soundly, for any sound sleeper, this bed would be truly delicious. But even for someone like myself, who is always tired but cannot sleep, it does some good, I spend a large part of the day in it, dispatching all my correspondence and questioning the parties. This works quite well. True, the parties have nowhere to sit, but that is something they get over since it's certainly more pleasant for them as well when they stand and the deposition taker feels good than when they sit there comfortably and get shouted at. So all I have to give away is this place on the edge of the bed, but it is not an official seat and is meant only for nighttime discussions. But you're so silent, Surveyor." "I'm very tired," said K., who, on hearing the invitation, had immediately sat down rudely and disrespectfully on the bed and had leaned against the post. "Of course," said Bürgel, laughing, "everyone is tired here. The work I did yesterday or even today, for instance, certainly wasn't insignificant. And now there's absolutely no possibility of my falling asleep, but even if that most unlikely event happened and I should fall asleep while you're still here, please remain still and do not open the door. But have no fear, I shall certainly not fall asleep, or at best only for a few minutes. Probably because I am so used to holding office hours, I find it easiest to fall asleep in company." "Go to sleep, please, Secretary," said K., delighted with this announcement, "then with your permission I too shall sleep a little." "No, no," Bürgel laughed again, "unfortunately I cannot fall asleep simply upon request, such opportunities can arise only during a conversation, a conversation is the likeliest means of putting me to sleep. Yes indeed, this business affects our nerves. Take me, for instance, I am a connecting secretary. You don't know what that is? Well, I'm the strongest connection"—

just then he rubbed his hands quickly in unintentional mirth—"between Friedrich and the village, I'm the connection between his Castle and village secretaries and am stationed in the village, though not permanently; at any moment I must be prepared to journey to the Castle, you see the travel bag, it is an unsettled life, not suitable for everyone. Still, it's true that I couldn't manage without this kind of work, I would find every other kind of work shallow. Now what is the situation concerning the land surveying?" "I'm not doing that kind of work, I'm not employed as a land surveyor," said K., who paid little heed since he was dying for Bürgel to fall asleep, but this too was simply out of a certain sense of obligation toward himself, for deep within he thought he knew that the instant when Bürgel would fall asleep was still unforeseeably distant. "That's astonishing," said Bürgel, tossing his head vigorously and pulling a pad from under the blanket to jot down something, "you are a surveyor, but you have no surveying work." K. nodded mechanically, he had stretched out his left arm on the bedpost and had leaned his head on it; he had already tried various ways of making himself comfortable but this was the most comfortable position of them all, and now he could also pay a little bit better attention to what Bürgel was saying. "I'm willing," Bürgel went on, "to pursue the matter further. After all, the situation here certainly isn't such that we can afford to let a skilled employee go idle. And it must also be hurtful for you, aren't you suffering from it?" "Yes, I am suffering from it," said K. slowly, smiling to himself, for right now he was not suffering from it at all. Besides, Bürgel's offer made little impression on him. It was really quite amateurish. Without knowing anything about the circumstances attending the summoning of K., the difficulties it had encountered in the community and at the Castle, about the complications that had already arisen during K.'s stay here or that were in the offing—without knowing anything about all this, without even showing that he had an inkling of it, which was the least one could expect of a secretary, he offered without further ado, simply with the help of his little notepad, to resolve the matter. "You do seem to have had a few disappointments,"

Bürgel then said, however, showing again that he actually did have a certain understanding of people, and indeed, ever since stepping into the room, K. had told himself several times not to underestimate Bürgel, but in his present state it was hard to be a fair judge of anything other than his own weariness. "No," said Bürgel, as if he were responding to a thought of K.'s and out of consideration wanted to save him the trouble of formulating it, "you shouldn't let those disappointments frighten you off. Here some things seem to be arranged in such a way as to frighten people off, and when one is new to the place those obstacles seem absolutely impenetrable. I don't want to get into the question of the true state of affairs, the illusion may actually correspond to reality, in my position I lack the distance that is necessary to establish that, but listen carefully to what I am saying, sometimes opportunities do arise that aren't altogether in keeping with the situation in general, opportunities through which more can be achieved with a word, with a glance, with a sign of trust, than with a lifetime of grueling effort. That is undoubtedly so. But then again these opportunities are actually in keeping with the situation in general inasmuch as nobody ever takes advantage of them. Now why does nobody ever take advantage of them, that's the very question I keep asking myself." K. had no idea; he did notice that the matters Bürgel was speaking about probably affected him greatly, but just now he very much disliked everything that affected him; he turned his head sideways a little, as if he were making way for Bürgel's questions and could no longer be touched by them. "There is," Bürgel went on, stretching his arms out and yawning, which was in confusing contradiction to the gravity of his words, "there is constant complaining from the secretaries that they are forced to conduct most village interrogations at night. But why do they complain about that? Because it's too much of a strain on them? Because they would rather use the night for sleeping? No, they certainly don't complain about that. Among the secretaries there are of course some who are diligent and others who are less so, just like everywhere else, but none of them ever complain about having to work too hard, especially not in public. That is simply not our style. In that respect we don't acknowledge any distinction between ordinary time and work time. Such distinctions are alien to us. Why then do the secretaries object to the nighttime interrogations? Perhaps it is even out of consideration for the parties? No, no, it isn't that either. The secretaries are always inconsiderate toward the parties, though not a bit more inconsiderate than they are toward themselves, but just as inconsiderate. This inconsiderateness, or in other words this iron-clad pursuit and performance of duty, is the greatest consideration that the parties could possibly desire. On the whole this is—though the superficial observer does not notice it—fully acknowledged; in this case, for instance, it is precisely the nighttime interrogations that are so welcome to the parties, no fundamental complaints about the nighttime interrogations have been received. So why then do the secretaries dislike them?" K. didn't know this either, he knew so little, he couldn't even determine whether Bürgel was serious or was only ostensibly demanding an answer, "If you let me lie on your bed," he thought, "I shall answer all your questions at noon tomorrow or, better still, in the evening." But Bürgel didn't seem to be paying attention to him, so excessively preoccupied was he with the question that he himself had raised: "As far as I can judge and as far as I myself have been able to establish, the secretaries have roughly the following concerns with regard to nighttime interrogations. Nights are not a suitable time for holding proceedings with the parties, for at night it is difficult or downright impossible to preserve the official character of the proceedings in full. That is not because of external factors, the formalities can of course be observed just as strictly by night as by day. So it isn't that; nevertheless, the capacity for making official judgments does suffer at night. At night one involuntarily inclines to judge matters from a more private point of view, the presentations of the parties are given more weight than should be the case, entirely irrelevant considerations about the parties' circumstances in other respects, their sorrows and their fears, interfere with the judgment, the necessary barrier between parties and officials, even if outwardly still intact, begins to crumble, and in places where usually, as should happen, there were only questions and answers going back and forth, the persons involved switched places in a strange and absolutely inappropriate manner. At least that is what the secretaries say, in other words, those people who, owing to their profession, are endowed with an altogether extraordinary sensibility in such matters. But even they themselves—and this is something we have often talked about in our circles—barely notice those detrimental effects during the nighttime interrogations; on the contrary, from the very beginning they go to great lengths to fight against that and they end up thinking that they have done especially good work. But later, on reading the depositions, one is often amazed at the glaring weaknesses that come to light. And these are errors, even half-unjustified gains secured over and over again by the parties, and they can no longer be made good, or at least not as specified in our regulations, in the usual speedy manner. Of course, a control agency will correct these errors, but this will only be for the sake of justice, since it is no longer possible to do that particular party any harm. Now, under such circumstances aren't the complaints of the secretaries quite justified?" For some time K. had been half-dozing, but now he was roused again: "What's the point of all this? What's the point of all this?" he asked himself, and from under his drooping eyelids he viewed Bürgel not as an official who was discussing difficult matters with him but merely as something that was keeping him from his sleep, and whose further significance couldn't be determined. But Bürgel, completely absorbed in his train of thought, smiled as though he had just managed to mislead K. somewhat. But he was prepared to put him back on the right track at once. "Well," he said, "one cannot simply say that these complaints are entirely justified. True, the nighttime interrogations are not expressly forbidden anywhere, and one isn't violating any regulation if one tries to avoid them, but the conditions, the overabundant work, the manner in which the officials are employed at the Castle, their indispensability, the regulation that no interrogations of the parties should be held until the rest of the investigation has been fully concluded, but then right away, all this and many other things have turned the nighttime interrogations into an unavoidable necessity. But if they have actually become a necessity, then—I would say—that is still, indirectly at any rate, a result of the regulations, and to carp at the nature of the nighttime interrogations would almost mean—I am naturally exaggerating a little and can therefore allow myself, simply as an exaggeration, to make the following remark—that would almost mean to carp at the regulations. On the other hand, the secretaries should be allowed to protect themselves as best they can within the framework of the regulations against the nighttime interrogations and their perhaps merely apparent drawbacks. They certainly go about this very thoroughly, permitting interrogations only on subjects that pose the least possible threat in that regard, examining themselves before the proceedings and, if the results of that examination make it necessary, canceling all interrogations even at the last minute, fortifying themselves often by summoning a party at least ten times before actually interrogating him, choosing to have themselves represented by colleagues whose jurisdiction doesn't extend to that particular case and who can therefore handle it more easily, setting the negotiations for the beginning or end of the night and avoiding the hours in between—there are many such measures; these secretaries don't let anybody get the better of them, and their resilience is almost equal to their vulnerability." K. slept, but it wasn't really sleep, he was still hearing what Bürgel was saying, perhaps better than earlier when he was still awake though dead tired, one word after the other accosted his ears, but that irritating awareness was gone, he felt free, it was no longer Bürgel who kept him, but he, K., who now and then groped about for Bürgel, he had not yet reached the depths of sleep, but he had dipped into it and now no one was going to steal this from him. And it seemed to him as though in this way he had achieved a great victory and a group of people was already there to celebrate it and he or even somebody else was raising a champagne glass in honor of the victory. And in order to let everybody know what it was all about, the battle and the victory were being repeated once again, or perhaps they weren't being repeated but were taking place for the first time and had been celebrated earlier and kept on being celebrated, because there was fortunately no doubt at all about the outcome. A secretary, naked, very like the statue of a Greek god, was being hard pressed by K. in battle. That was quite comical, and in his sleep K. smiled gently at the way the secretary was being constantly startled out of his proud posture by K.'s advances and quickly had to use his raised arm and clenched fist to cover up his exposed parts, but he was not yet quick enough. The battle didn't last long, for step by step, and very big steps they were too, K. advanced. Was this even a battle? There was no real obstacle, only every so often a few squeaks from the secretary. This Greek god squeaked like a girl being tickled. And then finally he was gone; K. was alone in a large room; ready to fight he turned around and looked for his opponent, but there wasn't anybody there anymore, the group of people had scattered as well, only the champagne glass lay broken on the ground, K. stamped on it. But the splinters hurt; with a start he woke up feeling sick, like a small child on being woken up; nevertheless, at the sight of Bürgel's bare chest a thought from the dream came to him: "There's your Greek god! So pull him out of the sack!" "But there is," said Bürgel, lifting his face pensively toward the ceiling, as though he were racking his memory for suitable examples but couldn't find any, "but there is an opportunity, despite all the precautionary measures, for the parties to take advantage of the nighttime weakness of the secretaries, assuming as always that it actually is a weakness. Of course this is a very rare opportunity, that is to say, one that virtually never arises. It entails the party's arriving unannounced in the middle of the night. It may surprise you that this opportunity, which appears to be a matter of course, should arise so rarely. But then of course you don't know what conditions are like here. But even you must have been struck by the seamlessness of the official organization. As a result of this seamlessness, though, everyone who has a request to make, or who must for some reason be interrogated about something, receives, immediately, without delay, usually even before he has thought the matter through, indeed even before he knows about it, a summons. This time he isn't interrogated, generally isn't interrogated, the affair usually isn't sufficiently mature for that, but he has the summons and can no longer arrive unannounced, that is, he cannot arrive entirely by surprise, he can at best arrive at the wrong time, and then he is simply made aware of the date and hour of the summons, and if he comes back at the right time, then he is generally sent away, this isn't a problem anymore since the summons in the hands of the party and the memorandum in the files are strong, though not always adequate, weapons in the hands of the secretaries. All this relates only to the secretary who is authorized to deal with the affair; approaching the others at night by surprise is something everybody would be free to do. But nobody is likely to do so, that would be almost pointless. Above all else, it would greatly embitter the secretary who is authorized; but in dealing with the parties, we secretaries certainly aren't jealous of one another when it comes to the work—everybody has an exceedingly heavy load, indeed one that is piled on without skimping, but in dealing with the parties we cannot tolerate any confusion about our jurisdiction. There are even people who have lost that round in the game because in the belief that they could get no further in the authorized office they tried to slip through at an unauthorized one. Such attempts inevitably fail because even if an unauthorized secretary is surprised by the party at night and is most willing to help, owing to his lack of jurisdiction any intervention he would make would scarcely be more effective than that of any lawyer, actually far less so, for he doesn't have the time, even if he were capable of taking some other step—and indeed he is more familiar with the secret ways of the law than all of those lawyerly gentlemen—but he has no time for matters over which he has no authority, he cannot even spare a moment for them. Who, faced with such prospects, would spend his nights going from one unauthorized secretary to the next; besides, the parties are fully occupied if, in addition to their usual professions, they attempt to respond to the summonses and signals from the authorized offices, but they are 'fully occupied' only according to the parties' understanding of that term, which is naturally by no means the same as 'fully occupied' in the secretaries' understanding of it." K. nodded, smiling; he thought that now he understood everything perfectly, not because it affected him but simply because he was convinced that in a few moments he would fall sound asleep, and this time without dreams or interruptions; surrounded on one side by authorized secretaries and on the other by unauthorized ones, and faced with the mass of fully occupied parties, he would fall into a deep sleep and thus escape from them all. He had become so used to Bürgel's soft, complacent voice, which was obviously trying in vain to put itself to sleep, that it would enhance rather than disturb his own sleep. "Chatter on, chatterbox," he thought, "you're chattering away just for me." "So where is it," said Bürgel, two fingers fidgeting at his lower lip, with widened eyes and craned neck, as though after a strenuous hike he were now coming to a delightful vista, "so where is the opportunity that I spoke of which rarely, and indeed almost never, arises? The secret lies in the regulations about jurisdiction. In fact, it is not true and in a great living organization cannot be true that there's only one authorized secretary for each case. It's just that one of them has chief authority, while many others have a lesser degree of authority. Who—even if he were the greatest worker—could keep together on his desk the ramifications of the smallest incident? Even what I was saying about the chief authority goes too far. Doesn't the least bit of jurisdiction contain all of it? Isn't the passion with which the matter gets tackled decisive? And isn't this passion always present to the same extent, isn't it always there in full force? There can indeed be distinctions between the secretaries in all matters, and there certainly are countless distinctions like that, but not in their degree of passion, there is not one of them who could restrain himself if he were approached with a request to deal with a case over which he has even the slightest jurisdiction. But outwardly it is necessary to establish an orderly means of negotiation, and therefore for each of the parties the primary responsibility is taken on by one particular secretary, whom they are to heed in official matters. But this authorized secretary needn't even be the one with most jurisdiction in the case; this is something the organization determines in light of its current needs. That's how matters stand. And now, Surveyor, consider the possibility that a party does succeed somehow or other, despite the generally adequate obstacles I have already mentioned, in surprising in the middle of the night a secretary who does have some jurisdiction in that particular case. You probably haven't even considered the possibility of something like that? I can believe that. But in any case there's no need to think about it since it virtually never happens. What a strange, precisely shaped, small, clever little grain such a party would have to be in order to slip through that incomparable sieve. You think this can never happen. You're right, it can never happen. But one night—who can vouch for everything?—it does happen. True, I don't have any acquaintances that this has ever happened to; now, that doesn't prove very much, since my circle of acquaintances is limited compared with the numbers involved here, and besides it is by no means certain that a secretary who has experienced anything like this would want to admit it; after all, this is a very personal matter, one that is closely tied to one's official sense of shame. Still, my experience may prove that it is so rare an occurrence—one that has actually only been rumored to take place and has never actually been quite confirmed—that one is exaggerating greatly if one actually fears it. Even if it did happen, one could—it would be reasonable to assume—render it quite harmless by showing it proof, as can easily be done, that there simply is no place on earth for it. In any case, it is morbid if out of fear of this somebody hides under the blanket and won't even dare to look out. And even if this perfect improbability had suddenly materialized, does that mean all is lost? On the contrary. That all should be lost is even more improbable than the greatest improbability. Of course, if the party is in the room, it's already bad enough. It does constrict one's heart. 'How much longer can you resist?' one asks oneself. But one knows that there will be no resistance. You just have to picture the situation correctly. Sitting there is the party whom one has never seen, always awaited, awaited with genuine thirst, and always quite wisely considered unreachable. Through his silent presence alone, he invites one to invade his poor life, to look about as though one were surrounded by one's own possessions, and to suffer along with him from the futile demands that he makes. On a quiet night an invitation like that is enchanting. One accepts it and has then actually ceased to be an official. The situation then is such that it soon becomes impossible to turn down a request. Strictly speaking, one is desperate, and speaking even more strictly, quite happy. Desperate, for the vulnerability with which one sits there waiting for the party's plea, knowing that one must grant it as soon as it is uttered, even if it should, at any rate insofar as one can perceive this oneself, literally tear apart the official system—this vulnerability must surely be the worst thing that can befall one in the course of one's duty. Especially since—leaving everything else aside—especially since the elevation in rank that one has forcefully claimed for oneself just then is beyond all comprehension. Our position is such that we are by no means authorized to grant requests of the kind at issue here, but through the proximity of the nocturnal visiting party our official powers increase, we promise to do things that are outside our own area and will actually fulfill them; at night, like a robber in the woods, the party forces from us sacrifices that we would never have been capable of otherwise—well, anyhow, that's the way it is right now while the party is still here, giving us strength and coercing us and spurring us on and everything is still half-unconsciously under way, but what will it be like afterward, when this is over, and the party, replete and indifferent, leaves us, and we stand here alone, helpless in the face of our abuse of office—it is absolutely unthinkable. And yet we are happy. How suicidal happiness can be! We could naturally make an effort to hide the real situation from the party. After all, he barely notices anything on his own. To his mind, it was probably only for indifferent, accidental reasons—

exhaustion, disappointment, inconsiderateness, and indifference—that he had out of exhaustion and disappointment penetrated into a room that was not the one he wanted, and sits there in complete ignorance, preoccupied with thoughts—if preoccupied with anything whatsoever—of his error or of his weariness. Cannot one simply let him be? One cannot. With the loquaciousness of the fortunate one must explain everything to him. Without sparing oneself in the least, one must show him exactly what has happened and why it has happened, how extremely rare and singularly great an opportunity this is, one must show the party how, even though he has stumbled into this affair in an utter helplessness that no being other than a party is capable of, he can now, if he wants, Surveyor, take control of the entire situation, and to this end need only somehow present his request, for which the fulfillment is ready and even heading toward him—one must show all this to him; for the official it's the most difficult hour. But, Surveyor, once one has done this, then the most necessary things have been done, and one must simply content oneself and wait."

That was all K. heard, he was asleep, cut off from everything around him. His head, which initially had rested on his left arm up on the bedpost, had slid off while he slept and now hung freely, sinking slowly; the support from the arm above no longer sufficed, K. involuntarily found a new hold by bracing his right hand against the blanket, thereby accidentally grasping Bürgel's foot, which stuck up under the blanket. Bürgel looked down and let him have his foot, no matter how bothersome that must have been.

Just then, there was knocking, a few heavy blows, on the side wall, K. gave a start and stared at the wall. "Isn't the surveyor there?" a voice asked. "Yes," Bürgel said, freed his foot from K.'s grasp, and suddenly stretched in a wild and willful manner, like a little boy. "Then he should finally come," the voice said again; it showed no consideration for Bürgel nor for the possibility that he might still need K. "It's Erlanger," Bürgel said in a whisper; the presence of Erlanger next door didn't seem to surprise him, "go to him at once, he's angry now, try to soothe him. He's a sound sleeper, but we spoke too loudly, one cannot control oneself or one's voice when one speaks of certain matters. Well, get going now, you seem unable to drag yourself out of your slumber. But do get going, what more do you want here? No, you needn't excuse yourself because of your sleepiness, why should you? One's physical strength has a certain limit, who can help it that this limit is significant in other ways, too. No, nobody can help it. That is how the world corrects its course and keeps its equilibrium. It's certainly an excellent, always unimaginably excellent arrangement, even if in certain other respects hopeless. Get going now, I don't know why you're looking at me like that. If you delay your departure any longer, Erlanger will come down on me, and that's something I would very much like to avoid. But get going now, who knows what awaits you there; here everything is full of opportunities. Except that some opportunities are, as it were, too great to be acted upon; there are things that fail through nothing other than themselves. Yes, that is amazing. Incidentally, I hope that now I can finally go to sleep for a while. But it's already five o'clock and the noise will soon start. If only you would at least go!"

Dizzy on being suddenly awakened from deep sleep, still immensely in need of sleep, his body hurting all over owing to the uncomfortable position, for a long time K. couldn't decide whether to get up, he put his hands on his forehead and gazed down into his lap. Even Bürgel's constant goodbyes couldn't have prompted him to leave; it was only a sense of the utter futility of remaining in this room that gradually led him to do so. How indescribably desolate this room seemed to him. Whether it had simply become like this or had always been like this he did not know. He wouldn't even be able to fall asleep here again. And that was the decisive thought; smiling slightly about this, he stood up, leaned against anything that would support him, against the bed, the door, and, as though he had long since taken leave of Bürgel, left without saying goodbye.

XXIV.

It's likely that he would have walked past Erlanger's room just as indifferently if Erlanger hadn't stood in the open door and signaled to him. A single brief signal with his index finger. Erlanger was already completely prepared to leave, he wore a black fur coat with a high-buttoned collar. A servant was handing him his gloves and still held his fur cap. "You should have come long ago," said Erlanger. K. was about to excuse himself, but Erlanger indicated by closing his eyes wearily that he did not want to hear it. "This has to do with the following matter," he said, "a certain Frieda used to serve in the taproom, I only know her name, I don't know Frieda herself, she is of no interest to me. At times this Frieda served Klamm his beer. There now seems to be another girl there. Well, this is of course a trivial change, probably for everyone and certainly for Klamm. But the greater the work, and Klamm's work is of course the greatest, the less energy is left for fending off the outside world, and as a result every trivial change in the most trivial matters can be a serious disturbance. The slightest change on Klamm's desk, the removal of a stain that was there forever, all of these things can disturb him, and so too can a new serving girl. Now even if this were to disturb everybody else and every other kind of work, it does not disturb Klamm, there can simply be no question of that. Still, we must guard Klamm's comfort so closely that we even dispose of disturbances that he doesn't regard as such—and for him there probably are no disturbances—if they strike us as possible disturbances. It isn't for his sake, not because of his work, that we dispose of these disturbances, but for ourselves, for our consciences and for our peace of mind. And Frieda must therefore return to the taproom at once, she will perhaps cause a disturbance by returning; then we shall send her away again, but for now she must return. You live with her, they tell me, so see to it at once that she returns. Personal feelings cannot be taken into account, that goes without saying, and I therefore refuse to engage in any further discussion of the matter. I'm certainly doing far more than is necessary by mentioning that if you prove yourself in this little affair, it may at some point help you get ahead. That is all I have to say to you." Nodding to K. in farewell, he put on the fur cap the servant had handed him and set off down the corridor, quickly but with a slight limp, followed by the servant.

At times the orders given here were quite easy to carry out, but this ease was not to K.'s liking. Not only because the order pertained to Frieda and, although it was indeed meant as an order, sounded like mockery to K., but also especially because he thought it foreshadowed the futility of all his efforts. The orders simply passed over him, the unfavorable and the favorable, and even the favorable ones probably had a final, unfavorable core, but in any case they all passed over him and he was in far too inferior a position to influence them, let alone to make them fall silent and ensure that his own voice be heard. If Erlanger waves you aside, what can you do, and if he shouldn't wave you aside, what could you say to him? True, K. remained conscious of the fact that his weariness today had done him greater harm than all the unfavorable circumstances; why couldn't he, who had believed that he could rely on his own body and who, if it hadn't been for that belief, wouldn't have set out at all, why couldn't he put up with a few bad nights and one sleepless one, why did he become so uncontrollably tired, here of all places, where nobody was tired, or rather where everybody was constantly tired, though it didn't harm their work and even seemed to further it. One had to conclude from this that it was by nature an entirely different kind of weariness from K.'s. Here it was probably weariness in the course of happy work, something that from the outside looked like weariness but was actually indestructible calm, indestructible peace. If you've become a little tired by noon, that is part of the benign, natural course of the day. For the gentlemen here it's always noon, K. told himself.

And this certainly tallied with the fact that now, at five o'clock, everything was coming alive on both sides of the corridor. This babble of voices from the rooms had something extremely cheerful about it. First it sounded like the jubilation of children getting ready for an excursion, then like wake-up time in a henhouse, like the joy of being in complete accord with the awakening day, somewhere there was even a gentleman imitating the crowing of a cock. Though the actual corridor was still empty, the doors were already moving, there was always one being opened a crack and then closed again quickly, the corridor was buzzing with all these door openers and door closers; K. saw here and there, above in the opening in the walls, which didn't quite reach the ceiling, disheveled early-morning heads appear, and then vanish. From a distance, guided by a servant, came a tiny little cart containing files. A second servant walked alongside, holding a list which he was evidently using to compare the numbers on the doors with those on the files. The little cart halted before most doors, which generally opened, and the relevant files, sometimes only a single sheet—in cases like that a brief conversation arose between the room and the corridor, the servant was probably being chided—were handed into the room. If the door remained closed, the files were carefully stacked on the threshold. In such cases it seemed to K. that the movement of the doors in the immediate vicinity was not lessening, even though the files had already been distributed there as well, but increasing. Perhaps the others were peering longingly at the files on the threshold, which still hadn't been picked up and were, incomprehensibly, still lying there; they couldn't understand how someone who had only to open his door to gain possession of his files could possibly fail to do so; perhaps it was even possible that any files left lying there were later distributed among the other gentlemen, who by making frequent checks were already trying to establish whether the files were still lying on the threshold and whether there was therefore still hope for them. Besides, most of the remaining files were in especially large bundles and K. assumed that they had been temporarily left there out of a certain boastfulness or malice or even out of justified pride, as a way to encourage their colleagues. Confirming him in this assumption was the tendency every now and then, always just when he wasn't looking, for the pile, after it had been put on show for a sufficiently long time, to be suddenly and hastily pulled into the room and then the door remained as quiet as it had been earlier; then the other doors in the vicinity also calmed down, disappointed or even satisfied that this object of constant annoyance had finally been disposed of, but they gradually started moving again.

K. observed all this not only with curiosity but with sympathy. He felt almost comfortable amid the bustle, glanced about here and there, and—from suitably far away—watched the servants, who had, to be sure, often turned toward him with a severe expression, lowered heads, pursed lips, as they distributed the files. The further the work advanced, the less smoothly it went; either the list wasn't entirely accurate or the servant couldn't make out the files, or the gentlemen objected on other grounds, in any case it turned out that some distributions had to be reversed, and then the little cart went back and negotiations for the return of the files were conducted through a crack in the door. These negotiations created sufficient difficulties, but it also happened often enough that whenever there was any question about files having to be returned precisely those doors that had previously moved the fastest remained implacably closed, as though they didn't want to have anything more to do with the matter. Only now did the real difficulties begin. The one gentleman who considered himself entitled to the files was extremely impatient, made much noise in his room, clapped his hands, stamped his feet, and repeatedly called out into the corridor through the crack in the door the number of a certain file. Then the little cart was often left quite abandoned. One servant was busy soothing the impatient gentleman, the other was standing in front of the closed door, fighting for the return of the files. Both had a difficult time of it. The impatient gentleman became even more impatient at these efforts to pacify him, could no longer endure the empty words of the servant, for what he wanted was not consolation but rather files; at one point one such gentleman emptied from the opening above a full washbasin on the servant. But the other servant, who was evidently of higher rank, had an even more difficult time. If the gentleman in question agreed to negotiate, then there were sober discussions in the course of which the servant quoted from his list, the gentleman from his memos and also from the files that he was supposed to return but that for now he still held tightly in his hand so that barely a corner of them remained visible to the servant's longing eyes. The servant also had to run back for new evidence to the cart, which in the slightly sloping corridor had kept rolling all by itself, or he had to go to the gentlemen who were claiming the files and exchange the objections of the previous owners for new counterobjections. Those negotiations took a long time, occasionally they came to an agreement, the gentleman gave up a portion of the files, or as compensation received another file since there had merely been a mix-up, but there were also times when somebody had to give up all the requested files without any fuss, either because the servant's evidence had driven him into a corner or because he had grown tired of the continual negotiations, but then he didn't hand the files to the servant, and instead threw them on a sudden decision along the corridor so that the strings came loose and the sheets went flying and the servants had great difficulty putting everything back in order again. But all this was still easy enough compared to when the servant received no answer to his repeated requests for the files to be returned, for then he stood before the closed door, requesting, pleading, citing from his list, quoting regulations, but all in vain, there wasn't a sound from the room, and the servant evidently had no right to enter without permission. And then even this excellent servant was sometimes abandoned by his self-control, he went to his little cart, sat down on the files, wiped the sweat from his forehead and for a while did nothing but swing his feet helplessly. All about him there was great interest in the affair, whispers came from all sides, scarcely a door stood still, and up at the molding following all these events were faces that, oddly enough, were almost completely masked by scarves and that, what's more, wouldn't stay in one place even for a second. During this commotion K. was struck by the fact that Bürgel's door had been closed the entire time and that even though the servants had already passed through this section of the corridor no files had been distributed to Bürgel. Perhaps he was still asleep, and in this noise it must have been a sound sleep, but why hadn't he received any files? Only very few rooms, probably unoccupied ones at that, had been overlooked in that way. By contrast, Erlanger's room was now occupied by a new and uncommonly restless guest who must have literally driven Erlanger away during the night; this wasn't exactly in keeping with Erlanger's cool, worldly-wise nature, but the fact that he had had to wait for K. on the threshold indicated as much.

From all these remote observations K. always returned before long to the servant; this particular servant truly had little in common with what K. had been told about the servants in general, about their idleness, their comfortable life, their arrogance, for even among the servants there were surely exceptions, or more likely diverse groups, for there were, as K. noticed, many different ranks here, of which he had up to now barely seen a hint. The intransigence of this servant was especially pleasing to him. In the battle against these stubborn little rooms—to K. it often seemed like a battle against the rooms, since he barely got to see the occupants—the servant never let up. True, he was becoming exhausted—who wouldn't have become exhausted?—but, recovering quickly, he slid down from the little cart and, erect, with clenched teeth, had another go at the door that had to be conquered. Twice, three times he was beaten back, actually by quite simple means, merely by the devilish silence, but he was not yet defeated. Since he saw that he couldn't achieve anything through an open attack, he tried another method, relying, if K. understood this properly, on cunning. He then seemed to leave the door alone, as if to exhaust its capacity for silence, turning to other doors instead, but after a while he came back, called the other servant, all this conspicuously and loudly, and began piling files on the threshold of the closed door, as though he had changed his mind and were now convinced that by rights the files should not be taken from the gentleman but rather allocated to him. Then he went ahead, keeping an eye on the door, and when before long, as usually happened, the gentleman cautiously opened the door to pull in the files, in a few leaps the servant was there, shoved his foot between door and jamb, and at least succeeded in forcing him to negotiate face to face, which usually led to a halfway satisfactory settlement. And if this didn't work or if it seemed to him to be the wrong method for one of the doors, he tried a different approach. Then he would turn, for instance, toward the gentleman who was demanding the files. Pushing aside the other servant, who was only working mechanically and was quite useless as an attendant, he began to address the gentleman, emphatically, in a whisper, secretively, sticking his head quite far into the room; most likely he was promising him that the other gentleman would be suitably punished during the next distribution, at any rate he pointed often to the opponent's door and laughed, insofar as his weariness allowed. Then there were some cases, though, one or two, where he did abandon all his efforts, but here too K. thought that was merely a seeming abandonment or at least a justifiable abandonment, for the servant went ahead, enduring the noise from the deprived gentleman without even looking around; only a rare, protracted closing of the eyes indicated that he was suffering from the noise. But then that gentleman too gradually calmed down; just as children's uninterrupted crying gradually turns into ever more isolated sobbing, so too with his shouting, but even after he had quieted down entirely, one could sometimes once again hear an isolated shout or a hasty opening and slamming of that door. In any case, it turned out that here too the servant had probably proceeded in an absolutely correct manner. Finally there was only one gentleman left who wouldn't calm down, he had remained quiet for quite a while, though only in order to recuperate, then started off again, no less loudly than before. It wasn't altogether clear why he was shouting and complaining like this, perhaps it hadn't anything to do with the distribution of the files. Meanwhile the servant had finished his work, only one file, actually only a scrap of paper, a note from a notepad, had been left lying in the cart through the fault of the attendant, and now they couldn't decide to whom it should be allocated. "That might well be my file," was the thought that went through K.'s head. The council chairman had always spoken of the smallest case. Arbitrary and ridiculous though this assumption seemed to K., he nonetheless tried to approach the servant, who was pensively examining the note; this wasn't exactly easy, since the servant repaid K. poorly for his sympathy; even throughout the hardest work he had always found time to glance angrily or impatiently, twitching his head nervously, at K. But now that the distribution was over, he seemed to have almost forgotten K., just as he had become more indifferent in other respects; his fatigue made this understandable, he didn't bother much with the note either, perhaps he hadn't even read it but had only pretended, and though he could probably have made each of the gentlemen here in the corridor happy by allotting him the note, he decided otherwise, for he was fed up with this task; with his index finger on his lips he motioned for his companion to be quiet—K. was still some distance away from him—tore the note into little pieces and put them in his pocket. That was probably the first irregularity in office operations that K. had ever noticed here, though it was possible that he misunderstood this, too. And even if it was an irregularity, that was forgivable, for under the conditions that prevailed here the servant could not work without error, and at some point the pent-up irritation, the pent-up unrest, would have to erupt, and if this expressed itself merely in the tearing up of a little note, that was still innocent enough. The voice of the gentleman who was impossible to calm down still rang out in the corridor, and his colleagues, who otherwise weren't exactly friendly to one another, seemed to be in complete agreement about the noise, it began to seem as if this particular gentleman had taken on the task of making noise for all the rest, who were merely encouraging him with nods and shouts to keep going. But the servant paid no attention to it, he had finished his work and now pointed to the cart handle, signaling to the other servant that he should grasp it, and so they left as they had come, only more content, and so quickly that the little cart went bouncing ahead of them. Only once did they flinch and look back as the gentleman—who was still shouting and at whose door K. now hung about because he would have liked to know what the gentleman actually wanted—must no longer have found shouting adequate and had probably discovered the button of an electric bell and, no doubt overjoyed to be thus relieved, had stopped shouting and now began to ring incessantly. At that, a great murmur went up in the other rooms, it appeared to indicate general agreement, the gentleman appeared to be doing something that all the others would have gladly done long ago had they not for some unknown reason been obliged to abandon the effort. Was it perhaps the servants, perhaps Frieda, whom the gentleman wanted to call with the bell? Well he could keep on ringing. For Frieda was busy wrapping Jeremias in wet compresses and even if he was now healthy again, she had no time, for then she lay in his arms. Still, the ringing had an immediate effect. Rushing over from some distance away came the landlord of the Gentlemen's Inn, dressed in black and buttoned up as usual; but it was as if he had forgotten his dignity, he was running so hard; his arms were half-extended, as if he had been called because of some great misfortune and came to seize it and smother it on his breast; and at every little irregularity in the ringing he seemed to do a little jump and then hurry even more. At some distance behind him, his wife now appeared as well, she too ran with her arms extended, but her steps were small and mincing and K. thought that she would arrive here too late, for by then the landlord would already have taken care of everything. And to make way for the landlord's dash, K. went and stood close to the wall. But the landlord stopped right next to K., as though he were the goal, and soon the landlady was there too and both inundated him with reproaches, which he couldn't understand in the bustle and surprise, especially since the gentleman's bell mixed in as well, and then other bells went into action, no longer out of necessity, but simply as a game and in an excess of joy. Because it was important to him to gain a proper understanding of his guilt, K. readily complied when the landlord took him under his arm and accompanied him away from the noise, which kept increasing, for behind them—K. didn't even turn around since the landlord and, even more so, on the other side, the landlady, were scolding him—the doors now opened fully, the corridor sprang to life, there was an increase in traffic as in a lively narrow alley, the doors before them were evidently waiting impatiently for K. to pass so that they could let out the gentlemen, and amidst all this pealed the bells, which were repeatedly rung as if in celebration of a victory. Now, finally—they were already back in the calm white courtyard, where some sleighs were waiting—K. gradually learned what it was all about. Neither the landlord nor the landlady could understand how K. could possibly have dared to do something like that. But what had he done? Repeatedly K. asked, but for a long time he could not elicit an answer, because his guilt was all too self-evident to them, and so they never even remotely considered that he might have acted in good faith. K. only slowly recognized all of these things. It was wrong of him to have been in the corridor, for in general he was at most allowed into the taproom, and then only as a favor, which could always be withdrawn. If summoned by a gentleman, he must of course go where he was summoned, but must always realize—surely he had at least normal human intelligence?—that he was in a place where he did not belong and to which he had merely been summoned by a gentleman, most reluctantly, and only because some official business demanded and excused it. So he had to appear there quickly to submit to the interrogation, but then he had to disappear, if possible, more quickly still. Hadn't he had a feeling of grave impropriety there in the corridor? But if that were so, how could he have hung around there like an animal in pasture? Hadn't he been called to a nighttime interrogation and did he not know why nighttime interrogations had been introduced? The sole purpose of the nighttime interrogations—and here K. received a new explanation of what they meant—was to ensure that those parties whom the gentlemen couldn't stand to see by day were quickly examined at night under artificial light, so the gentlemen would get a chance right after the hearing to forget all that ugliness in their sleep. But K.'s behavior had made a mockery of all of the measures. Even ghosts disappear toward morning, but K. had remained there with his hands in his pockets, as though he expected that since he was not going away the entire corridor with all the rooms and gentlemen would go away instead. And this would certainly have happened—he could be sure of this—had it been at all possible, for the gentlemen's delicacy of feeling was boundless. Nobody would, for instance, drive K. away, or even tell him what was so obvious, namely, that he should finally go, nobody would do so, even though they probably trembled with excitement while K. was around, and so the morning, their favorite time, was spoiled for them. Rather than take action against K., they preferred to suffer, though no doubt partly in hopes that K. would finally have to recognize the most glaringly obvious thing and would have to suffer, in a way that matched the gentlemen's sufferings, by being obliged to stand in the corridor in the morning, so terribly out of place, so visible to all. Vain hope. They don't know or in their friendliness and disdain don't want to know that there are insensitive, hard hearts that cannot be softened even by reverence. Does not even the night moth, poor creature, when day comes, seek a quiet corner and flatten itself out, preferring to disappear and unhappy that it cannot. K., by contrast, goes and stands where he is most visible, and if in this way he could prevent the day from dawning, he would do so. He cannot prevent that, but unfortunately he can postpone it and make it more difficult. Didn't he watch the files being distributed? Something that nobody was allowed to watch, except for the immediate participants. Something that the landlord and the landlady weren't even allowed to watch in their own house. About which they had heard only a few hints, such as today, for instance, from the servant. So he hadn't noticed the difficulties under which the distribution of files had taken place, which were actually incomprehensible, for, after all, each gentleman serves only the cause, never thinks of personal gain, and therefore had to work with all his strength to ensure that the distribution of files, this important, essential work, proceed quickly, easily, and without error? And had it really never even remotely dawned on K. that the main thing about all the difficulties was that the distribution had to be carried out with the doors almost closed, without the possibility of direct contact between the gentlemen, who could of course signal to one another in a flash, whereas the distribution through the servants necessarily has to go on for hours, can never take place without complaints, is a constant source of torment to the gentlemen and to the servants, and will probably have harmful consequences for the work later on. And why couldn't the gentlemen have any contact with one another? So K. didn't understand this yet? Nothing like this had ever happened to the landlady—the landlord confirmed that this was also true of him—though they had had to deal with quite a few unruly people. Things that otherwise one didn't dare to say had to be said to him openly, for otherwise he did not understand the most important point. Well now, since it had to be said: because of him, simply and solely because of him, the gentlemen couldn't emerge from their rooms, for early in the morning, shortly after sleep, they are too modest, too vulnerable, to be able to expose themselves to the eyes of strangers; they feel too bare, even if they're completely dressed, to show themselves. It's certainly hard to say why they're ashamed, perhaps they're ashamed, these eternal workers, simply because they have slept. But perhaps they are even more ashamed of seeing strangers than of being seen; the very thing that they had happily overcome with the help of the nighttime interrogations, namely, the sight of the parties—whom they find hard to stand—they do not want intruding on them in the morning, suddenly, abruptly, in all of nature's truth. They are simply not up to that. What kind of person would fail to respect this! Well, it could only be a person like K. Somebody who puts himself above everything, above the law and above the most ordinary human consideration with that stolid indifference and drowsiness of his, who doesn't care that he not only makes it almost impossible for the files to be distributed and damages the reputation of the inn and who brings about an entirely unprecedented situation, namely, that the gentlemen, who have been reduced to despair, begin to fight and after an inner struggle inconceivable to ordinary people reach for the bell and call for help in order to drive away the otherwise unshakable K. They, the gentlemen, call for help! Wouldn't the landlord and the landlady and their entire staff have come running over a long time ago if they had only dared to appear unsolicited before the gentlemen in the morning, even if only to bring help and then to disappear at once. Trembling with outrage at K., inconsolable because of their impotence, they had waited here at the entrance to the corridor, and the utterly unexpected ringing had been like a deliverance for them. Now the worst was over! But if only they could steal a look at the joyous antics of the gentlemen who had been finally liberated from K.! But this wasn't the end of it for K., for he would certainly have to answer for what he had gone and done here.

They had meanwhile reached the taproom; why the landlord,

angry though he was, had brought K. here wasn't entirely clear, perhaps he had actually noticed that right now K.'s weariness made it impossible for him to leave the inn. Without waiting for an invitation to sit down, K. literally sank onto one of the barrels. It felt good to be in the dark. In this large room there was only a single weak electric bulb burning over the beer taps. Outside, too, it was still completely dark, and there seemed to be snow flurries. Once inside in the warmth, one had to be grateful and make sure one would not be thrown out. The landlord and the landlady were still standing in front of him, as though he actually posed a certain threat, as though one could not rule out the possibility, given his utter unreliability, that he would suddenly jump up and attempt to invade the corridor again. Besides, they themselves were tired after the nighttime fright and the early rising, especially the landlady, who wore a rustling silklike, carelessly buttoned and tied, full-skirted brown dress—where had she found it in the rush?—and, resting her head, as if it had snapped, upon her husband's shoulder, she dabbed her eyes with an elegant little handkerchief while now and then aiming childishly nasty looks at K. In order to calm the couple, K. said that everything they had just told him was completely new to him but that though he had not known about that he hadn't wanted to stay so long in the corridor, where he really had nothing to do and certainly hadn't wanted to torment anybody, all this had happened merely because of his extreme weariness. He thanked them for putting a stop to that embarrassing scene. If he were called to account, he would welcome the opportunity, for only in that way could he ensure that his conduct would not be generally misinterpreted. Only weariness was to blame. But this weariness came from his still not being used to the strain of the interrogations. After all, he hadn't been here all that long. Once he had more experience at this, nothing like that would ever be possible again. Perhaps he was taking the interrogations too seriously, but that alone was hardly a drawback. He had had to go through two interrogations, one shortly after the other, the first with Bürgel and the other with Erlanger, the first especially had exhausted him, but the second hadn't lasted long, Erlanger had simply asked him for a favor, but the two together were more than he could bear at once, perhaps this sort of thing would also be too much for anybody, for instance, the landlord. After the second interrogation all he had managed to do was stagger out. It had almost been a sort of drunkenness—that was the first time he had seen and heard the two gentlemen, and he also had to come up with answers for them. So far as he knew, everything had turned out rather well, but then there had occurred that misfortune which, after what had happened earlier, they could scarcely blame him for. Unfortunately, only Erlanger and Bürgel had known about his condition and would certainly have taken care of him and averted everything that had subsequently occurred, but Erlanger had had to leave right after the interrogation, evidently to go to the Castle, and Bürgel, probably exhausted from that same interrogation—so how could K. have survived it without weakening?—had fallen asleep and even slept right through the distribution of the files. Had K. been given a similar opportunity he would have used it with pleasure and gladly given up all forbidden glimpses, and this all the more readily, given that he had been in such a state that he couldn't see anything, so even the most sensitive gentlemen could have appeared before him without fear.

The mentioning of both interrogations, especially that of Erlanger, and the respect with which K. had spoken of the gentlemen, made the landlord more favorably disposed toward him. He already seemed prepared to fulfill K.'s request for permission to put a board over the barrels and to sleep there, at least until dawn; the landlady clearly opposed that and, vainly tugging here and there at her dress, which she had only just noticed was in disarray, shook her head repeatedly; a seemingly long-standing quarrel about the cleanliness of the house was about to break out. To K. in his weariness the couple's conversation seemed far more significant than usual. Being driven away from here seemed to him a misfortune that surpassed everything he had experienced up to now. That must not be allowed to happen, even if the landlord and landlady were to be united against him. K. lay in wait, doubled up on the barrel, watching the two of them. Until the landlady, who with her unusual sensitivity, which had struck K. a long time ago, suddenly stepped aside and—most likely she had begun talking to the landlord about other matters—cried: "See how he's looking at me! It's about time you sent him away!" But K., seizing this opportunity, for by now he was absolutely confident, even almost to the point of indifference, that he would stay, said: "I'm not looking at you, only at your dress." "Why my dress?" asked the landlady, agitated. K. shrugged. "Come," said the landlady to the landlord, "he must be drunk, the lout. We'll let him sleep off his stupor here," and she gave an order that Pepi, who had at a call from her appeared out of the dark, unkempt, tired, casually holding a broom, should throw K. a cushion.

XXV.

When K. awoke, he thought at first that he had barely slept, the room had not changed, it was empty and warm, the walls in the dark, a single lightbulb over the beer taps, and outside the windows too, night. But when he stretched out, the pillow fell to the floor and the board and barrels creaked, Pepi came at once and he learned that it was already late evening and that he had slept for well over twelve hours. The landlady had asked for him several times during the day, as had Gerstäcker, who had waited here in the dark in the morning over a beer while K. spoke with the landlady, but then hadn't dared to disturb K., had since come back once looking for K., and finally even Frieda had supposedly come in and had stood for a moment beside K.; still, she had scarcely come because of K. but rather because she had to get some things ready here, for this evening she was supposed to take up her old duties again. "So she doesn't like you anymore?" Pepi asked, while bringing him coffee and cake. Yet she didn't ask maliciously, as she used to do, but sadly, as though she had meanwhile become acquainted with the malice of the world, in the face of which all one's own malice gives way and becomes meaningless; she spoke to K. as though to a fellow sufferer, and when he was sipping the coffee and she thought she saw that it wasn't sweet enough for him, she ran to get him a full sugar bowl. Still, her sadness hadn't prevented her from prettying herself perhaps even more today than last time; she had a wealth of bows and ribbons, which were plaited through her hair, and along the forehead and temples her hair had been carefully crimped, and around her neck she wore a small chain, which hung down into the low neckline of her blouse. When K., satisfied because he had finally had enough sleep and was able to drink some good coffee, stealthily reached for a bow and attempted to undo it, Pepi said wearily: "Would you leave me alone," and sat down on a barrel next to him. And K. didn't even have to ask her about her sorrow, she herself began to talk right away, fixing her gaze on K.'s pot of coffee as though she needed some distraction even while she was talking, as though she were incapable, even while preoccupied with her sorrow, of abandoning herself completely to it, for that would exceed her strength. In the first place K. found out that he himself was to blame for Pepi's misfortune but that she wasn't reproaching him for that. And she nodded eagerly as she spoke in order to forestall K.'s objections. First, he had taken Frieda from the taproom and thus enabled Pepi to advance. It would otherwise be difficult to imagine what could have induced Frieda to give up her post, she was just sitting there in the taproom like a spider in its web, had threads everywhere that only she knew of; stealing her away against her will would have been absolutely impossible; only love for an inferior, something in other words that was incompatible with her position, could drive her from her post. And Pepi? Had she ever thought of securing the position for herself? She was a chambermaid, had an insignificant and scarcely promising post; like all girls, she dreamed of a great future, one cannot prevent oneself from dreaming, but gave no serious thought to moving on, she had resigned herself to what she had already achieved. And then all of a sudden Frieda disappeared from the taproom; that had happened so suddenly that the landlord didn't have a suitable replacement at hand, he looked about and his eye fell on Pepi, who had admittedly pushed her way to the fore. At the time she loved K. as she had never loved anybody else, for months she had sat downstairs in her tiny dark bedchamber and was prepared to spend years there unnoticed and at worst her entire life, and then all of a sudden K. had appeared, a hero, a rescuer of maidens, and had opened the way to the top for her. True, he didn't know anything about her, hadn't done it for her sake, but this didn't lessen her gratitude, the night before she was taken on—it was not yet clear that she would be taken on, but it was quite likely—she spent hours talking to him and whispering thanks in his ear. And his deed became even more exalted in her eyes, for it was precisely Frieda with whom he had burdened himself; there was something incomprehensibly selfless about his having, with the aim of bringing Pepi to the fore, made Frieda his mistress, Frieda, an unattractive, oldish, thin girl with short, sparse hair, and, what's more, a devious girl who always has some secret or other, which surely has something to do with her looks; if the wretchedness of her face and body is incontestable, then at least she must have some other secrets that nobody can check on, such as her supposed relationship with Klamm. And at the time Pepi even had thoughts such as these: is it possible that K. really loves Frieda, is he not deceiving himself, or could it be that he might only be deceiving Frieda, and so all that will happen is that Pepi will advance, and will K. then notice the mistake or no longer wish to hide it and no longer see Frieda, but only Pepi, which wasn't necessarily an insane idea of Pepi's, for she was certainly well able to compete with Frieda, one girl against another, nobody could deny it, and it was above all else Frieda's position and the brilliance that Frieda had been able to give it that had blinded K. just then. And then Pepi had dreamed that once she had the position K. would come and plead with her, and then she would have the choice of either granting K.'s plea and losing the post, or rejecting him and climbing higher. And she had planned to give up everything and to go down to him and to teach him the true love that he could never experience with Frieda and that is independent of every position of honor in the world. But that is not what happened. And what was to blame for that? K. above all, and then of course Frieda's slyness. K. above all, for what does he want, and what sort of strange person is he? What is he striving for, what are the important things that make him so preoccupied and make him forget what is nearest and best and most beautiful? Pepi is sacrificed and everything is idiotic and everything is lost, and anybody who had the strength to set the entire Gentlemen's Inn on fire and burn it down, without leaving a trace, to burn it up like a sheet of paper in a stove, today he would be Pepi's chosen one. Well, so Pepi came to the taproom, it was four days ago today, shortly before lunch. The work here isn't easy, it is almost murderous work, but then the things to be gained aren't insignificant either. Pepi hadn't simply lived from day to day before that, and in her wildest thoughts she would never have claimed this post for herself, but she had already made numerous observations, knew what was involved in the post, and hadn't taken it on unprepared. You certainly couldn't take it on unprepared, for if you did, you would lose it in the first hour or two. Even if you were willing to conduct yourself like the chambermaids here. As a chambermaid, you do after a while feel quite lost and forgotten, it's like working in a mine, at least it's like that in the secretaries' corridor, for days you see nobody other than the odd daytime parties, who flit about and don't dare look up, nobody except for two or three other chambermaids, and they are just as embittered. In the morning you aren't even allowed out of your room, the secretaries want to be left to themselves, the domestics carry in their meals from the kitchen, the chambermaids usually don't have anything to do with that and during mealtimes they aren't even allowed to appear in the corridor. It's only while the gentlemen are at work that the chambermaids are allowed to tidy up, though not of course in the occupied rooms, but only in those that happen to be empty, and that work must be done very quietly so that the gentlemen's work is not disturbed. But how is it possible to tidy up quietly if the gentlemen occupy the rooms for days at a time, and what's more if the domestics, that dirty riffraff, also go about their business in there so that when the room finally is turned over to the chambermaids, it is in such a state that not even the Flood could make it clean. Truly, they are high-ranking gentlemen, but you have to struggle hard to overcome your revulsion in order to be able to tidy up after them. The chambermaids really don't have too much work, but it is strenuous. And never a kind word, nothing but constant reproaches, especially this, the most tormenting and most frequent of them all: that in the course of the tidying-up files have been lost. In reality nothing is ever lost, every scrap of paper is handed to the landlord, but files naturally do get lost, only not by the girls. And then commissions come and the girls have to leave their room while the commission is rummaging through their beds; of course the girls don't have any possessions, their few things fit in a rucksack, but the commission searches for hours all the same. Of course it doesn't find anything; how could files possibly end up there? What interest could girls have in files? Once again, though, the only results are the insults and threats conveyed by the disappointed commission through the landlord. And never any peace—not by day, not by night. Noise half night long and noise from earliest morning. If only one didn't have to live there, but one must, for in between mealtimes it's the chambermaids' job to go and get little things from the kitchen when given the order, especially at night. Always the sudden banging of a fist on the chambermaids' door, the dictating of the order, the rushing down to the kitchen, the shaking of the sleeping kitchen lads out of their sleep, the placing of the tray with the things that have been ordered outside the chambermaids' door, where the domestics pick it up—how sad all of this is. But that isn't the worst thing. The worst thing rather is when we get no orders; deep at night, sometimes at a time when everybody should be asleep and most people are finally asleep, something or other starts creeping about outside the chambermaids' door. Then the girls climb out of their beds—the beds are arranged one above the other, there is really very little space, the entire maids' room is actually no more than a large cabinet with three compartments—listen at the door, kneel down, and embrace one another in fear. And all this time you can hear the prowler at the door. By now everyone would be glad if he would finally come in, but nothing happens, nobody comes in. And you have to remind yourself that there doesn't have to be any danger lurking there, maybe it's only someone walking to and fro outside the door, wondering whether or not to place an order and in the end unable to decide to do so. Maybe that's all it is, but maybe it's something quite different. Actually you don't even know the gentlemen, you have barely seen them. In any case, the girls inside are dying of fright and when it has finally become quiet outside they lean against the wall and don't have the strength to climb back into their beds. That life again awaits Pepi, this very evening she's supposed to take up her old place in the chambermaids' room again. And why? Because of K. and Frieda. Back to the life she's barely fled, not only with the help of K. but also through great efforts of her own. For while serving there the girls neglect their appearance, even those who are most careful otherwise. Who should they pretty themselves for? Nobody sees them, at most the kitchen staff; anybody happy with that is perfectly free to pretty herself. For the rest, though, to have to be constantly in their small room, or in the gentlemen's rooms, which it's silly and a waste to enter even just with clean clothes on. And always in that artificial light and stuffy air—the stove is constantly lit—and certainly always tired. The best way to spend the one free afternoon in the week is to sleep through it in some pantry off the kitchen, calmly and fearlessly. So why pretty oneself? You barely even get dressed. And then all of a sudden Pepi was transferred to the taproom, where, if you wanted to establish yourself, precisely the opposite was needed, where you were constantly being observed by people, including some quite spoiled and attentive gentlemen, so you always had to be as refined and pleasant-looking as possible. Well, that was quite a change. And Pepi may say of herself that she spared no effort. What would happen later on was of no concern to Pepi. She knew that she had the qualities needed for this post, was quite certain of it, and still had that belief, which nobody can take from her, not even today on the day of her defeat. Only having to prove herself in the early days, that was difficult, because she was after all only a poor chambermaid without clothes or jewels, and because the gentlemen hadn't the patience to wait and see how you turn out but wanted a barmaid right away, without any gap, as is only appropriate, for they turn aside if that isn't the case. One might think their demands weren't all that great, for after all even Frieda could satisfy them. But that is not so. Pepi often thought about this, often got together with Frieda, and for a time even slept with her. It is not easy to figure out Frieda and anybody who doesn't pay close attention—well, do any of the gentlemen pay close attention?—is immediately misled by her. Nobody realizes as keenly as Frieda herself how wretched she looks; the first time you see her letting down her hair, say, you clutch your hands with pity, and if everything were done by rights, a girl of that sort should not even be a chambermaid; she knows it too, and many nights she wept over it, pressed herself up against Pepi and wound Pepi's hair around her own head. But when she's on duty, all her doubts disappear, she thinks she's the most beautiful of all and knows how to convince everybody of that. She understands people, and that is her true skill. And is quick to lie and deceive so that people don't have time to take a closer look at her. Of course in the long run that isn't enough, people do have eyes, and in the end they would be proved right. But no sooner has she noticed this kind of danger than she comes up with some other measure, most recently, for instance, her relationship with Klamm. Her relationship with Klamm! If you don't believe that, you can always check, go to Klamm and ask him. How sly, oh how sly! And if, say, you don't dare go to Klamm with a question like that, and if you aren't admitted with some infinitely more important questions and Klamm shuts himself off completely from you—only from you and people of your sort, since Frieda, for instance, skips in to see him whenever she likes—if that is so, then you can still check the matter, all you need do is wait. Klamm won't be able to tolerate such a false rumor for long, he must after all be wildly eager to discover what is being said about him in the taproom and in the public rooms, all this is of the greatest importance to him, and if it's wrong, then he will correct it at once. But he hasn't corrected it, so it doesn't need to be corrected, it is the utter truth. All you actually see is Frieda taking beer into Klamm's room and then coming out with the payment, but Frieda describes what one cannot see, and one has to take her at her word. But she doesn't even describe it, she isn't about to blurt out secrets like that, no, all around her the secrets blurt out on their own and once they're blurted out, she herself no longer hesitates to talk about them, modestly, without making claims, referring only to matters that are already common knowledge. But not to everything, not, for instance, to the fact that ever since she came to the taproom Klamm has been drinking less beer than he used to, not a great deal less, but clearly less all the same, she says nothing about this; well, there may be various reasons for that, beer has lost its appeal for Klamm just now or maybe he even forgot all about beer drinking over Frieda. So at any rate, however astonishing this may seem, Frieda is Klamm's mistress. How could anything that is good enough for Klamm fail to draw admiration from the others, and so, before you know what is happening, Frieda has become a great beauty, a girl who is made to fit the needs of the taproom and is almost too beautiful, too powerful; but now the taproom is barely good enough for her. And people even find it odd that she's still in the taproom; to be a barmaid is no small thing; from that point of view her relationship with Klamm seems quite credible; but once the barmaid has become Klamm's mistress, why does he leave her in the taproom, especially so long? Why doesn't he lead her higher? One can say to people a thousand times that there's no contradiction here, that Klamm has definite reasons for acting like this, or that Frieda will be raised all of a sudden, perhaps even in the very near future, but this has barely any effect, people have definite ideas and in the end they refuse to let sleight-of-hand of any kind distract them from them. Nobody even doubted anymore that Frieda is the mistress of Klamm, even those who obviously knew better had become too tired to doubt it, "In the name of the devil, be Klamm's mistress," they were thinking, "but if you are that already, we want to see signs of it in your rising up." But they saw no such signs and Frieda remained in the taproom and secretly she was even quite happy that everything remained as it was. But she lost prestige among the people; this couldn't of course have escaped her notice, she usually notices things even before they happen. A really charming beautiful girl, once settled in the taproom, doesn't have to use tricks; so long as she is beautiful, barring some particularly unfortunate coincidence, she will remain a barmaid. But a girl like Frieda has to worry constantly about her position, though of course she doesn't show it, understandably enough, instead she usually complains and curses the post. But in secret she is constantly observing the general mood. And so she saw that people were becoming indifferent, that they no longer thought it worthwhile to lift up their eyes when Frieda came in, that even the domestics no longer bothered with her but rather clung for understandable reasons to Olga and girls of that sort, and she also saw from the landlord's conduct that she was becoming less and less indispensable, one couldn't continue inventing new stories about Klamm, there's a limit to everything—and so dear Frieda decided to try something new. But who could possibly have seen through that right away! Pepi suspected it, but unfortunately she failed to see through it. Frieda decided to create a scandal; she, Klamm's mistress, would throw herself at the first comer, if possible at the lowest of the low. This would cause a stir, they would talk about it a long time and finally, finally they will once again remember what it means to be Klamm's mistress and what it means to reject this honor in the intoxication of a new love. The only difficulty was how to find the appropriate man with whom this clever game could be played. It couldn't be an acquaintance of Frieda's, not even one of the domestics, he would probably have stared wide-eyed at her and gone his way, above all else he wouldn't have maintained sufficient seriousness and it would have been impossible even with the greatest eloquence to spread the rumor that Frieda had been accosted by him, hadn't been able to ward him off, and had in a moment of oblivion succumbed to him. And even if it had to be the lowest of the low, it still had to be someone of whom one could credibly claim that despite his dull and unrefined manner he longed for nobody but Frieda and had no higher wish—good heavens!—than to marry Frieda. But even if it had to be a common man, perhaps lower even than a laborer, far lower than a laborer, then he would still have to be a man who wouldn't make you the laughingstock of every girl and might even seem attractive to some judicious girl. But where do you find a man like that? Another girl would probably have spent her entire life vainly looking for him, but Frieda's good fortune guides the surveyor into the taproom, perhaps on the very evening that the plan first crosses her mind. The surveyor! So what is K. thinking of? What extraordinary ideas go through his head? Is there something special that he wants to achieve? A good appointment, a prize? Does he want something of that sort? Well then he should have gone about the whole thing very differently from the very start. He is nothing, though; it's painful even to think about his situation. He's a surveyor, perhaps that is something since he has learned a trade, but if you don't have any idea what to do with it, it's still nothing. And he still makes demands; without having the least bit of support he makes demands, not directly, but you can still see he's making certain demands, and naturally this is irritating enough. For did he not know that even a chambermaid demeans herself somewhat if she talks to him at any length. And then with all these special demands of his, on that very first evening he goes and falls into the crudest trap with a thud. So is he not ashamed of himself? Well, what was it about Frieda that won him over? For he could own up to it now. Had she really succeeded in pleasing him, that thin yellowish creature? Oh no, he never even looked at her, she simply told him that she was Klamm's mistress; that still struck him as a novelty at the time and so he was lost. But then she had to move out, there was naturally no room for her at the Gentlemen's Inn anymore. Pepi saw her again the morning before the move, the staff had come running, everybody was eager to get a look. And she still had such power that people pitied her; everybody, even her enemies, pitied her; so at the very beginning her calculation proved correct; her having thrown herself away on a man such as that seemed incomprehensible to everyone, a stroke of fate; the little kitchen maids, who of course admire every barmaid, were inconsolable. Even Pepi was affected by it, even she couldn't completely resist, though her attention was actually directed elsewhere. She noticed that Frieda wasn't all that sad. But basically it was a terrible misfortune that had befallen her, she herself acted as though she were very unhappy, but that wasn't good enough, Pepi wouldn't allow herself to be deceived by that game. What kept her going? Perhaps the happiness of her new love? Well, there could be no question of that. But what else could it be? Where did she get the strength to be as coolly amicable as ever, even with Pepi, who was regarded as her successor. Pepi hadn't the time to think about all this just then, she had too much to do with the preparations for the new post. She was probably supposed to start in a few hours and had no beautiful hairdo, no elegant dress, no fine underclothing, no serviceable shoes. All of that had to be put together in a few hours; if you could not fit yourself out properly, then it was better to relinquish the post entirely, for you would certainly lose it otherwise before half an hour had gone by. Well, she almost managed. She has a special talent for hairdressing, the landlady once asked her for a hairdo, it's a special nimbleness with her hands that has been given to her, but then her thick hair is easy to manage. For the dress too there was help at hand. Her two colleagues remained loyal to her, they regard it as something of an honor when a girl from within their own group becomes a barmaid, and besides, later on, if Pepi had gained power, she could have provided them with some advantages. One of the girls had left some precious material, her treasure, lying around for a long time, she had often let the others admire it and probably dreamed of putting it to splendid use at some point, but then—and that was nicely done on her part—since Pepi needed it, she gave it up. And both of them helped her very eagerly with the sewing; had they been sewing for themselves, they couldn't have shown greater zeal. It was even cheerful and gratifying work. They sat there, each on her own bed, one above the other, sewing and singing, passing the finished pieces and accessories up and down. When Pepi thinks about it, her heart grows even heavier at the thought that everything was in vain and that she is going back empty-handed to her friends. What a misfortune and how frivolously it had been brought about, especially by K. How pleased everyone had been about the dress. It seemed a guarantee of success, and after it was finished and they found room for one more small ribbon, the last doubts vanished. And isn't the dress really beautiful? It's already crushed and a little stained, Pepi didn't even have a second dress, she had to wear this one day and night, but you can still see how beautiful it is, it's something not even that accursed Barnabas woman could have come up with. And then the way you can draw it tight and loosen it again as you wish, at the top and the bottom, and the way, although it's only a dress, it can be so easily changed, was a particular advantage and was actually something she had invented. Of course she isn't difficult to sew for, Pepi wasn't boasting about this, anything will look good on healthy young girls. It was far more difficult to get hold of underclothing and boots and this actually is where the misfortune commences. Here, too, her girlfriends helped out as best they could, but they weren't able to do much. For it was only coarse underclothing that she gathered and sewed, and instead of boots with high heels she had to make do with slippers, which you feel better hiding than showing. They consoled Pepi: after all, Frieda didn't dress very prettily either and traipsed about so sloppily at times that the guests would rather be served by the cellar boys than by her. That was true, but this was something Frieda could permit herself, for she had already won favor and prestige; if at some point a lady shows up dirty and carelessly dressed, that only makes her all the more enticing, but what about a novice like Pepi? And in any case Frieda was completely incapable of dressing well; she's utterly lacking in taste; if a person happens to have yellowish skin, then she is of course stuck with it; she needn't, like Frieda, deck herself out in a cream blouse with a low neckline, and almost blind you with the sight of all that yellow. And even if that hadn't been so, she was really too stingy to dress well; everything she earned she held on to, nobody knew what for. On duty she didn't need money, she made do with lies and dodges, Pepi could not and would not follow this example; she was therefore justified in prettying herself in this way so as to show herself to her best advantage, especially at the start. Had she had great resources to draw on, she would, in spite of Frieda's slyness, in spite of K.'s foolishness, have emerged the victor. Things certainly got off to a good start. She had already acquainted herself with the few little skills and bits of knowledge that were necessary. No sooner was she in the taproom than she had settled in. At work nobody missed Frieda. It wasn't until the second day that a number of guests asked where Frieda was. There hadn't been any mistakes, the landlord was satisfied; on the first day in his anxiety he was always in the taproom, later on he came only now and then, and finally, since the cashbook tallied—the receipts were even a little higher on average than in Frieda's day—he handed everything over to Pepi. She came up with a few innovations. Frieda had, not out of diligence but rather out of stinginess, imperiousness, and fear of giving up her rights to others, supervised the domestics, to some extent anyhow, particularly when there was somebody looking; by contrast, Pepi assigned that entire task to the cellar boys, who are more adept at it. That way she could spend more time on the gentlemen's rooms; the guests were quickly served, but she could still say a few words to each one, unlike Frieda, who claimed that she was reserving herself for Klamm alone and took every word, every approach from other men to be an insult to Klamm. But of course that was clever of her, for if she ever let anyone approach her, it was an enormous favor. But Pepi hates tricks like that, and in any case they're not useful when you're just starting there. Pepi was friendly to each of the customers and each one repaid her with his friendliness. All of them were clearly pleased with the change; when the exhausted gentlemen finally manage to sit down over beer for a moment, you can literally transform them with a glance or a shrug of the shoulders. So eagerly did all of them run their hands through Pepi's curls that she probably had to redo her hair ten times a day; nobody can resist the lure of these curls and bows, not even K., who is so absentminded otherwise. And that's the way those exciting, strenuous, but successful days flew by. If only they hadn't flown by so quickly, if only there had been a few more of them! Four days are too few, even when you're exerting yourself to the point of exhaustion, perhaps a fifth day would have been enough, but four days were too few. True, in those four days Pepi had found some patrons and friends; if she could have trusted all of the looks she was given every time she came in with mugs of beer, she would be awash in a sea of friendship; a clerk called Bratmeier is crazy about her, he bestowed on her this small chain and a pendant, which he had put his portrait into, that certainly was cheeky of him—that and a few other things had happened, but still it had only been four days; but if Pepi put her mind to it, in four days Frieda could almost be forgotten, though not completely, but she would have been forgotten all the same, perhaps even earlier, if she hadn't taken the precaution of putting her name on people's lips with her big scandal; in this way she had become a novelty to people, simply out of curiosity they would have liked to see her again; the very thing they had grown sick and tired of now held some attraction for them again, thanks to K., whom they regarded with utter indifference otherwise, though they wouldn't have given up Pepi in exchange, so long as she was there making her presence felt in the taproom, but they are mostly older gentlemen, cumbersome in their habits, it does take a few days for them to get used to a new barmaid, no matter how advantageous the change may be; quite against the wishes of the gentlemen themselves it does take a few days, maybe only five, but four aren't enough, for despite everything they regarded Pepi merely as a temporary. And then possibly the greatest misfortune, that in those four days, Klamm, even though he had been in the village those first two days, didn't come down to the public room. Had he come, that would have been the decisive test for Pepi, a test, incidentally, that she was least afraid of and even looked forward to. She wouldn't—but of course it's best not to go near matters like that with words—wouldn't have become Klamm's mistress and wouldn't have lied her way up to a position like that, but she could have put the beer glass down on the table at least as nicely as Frieda had done, could have welcomed the guests in a pleasant manner and taken leave of them just as pleasantly, without any of Frieda's pushiness, and if Klamm ever looks for anything in a girl's eyes, then Pepi's eyes would have completely satisfied him. But why did he not come? By chance? Pepi had even believed that at the time. During those two days she expected him any moment, and even during the night she waited for him. "No, Klamm will come," she thought constantly, running back and forth simply out of restless expectation and the wish to be the first to see him the moment he came. This constant disappointment made her tired, perhaps that's why she did not accomplish as much as she might have accomplished. When she had the time, she sneaked up to the corridor, which the staff is strictly forbidden to enter, squeezed into an alcove, and waited. "If Klamm would only come," she thought, "if only I could take the gentleman out of his room and carry him in my arms down to the public room. I wouldn't collapse under the burden, no matter how big it was." But he did not come. In those corridors upstairs it's so silent, one cannot imagine it if one hasn't been there. It's so silent that one cannot stand it there for long, the silence drives one away. Again and again, ten times, Pepi was driven away, but ten times she went back up. That was quite pointless. If Klamm wanted to come, then he would come, but if he did not want to come, Pepi would not entice him out, even though with her pounding heart she was almost suffocating in the alcove. It was pointless, but if he didn't come, then almost everything else was pointless, too. And he did not come. Pepi now knows why Klamm didn't come. Frieda would have been wonderfully amused had she been able to see Pepi in the alcove in the corridor, with both hands on her heart. Klamm didn't come down because Frieda wouldn't let him. It wasn't through her pleas that she had accomplished this, her pleas don't reach Klamm. But she, the spider, has connections nobody knows anything about. When Pepi says something to a guest, she says it openly, the next table can hear it; Frieda has nothing to say to them, she puts the beer on the table and leaves; all one can hear is the rustling of her silk petticoat, the only thing she spends money on. But when she does say something, she does not do so openly, she whispers it to the guest, bending down so that the people at the next table prick up their ears. The things she says are probably quite trivial, but not always, she does have connections, uses some to support others, and if most of them lead nowhere—who would want to have to bother about Frieda all the time?—one or the other of those connections does work. And she now began to exploit these connections, K. gave her the opportunity to do so; instead of sitting with her and keeping watch over her, he hardly ever stays at home, wanders about, has discussions here and there, is attentive to everything, only not to Frieda, and in order to give her even more freedom moves from the Bridge Inn into the empty schoolhouse. What a wonderful way to begin a honeymoon. Well, Pepi is certainly the last one who will reproach K. for not being able to stand being with Frieda; one simply cannot stand being with her. But then why hasn't he left her altogether, why has he gone back to her again and again, why has he created the impression through his wanderings that he is fighting for her. It even looked as if it was only through his contact with Frieda that he had discovered his actual paltriness and in an effort to make himself worthy of Frieda and somehow claw his way to the top had abandoned their life together temporarily, but only in order to be able to make up later on for the privations without being disturbed. Meanwhile Frieda loses no time, she sits in the schoolhouse, to which she probably steered K., and observes the Gentlemen's Inn and observes K. She has excellent messengers at hand, namely, K.'s assistants, whom K.—this is incomprehensible, even if you know K. it's incomprehensible—leaves entirely to her. She sends them to her old friends, reawakens their memories of her, complains of being held captive by a man such as K., agitates against Pepi, announces she'll soon be back, asks for help, begs them not to reveal anything to Klamm, acts as though Klamm has to be protected and can therefore on no account be allowed down to the taproom. What to some she makes out to be consideration for Klamm, she uses with the landlord as an example of her success, pointing out that Klamm doesn't come down anymore; how could he come if the person serving in the taproom is only a Pepi; true, it isn't the landlord's fault, for this Pepi was the best replacement he was able to find, only she won't do, not even for a few days. K. knows nothing about all these activities of Frieda's; when he's not wandering about, he lies at her feet unawares while she counts the hours that keep her from the taproom. But the assistants do more than carry messages, they also serve to make K. jealous and to keep his blood warm. Frieda has known the assistants since childhood, they certainly don't have secrets to keep from one another anymore, but in K.'s honor they begin to long for each other, and the danger arising for K. is that this will turn into a great love. And K. does everything Frieda wants, even the most contradictory things, allows himself to become jealous because of the assistants, but permits the three of them to stay together while he wanders off on his own. It's almost as if he were Frieda's third assistant. Finally Frieda decides, on the strength of her observations, to strike a great blow, she decides to return. And it actually is high time for that, it's admirable how this sly Frieda senses it and takes advantage of it, Frieda's inimitable skill lies in her powers of observation and resolve; if Pepi had that, how different her life would be! Had Frieda only stayed in the schoolhouse another day or two, Pepi cannot be driven out, is a barmaid for good, loved and kept by all, has earned enough money to add some splendid things to her meager wardrobe, and in another day or two Klamm can no longer be kept from the public room by means of intrigue, comes, drinks, feels comfortable, and, if he even notices Frieda's absence, he is extremely pleased with the change, another day or two and Frieda with her scandal, her connections, the assistants, all of that, is completely forgotten, she's never mentioned again. Then she might cling to K. all the more tightly and might, if she were capable of this, truly learn to love him? No, that wouldn't happen either. For even K. doesn't need more than a day to become tired of her and to recognize how dreadfully she deceives him in everything, her so-called beauty, her so-called fidelity, and most of all her so-called love of Klamm; only one day more, that's all it takes for him to chase her and that whole filthy assistant mess from the house, even K. doesn't need any more than that. And just then, between these two dangers, when the grave is beginning to close above her, K. in his simplemindedness keeps the last narrow path open for her, just then she takes to her heels. All of a sudden—and this is something hardly anybody was expecting anymore, it goes against nature—all of a sudden it is she who is pushing away K., who still loves her and constantly pursues her, and it is she who with some helpful pressure from friends and assistants appears to the landlord as a savior, all the more enticing owing to her scandal, desired by the lowest as well as the highest, as has been proved, but who was only enthralled with the lowest for a moment and soon pushed him away, as is only fitting, and is as unattainable for him and for everyone else as she used to be, except that earlier one had just doubted all this but now one had been persuaded again. So she returns, the landlord with a side glance at Pepi hesitates—should he sacrifice the barmaid who proved her worth?—but he's soon persuaded, so much speaks in favor of Frieda, especially since she'll woo Klamm back to the public rooms. And now it's already evening. Pepi won't wait until Frieda comes and makes a triumphant show out of taking on the post. She has already handed over the cashbook to the landlady, she can leave. The bed compartment in the chambermaids' room downstairs is prepared for her, she will go down, bc greeted by her tearful friends, rip the dress from her body, the ribbons from her hair, and stuff everything into a corner where it is well hidden and doesn't needlessly remind her of times that ought to be forgotten. Then she will take the big bucket and the broom, clench her teeth, and get down to work. But first she had to tell all this to K., who even now couldn't have made this out without some help, so that he for once would see clearly how horribly he has treated Pepi and how unhappy he has made her. Of course he too has been subjected to nothing but mistreatment.

Pepi had finished. Breathing deeply, she wiped a few tears from her eyes and cheeks and looked at K., nodding her head as though she wanted to say that this had really nothing at all to do with her misfortune, she would bear it and did not need help or consolation from anybody, least of all from K., for she knew a great deal about life, despite her youth, and her misfortune only confirmed her knowledge, but it certainly had to do with K.; she had wanted to hold a mirror up to him, and even after all her hopes had been dashed she had thought it was still necessary to do so.

"What a wild imagination you have, Pepi," said K. "It's not at all true that you've only just discovered all this, those are only dreams from your dark narrow chambermaids' room downstairs, which are not out of place there, but here in the public taproom they sound odd. You couldn't make your mark here with ideas like that, well, that's quite understandable. Even the dress and hairdo you boast about are nothing but the evil spawn of that darkness and of those beds in your room; they're no doubt all very fine down there, but here everyone laughs at them, secretly or openly. And what else were you saying? That I was mistreated and deceived? No, dear Pepi, I was as little mistreated and deceived as you were. It's true, for the moment Frieda has left me, or has, as you put it, taken to her heels with an assistant, you have certainly caught a glimmer of the truth, and it is also really quite unlikely that she will ever become my wife, but it is absolutely untrue that I would have grown tired of her, let alone that I would have driven her away the very next day or indeed that she would have deceived me, as otherwise a woman might deceive a man. You chambermaids are used to spying through a keyhole, and so from the tiny details that you actually see you often draw grand but false conclusions about the whole thing. The result is that, for example in this case, I know far less than you do. I certainly cannot give as detailed an explanation as you can of the reasons why Frieda left me. The most likely explanation, it seems to me, is the one you mentioned but didn't use, namely my neglect of her. That's unfortunately true, I did neglect her, but there were specific reasons for that, which are irrelevant here; I would be happy if she returned, but then I would immediately start neglecting her again. That's how it is. When she was with me, I was always away on those wanderings that you ridicule; now that she's gone, I have almost nothing to do, am tired, and I desire to have even less to do. Don't you have any advice for me, Pepi?" "Oh, yes," said Pepi, becoming animated all of a sudden and seizing K. by the shoulder, "both of us were deceived, let's stay together, come on down with me to the girls." "So long as you complain about being deceived," said K., "I cannot reach an understanding with you. You're constantly wishing to have been deceived, because it's flattering and because it moves you. But the truth is that you aren't suited for that position. How clear that unsuitability must be if even I, the most ignorant person in your opinion, can see it. You're a good girl, Pepi, but it isn't so easy to see that; I, for one, initially considered you cruel and arrogant, but you're not, you're simply confused by this position, which confuses you because you aren't suited to it. I don't want to say that the position is too lofty for you, it's really not such an exceptional position, but looked at more closely, perhaps it is somewhat more honorable than your previous position; but on the whole, there is no great difference, the two are really confusingly similar, one could almost claim that it would be preferable to be a chambermaid rather than serve in the taproom, for one is always surrounded by secretaries there, while here, though one may serve the superiors of the secretaries in the public rooms, one must waste one's time with the lowest riffraff, like me, for instance; by rights I'm not allowed to spend my time anywhere except here in the taproom, so is it such an enormous honor to associate with me? Well, it seems so to you and you may have your reasons for that. But that's why you are unsuitable. It's a position like any other, but to you it is heaven, so you seize everything with exaggerated eagerness and pretty yourself just as, in your opinion, the angels pretty themselves—but in reality they're different—you tremble for the position, feel you're constantly being hounded, seek to win over through exaggerated friendliness everyone who could to your mind support you, but you only disturb and disgust them, for what they want at the inn is peace, and not the barmaids' worries on top of their own worries. It is possible that after Frieda's departure none of the high-ranking guests noticed what had happened, but today they know it and really long for Frieda, since Frieda must have managed everything quite differently. No matter how she is otherwise and no matter how high a regard she had for her position, on duty she was highly experienced, cool and restrained, you even stress that yourself, though you obviously haven't learned anything from the example. Did you ever notice that look of hers? That surely was no longer the look of a barmaid, it was almost the look of a landlady. That look of hers swept over everything, but also took in each person, and the glance accorded to each one was still sufficiently strong to conquer him. Who cares that perhaps she was rather thin, rather old, that one could imagine more plentiful hair; those are trifles compared with what she really had in her possession, and anybody who found these shortcomings disturbing would simply have demonstrated his incapacity to appreciate higher things. One certainly cannot reproach Klamm for that; it's only because of your mistaken point of view as an inexperienced young girl that you cannot believe in Klamm's love for Frieda. To you, Klamm seems unattainable—and rightly so—you therefore think Frieda couldn't have approached Klamm either. You are mistaken. On this question I would rely solely on Frieda's word even if I didn't have unmistakable proof. No matter how unbelievable this may seem to you, and no matter how difficult it may be for you to reconcile it with your notions of the world, of officialdom, of refinement, and of the effect of female beauty, it is true all the same that just as we sit here and I take your hand in mine they sat there side by side, Klamm and Frieda, as if it were the most natural thing in the world, and he came down here of his own free will, even hurried down, nobody was lying in wait for him in the corridor and leaving other tasks undone, Klamm himself had to go to the trouble of coming down, and the defects in Frieda's clothing that would have horrified you did not disturb him at all. You don't want to believe her! And you don't realize how you're exposing yourself, and the lack of experience you are revealing in this way. Even someone who knew nothing of her relationship with Klamm would certainly have to recognize by observing her nature that it had been molded by someone who was more than you and me and all of the people in the village, and that the conversations between them went beyond the jokes that go back and forth between guests and waitresses and that seem to be your goal in life. But I'm being unjust toward you. You do recognize Frieda's good qualities yourself, only you're interpreting everything incorrectly, you think she's simply using all of this for her own purposes and to some evil end, or even as a weapon against you. No, Pepi, even if she had arrows like that, she could not shoot them at such close range. And selfish? One could rather say that by sacrificing the things she already owned and the things she might have expected to gain she gave the two of us the chance to prove ourselves in a higher position, but we have disappointed her, and we're even forcing her to come back. I don't know whether that is so, nor am I certain of my guilt, it's only when I compare myself with you that such things come to mind; it is as if both of us had struggled too hard, too noisily, too childishly, too naively to obtain something that can be easily and imperceptibly gained through, say, Frieda's tranquillity and Frieda's reserve, and had done so by weeping, scratching, and tugging, just as a child tugs at the tablecloth but doesn't gain anything and only tears down all that splendor and puts it out of his reach forever—I don't know whether that is so, but I certainly do know that it's more like that than as you say." "Oh, well," said Pepi, "you're in love with Frieda because she ran away from you, it's not hard to be in love with her when she's gone. But even if everything is as you would have it, and even if all this, even your ridicule of me, is justified—what are you going to do now? Frieda has left you, neither my explanation nor yours gives you any hope that she'll return, and even if she does, in the meantime you'll have to stay somewhere, it's cold and you don't have work or a bed, so come to us, you'll like my friends, we'll make you comfortable, you'll help us with our work, which is really too heavy for girls to do on their own, we girls won't have to fend for ourselves anymore, and we will no longer be afraid at night. Come to us! My friends know Frieda too, we'll tell you stories about her until you have grown tired of them. Do come! We have pictures of Frieda too and we'll show them to you. In those days Frieda was even more unassuming than she is now, you'll barely recognize her, at most by her eyes, which had a sly expression even then. So will you come?" "Is that permitted? Yesterday there was after all a big scandal because I was caught in your corridor." "Because you were caught; but when you are with us, you won't be caught. Nobody will know about you, except for the three of us. Ah, it'll be fun. Life there now seems more bearable to me than it did only a moment ago. Perhaps I won't even lose that much by having to go away from here. Listen, even with only the three of us we weren't bored, one must sweeten the bitterness of life, it's already been made bitter for us in our youth to ensure that our tongues don't get spoiled, the three of us stick together, we live as pleasantly as possible there, you will like Henriette in particular, but Emilie too, I have already told them about you, there one listens to such stories with incredulity, as though nothing could ever happen outside that room, it's warm and narrow, and we huddle all the more closely; no, even though we depend on each other, we haven't become tired of each other; on the contrary, whenever I think of my friends I'm almost glad to be returning; why should I climb any higher than they; that's precisely what kept us together, that for all three of us the future was blocked off in the same way, but then I broke through and was separated from them; I didn't forget them of course and my first concern was how to help them; my own position was still uncertain—I had no idea just how uncertain—and it wasn't long before I talked to the landlord and Henriette and Emilie. Concerning Henriette, the landlord wasn't altogether intransigent, but for Emilie, who's much older than the two of us, she's about Frieda's age, he held out no hope. But, believe it or not, they have no wish to leave, they know the life that they're leading there is miserable, but they've already reconciled themselves to it, the dear souls; I think their tears over my departure were mostly out of grief that I had to leave the room we share and go out into the cold—there, everything outside the room seems cold—and that I had to cope with strange tall people in strange tall rooms for the sole purpose of making a living, which after all I had been doing quite successfully in our common household. They probably won't be at all astonished when I return and will weep for a while and bewail my fate only so as to let me have my way. But then they'll see you and realize that it was actually a good thing that I went off. It'll make them happy to see that we now have a man who will help us and protect us and they'll simply be delighted that all this must be kept secret and that through this secret we will be bound together even more closely than we were before. Come, oh please, come to us! There will be no obligation, you won't be confined to our room all the time, as we are. Then, when spring comes and you find a refuge somewhere else and don't like being with us anymore, you can of course leave, but even then you must keep this secret and not give us away, since that would be our last hour at the Gentlemen's Inn; and in other ways, too, you must naturally be careful while you are with us and not go showing yourself anywhere, unless we've said that there's no danger there, and in general you must follow our advice; that's the only thing that binds you and surely you're just as keen about this as we are, but otherwise you're completely free, the work we'll assign you won't be too difficult, you need have no fear of that. So will you come?" "How much longer is it till spring?" asked K. "Till spring?" repeated Pepi, "the winter here is long, a very long winter, and monotonous. But we don't complain about that down there, we're safe from the winter. Of course at some point spring does come and summer too, and they certainly have their day, but in one's memory spring and summer seem so short, as if they didn't last much longer than two days, and sometimes even on these days, throughout the most beautiful day, snow falls."

Just then the door opened, Pepi gave a start, her thoughts had strayed too far from the taproom, but it was not Frieda, it was the landlady. She feigned surprise on finding K. still here, K. excused himself by saying that he had been waiting for the landlady, he also thanked her for the permission he had been given to spend the night here. The landlady could not understand why K. had waited for her. K. said he had the impression that the landlady wanted to say something else to him, and he begged her pardon if he had been mistaken, besides he had to leave, he had left the school, where he was janitor, to its own devices for too long, that summons yesterday was to blame for everything, he didn't have enough experience in such matters yet, it would certainly never happen again, never again would he create unpleasantness for the landlady, like yesterday. And he bowed with the intention of leaving. The landlady gazed at K., as if she were dreaming. Her gaze detained K. longer than he had intended. And now she was even smiling a little, having only just been awakened, as it were, by the astonished expression on K.'s face; it was as though she were expecting an answer to her smile and woke up only because the answer failed to come. "Yesterday, I think it was, you were so cheeky as to say something about my dress." K. couldn't remember. "You cannot remember? Cheekiness is often followed by cowardice." K. excused himself, yesterday he had been tired and might have said something like that, in any case he couldn't remember anymore. Besides, what could he have said about the landlady's clothes? That they were so beautiful that he had never before seen anything like them. At any rate he had never seen a landlady working in such clothes. "Stop making comments like that," the landlady said quickly, "I do not want to hear another word from you about the clothes. My clothes are no concern of yours. I forbid you to talk about them, once and for all." K. bowed again and went to the door. "Well, what does that mean," the landlady called after him, "that you've never seen a landlady working in such clothes. What's the point of senseless comments like that? That makes no sense at all. What are you trying to say?" K. turned around and asked the landlady not to get upset. Of course it was a pointless comment. Besides, he knew absolutely nothing about clothes. In the situation he was in every clean, unpatched dress seemed valuable to him. He had simply been surprised to see the landlady appear at night in the corridor in such a beautiful evening dress among all those barely dressed men, that was all. "Well, then," said the landlady, "you finally seem to have remembered the comment you made yesterday. And you're now topping it off with some more nonsense. As for your not knowing anything about clothes, that is true. But in that case—and I am requesting this of you in all seriousness—do also refrain from passing judgment on the valuableness of clothes or the inappropriateness of evening dresses and so on. Besides"—it was if a cold shudder went running through her—"you may have nothing to do with my clothes, do you hear?" And since K. was about to turn away again without saying a word, she asked: "So where did you acquire your knowledge of clothes?" K. shrugged and said that he had no such knowledge. "You have no such knowledge," said the landlady, "then you shouldn't act as though you do. Come to the office, I'll show you something, and then you will, I hope, cease being cheeky for good." She went through the door first; Pepi leaped over to K.; under the pretext of settling K.'s account, they quickly reached agreement; this was quite easy since K. knew the courtyard, which had a gate leading into the side street; by the gate was a small door behind which Pepi would be standing in about an hour and which she would open on the third knock.

The private office was opposite the taproom, all he had to do now was cross the corridor, the landlady already stood in the illuminated office, looking impatiently in K.'s direction. But there was another interruption. Gerstäcker had been waiting in the corridor and wanted to speak to K. It wasn't easy to shake him off, even the landlady helped out by chiding Gerstäcker for his intrusiveness. "So where to? So where to?" Gerstäcker could still be heard calling even after the door had been closed, and his words were disagreeably interspersed with sighs and coughs.

It was a small overheated room. By the end walls were a reading stand and an iron safe, along the side walls a cabinet and an ottoman. Most of the room was occupied by the cabinet, which not only took up the entire side wall but was so deep that it made the room much narrower, three sliding doors were needed to open it completely. The landlady pointed to the ottoman, K. should take a seat, she herself sat on the swivel chair by the desk. "Have you never even learned anything about clothesmaking?" asked the landlady. "No, never," said K. "Well, then, what are you?" "A surveyor." "And what's that?" K. explained, the explanation made her yawn. "You're not telling the truth. So why aren't you telling the truth?" "You are not either." "I'm not? You're becoming cheeky again. And even if I weren't telling the truth—must I answer to you? And in what way am I not telling the truth?" "You are not only a landlady, as you claim." "Look here, you're full of discoveries. So what else am I? But your cheekiness is really getting out of hand." "I don't know what else you are. I can see only that you are a landlady and besides that you are wearing clothes which aren't suitable for a landlady and which, so far as I know, no one else in the village wears." "Well then we finally are getting to the heart of the matter, you cannot even conceal it, perhaps you are not cheeky, you are like a child who knows some silly thing and cannot be kept silent. So speak. What's special about these clothes?" "You'll be angry if I tell you." "No, I shall laugh, it'll be nothing but childish talk. What kind of clothes are they?" "So you do want to know. Well, they are made of good material, quite costly, but they are outmoded, overdone, they've been frequently altered, are worn out, and aren't suitable for your age, your figure, or your position. They struck me at once when I first saw you, it was about a week ago, here in the corridor." "Oh, so that's it, then. They're outmoded, overdone, and what else? And how do you come to know all this?" "I can see it. No training is required." "So you can see it that easily. You do not need to ask, you simply know immediately what fashion demands. Then you will become indispensable to me, since I do have a weakness for beautiful clothes. And now what will you say once you see that the wardrobe here is full of clothes." She pushed aside the sliding doors, one could see the dresses pressed tightly together throughout the length and breadth of the wardrobe, they were mostly dark-colored, gray, brown, or black dresses, all of them had been carefully hung up and spread out. "These are my dresses, they are all in your opinion outmoded and overdone. But these are simply the dresses I have no space for in my room upstairs, I have two more full wardrobes there, two wardrobes, each one almost as large as this one here. You are amazed?" "No, I was expecting something like that, for, as I said, you are not only a landlady, you have other goals." "My only goal is to dress beautifully, and you are a fool, or a child, or a very malicious, dangerous person. Off with you now!" K. was already in the corridor and Gerstäcker had again caught hold of his sleeve when the landlady called after him: "I am getting a new dress tomorrow, perhaps I shall send for you."

Gerstäcker, waving his hand angrily, as if determined to silence from afar the landlady, who was bothering him, asked K. to go with him. Initially he refused to give any further explanation. He paid scarcely any attention to K.'s objection that he needed to go to the school. Only when K. began to resist being dragged did Gerstäcker tell him that he shouldn't worry, that he would be given everything he needed at his house, that he could give up his position as school janitor but should finally come, he had spent all day waiting for him, his mother had no idea where he was. Gradually giving way to him, K. asked what he wanted in return for food and lodgings. Gerstäcker gave only a cursory answer, he needed K.'s help with the horses, he himself now had other business, but K. shouldn't let himself be dragged along like this and make things needlessly difficult for him. If he wanted to be paid, he would be paid. But K. now came to a halt, despite all the dragging. He didn't know anything at all about horses. That wasn't necessary, Gerstäcker said impatiently, clasping his hands angrily in order to induce K. to go with him. "I know why you want to take me with you," K. said finally. What K. knew was of no concern to Gerstäcker. "Because you think I can get something out of Erlanger for you." "Certainly," said Gerstäcker, "why else would I be interested in you?" K. laughed, took Gerstäcker's arm, and let himself be led through the darkness.

The room in Gerstäcker's cottage was only dimly illuminated by the fire in the hearth and by a candle stump in the light of which someone deep inside an alcove sat bent under the crooked protruding beams, reading a book. It was Gerstäcker's mother. She held out her trembling hand to K. and had him sit down beside her, she spoke with great difficulty, it was difficult to understand her, but what she said

Appendix

AFTERWORD TO THE GERMAN CRITICAL EDITION

BY MALCOLM PASLEY

Kafka began *The Castle* in January 1922, in a mountain village where he had sought refuge after a severe breakdown. On the evening of his arrival he notes in his diary: "The strange, mysterious, perhaps dangerous, perhaps redeeming consolation of writing." He had long been unproductive, and it was many years since he had attempted a substantial piece of work.

He continued work on the novel in Prague (where he read parts of it to Max Brod), and then at his sister Ottla's house in the country; but in September he writes to Brod: "I have not spent this past week very cheerfully, for I have had to give up the Castle story, evidently for good." Like all the novels he had previously embarked on, this last and most ambitious one remained a fragment.

When Kafka died in 1924, Brod rapidly began to make his unpublished works known. He brought out the *The Trial* in 1925, *The Castle* in 1926, and *Amerika* in 1927. Of his first edition of *The Castle* Brod later declares: "At that time my aim was to present in accessible form an unconventional, disturbing work which had not been quite finished: thus every effort was made to avoid anything that might have emphasized its fragmentary state." In order to achieve this he brought the novel to a close at a point which suggested to him that the hero had suffered a "probably decisive" defeat, namely when K. loses Frieda (end of

---

This afterword is a translation of that which was written for the paperback edition of the novel in the German critical edition (Franz Kafka, *Das Schloß*, Roman in der Fassung der Handschrift [Frankfurt am Main: Fischer Taschenbuch Verlag, 1994], 385–90).

chapter 22 in the critical edition). Almost a fifth of Kafka's text was thus omitted.

Brod's second edition, which restored most of what he had left out, went virtually unnoticed for political reasons. It was published in 1935 in Berlin, by Schocken Verlag, which was only permitted to issue its books in limited editions (and with sales restricted to Jewish readers); that same year Kafka's work as a whole was entered in the notorious "List of Harmful and Undesirable Literature." So it was not in the original German that this novel by a writer rejected in the Third Reich became world famous, but through translations—above all the English translation by Willa and Edwin Muir (1930). But all these translations were based on the text of Brod's severely abridged first edition. The fuller text which he presented in 1935 did not become widely known until much later, when it was republished in 1946 (by Schocken Books, New York) and in 1951 (by S. Fischer, Frankfurt am Main).

After Brod had completed his own editorial work and most of Kafka's manuscripts had become available for study (in 1961), it was possible to undertake the critical edition of his writings, diaries, and letters. The first volume to appear was *The Castle* (with the accompanying critical apparatus in a separate volume) in 1982.

In this edition the chaptering of the novel differs markedly from Brod's. A list of numbered chapter headings in Kafka's hand, together with marks in the manuscript indicating chapter divisions, makes clear what the author intended. (Since Kafka wrote on principle without advance planning—"open-endedly," as he put it—the chaptering of a story could only be determined retrospectively, as the story developed: thus at the time he abandoned the novel the question of dividing up the last part of the text he wrote had not yet arisen.)

Kafka never prepared his "Castle story" for publication. He merely brought it to the stage at which he could read aloud from it if occasion arose. This informal character of his text is of course preserved in the critical edition, for the sake of authenticity, but Brod was governed by other considerations: when he produced his fuller version of the novel in 1935 the prime need was still to make the existence of Kafka's unpublished works more generally known. He and his co-editor, Heinz Politzer, wished to make the text of the novel as easy of access as possible; they therefore emended, among other things, such local "Prague and Austrian forms" as might "impede the diffusion of Kafka's writings."[1] If Kafka had prepared the work for press, he might indeed have taken some steps in this direction himself. However, the attempts to correct Kafka's supposed mistakes sometimes proved thoroughly misleading. For example, in the first paragraph of the novel Kafka wrote: "For a long time K. stood on the wooden bridge which *leads* from the main road to the village . . . " This is "corrected" to read: " . . . which *led* from the main road to the village . . . " But the present tense is by no means an error on Kafka's part: on the contrary, it signals the presence of a narrator who is not wholly shackled to his hero's awareness, but who can oversee more and vouch for more than he can.

Finally, a word needs to be said about Kafka's light and sometimes unconventional punctuation. When a continuous sequence of the hero's experiences and thoughts is narrated, this is done in a single sentence, divided by commas only, so as not to interrupt the flow:

> Actually, they had only moved out the maids, aside from that the room was probably unchanged, there were no sheets on the one bed, just a few pillows and a horse blanket left in the same state as everything else after last night, on the wall there were a few saints' pictures and photographs of soldiers, the room hadn't even been aired, they were evidently hoping the new guest wouldn't stay long and did nothing to keep him.

In the Brod/Politzer edition one clause is detached from this chain to form a separate sentence, so that the impulse of the passage is lost.

Kafka's unorthodox punctuation serves not so much to clarify the grammatical structure of his sentences as to convey the rhythm of the events and thoughts recounted. It is related to the predominantly oral quality of his narrative style. He is known to have judged his own stories above all by the effect which they had when read aloud. "Readers would do well," remarks one critic, "to try and restore to his language the sound pattern which he gave it, and not to remain content with the poor substitute of silent reading."[2]

Notes

1. Heinz Politzer, "Zur Kafka-Philologie," *Die Sammlung* 2 (1935): 386f.
2. Richard Thieberger, "Sprache," in *Kafka-Handbuch*, ed. Hartmut Binder (Stuttgart, 1979), 2: 198.

CHRONOLOGY

1883	July 3: Franz Kafka is born in Prague, son of Hermann Kafka and Julie, née Löwy.
1889	Enters a German primary school. Birth of his sister Elli Kafka, his first surviving sibling.
1892	Birth of his sister Ottla Kafka.
1893	Enters Old City German Secondary School in Prague.
1896	June 13: Bar mitzvah—described in family invitation as "Confirmation."
1897	Anti-Semitic riots in Prague; Hermann Kafka's dry goods store is spared.
1899–1903	Early writings (destroyed).
1901	Graduates from secondary school. Enters German University in Prague. Studies chemistry for two weeks, then law.
1902	Spring: Attends lectures on German literature and the humanities. Travels to Munich, planning to continue German studies there. Returns to Prague. October: First meeting with Max Brod.
1904	Begins writing "Description of a Struggle."
1905	Vacation in Zuckmantel, Silesia. First love affair.
1906	Clerk in uncle's law office. June: Doctor of Law degree.
1906–1907	Legal practice in the *Landesgericht* (provincial high court) and *Strafgericht* (criminal court).
1907–1908	Temporary position in the Prague branch of the private insurance company Assicurazioni Generali.
1908	March: Kafka's first publication—eight prose pieces appear in the review *Hyperion*. July 30: Enters the semi-state-owned Workers Accident Insurance Company for the Kingdom of Bohemia in Prague; works initially in the statistical and claims departments. Spends time in coffeehouses and cabarets.

1909 Begins keeping diaries. April: Kafka's department head lauds his "exceptional faculty for conceptualization." September: Travels with Max and Otto Brod to northern Italy, where they see airplanes for the first time. Writes article "The Aeroplanes in Brescia," which subsequently appears in the daily paper *Bohemia*. Frequent trips to inspect factory conditions in the provinces.

1910 May: Promoted to *Concipist* (junior legal advisor); sees Yiddish acting troupe. October: Vacation in Paris with Brod brothers.

1911 Trip with Max Brod to northern Italy and Paris; spends a week in a Swiss natural-health sanatorium. Becomes a silent partner in the asbestos factory owned by his brother-in-law. October 4: Sees Yiddish play *Der Meshumed* (The Apostate) at Café Savoy. Friendship with the Yiddish actor Yitzhak Löwy. Pursues interest in Judaism.

1912 February 18: Gives "little introductory lecture" on Yiddish language. August: Assembles his first book, *Meditation*; meets Felice Bauer. Writes the stories "The Judgment" and "The Transformation" (frequently entitled "The Metamorphosis" in English), begins the novel *The Man Who Disappeared* (first published in 1927 as *Amerika*, the title chosen by Brod). October: Distressed over having to take charge of the family's asbestos factory, considers suicide. December: Gives first public reading ("The Judgment").

1913 Extensive correspondence with Felice Bauer, whom he visits three times in Berlin. Promoted to vice-secretary. Takes up gardening. In Vienna attends international conference on accident prevention and observes Eleventh Zionist Congress; travels by way of Trieste, Venice, and Verona to Riva.

1914 June: Official engagement to Felice Bauer. July: Engagement is broken. Travels through Lübeck to the Danish resort of Marielyst. Diary entry, August 2: "Germany has declared war on Russia—swimming club in the afternoon." Works on *The Trial*; writes "In the Penal Colony."

1915 January: First meeting with Felice Bauer after breaking engagement. March: At the age of thirty-one moves for the first time into own quarters. November: "The Transformation" ("The Metamorphosis") appears; Kafka asks a friend: "What do you say about the terrible things that are happening in our house?"

1916 July: Ten days with Felice Bauer at Marienbad. November: In a small house on Alchemists' Lane in the Castle district of Prague begins to write the stories later collected in *A Country Doctor*.

1917 Second engagement to Felice Bauer. September: Diagnosis of tuberculosis. Moves back into parents' apartment. Goes to stay with his favorite sister, Ottla, on a farm in the northern Bohemian town of Zürau. December: Second engagement to Felice Bauer is broken.

1918 In Zürau writes numerous aphorisms about "the last things." Reads Kierkegaard. May: Resumes work at insurance institute.

1919 Summer: To the chagrin of his father announces engagement to Julie Wohryzek, daughter of a synagogue custodian. Takes Hebrew lessons from Friedrich Thieberger. November: Wedding to Julie Wohryzek is postponed. Writes "Letter to His Father."

1920 Promotion to institute secretary. April: Convalescence vacation in Merano, Italy; beginning of correspondence with Milena Jesenská. May: Publication of *A Country Doctor*, with a dedication to Hermann Kafka. July: Engagement to Julie Wohryzek broken. November: Anti-Semitic riots in Prague; Kafka writes to Milena: "Isn't the obvious course to leave a place where one is so hated?"

1921 Sanatorium at Matliary in the Tatra mountains (Slovakia). August: Returns to Prague. Hands all his diaries to Milena Jesenská.

1922 Diary entry, January 16: Writes about nervous breakdown. January 27: Travels to Spindlermühle, a resort on the Polish border, where begins to write *The Castle*. March 15: Reads beginning section of novel to Max

Brod. November: After another breakdown, informs Brod that he can no longer "pick up the thread."

1923 Resumes Hebrew studies. Sees Hugo Bergmann, who invites him to Palestine. July: Meets nineteen-year-old Dora Diamant in Müritz on the Baltic Sea. They dream of opening a restaurant in Tel-Aviv, with Dora as cook and Franz as waiter. September: Moves to inflation-ridden Berlin to live with Dora. Writes "The Burrow."

1924 Health deteriorates. March: Brod takes Kafka back to Prague. Writes "Josephine the Singer." April 19: Accompanied by Dora Diamant, enters Dr. Hoffman's sanatorium at Kierling, near Vienna. Corrects the galleys for the collection of stories *A Hunger Artist*. June 3: Kafka dies at age forty. June 11: Burial in the Jewish Cemetery in Prague-Strašnice.

BIBLIOGRAPHY

Primary

While all of Kafka's works are interrelated, the following titles have a direct bearing on *The Castle*:

Kafka, Franz. *The Complete Stories*. Ed. Nahum N. Glatzer. New York, 1983.

———. *The Diaries, 1910–1923*. Ed. Max Brod. New York, 1988.

———. *Letters to Milena*. Trans. Philip Boehm. New York, 1990.

Secondary

BIOGRAPHICAL

Brod, Max. *Franz Kafka: A Biography.* Trans. G. Humphreys Roberts and Richard Winston. New York, 1960.

Citati, Pietro. *Kafka.* Trans. Raymond Rosenthal. New York, 1990.

Karl, Frederick. *Representative Man: Prague, Germans, Jews, and the Crisis of Modernism.* New York, 1991.

Northey, Anthony. *Kafka's Relatives: Their Lives and His Writing*. New Haven, Conn., 1991.

Pawel, Ernst. *The Nightmare of Reason: A Life of Franz Kafka*. New York, 1985.

Wagenbach, Klaus. *Franz Kafka: Pictures of a Life.* Trans. Arthur S. Wensinger. New York, 1984.

THE CASTLE

Bloom, Harold, ed. *Franz Kafka's "The Castle."* New York, 1988.

Cohn, Ruby. "*Watt* in the Light of *The Castle.*" *Comparative Literature* 13 (1961): 154–66. (On the literary relationship between Kafka and Beckett.)

Dowden, Stephen D. *Kafka's "Castle" and the Critical Imagination.* Columbia, S.C., 1995.

Gray, Ronald. *The Castle.* Cambridge, 1956.

Harman, Mark. "'Digging the Pit of Babel': Retranslating Franz Kafka's *Castle*." *New Literary History* 27 (1996): 291–311.

———. "Approaching K.'s *Castle*." *Sewanee Review* 105, no. 4 (Winter, 1997):513–23.

Neumeyer, Peter F., ed. *Twentieth Century Interpretations of "The Castle."* Englewood Cliffs, N.J., 1969.

Robert, Marthe. *The Old and the New: From Don Quixote to Kafka*. Trans. Carol Cosman. Berkeley, 1977.

Sebald, W. G. "The Law of Ignominy: Authority, Messianism, and Exile in *The Castle*." In *On Kafka: Semi-Centenary Perspectives,* ed. Franz Kuna. New York, 1976.

Sheppard, Richard. *On Kafka's "Castle."* London and New York, 1973.

GENERAL

Adorno, Theodor. "Franz Kafka." In *Prisms,* trans. Samuel and Shierry Weber. London, 1967.

Alter, Robert. *Necessary Angels: Kafka, Benjamin, Scholem*. Cambridge, Mass., 1990.

Anderson, Mark, ed. *Reading Kafka*. New York, 1989.

———. *Kafka's Clothes: Ornament and Aestheticism in the Habsburg "Fin de Siècle."* Oxford, 1992.

Arendt, Hannah. "Franz Kafka: A Revaluation." *Partisan Review* 11 (1944): 412–22. Reprinted in *Essays in Understanding, 1930–1945,* ed. Jerome Kohn. New York, 1994.

Beck, Evelyn Torton. *Kafka and the Yiddish Theater: Its Impact on His Work*. Madison, Wis., 1971.

Benjamin, Walter. "Franz Kafka on the Tenth Anniversary of His Death." In *Illuminations,* ed. Hannah Arendt. New York, 1969.

Bernheimer, Charles. *Flaubert and Kafka: Studies in Psychopoetic Structure*. New Haven, Conn., 1996.

Boa, Elizabeth. *Kafka: Gender, Class and Race in the Letters and Fictions*. Oxford, 1996.

Canetti, Elias. *Kafka's Other Trial*. Trans. Christopher Middleton. New York, 1974.

Corngold, Stanley. *Franz Kafka: The Necessity of Form*. Ithaca, N.Y., 1988.

Crick, Joyce. "Kafka and the Muirs." In *The World of Franz Kafka,* ed. J. P. Stern. New York, 1980.

Deleuze, Giles, and Félix Guattari. *Kafka: Toward a Minor Literature*. Trans. Dana Polan. Minneapolis, 1986.

Gilman, Sander. *Franz Kafka, the Jewish Patient.* New York, 1995.

Grözinger, Karl Erich. *Kafka and Kabbalah.* Trans. Susan H. Ray. New York, 1994.

Harman, Mark. "Irony, Ambivalence, and Belief in Kleist and Kafka." *Journal of the Kafka Society* 1/2 (1984): 3–13.

———. "Biography and Autobiography: Necessary Antagonists?" *Journal of the Kafka Society* 1/2 (1986): 56–62.

———. "Life into Art: Kafka's Self-Stylization in the Diaries." In *Franz Kafka (1883–1983): His Craft and Thought,* ed. Roman Struc and J. C. Yardley, 101–16. Calgary, Alberta, 1986.

———. "Joyce and Kafka." *Sewanee Review* 101, no. 1 (1993): 66–84.

Kundera, Milan. *Testaments Betrayed: An Essay in Nine Parts.* Trans. Linda Asher. New York, 1995.

Politzer, Heinz. *Franz Kafka: Parable and Paradox.* Ithaca, N.Y., 1966.

Robert, Marthe. *As Lonely as Franz Kafka.* Trans. Ralph Manheim. New York, 1982.

Robertson, Ritchie. *Kafka: Judaism, Politics, and Literature.* Oxford, 1985.

Rolleston, James. *Kafka's Narrative Theater.* University Park, Pa., 1974.

Sokel, Walter H. *Franz Kafka: Tragik und Ironie.* Munich and Vienna, 1964.

———. *Franz Kafka.* New York, 1966.

ILLUSTRATION

Mairowitz, David Zane, and Robert Crumb. *Introducing Kafka.* Cambridge, 1993.

THEATER

The Castle. Adapted by Max Brod. Trans. James Clark. London, 1963.

FILM

Nears, Colin. *The Castle.* London (BBC), 1974.

Noelte, Rudolf. *Das Schloß.* Germany, 1968.

OPERA

Reimann, Aribert. *Das Schloß.* Berlin, 1992.

读 者 调 查 问 卷

姓名		性别		年龄		文化程度/专业	
职业		地址				邮编	

1 您买的书是：

2 您购买此书是因为：

a. 对本书内容感兴趣　　b. 喜欢本书的作者

c. 喜欢封面、装帧设计　　d. 其它

3 您认为本书的价格：

a. 适中　　b. 较高　　c. 太高

4 您从何处得知此系列图书？

a. 书店　　b. 广告　　c. 朋友　　d. 其它

5 您希望在我社的"二十世纪外国文学精选"的第二辑、第三辑中读到哪些作品？

6 您对我社哪种图书印象深刻？为什么？

7 您认为我社今后应多出哪类图书？有何建议和要求？

我们将根据收到问卷的时间先后，对前 100 名读者给予小小的奖励，赠送本系列中的一本图书。

感谢您的关心，问卷请寄：

北京市西三环北路 19 号外语教学与研究出版社　国际合作部
邮编：100089
Tel：68917198　Fax：68917889